THE DAUGHTERS OF ERIEToWN

THE
DAUGHTERS OF
ERIEToWN

A NOVEL

CONNIE SCHULTZ

RANDOM HOUSE
NEW YORK

Copyright © 2020 by Connie Schultz

Published in the United States by Random House, an imprint and division of Penguin Random House LLC, New York.

RANDOM HOUSE and the HOUSE colophon are registered trademarks of Penguin Random House LLC.

LIBRARY OF CONGRESS CATALOGING-IN-PUBLICATION DATA
Names: Schultz, Connie, author.
Title: The daughters of Erietown: a novel / Connie Schultz.
Description: First edition. | New York: Random House, [2020]
Identifiers: LCCN 2019034976 (print) | LCCN 2019034977 (ebook) | ISBN 9780525479352 (hardcover; acid-free paper) | ISBN 9780525479499 (ebook)
Subjects: GSAFD: Love stories.
Classification: LCC PS3619.C4774 D38 2020 (print) | LCC PS3619.C4774 (ebook) | DDC 813/.6—dc23
LC record available at https://lccn.loc.gov/2019034976
LC ebook record available at https://lccn.loc.gov/2019034977

Printed in the United States of America on acid-free paper

randomhousebooks.com

9 8 7 6 5 4 3 2 1

First Edition

Chapter- and part-opener line drawings: iStock.com/KrulUA

Book design by Elizabeth Rendfleisch

For Clayton, Leo, Jackie, Carolyn, Milo, Ela, and Russell, always

For my brother, forever Chuckie

Gently, Teacher explained the difference between a lie and a story. A lie was something you told because you were mean or a coward. A story was something you made up out of something that might have happened. Only you didn't tell it like it was; you told it like you thought it should have been.

—Betty Smith, *A Tree Grows in Brooklyn*

THE DAUGHTERS OF ERIETOWN

PROLOGUE

1975

Samantha McGinty pressed her cheek against the cold window and exhaled slowly to cloud the glass. She glanced at the back of her father's head in the front seat before lifting her finger to write in big block letters: LUCKY.

Every Saturday, for as long as she could remember, her father had spritzed the windows of his car with a mix of vinegar and water and wiped them clean with pages of the previous week's *Erietown Times*. When she was little, in the coldest months of northeast Ohio, she would breathe on her backseat window and draw messages for her dad. A smiley face, maybe, or a star with sticks exploding from its five tips. Her father never said a word about them, but she was sure he saw them.

After that awful day in the summer of '69, when she was twelve, everything changed. Her father stopped cleaning the car windows every weekend and sometimes went as long as two weeks without washing his Chevy in the driveway. It was too warm for window notes, which made it easier for Sam because it didn't feel right to do anything nice for her father anyway.

Then autumn came, frosting car windows every night. One morning before dawn, Sam slipped out the back door before her father left for work and scrawled a message on her car window—SAD, inside a heart—and ran back into her bedroom.

Her father didn't even bother to knock before storming into her room just minutes later. "Stop leaving your fingerprints all over the car window, Sam," he said. "You're too old for that shit."

He was standing at the foot of her bed, a dark silhouette against the window as he jingled the coins in his pocket, which Sam knew to be the soundtrack of his rising discontent. "Dad," she said, about to apologize, but then her mother appeared in the doorway and turned on the light. In unison, father and daughter looked at her and said, "Are you all right?"

Ellie stood there, staring at Brick. "Let's go downstairs," he said.

Sam slipped out of bed and stood in her doorway as her father, towering over her tiny mother, walked Ellie down the stairs. "What did Sam draw on the window?" she heard her mother say.

"Nothing," Brick said. "Just fingerprints."

Sam never drew on her father's car window again. Until today.

He would understand why.

She shifted in her seat and hugged the powder blue train case on her lap, curling her fingers around its handle. She squeezed her eyes shut and whispered in the dark, "I am going to college."

Her mother's beehive bobbed slightly over the top of the seat in front of her. "What's that, Sam?"

"Nothing," Sam said, bolting upright.

She shoved the shoeless feet of her sleeping brother away from her hip and peered out her window. The sun wouldn't rise for another hour, but she could see life stirring in this rural patch of Ohio. Kitchen windows were aglow, bracketing lives like the frames of a movie reel. She saw a man in a barn coat reach for his hat on a hook. Three frames later, another man opened a door and a small dog slipped out and quickly squatted. A woman lifted a coffee mug, and in the very next frame another woman poured coffee into a raised cup. The early hours have an easy rhythm no matter where you are. *It's the rest of life,* Sam thought, *that gets away from you.*

Sam shook her head in silent reprimand. *Not today. I'm going to college.*

Her brother stirred in his sleep and rammed his feet into her hip again. She reached down to grab the top of first one sock, and then the other, pulling them higher over his bony ankles before easing his feet away. Reilly groaned and curled up like a cat resisting a nudge. "Reill could sleep through a tornado," Sam said.

"Let him be, Sam," her mother said. "He got out of bed at four-thirty for you. That's mighty early for an eleven-year-old boy. On a Saturday, no less."

Sam rolled her eyes. God, the unearned dispensation her mother granted the males in this family. She raised her left wrist and tipped the face of her Timex into the lingering moonlight. Not even six yet. "Why'd we have to leave so early?" she said. "It's only an hour and a half away, and I can't even pick up the key to my dorm room until nine."

"Your father wanted to make sure we had plenty of time to get there and find the place," Ellie said. "We've never done this before. We're all doing this for you, Sam."

"Ellie," her father said.

"Well, we are, Brick. This is new for all of us."

Sam's father glanced at her in the rearview mirror. "I always leave early, Sam. You know that. That way, if you get a flat tire or have to wait for a train, you're still on time for work."

Sam pressed her back against the seat. "Mom, I appreciate everything you and Dad are doing."

Her father smiled in the mirror. "Nobody said you didn't," he said.

Really, Mom, Sam thought, but she didn't say anything. She touched the back of her mother's seat and mouthed, *I get it. I'm going to miss you, too.*

She ran her fingers along the stitching on the train case lid. For all of Sam's life, the powder blue leather case had sat on the top shelf in her parents' bedroom closet, loosely covered in faded gold tissue paper. Sam and Reilly were not allowed to touch the case, let alone play with it.

Two nights ago, her mother had called Sam into the bedroom and patted the spot next to her on the bed. She reached for the train case sitting beside her and placed it on the bed between them.

"You remember Aunt Nessa," she said.

"Sure," Sam said. "She was a teacher, and she was really nice. She saved her prettiest Christmas cards for me. The ones with glitter or that velvety snow stuff. So that I could cut them up and make new cards."

Ellie nodded. "She saw early talent in you, the way you liked to draw. She wanted to encourage you to be an artist."

Sam shrugged. "Guess I would have disappointed her on that score."

Her mother sighed. "Aunt Nessa sometimes overestimated the ones she loved."

"There are worse habits to have."

"That's right," her mother said. "But it can get your hopes up."

Sam ran her hand across the smooth leather. "So, Aunt Nessa gave you this?"

Ellie nodded. "She took me to Higbee's department store in downtown Cleveland to buy it, a couple of months before I graduated from high school. We shopped in the personal leather goods department, and then had lunch at the Silver Grille. It was a famous restaurant there."

Sam pulled the case onto her lap and was surprised by the force when its metal latches sprang open. "It feels so new," she said, opening the case. She leaned in and sniffed the silky gray lining. "Smells new, too."

Sam tilted the case back to see herself in the mirror inside the lid. A diamond of ruffled elastic framed her face. "I've never seen a mirror in a suitcase before."

"To check your makeup," Ellie said. She leaned in to peer at Sam's reflection. "To make sure you look your best before you get off the train." She pushed back a strand of hair from Sam's face. "Or off the plane now, I guess." Ellie dropped her hand into her lap. "So many people flying now."

Sam closed the lid and pressed down the latches. "How come you never used it, Mom?"

"I did, once, when your father and I—" She stood up. "I stayed home. Never needed it." She slid her hands down the sides of her hips and smoothed the pockets of her capri pants. "Anyway, it's yours now," she said, walking toward the doorway. "For this big adventure of your life."

Sam spent the rest of that day figuring out what to pack in the train case. "The must-haves," her mother had said, "the things you don't want to be without."

Things you don't want to leave behind, too, Sam had decided.

Now, in the car, she cupped the latches with her hands to muffle the sound as she opened the lid and started pulling out one item at a time. A comb and hairbrush, a small box of tampons, two plastic eggs of L'eggs sheer-toe pantyhose, a new tube of Maybelline Great Lash mascara, and a half-empty bottle of Love's pink Baby Soft. She smiled at the small sewing kit, a gift from her former 4-H adviser, Mrs. Sandstrom. Mrs. Sandstorm, they used to call her, because she got so worked up whenever the girls failed to take seriously their "marital futures."

"Our future as domestic slaves, she means," Val Murphy had said to Sam.

Sam had laughed at the time, but now the memory made her sad. Val's baby was almost six months old already. Before she got pregnant, she and Sam had dreamed of going together to Smith College, just like Gloria Steinem had. Val's father owned four car lots and could afford to send her anywhere she wanted to go. Val's dream died the day her parents said they'd disown her if she went to Cleveland and got an abortion.

"It's over for me," Val told Sam through tears after she'd dropped out of high school. "But you, Sam? You could still apply to Smith. Remember what Mrs. Sandstorm's husband told you at the state fair booth. 'They've got scholarships for girls like you.'"

"He was making a point about my lack of sewing skills."

Val shook her head. "He was also right. Which is why you've got to write that essay. Go for both of us."

Val wouldn't let up on her, badgering her to fill out the application and even editing her essay. To Sam's shock, Smith College offered her a full ride.

Her father killed the deal. "You know what this is," he said, waving the admission letter. "Charity. Pure and simple. They feel sorry for you."

"It's a full scholarship, Dad. They said they liked my essay. They said I had *great potential.*"

"That's rich people talk for pity. What they mean is they'll get to show you off like a prize monkey."

Sam squeezed her eyes shut, willing herself not to cry. "But it's free, Dad. It's where I want to go."

"Sam, nothing worth having is free. They'll own you for the rest of your life. No matter what you accomplish, it will never feel like you did it on your own because you owe that school something you can't ever pay back."

"We'll owe money if I go to Kent State," Sam said. "You wouldn't even let me apply for a federal grant."

"And what did you learn after you went behind my back and did it anyway?"

She shrugged.

"Answer me. What did they tell you?"

"I didn't qualify," Sam said softly.

Brick shook his head. "That's right. You didn't qualify because I make too much money. Your old man may work in maintenance at Erietown Electric, but I still make too much money for you to go to college for free. That's who you come from. Don't you ever forget that."

"We'll still have the student loan."

"That we'll pay back, with interest," he said. "That's how it works."

Sam gave it one last try. "They killed four students there."

Brick shrugged. "That was five years ago, and they haven't killed one since. You'll be fine." He walked over to her and squeezed her shoulder. "Don't worry, kid. Kent State is a great college, with no strings attached. That's why your mother got her job, so we could afford this."

Until then, Sam's mother had been sitting silently on the sofa. Ellie cleared her throat and said, "That's not why—" She waved her hand and stood up. "Never mind."

That was the end of it. The next morning Sam stepped on the lever to open the flip top of the kitchen trash can and saw Smith's acceptance letter crumpled and covered in bacon grease.

"The end of a dream," she told her other close friend, Lenny Kleshinski, her eyes red and swollen. "So much for us being just a train ride apart."

Sam and Lenny had known each other since kindergarten, when his large family moved two houses down. They became best friends the day Sam decided he was the only friend her father would never ban on a whim because his dad was a union brother at Erietown Electric.

For years, Lenny and Sam had talked about going to the same college. Now she was headed for Kent, and Lenny was already at Boston College. "Home of the Kennedys," Brick said, pointing to the framed picture of the president hanging next to one of Christ on the Jack-and-Jesus wall in the living room. "Good for Lenny."

"The Kennedys lived in Boston, Dad. They went to Harvard. I read about it in the Rose Kennedy book you gave me last year for Christmas."

Her father shook his head. "The point, Sam, is that you'll sprout where you're a seed, like your mother always says."

Sam groaned. "Bloom where you are planted, you mean."

Her father smiled. "See? You don't need Harvard."

Maybe leaving home was like what they say about dying, Sam thought, with snapshots of your life flashing before you.

She lifted from the train case the small bundle of new underpants, a gift from her mother's best friend, Mardee. She set them aside and unrolled the picture Reilly had drawn for her. "To hang on your wall," he'd told her last night. "So you won't forget me." Reilly had depicted himself as a head taller than Sam, with his arm wrapped around her shoulders. "Nice try, shrimp," she had said, pointing to his self-portrait as they sat on the edge of her bed. He'd laughed and bumped against her. "I will be bigger than you by the time you come home." She'd fluffed his bushy red hair and kissed his cheek. "I'll be home for Thanksgiving, you boob."

She glanced at her sleeping brother. "Thank you, God," she whispered. "Thank you for helping me protect Reilly from the worst of it."

A newspaper clipping and drawing lined the bottom of the train case. She couldn't part with them, and she sure didn't want her mother to know she had them. For six years, Sam had held up her end of the unspoken agreement with her parents: That day had never happened to them, even though it had changed all of them.

She piled everything back into the case and closed the lid.

PART I

CHAPTER

1

1947

Ada Fetters walked to the kitchen table and set down her laundry basket with the sigh of an expired hope. The morning's conversation with her youngest son grew heavier with each passing hour. *I raised that boy to be better than this. I raised him, and I failed.*

She walked to the window over the sink and searched for her husband. Wayne was stepping off the tractor, and she could hear him whistling for Sheba. The dog ran to Wayne's side and leapt for the last piece of beef jerky in his hand. Wayne rubbed the dog's head, and both of them turned toward the house with the red sun behind them, two shadows walking into bad news.

She went over to the stove and flipped the chicken pieces sizzling in the skillet, scraping bits of char from the sides. This pan had helped her raise four kids. She had cooked with it every day for more than forty years, and brandished it countless times to bring a shaky peace to the Fetters household.

Larry was the problem. Always had been. And now this.

Wayne pushed open the back door, followed by the tap-tap-tap of Sheba's nails on the hardwood floor. "Go see Mommy," he said, chuckling. "Go see what she's got for ya."

The dog raced across the room and slid to a stop at the stove, her fat tail thumping against Ada's legs.

"Sit," Ada said. "Sit, girl." She picked up the boiled chicken heart on the stove and popped it into the dog's mouth.

Wayne walked up behind her and kissed her neck. "Anything for me?"

"Supper's almost ready." She wiped her hands on her apron and reached for the two plates they used every night for dinner, her mind full of the changes her husband didn't even know were coming. She'd be stacking three plates soon, setting another place. She looked over at Wayne and let out a long, slow breath.

"What?" he said.

"Larry was here today," she said, avoiding his eyes as she set down the plates.

"What'd he want this time?"

Ada almost started to chastise him, as she always did when they talked about their youngest child, but stopped herself. *No point. No defense. Not this time.* She pulled out two faded napkins from the basket in the middle of the table, slid one beside each plate, and added forks and knives.

"Ada, I asked you a question. What did Larry want?"

Ada silently rehearsed her lines one more time as she emptied the pot of boiling potatoes into a bowl and pulled out a tray of biscuits from the oven. She slid them into a basket lined with a checkered napkin, then reached for a platter and started scooping up the chicken with a fork.

"Larry and Alice are getting a divorce," she said finally, without looking up. She set the platter of chicken on the table.

"Well, that's hardly news, is it?" Wayne said, shifting in his chair. "Even Larry can't stay married to a woman who's decided her hobby's being a whore."

"It's worse than that, Wayne," Ada said, setting the pitcher on the table. "Alice was arrested. Found drunk and naked in the fountain in downtown Andover."

"Jesus Christ."

Ada pulled off her apron and sat down at the table. She folded her hands and bowed her head. Wayne sighed, put down his fork, and folded his hands, too. "Bless, O Lord, this food to our use and us to thy loving service," Ada said. She glanced at Wayne. "And keep us ever mindful of the needs of others. Amen."

"Amen," Wayne said as he poked a chicken thigh with his fork and dropped it on his plate. "What did Larry want today? Besides pity."

"It's about Ellie," she said.

Wayne bit off a chunk of chicken. "What about Ellie?"

"Larry wants us to take her in."

Wayne stopped chewing. "What?"

Ada set down her fork.

"What do you mean 'take her in'? For how long?"

"For good, Wayne. Larry wants us to raise her."

Wayne slammed a fist on the table. "Raise her! *Raise her?* We can raise her. And what about his other kids?"

Ada shrugged her shoulders. "Well, Larry's got a lady friend, as it turns out. Name's Florence. They want to get married. She likes little Chrissy and Beth, but she thinks Ellie's too old."

"Ellie is only eight," Wayne said.

"Old enough to grow up remembering when Florence wasn't her mother, I guess."

"So, he's just gonna dump her?"

"No, honey," Ada said, locking eyes with him. "We're going to welcome her into our home. We're going to raise her."

Wayne slammed his fist on the table again, but Ada did not flinch. He was angry, but he was just making noise. In nearly forty years of marriage, Wayne had never raised a hand to her.

"We're done raising children, Ada. I'm sixty, and you're fifty-six, for Christ's sake."

"She's our granddaughter, Wayne. Either we take her, or strangers are going to raise her. Think about that. Our Ellie with a bunch of people we don't know. What kind of people adopt a seven-year-old girl? Who knows what they'd do to her?"

Wayne pushed his plate away and threw his napkin on it. "I'll be damned."

"Eat your dinner," Ada said, reaching for his hands. He pulled away and stood up. "You spoiled that boy, Ada," he said. "Always made excuses for Larry, because he was the baby. Twenty-five, and he still hasn't grown up." He walked over to the kitchen window and grabbed his Marlboros from the sill. "You want her, you raise her," he said. "I'm done. I don't want anything to do with this."

Ada walked over to him and held him from behind. "You don't mean that," she said, pressing her cheek against his back.

He shrugged. "I do right now." He whistled for Sheba. "C'mon, girl," he said. "Let's get out of here." The dog jumped up and followed him out the door.

Ada watched Wayne march to the shed in a cloud of cigarette smoke, Sheba at his heels. She'd won, but she could already feel the cost of this victory. She walked over to the telephone on the kitchen wall, picked up the receiver, and waited for the operator's voice.

"Yes, Joanie, get me Andover 457, please," she said. "That's right. Larry."

CHAPTER

2

1956

Ellie leaned into the mirror and waved a finger at the face scowling back at her. "Give him five more minutes," she said. "Five more minutes, and then Brick McGinty is histor-y."

She tossed back her dark curly hair and tried again.

"Five minutes, Brick McGinty. If you aren't here by then, Arnie Scribner's name will be in every slot on my dance card."

Ellie sighed. She'd never even seen a dance card, not in Clayton Valley, but she loved the thought of it. What sixteen-year-old girl wouldn't? All those boys lining up to sign a little piece of paper dangling from your wrist, just like in the movies. Acting surprised. *Why, Freddie Carpenter, let me see if I can squeeze you in.*

How Brick would hate that. He was a jealous boy, which thrilled her. He made her feel worth fighting over for the first time in her life. And he wasn't just any boy. He was six-feet-two Brick McGinty, point guard on the basketball team, top scorer in the county, and one of the most popular boys at Jefferson High School. Thirty-seven other girls in their senior class, but he picked her. At four feet eleven, her head didn't even reach his shoulders. She had to stand on her tiptoes to kiss him, and even then she had to tilt her head back and raise her chin.

"My pint-size Ellie," he called her. She loved that, how he used the word "my."

She scowled again at the mirror. "Thinking like this is how you lose your resolve," she said, pointing her finger again. She walked to the bedroom window, pushed apart the curtains, and poked her head out. The frigid air stung her face as she leaned out as far as she could to see the patch of gravel where Brick's truck always came to a stop.

Ellie heard her grandmother's voice before she saw her, standing beneath the window. "Eleanor Grace, have you lost your mind? Get out of that window before you fall and break your neck." Ellie grabbed her books and flew down the stairs just as a gust of air ushered her grandmother through the door. "Look at you," Ada said, "waitin' on that boy like a lovesick hound dog."

"I'm not waiting for anybody, Grandma. I was just checking to see if I needed a coat this morning."

Ada sat on the bench and pulled off her boots. "I guess you think there's nothing but corn husks rattling around in this old head of mine," she said. "It's snowing, Ellie. And you're wondering if you need a coat?" She pulled off her knit cap and shoved it into her coat pocket before hanging the coat on the hook by the door. "Brick McGinty's not picking you up for school today, honey."

"Brick always picks me up on Wednesdays, Grandma."

"Not anymore. Grandpa told that boy's mother that Brick is not to come anywhere near this property again."

"What?" Ellie said. "Why, Grandma? Why would he do that? I love Brick." Ellie sank into her chair at the table.

"You're sixteen," Ada said, tying her apron around her thick waist. She shoved a basket of potatoes next to her chair, sat down opposite Ellie, and started peeling. "You don't know love."

"I love you," Ellie said. "I love Grandpa."

"That's different," Ada said. Ellie walked over to the counter and yanked open the silverware drawer to grab another paring knife. She slammed the drawer shut and sat down.

"Grandma," she said, plucking a potato. "You were sixteen when you married Grandpa. Same age as me. How old were you when you fell in love with him?"

"I'll let you know," Ada said.

"Grandma."

"It was different back then. All the girls married early, except for your aunt Nessa, who was born with a mind of her own. We only had five or six boys to pick from, and two got eliminated for inbreeding."

Ellie dropped a peeled potato into the bowl. "Grandpa says it was love at first sight."

"Grandpa's talking about the first time he looked in the mirror, honey."

Ellie smiled. "Brick and I have been together for three years now. That's a long time to get to know someone. He's smart. And he's funny, too."

"Never trust funny, Ellie," Ada said. "Your father was always funny. We see how Larry worked out." Ada regretted it as soon as she said it. Ellie pretended to pick at a tough patch of skin on the potato.

"I don't mean your daddy doesn't love you, Ellie," Ada said. "He just has a hard time showing it."

Ellie tossed another peeled potato into the bowl.

"Ellie, look at me."

"I heard you, Grandma. He loves me. He just didn't want to raise me. Didn't want to have to see me much, either."

"That doesn't mean he isn't your father. He's still family."

"Sure, Grandma."

Ada picked up another potato, silently cursing herself for bringing up her son. In the nine years that Ellie had lived with them, she'd seen her father only once a month, at best, and even then he always made it clear that he was just stopping by to say hello. Larry hurt Ellie as only a father could, and it made Ada feel guilty, as if she'd missed something in him when he was little. Something she could have fixed if only she'd paid attention. There was a special kind of guilt for the mother whose child turned out wrong.

Ada's chest ached at the sight of her heartbroken granddaughter, whose only sin was to want her father to act like one. "It's like he doesn't even remember Ellie's his daughter," Wayne said one evening as they were getting ready for bed. "Like she never happened."

Ada knew why. With each passing year, Ellie looked more like Alice, her mother. Same thick, curly hair and pale Irish skin. Same big blue eyes, so large that Ellie spent the first two years of her life looking like a child shocked with the state of things. She was built like her mother, too, short and busty, with the tiny hands of a porcelain doll. As a result, Ellie was growing up as an only child, kept from her younger sisters because Larry's second wife couldn't bear to look at her. "You know Ellie looks like Alice," Larry once explained to his incredulous mother. "Makes Florence think about Alice and me together when we were young. We can't deal with all that."

Ada had sometimes worried that, as Ellie grew older, she would become bitter after she understood what her parents had done to her. Instead, she became God's great apologist. Making excuses for other people's bad behavior, always granting second and third chances. "We don't know what happened to them before they got to us," Ellie always said. "We don't know what made them that way."

"Not a mean bone in her body," Ada often said to Wayne.

"Closest to God and carrying the cross for the rest of us." It broke Ada's heart how hard Ellie tried to please everyone, and how skittish she could be, particularly around her grandfather. It was as if Ellie always thought she was just one mistake away from being traded again.

Ada smiled at her granddaughter as she reached for the half-peeled potato in her hands. "You haven't touched your toast, and the bus will be here any minute. Go get your books and get your coat on. I'll wait outside in case Clarence is early. It'll give me a chance to make sure he's not drinkin' and drivin' that bus again."

Ellie stood up. "He's not."

"Oh, really. And how would you know that?"

"Becca Gilley and I threw out his bottle of Jameson's last week. He didn't even see us reach under his seat and grab it."

"You what? Oh, Lord, that man." Ada pulled on her coat and opened the door. "C'mon, Sheba."

Ellie pulled on her coat. Barely 7:30, and the day was already ruined. No Brick. She stared at her face in the mirror by the door, playing her usual game of imagining how Brick might see her.

"Well, that won't do." She stood straighter and smiled. "Someday," she whispered. "Someday, Brick McGinty, you and I are going to marry and live in our own house, with our own front porch, and lots of kids." Sons for him, she decided, and a daughter all her own. "And I promise you this, little girl," Ellie said, weaving the scarf around her neck, "we will never, ever give you away."

CHAPTER

3

Brick McGinty had finished feeding the pigs and was washing up at the kitchen sink when he felt his father's fingers curl around his collar.

"You stay away from the Fetters house," Bull hissed into his ear. "That girl's grandpa came by here yesterday. Says he doesn't want you or your fancy truck anywhere near their granddaughter again." He tightened his grip on Brick's collar, pulling it taut enough to pop the top button. "To hell with 'em. A McGinty doesn't go where he isn't wanted."

Brick jerked his father's hand away, unaware of the other fist coming at his head. His forehead grazed the hot-water faucet as his head plowed into the bottom of the cast-iron sink. Brick winced and gripped both faucets, managing to stand despite the next punch to his head. His nostrils flared as he panted. Damned if he'd give the old man the pleasure of his pain. He made a show of lifting his face and sniffing the air. "You stink," Brick said over his shoulder. "Least you could do is wash her off before you come home to Ma."

"You little—" Bull twisted Brick's right arm behind his back, spun him sideways, and shoved his son's face against the kitchen doorjamb. He leaned in and growled in Brick's ear.

"Just because you can drive Harry's truck now doesn't mean you're anything like Harry. Your brother-in-law had no business holding on to that truck for you. It should've been mine after Harry died."

Brick's shoulder was on fire. He tried to wriggle out of the hold, but Bull grabbed harder and pushed Brick's wrist up toward the back of his neck. "You think your shit don't stink. Cuz you're bigger'n me, cuz you're a big basketball star in this nothing town. I'm your daddy and nothin' you can do will ever change that. You show some respect, or I'll beat the shit out of you until you scream for your mommy. Make you pee like a little boy again."

Brick's eyes began to sting.

"You hear me?"

Brick gritted his teeth and said nothing.

"Answer me," Bull said, twisting his arm harder.

"Bull!"

Brick heard the clothes basket drop to the floor and the clack of his mother's shoes against the linoleum as she ran to wedge herself between her son and her husband. She was two inches taller than Bull, and at least twenty pounds heavier. She flattened her palms against Bull's chest. "Bull. Stop."

"This don't concern you, Angie," Bull growled, but Brick could tell by the lightening weight against his back that his father had taken a step back. "Go back to your laundry."

Angie McGinty did not move. "He's getting ready for school," she said, her arms extended behind her now to embrace Brick's waist. "He can't miss any more days if he's going to stay on the team. Let him be."

"The *team*," Bull said, laughing. "Do you hear yourself? It ain't a job, Angie. It's a bunch of pansy-ass boys chasing a little ball." Brick slid out from behind his mother and turned to face them, as his father pointed at him and said, "That boy of yours gave me back talk. He pays for that. No son of mine is gonna mouth off to me."

Angie's eyes were riveted on Bull as she spoke. "Brick, apologize to your father."

"I'm not the one who did anything wrong," Brick yelled.

"You sonnuvabitch."

"Please, Son," Angie said. "Just say you're sorry. Say it for me."

Brick squeezed his eyes shut and flexed his hands. Open, closed. Open, closed.

"Say you're sorry, honey. He'll leave us alone if you just say you're sorry."

Brick hated that she was right.

"All right, Ma," he said. "For you." He glared at Bull as he slid his mother's hands off his shoulders. "I'm sorry."

"Dad," Bull said. "I'm sorry, *Dad."*

Angie patted her son's back.

"I'm sorry, Dad," Brick said, his face a map of contempt. Bull lunged and Brick tumbled backward onto the floor. "You just remember who's boss, mama's boy," Bull said, pinning Brick's shoulders to the floor as he spit on Brick's face. "You just remember who's the man in this house."

Bull swatted Angie's grip off of his shirt. "You, too," he said, snapping his ball cap on and pulling open the door.

The door slammed, and Bull was gone.

Angie grabbed the wet dishrag hanging on the cold-water faucet and held on to the oven door handle as she eased herself down onto her knees next to Brick. "Let me get a look at that," she said, reaching for the cut over his eye.

"No, Ma," Brick said, rising to his feet. He held out his hand and pulled his mother up. She handed him the rag and he wiped the spittle from his face, rinsed the rag out, and dabbed at his eye.

"Brick, you need to put ice on that. It's already starting to swell."

"I don't want any ice," he said. He looked at the bloody rag and threw it into the sink. Several drops of blood drew a scarlet line down the side of his freckled face. How many times? Angela McGinty wondered. How many times would this happen to her boy before he left for good?

Brick was her second son, her only living boy, the youngest of twelve. She'd almost died after the birth of her tenth child, Margaret. "This has to be your last, Angie," Dr. Stevens told her before he discharged her from the hospital. "Your next child won't have a mother to hold on to."

Having no more children meant saying no to Bull McGinty, and nobody did that in his house, especially when he came home drunk. She had Louise at age thirty-six, and got pregnant again before the baby was six months old. Brick was born on Thanksgiving Day in 1938, all ten pounds, seven ounces of him.

Brick was all hers, from the day he was born. Bull had insisted on naming the boy Richard, for a drinking buddy from his jazz band days, but Bull was nowhere to be found when it was time to sign the birth certificate. She wrote in Paull for his middle name, after her only brother, who had died of tuberculosis when he was fourteen.

By the time he was three, everyone called him Brick because of his red hair and tank of a build. He was seventeen now and still called Brick, but for different reasons. Brick was six feet two, a towering brawn of a man, and a relentless target of her husband's rage ever since their oldest son, Harry, was killed in World War II.

She kept the Navy's telegram informing her of Harry's death wrapped in a hankie in the top drawer of her dresser. The Western Union had spelled his name wrong—MacGinty, instead of McGinty—but she couldn't part with the letter because it was the last time she ever opened an envelope thinking her beautiful Harry was still alive.

Almost overnight, Bull turned on Brick. Angie always thought it was because his face looked so much like Harry's. Same red hair and freckles, same ice-blue eyes, but Brick was different from Harry. Bigger boned, and less easygoing. By the time he was fourteen, Brick was two inches taller than Bull. At fifteen, he took his first swing to defend himself. Bull backed off for a while after that, but lately he'd begun picking fights with Brick again, and threatened to start hitting Angie again, too. Brick towered over his father now, and he was protective of his mother. Angie knew that no good could come of that. There'd be no peace as long as Bull and Brick McGinty lived in the same house.

She pulled a clean rag out of the drawer and ran it under cold water. "Let me just clean you up," she said, reaching up to dab Brick's eye. "You don't want Ellie seeing you with blood on your face." At the sound of Ellie's name, Brick surrendered. He slouched into a chair at the table and raised his face toward his mother. "Her grandparents don't think I'm good enough for her, Ma. They want me to stay away from her."

Angie dabbed at the cut, then leaned in and kissed him between the eyes.

"That's all Wayne, I'll bet," she said. "He doesn't think any-one's good enough for his little girl." She sat opposite her son and grabbed an apple out of the bowl on the table. She rolled it toward him. "Stick that in your pocket."

"Why don't they like me, Ma?" Brick said.

"The Fetters? Oh, honey, they're just trying to protect Ellie from more hurt. She was a child when her parents abandoned her. Their own son treated her like trash for the dump."

"Don't talk about Ellie like that, Ma."

Only at the mention of Ellie did her son's eyes start to tear up. How he loved that girl. "I'm sorry, honey," she said. "I know you love her, and this is hard."

"There have to be some good fathers out there," he said. He jabbed his finger toward the door. "They can't all be like that. Like him. And like Ellie's dad. Like your father, too."

What could she have been thinking, confessing such hard secrets to her child? He was barely ten at the time, and Bull had just whipped him so hard he'd wet his pants in front of the Matthews boys. He was so humiliated he ran into the field and didn't come home until after supper.

She had been desperate to ease his shame, to make him see that she really did understand how he felt, and that God would help him through it. "I know what this feels like," she had told him that night. "I know how you feel." She'd described how her own father used to beat her till she peed, and left her covered in bruises. "For nothing," she'd whispered to him that night as Brick softly wept. "For no reason at all."

Angie would never forget the look of betrayal on her little boy's face. "And you went and married someone just like him, Ma?" he'd said, tears running down his face. "Why'd you go and do that? Why didn't God stop you?" Angie had no answer for him.

"Ma?"

Angie startled now. "I'm sorry, honey. What?"

"I said I've got to get to school."

Angie grabbed the edge of the table and rose to her feet. Every inch of her ached all the time now. "Press the rag to your cut while you drive," she said. "The longer you keep it there, the less likely people will notice it when you get to school."

"Ellie will notice," Brick said, standing up. "Ellie notices everything." He grabbed his jacket off the hook, pulled it on, and stuck the apple in his pocket. "Seeya, Ma."

Angie stood at the door and watched Brick climb into his truck and pull away. A cloud of gravel dust rose and scattered over the snow. Angie clutched the small gold cross dangling on the chain around her neck. "And wherever they do not receive you," she whispered, "when you leave that town, shake off the dust from your feet as a testimony against them."

Her fingers traced the lines of the cross. "Please, God, watch over my boy. Keep him safe."

CHAPTER

4

Ellie shivered in the school parking lot, jumping from one foot to the other, her bare legs blotchy and red. "C'mon, Brick," she whispered into the wool scarf around her neck. "Where are you?"

"Ellie!"

Ellie turned and saw Becca Gilley waving a bright purple mitten. "Bell's about to ring. You're going to be late." Ellie clutched her books closer to her chest and looked at the road. No truck. No Brick.

"I'm coming," she yelled over her shoulder. "Just one more minute." The sound of busybody Becca's saddle shoes slapping against the pavement grew louder. "Whew," Becca said, leaning on Ellie's shoulder. "I can't breathe in this weather." She tugged on Ellie's sleeve. "You have got to stop waiting around for Brick. He's supposed to stay away from you. You could get him in trouble."

Ellie shrugged off Becca's hand and thought, not for the first time, that she looked like a fifty-four-year-old teenager in her blue, cat-eye frames. "So now everybody knows my business? How did you find out?"

"Like you weren't going to tell me anyway. Daddy said

Brick's father was carryin' on about it last night at O'Doole's. Said you had some nerve thinking you were better than Brick when your mother is—"

Ellie turned toward her. "My mother is what?"

Becca looked away. "Never mind. He's a mean man, Ellie, that Bull McGinty. Daddy says he's always tryin' to pick a fight. Talks terrible about his own son, too. Says he should've drowned him when he was born. Can you imagine saying that about your own son?"

The snow was coming down harder now. "Becca, next time you're thinking of saying something to make someone feel bad, maybe think again."

"I'm sorry, El. I was just sharing information."

"Nobody understands Brick like I do," Ellie said. "I know who he really is."

"Oh, El. Don't do this. Brick's not long for this town. Everyone knows he's going to get a basketball scholarship and be the first basketball player from Jefferson High to go play at college."

Ellie turned her back to Becca and looked out at the road. "So, he has plans. What makes you think I don't have plans, too? That we don't have plans together?"

Both of them turned to the sound of wheels crunching on packed snow. Ellie waved at Brick. "Oh, boy," Becca said. "Now you're going to be late for sure. I'll see you inside."

As soon as Ellie saw Brick's truck, she went from worried to wounded. So what if Grandpa said Brick couldn't pick her up anymore? Did that mean he could just wander in anytime he wanted? He should have been here a half hour ago. "If you were in a hurry to see me," she said. "Which you obviously aren't." One look, she told herself. She'd let him get one good look at her, and then she'd turn and run off to class.

Brick waved at her through the windshield as she raised her eyebrows and jutted out her chin in silent reprimand. She turned and started stomping toward the school's front entrance. She heard his truck door open and slam shut.

"Ellie!"

She kept walking, but slowed down at the sound of his running.

"Ellie, please."

Please? That didn't sound like Brick McGinty.

She turned around and saw blood crusted over his swollen left eye, and a bruise under it pooling in a deep shade of violet. "Brick, what happened to you?" She pulled off a glove and started to reach for his swollen eye. He dodged her hand and pulled her into a hug. "Nothing. It looks worse than it feels."

"Who did this to you?"

"I told you. It's nothing."

Ellie looked up at his face. "He did this. Your father." She licked her fingers and rubbed his cheek. "You've still got blood on your face."

"Let's get you inside, Pint. Your legs are so red, they look like they're going to snap in two."

Ellie stepped back to look at him. He was wearing his letterman's jacket, but no gloves or hat, no scarf. The ridges in his red hair were sculpted with his usual dab of Brylcreem, and looked sharp as ice. "I don't care if I freeze to death," she said as she unwound her scarf and tossed it around his neck.

"I don't need your pity."

"Good," she said, forcing a smile. "Because I'm not offering it. You're my mighty Brick. Let's go inside. We can talk later." The second bell rang. Brick squeezed her hand and with his other hand grabbed the leather strap buckled around her books. "C'mon, we gotta get in there or both of us will be banned from tonight's game."

Across the street, Wayne Fetters's breath clouded the windows as he sat in his pickup truck, waiting to see when his granddaughter would go inside. He saw her shade her eyes as she waited in the parking lot, talking to Becca Gilley. He saw her stomp her feet in the snow trying to keep her legs warm. He saw her drop her books and run into the arms of Bull McGinty's boy.

Ellie rising on tiptoes to touch his face. Looping her arm through his. Kissing him, twice, before running with him into the building.

Wayne Fetters saw it all.

"Goddamn him," he said, turning the key in the ignition and pulling away.

CHAPTER

5

Ada wiped her hands on her apron as she walked into the living room and sat in the rocking chair facing her husband. The chair creaked as she lowered herself into it with an audible sigh. Wayne raised the evening newspaper a little higher in front of his face.

"You know I'm sitting here, Wayne," she said. "And we both know there's no way you can't hear that child crying her heart out upstairs." Wayne shifted in his chair and rustled the paper, saying nothing.

Ellie started pounding again on her bedroom door, her every wail punctuated with Sheba's howls. "Let me come down! Please let me out! Grandma! Grandpa!"

Ada covered her face with her hands. "Oh my Lord. I can't take this a minute longer. Wayne, you can't keep her up there forever."

Wayne flipped down a corner of the paper. "She was kissing him, Ada. I saw it with my own eyes this morning. Not even an hour after you told her she was not to see that boy again, she was holding his hand and kissing him. I saw her."

He rattled his paper again and tried three times to snap it upright before throwing it to the floor. He reached for the radio perched next to them on a step stool Ada had made out of coffee cans and upholstery remnants. He turned it on and fidgeted with the dial.

Ada rested her hand on his. "We need to talk, Wayne."

Wayne stared at his wife's hand. This was not like his Ada. She'd always known when to let him be. They had their understandings. He didn't touch a kitchen appliance except to repair it. Never complained about any meal she cooked or budget decision she made. In return, she stayed away from the toolshed, left the driving to him, and trusted Wayne to pick their programs on the radio. Not once had she ever so much as suggested he adjust the volume.

"Thought we'd listen to a little *Gunsmoke*." He locked eyes with his wife and saw a stranger looking back at him. He turned off the radio. "Go on," he said. "Say your bit."

"She's still a child, Wayne. A sweet girl. You act as if she's suddenly this sinister creature trying to betray us. Like she's—"

"Grandpa!" Ellie yelled. "Please let me come downstairs!"

Wayne pointed to the ceiling. "Remember how much I didn't want her livin' with us nine years ago? This is what I worried about. It wasn't that I didn't want that little girl in our house." He pointed to the ceiling again. "I didn't want this."

Ada pulled a hankie from her pocket and dabbed at her eyes. "This isn't like you, Wayne. Do you ever look at Ellie's face, see how hard she's always trying to please us. She's spent the last nine years afraid you'd kick her out, Wayne. Our own granddaughter."

Wayne leaned forward. "I can't remember the last time I've seen you cry, Ada. You know I'd never do that to her. Why didn't you ever say anything to me?"

Ada pulled off her horn-rimmed glasses and wiped them with the hem of her apron. She laid them on her lap and looked up at her husband. "I guess a little part of me is afraid you're going to kick her out, too. I couldn't bear it, Wayne. I couldn't bear to lose her."

They heard Ellie wailing again. "Please, Grandpa!"

They looked up at the ceiling. "She was kissing that McGinty boy, Ada. A McGinty."

"She's a teenager, and she's in love. Don't you remember us at that age?"

"I never touched anything but your face and your hands before we were married," he said. "Maybe once or twice I wrapped my arm around your shoulder, but I knew what was expected of me. I'm not saying that was easy. You walk the fields alone till midnight, if you have to. Go swim in the ice pond. Drive your gas tank empty." He winked at her. "Whittle a whole set of dolls for your girlfriend's sister."

Ada smiled. "Nessa still has those dolls, you know. Keeps 'em in her breakfront in the dining room."

Wayne shook his head, but he was smiling now, too. "Women. You girls are all crazy."

"Times are changing, Wayne. You see how the kids are dressing these days. How they dance when we chaperone. But not our Ellie. She's still a good girl. Her skirts are the longest in the class."

"Not that cheerleading thing she wears," Wayne said. "That's why I don't go to her games. Can't stand the way boys look at her."

"Oh, Wayne. She's got no control over that. She still goes to church on Sundays, and in the summer she still likes to walk to the church with me every Thursday for quilting bee."

Wayne looked up at her. "Quilting bee. She goes for the gossip, just like her grandma."

"She's a good girl, Wayne. And she'd give anything to make you proud. She'd do anything just to make you like her."

"Dammit, stop that, Ada. I love that child. I love her as much as I've loved anyone but you."

Ada grabbed his hand and pressed it against her heart. "Then you have to stop hiding it. You have to stop being afraid she'll hurt you."

"Hurt me? I'm not afraid of anyone or anything."

Ada patted his hand. "Of course not, honey. Please, Wayne. You have to let her know you trust her. That she matters to you. It breaks my heart to say this: She's Larry's daughter, but you're the only father she'll ever have."

Wayne studied his wife for a moment. She was not one to show physical affection outside the bedroom, certainly not in front of their living room window. But there she was, holding his hand against her bosom. Overhead, he could still hear his granddaughter's sobs. Under his hand, he felt his wife's heartbeat. "I'm seventy, Ada. I'm an old man. I can't change my ways now."

Ada patted his hand again before releasing it. "I'm not asking you to change. I'm just asking you not to hide the best parts of you." She looked up at the ceiling. Ellie's cries had softened to whimpers. "She's exhausted. She needs to eat something." Ada shook her head. "Isn't it time you two stopped being so afraid of each other?"

Wayne sat in silence as Ada stood up and walked into the kitchen. Then he joined her. She pulled out of the icebox the bowl of leftover wilted lettuce with bacon, his favorite, and set it on the counter. She walked to the stove, and he took the box of matches from her. "I got this," he said, striking a match to light the burner under the pot of beef stew. Ada lifted the lid and started stirring with the wooden spoon Wayne had made for her ten Christmases ago. He stood behind her and wrapped his arms around her, breathing in the scent of lilac powder, her one indulgence. "This will be warm in a few minutes," she said. "How about you go fetch our Ellie?"

He kissed the top of her head. "You're a good woman, Ada." She leaned into him ever so slightly and closed her eyes, the thickness of his chest warming her back. "Go talk to her, honey," she said.

Wayne headed for the stairs. He could hear the sound of Ellie's whimpers. "Goddammit," he whispered, and plodded up the steps. Sheba was lying in the hallway, wedged against Ellie's door.

Wayne touched the cross of Irish peat hanging on the wall next to the doorframe. His mother had mailed it to him from Ireland after his first son was born. For more than forty years it had rested against the framed picture of his mother on top of his chest of drawers. Ellie had loved the cross from the first time she saw it. "Tell me about them, Grandpa," she said, caressing the cross in her hands. "Why did your parents stay in Ireland but send you away?"

Ellie was the first person besides Ada to show an interest in his parents. They were too Irish, they'd told him, too set in their ways. But they wanted a better life, an American life, for their children. "I was twelve, the oldest," Wayne told Ellie, "so I was the first to go. I lived with my uncle, who had already settled in Ohio."

"They loved you that much," Ellie said, oblivious to the fear he'd felt when he turned around at the dock that day and his mother was already gone. He looked at his granddaughter's wide, imploring eyes, and it hit him. Ellie wanted a different version of her parents' abandonment. Time and again, she had reached for the cross and asked for another story about his long-ago life in Ireland. "Your mother loved you so much, Grandpa," she often said. "She loved you enough to give you away."

One evening, after one of their talks, Wayne had decided to hang the cross on the wall next to Ellie's bedroom door. She had noticed it right away the following morning, and raced to hug him in the kitchen without saying a word. Every night before bed, she touched the cross and he could hear her whisper his mother's name. "Good night, Evelyn Joy." The first time he saw her do that he had to walk away.

Ada was wrong about one thing: He had always loved Ellie.

He touched the cross again, and this time Sheba whimpered and slowly rose to her feet. He tapped on the door and heard the springs of Ellie's bed creak. She cracked open the door, and the sight of her red, puffy face weakened his knees. Sheba stuck her nose through the doorway and thumped her tail against his calves.

"Can I come in?"

Ellie nodded and walked across the room, facing him with her back pressed against the window. Wayne sat on her bed and patted the spot next to him. "I won't bite."

She pulled her cardigan tight around her. "I know, Grandpa," she said, sniffling. She walked over to him and sat down. He glanced at the two feet of distance between them and smiled. Ellie crossed her arms and stared straight ahead.

"Your grandmother's worried about you, you know that. She's worried that you're going to run off with that McGinty boy."

"I'm not running anywhere, Grandpa. I'm still in high school. I'm going to graduate."

"Well, that's good," he said. "We want you to graduate. We want you to have a better life."

"Brick wants to graduate, too, Grandpa. And he wants to go to college."

Steady, Wayne warned himself. *Don't get too excited.*

"Brick's going to college?"

She looked at him with a patient smile. "Everybody says he's going to be Jefferson High's first basketball star to go to college."

"Is that what Brick wants?"

Ellie nodded and started picking at threads on her quilt. "He talks about it all the time."

"College. Well, how 'bout that. Any other secrets you want to share with me?"

"I'd like to go, too, Grandpa," Ellie said, slowly. "I'd like to go to college and become a nurse."

"What do you need that for? Grandma has always said you were a born mother. It's only a matter of time before you're married and giving us great-grandchildren to spoil."

"Lots of women go to school and become nurses. Mrs. Lammer, for example. She works with Dr. Lammer."

Wayne nodded. "It's the family business for them."

Ellie pulled her sweater tighter. "You don't have to be married to a doctor to work with one."

Wayne stood up. "Well, Brick going to college solves our immediate problem, doesn't it?"

"Your problem, you mean," Ellie said, looking up at him. "He's coming back for me, Grandpa. We're going to build a life together, Brick and me."

Wayne held out his hand and pulled her to her feet. "Of course he will, Ellie," he said. "Only a fool would let a girl like you get away."

CHAPTER

6

Brick took a long drag on his cigarette and lifted his face, blowing smoke at the moon. It was early March, still the dead of winter in snowbelt Clayton Valley, but spring was flirting. For two days now, the mercury in the thermometer outside the kitchen window had crawled into the mid-sixties by afternoon. Happened every winter. You started the day stomping ice off your boots and by midafternoon you were counting crocuses peeking out of the snow. The warmth hovered just long enough to get everybody's hopes up before another snowstorm buried them.

We never learn. Brick took another drag on his cigarette. *Town full of suckers.*

The sun had gone down more than two hours ago, taking the tease of warmth with it. He'd been sitting for more than an hour on his cold patch of ground that offered no mercy, leaning against the shed as the wind played with his hair.

He squinted into the moonlight. Who up there might be watching him? An alien on the moon seemed more likely to be real than any God he could imagine. His mother had believed in God all her life. Look what that got her.

Brick looked down at the envelope in his lap. He ran his fingers again over the embossed return address:

Carl R. Swartz
Kent State University
Varsity Athletic
Kent, Ohio

He touched his name: *Mr. Richard P. McGinty.*
Mister. That was a first.

He stared at the envelope until the cigarette singed his fingers. "Shit," he said, throwing the butt. He watched the ember as it hissed in the wet grass and died. His dog, Patch, wedged against his thigh, groaned from the interruption and snuggled closer, burrowing his head into Brick's lap. The feathers of his thick brown fur fanned across the envelope, hiding it from view.

"Not you, too, Patch," Brick said. "Don't tell me you don't want me to leave, either."

What would happen to Patch if he went away to college? He scratched the dog's head before tracing with his finger the thin, furless scar where Patch's left eye used to be. Another victim of Bull McGinty. Brick's throat tightened at the memory.

Brick had been twelve years old, on an errand for his mother, when he found the abandoned puppy in the parking lot of Thompson's Dry Goods. He had scooped him up and named him Lucky by the time he'd carried him home. "No, no, no," Angie said when he walked into the kitchen, but her resistance was no match for the look on her son's face. "Well, every boy needs a best friend," she said, scratching Lucky's head. "But he's your responsibility."

About a month later, Lucky mangled a tin of Bull's chewing tobacco that he'd left on the back stoop. Brick saw it all happen. Lucky dropping the tin, the outline of his mouth speckled with bits of tobacco. His father, red with rage, scream-ing at the dog. Lucky cowering as Bull picked up a fist-size rock and threw it straight at the puppy's head.

Lucky yelped and started running in circles as the blood seeped into the sandy colored fur on his face. Brick dove for the puppy and pulled him into a huddle. His shirt was covered in blood by the time his father walked away, vowing to kill the dog. Brick held Lucky to his chest as he ran nearly two miles down the road to Doc Waverly.

"His eye's mush, son," the veterinarian said, "and he's lost a lot of blood. Best chance for survival is to clean out the socket and stitch it shut." Brick never forgot how it felt to have a man's gentle hand on his shoulder, and his shock when Doc Waverly refused to let Brick work off the money he owed him.

"Just remember this moment, Brick," Doc said as he washed his hands after stitching up Lucky. "Remember the harm we can do in this world when we lose our temper." It was the first time an adult outside the family had been willing to say to Brick what he already knew about his father.

Brick pointed to the large swath of gauze taped over the dog's missing eye. "Guess I'll change his name, Doc," he said. "Think I'll call him Patch now."

"I think that's just right, Son," Doc said.

Two weeks later, Brick was on his knees in the backyard brushing Patch with his mother's old hairbrush when his father came out of the barn carrying his shotgun. Brick lunged for the dog and enveloped him with his arms and legs. "No!" he screamed. "Don't shoot him!"

"The dog's blind," Bull said. "He's worthless."

Brick pulled the trembling dog closer against his chest. "He can still see. He can see out of the other eye."

"We ain't running a home for cripples," Bull said as he

cocked the gun and aimed at the dog's head. "Get outta the way."

Brick started to sob, burying his head in the dog's neck. If Patch had to die, Brick was going with him. "No! No, please! Please don't shoot him!" He closed his eyes tight and whispered into the dog's ear, "I love you, Patch. I'm so sorry, boy."

He heard the kitchen door slam.

"Bull."

It was his mother's voice.

"Bull, put the gun down."

Brick peered over the top of Patch's fur and saw his mother standing in the doorway with her hands on her hips. Bull widened his stance and aimed again at the dog. Angie fled down the steps and stood in front of him.

"*No, Bull*," she said, low and slow. "Not *this* dog. Not *this* boy."

Brick held his breath, afraid to make the slightest sound.

Bull could have taken one look at this wife, this *woman* who dared to defy him, and decided to teach her another lesson. Brick had seen him do that plenty of times in the past, hurling his mother across the room and laughing as she stumbled to get up. But on that day, on that dusty afternoon with the sun beating down on them as Brick whimpered in the dirt, Bull looked up at his wife towering over him and backed down. He lowered his gun and bent over Brick.

"Look at you, like a little girl," he said, spitting on the boy. "Just like a goddamn little pussy." Brick held the dog tight, afraid to move as the spittle slid down his cheek. He buried his face deeper into the dog's neck. Patch wriggled and turned his head, and started licking Brick's face with his wet, warm tongue.

Bull kicked dirt on the huddling pair and then turned to face his wife. "You are one sorry, dried-up, useless bitch." She didn't say a word. Didn't budge or blink. She just kept standing with her hands on her hips, glaring at her husband as small beads of sweat streaked down the sides of her face. Bull spit in the dirt and walked away.

Brick heard his father's truck peel out of the driveway, but he didn't move until he felt his mother's hand on his head. "You can get up now, Son. He's gone."

Bull would always remember that day as the time Angie McGinty took on the monster in their lives, and she won. He saw his mother differently after that. She'd always seemed so beaten down, so defeated. He had never seen her hit back when Bull punched her, or even raise her voice. She just took the abuse, over and over. Until that day when Bull McGinty aimed a gun at her son's dog.

Five years later, Brick could still see his mother standing between him and his father, her voice low and strong as she told her husband, "Not *this* dog. Not *this* boy." He could tell by the look on Bull's face, by the way he crumbled, there was a different reason she had won.

"Every marriage has its secrets," she'd told Brick when he asked about it right before dinner later that day.

"What kind of secrets?"

"Grown-up secrets, Son," she'd said, running a towel under the kitchen faucet and wiping it roughly across his dirty face. "Just be glad you've still got that one-eyed puppy of yours. He's your responsibility. Every day, all day, till he dies—of natural causes, if he's lucky. Don't you forget it."

From then on, after Patch's dodge-the-bullet day, as Brick always called it, he snuck him into his bed at night, terrified that Bull would finish him off in the dark, out of spite. Bull had forbidden the dog to be in the house, but Brick slept in the attic, and his father had never bothered to check on him there. Whenever Angie climbed the stairs to kiss Brick good night, she patted Patch's head and whispered, "Good boy."

Patch was almost six now, and spent most of his waking hours either tagging along with Brick or waiting for him to come home. What was he going to do with Patch if he went to Kent State?

The wind was picking up. Brick shivered and reached for the pack of cigarettes in his shirt pocket. Patch groaned again. "Shh, boy." He lifted his face to take a long drag and shook his head. He had a lot more than Patch to worry about if he was ever going to leave Clayton Valley.

"Ellie," he whispered, pressing his back against the barn.

He slid the envelope from under Patch's head and pulled out the letter. He'd read it dozens of times, but it was still pristine. Every time he opened it, he held the envelope with his fingertips and edged the letter out between his fingernails. Slowly, he unfolded it. A postcard slipped out and fluttered to the ground. Brick picked it up, blew on it, and slid it into his shirt pocket.

Kent State University
Kent, Ohio

February 15, 1957

Mr. Richard P. McGinty
R.D. #3
Jefferson, Ohio

Dear Richard:

It was a pleasure to receive your card which indicates your interest in Kent State. We have a fine growing school where one may secure a good education. The athletic program is getting better all the time. Playing in the strong Mid-American Conference, whose basketball teams are listed as major college teams by the N.C.A.A., we are building to the point where we can become a definite factor.

I would like to invite you to visit our campus and examine our facilities and to discuss the possibility of your enrolling. I realize that you are busy now with your own games and with the tournaments coming soon you will be even busier. While I don't want to interfere with the chances of your team's success, you may have time to visit in the future.

Enclosed is a card for your convenience to indicate the date and approximate time of arrival. Almost any day is satisfactory, but I should receive the card in time to confirm that I will be able to meet you. Usually any day including Saturday is a good day by afternoon.

Best of luck to you and your team in the game and tournaments.

Very truly yours,
Carl R. Swartz
Basketball Coach

CRS: bms
encl. (1)

Encl. It took Brick two days to figure out what that meant. He finally went to the school library and searched the dictionary for words beginning with "e-n-c-l." Felt like a fool once he realized it stood for "enclosure." There was so much in this world he didn't know.

Brick pulled the postcard out of his pocket. It was addressed to Coach Swartz. Thomas Jefferson's profile was embossed in burgundy on the two-cent stamp.

The back of the card was a blank slate of possibilities.

I will visit Kent on _____
  (date)
and will arrive _____
  (time)
_____
  signed

Brick folded the letter around the postcard and slid both back into the envelope. He tucked it in his shirt pocket, behind the pack of Kents, his new cigarette brand since the day after he'd opened the letter. He rested his head against the shed and closed his eyes. Three weeks had passed, and he still hadn't responded to the letter. Until today, he hadn't told a single soul about it. Not his mother, and certainly not his father. Not even Ellie.

Finally, early that morning, he'd decided to talk to Coach Bryant. He showed up early for practice and found Sam Bryant in his usual spot on the bench, hunched over a clipboard on his lap. Just the sight of the old man made Brick relax.

"Hi, Coach."

Coach's furrowed brow softened at the sight of his star player. "Brick. What are you doing here? Can't get enough of me, eh?"

Brick returned his smile and threw his jacket on the bench before reaching into his shirt pocket. "You got a minute, Coach? I wanted to show you something."

Coach set the clipboard on the bench and reached for the letter in Brick's hand. Within seconds he was on his feet, his eyebrows arching as he read.

"Jeeeeesus Christ," he said. "Brick, this is big. This is bigger than big. This is the damn biggest letter any Jefferson High School player has ever gotten in the history of Jefferson High School."

Brick laughed. "Really, Coach?"

Coach set the letter down on the bench and grabbed Brick's shoulders. "Son, listen to me. If Carl Swartz is asking you to come visit Kent State, that means he's watched you play at least a half-dozen times." He looked up at the empty bleachers. "Huh. I know exactly where he sat, now that I think about it. He was the guy in the dark green overcoat sitting behind Buddy Clark's family. Wore a fedora that he never took off, which is why I remember him. I heard he's like that. Pretends to be someone else when he's checking out players."

He shook Brick's shoulders. "Brick, Coach Swartz wants you to play for Kent State and he's got the scholarship money to make it happen. Your life just changed."

Brick could feel the hairs on the back of his neck stand to attention. "I don't know, Coach. No one in my family's ever gone to college. And I've always had a hard time with studying. You know that better than anybody. How many times have I sat at your kitchen table so's Mrs. Bryant could help me with biology?"

"The point is, you knew when to ask for help," Coach said. "Loretta says you know more than you think. You're my point guard for a reason. You're the smartest boy on the team."

Coach started fidgeting with his tie. "Look, Brick, I don't know how to say this any other way: You need to get out of here. You need to get away from this town. Hell, I'm just gonna say it. You need to get away from that house. From him. Fear has a way of blinding a person to his own potential. You can't spend your life worrying when the next punch is coming."

"I'm not afraid of anyone," Brick said. "I'm sure as hell not afraid of *him*."

Coach locked eyes with Brick. "I've seen the bruises on your face." He pointed to Brick's eye. "You had a nasty cut goin' there just last month. I wouldn't treat a dog that way. It has to get to you, being thrown around like that. I hope you're afraid. Your fear will keep you alive."

Brick took a step back. "Coach, I—"

Coach held up his palm. "I don't need to know your business. But I do need you to know that this"—he picked the letter up off the bench, waved it—"*this* is your one chance to find out who you are, and what you can really do. You can't do that here. You have to leave this school, this town. You have to leave this life behind you."

Brick slid his left hand into his pocket and started jingling his coins. Coach pointed to his pocket. "Hear that, Brick? That's the sound of pocket change. If you don't take advantage of this opportunity, that's all you're ever going to have. A pocket full of change and a life of broken dreams."

"Maybe my dream isn't about playing basketball."

Coach laughed. "Who're you talking to here? I see you out there. I see how hard you work to make those shots look easy as a sneeze. I've never known a boy who glides across the floor like you. You're a born leader, too. Whole team looks up to you. You were made to play this game. It's the only time you look happy."

Brick looked up at the basketball hoop and said nothing.

"I know what you're thinking," Coach said. "Ellie's a sweet girl. If she loves you, she's going to tell you to go to Kent State. If she loves you, she won't want to hold you back."

"She'd never hold me back, Coach. Ellie believes in me more than—" His eyes darted quickly to Coach's face then looked away. "I gotta go change for practice," Brick said, folding the letter back in the envelope and sliding it into his shirt pocket.

Coach grabbed his arm. "Brick, I don't want to overstep here. It's just that I want everything for you." He loosened his grip. "What does Ellie say?"

"I haven't told her yet. She hasn't seen the letter."

"Well, son, it's time to let her know about it, don't you think? Give her a chance to get excited for you."

Brick reached for his jacket on the bench. "Yeah, I guess so. I'm driving her home after practice. I'll tell her then."

"I'm sure she'll be happy for you," Coach said. "How could she not? Take it from me. Nothing is impossible when your woman believes in you."

Brick had lied about driving Ellie home. He wasn't even allowed to pull his truck into her driveway. He lied to Ellie, too, the next morning when she asked why he hadn't waited with her at the bus stop after school. "Coach wanted to go over last's week game to prepare for the one coming up with Glenville," he told her, avoiding eye contact.

Ellie didn't even question him. He wasn't sure what to make of her lately. She seemed always on the verge of tears, like she had some bad news she was keeping to herself. Normally he was willing to do whatever it took to make Ellie smile. He just didn't have it in him right now.

Brick raised his coat sleeve to look at his watch. Barely twenty-four hours had passed since he'd talked to Coach, but it felt like a week. He wasn't sleeping, and he had no appetite, which his mother had noted at breakfast. "I know you're upset about Ellie's grandpa, but you have to eat," she told him, handing him a plate of eggs and toast. "You need your energy for the game."

He felt so guilty, he couldn't look at her. His mother would love to know he got the scholarship, but she'd be just like Coach and tell him to get going and forget about Ellie. How could they not see that everything good about him came to life only after Ellie named it? In her eyes he was handsome and smart. "Clever-smart," she always said, "and nobody's fool." She said he was brave, too, the way he didn't let his father hold him back. She was the only person in his life who made him believe his father was wrong about him. Even his mother couldn't do that.

Brick pulled out another cigarette and flipped open the silver lighter Ellie had bought him with her babysitting money for Christmas last year. He flicked on the flame, held it under the cigarette, and snapped the lighter shut. He angled it so that he could read the engraving: LOVE, PINT. He slid the lighter back into his pocket and threw the cigarette at the moon.

CHAPTER

7

Ellie yanked her skirt around her knees and slid across the front seat, pressing her back against the passenger door. "Brick, I've told you over and over, I can't do that."

"I wasn't doing anything, Ellie."

"Maybe *you* weren't, but your hand was breaking every rule from A to Z."

"What rule starts with 'Z'?"

Ellie looked out the windshield and stared at the ice caps on Lake Erie. "Zoo," she finally said. "Don't act like you live in a zoo."

Brick laughed, and the briefest of smiles disrupted Ellie's scowl. He cracked open his window and reached under his jacket to pull out the pack of cigarettes tucked into his shirt pocket. Ellie glanced at the brand and shook her head. "Kents," she said, softly. "Of course, you're smoking Kents now." She pulled up the collar of her coat and shivered. "It's freezing outside, Brick."

Brick flicked open his lighter. "It isn't much warmer in here, if you ask me."

Ellie squeezed her eyes shut. The last thing she wanted to do was to start crying. "Brick, you said yourself we don't want to take any chances of ruining your scholarship. You said it yourself."

"All right, Ellie. I said it once, and you've said it a hundred times since."

Ellie said nothing. She was done talking, done explaining herself to anybody. Brick was going to Kent State, no matter how many times he said he hadn't decided. And everyone but Ellie McGinty would celebrate. She spread her damp hankie across her lap and ran a finger over the cluster of her grandmother's embroidered lilacs, French knots of pink and lavender. Yesterday morning she had walked into the kitchen and, at the sight of Grandma standing at the stove frying bacon, felt such a wave of sadness. Her grandmother's dress was made from the same fabric she had used for many of the squares in Ellie's quilt, and for two of the pot holders hanging on the hook by the stove.

"Grandma, have you ever bought a brand-new dress? From a store. One that's already made."

Ada turned around and looked at her granddaughter. "Why would I waste my money on that?" she said, and turned back to the stove.

"I just wondered if you ever wished you had one dress you didn't have to make."

"You're going to wish you knew how to sew someday, young lady. I won't always be around to make sure you have clothes that fit."

"I'm going to buy mine, Grandma," Ellie said as she pulled out her plate and coffee cup. "I'm going to go shopping, and I'm going to wear dresses just like the ones in *Ladies' Home Journal*."

"Is that right," Ada said, cracking two eggs into the skillet. "Guess you're going to be marrying up then."

Ellie walked over to the stove and lifted the percolator off the back burner to pour a cup of coffee. "Or maybe," she said, setting the percolator back on the burner, "maybe I'm going to get a good job myself. With my own paycheck. Maybe buy my own dresses."

"Is that right? Is this because Brick's going to go to college?"

Ellie sat down at the table and started picking at the hem of her jumper. "I wasn't talking about Brick. He'll go if he wants. But who says I'm not going to college, too? Plenty of girls go to college now. I could be a teacher. Or a nurse. You always say I'm good at taking care of people. That I anticipate other people's needs." Ada carried the skillet to the table and slid the bacon and eggs onto Ellie's plate. "You can do that as a mother, too."

Now Ellie scrunched up the hankie and silently berated herself. Here she was, slumped in Brick's pickup truck, pouting because he had a chance to make something of himself. What was wrong with her?

They'd had a terrible fight the day before, after Brick showed her the letter from Kent State. It was the way he kept reprimanding her. *Be gentle with the envelope. Don't muss up the paper. Watch your fingerprints there.*

"That's my future you've got in your hands, Ellie," he'd said. *My* future. Not *our* future. She'd started to cry, and he shut down. Drove her to Becca Gilley's house and didn't even say goodbye.

After a sleepless night for both of them, they rushed to each other at the school entrance. "I just need to talk to you, Pint," he said. "Once we talk you'll know everything's going to be fine."

Ellie spent the day fantasizing about how he would take her hand and confess that he could never leave her. Then he would ask her to marry him. What an idiot she was. She turned to look at Brick. "If you go to Kent, what's going to happen to us?"

Brick's face relaxed. "What's going to happen? Ellie, we're going to get married, that's what's going to happen. That's what I tried to tell you yesterday, but as soon as you saw the letter you were all cryin' and stuff and wouldn't listen to anything I said."

She looked at him, waiting.

"I'm going to get a college degree, and then I'm going to marry you and be head basketball coach at one of those big high schools in Cleveland. I might have to start by coaching JV, but Coach has taught me everything he knows. I'll be coaching varsity before you know it. You'll be there every game, cheering for me just like you do now, only you won't be standing on the sidelines in that cheerleading dress. You'll be the coach's wife. And you'll be sitting with all of our sons."

Ellie giggled. "I'd like at least one girl. I want to have a daughter and name her Joy. It was Grandpa's mother's middle name."

"Then we'll have a girl, too," Brick said. "I want you to have everything you've ever wanted, Ellie."

She looked at Brick and smiled. "Coach McGinty."

"And his lovely wife, Mrs. Brick McGinty," he said, grabbing her hand. "I'll teach history. Or biology, maybe."

She slid up next to him, and he wrapped his right arm around her. "It's different when you're the one giving orders, Ellie. Everything's different when you're the one in charge."

She looked out the window and sighed at the sight of so many barren trees. "What am I supposed to do while you're gone?"

"Write me lots of letters," he said. "And you'll come down on the bus to watch my games."

"What if I go to college, too? What if I want to become a nurse?"

Brick stiffened. "Well, this is new."

"Well, I was just thinking, why not do something useful

with myself while you're away at school? I've got the best grades in the class. You know that. Maybe there are scholarships for that, too?"

Brick took a deep breath and slowly nodded. "Well, sure. This is *our* dream, right? Together. Neither one of us wants to be stuck in this tiny hellhole of a town for the rest of our lives."

She laid her head on his shoulder. "I'm sorry I didn't act excited when you showed me the letter, Brick. I'm just trying to figure out where I fit in. You think so much bigger than others. Some of the boys are fine with getting jobs on the docks. Like Richard Ryan. He's going to work at the power plant, for EEI. Marcia says he's going to join the union, make more money than both of their fathers put together."

"And be a slave for the rest of his life," Brick said. "Workin' for someone else, taking orders from some dumb-ass nobody. That may be good enough for them, but it's not good enough for me."

Ellie squeezed his arm. "If you teach, even if you coach, you still have to take orders. It's not like you own the school."

Brick turned to face her, his eyes glistening. "Ellie, you know how it feels when you stand in the middle of that gym? When you're doing one of your cheerleading routines and everyone's cheering for you? Everybody's looking right atcha?"

She nodded.

"That's what it feels like every time I'm on the basketball court. All eyes on me. I want to feel like that for the rest of my life. I want to feel that buzz when I walk into a room, when I see you there in the center of it all, cheering for me, louder than anyone."

She pulled her hankie out of her sleeve and wiped the tears from his eyes. She no longer cared about being late, or any stupid school penalties she was about to outgrow anyway. She just wanted to hear more about the life waiting for them away from Clayton Valley.

"What else do you want, Coach McGinty?"

He pulled her close, and started kissing her eyelids, her cheeks. She leaned back as he pushed her hair from her face, cupping her chin, lifting her mouth to his.

"Ellie," he whispered, as he rolled her coat off her shoulders. "My Ellie."

CHAPTER

8

Grandma Ada's younger sister, Nessa, was the only person Ellie knew who brought no judgment to other people's bad news. She was sixty-three and had never married, a single fact about her life that she often mentioned to friends and strangers alike as evidence of her sound judgment and independence. They could call Nessa Travis an old maid and a spinster all they wanted. She was one of the lucky ones, she insisted to Ellie—a woman exempt from other people's low expectations.

Nessa was the only person in Ellie's extended family to have gone to college. She'd graduated from Reynolds Teachers College in 1915 and for more than four decades taught senior English at Erietown High School. Every summer, she had traveled alone by train to explore "this great country of ours." Ellie had filled two shoe boxes with Aunt Nessa's postcards, each one crammed with facts about the region delivered in her tiny, precise handwriting, ending with the same postscript: "Put this on your list of places to see before you die."

When Ellie was little, she sometimes overheard her grandmother describe her sister's "barren life" and how sad it was that Aunt Nessa had no children of her own. Ellie used to wince in silent agreement. What was a woman's life worth if she couldn't be a wife and mother? It wasn't until last December that Ellie had seen it differently, when she was visiting Aunt Nessa. Ellie marveled aloud at the hundreds of Christmas cards hanging from string draped across three doorways and along the crown molding in both the dining and living rooms.

"My children," Aunt Nessa said, waving her arm under one of the curtains of cards. "I've launched so many of them into the world. They like to let me know what they're up to. They've got a lot of children of their own now." She looked at Ellie's confused face and smiled. "Never feel sorry for me, sweetheart. I have lived an amazing life."

"I never said I—"

Aunt Nessa waved her off. "I know what my big sister thinks of my choices. I don't expect her to understand. Just don't you believe it."

It was that one word that burrowed into Ellie's mind and took hold. *Choices.* It had never occurred to Ellie that her great-aunt had ever had options. She had always assumed that Aunt Nessa was an old maid by fate, not choice. What if she could have married, and chose not to? The more Ellie stewed about her own future, the more she wanted to talk to Aunt Nessa about her "choices."

A month later, Ellie got her chance. "Aunt Nessa called," Grandma Ada said one day after school. "Says she wants to pick you up and take you to Cleveland for lunch on Saturday."

Ellie could not contain her excitement. "Just the two of us?"

Ada was at the stove, mashing a pot of potatoes. "That's what she said. I don't know that you need to go all the way to Cleveland for a sandwich, but if Nessa wants to waste her money like that, who am I to stop her?"

Early on Saturday morning, Nessa had barely pulled her arctic blue Oldsmobile into the Fetterses' driveway before Ellie was shouting goodbye to her grandparents and running out the door. On the drive to Cleveland, Aunt Nessa made small talk about school and her plans for next summer's train trip, but after they parked and the doorman ushered them into Higbee's department store, she was all business.

"It's time you had your own train case," Aunt Nessa said, guiding her toward the escalator.

Ellie watched her aunt step on the grated stair and slide her hand onto the railing. "Okay," she whispered to herself. "You can do this." She jumped onto the bottom stair with both feet and grabbed the railing. On her way to the mezzanine, Ellie tried to memorize everything on the first floor. The smell of dried rosebuds wafting from silver bowls on countertops. Gleaming glass tops reflecting the spray of chandelier lights. The fine wools and silks, and chirpy greetings from one saleslady after another.

"Aunt Nessa," Ellie said, stepping off the escalator. "I don't even know what a train case is." Nessa pointed to the Personal Leather Goods sign. "Every girl needs a train case," she said, leading her through the archway. "I've had mine for decades. If you buy a top-notch one, it will last you a lifetime."

"Afternoon, Miss Reilly."

Aunt Nessa smiled at the young woman standing behind the glass counter. "Hello, Melissa," she said. The brass name tag pinned to the clerk's cardigan was bigger and shinier than any piece of jewelry Ellie owned. The clerk lowered her chin and peered at Ellie from under her bangs. "Is this your niece we've heard so much about?"

Ellie looked at her aunt. "You *talk* about me, Aunt Ness?"

The salesclerk smiled. "*Does* she."

"Why wouldn't I?" Aunt Nessa said, coaxing Ellie to the counter. Another saleswoman, older and with a small diamond embedded in her name tag, approached them. "Miss Reilly, what brings you here today?"

Aunt Nessa unlocked arms with Ellie and wrapped an arm

over her shoulder. "Hello, Kristina. My niece here needs a train case in"—she looked at Ellie—"what color would you like?"

Ellie looked around the room, which smelled of leather and lavender potpourri. "There's so much here," she said, staring at the racks of suitcases and purses. "I don't know where to begin."

"Well," Kristina said, "let's start with your favorite color."

"Grandma says that blue's my color."

Aunt Ness lifted her gloved hand and pushed a lock of curls from Ellie's forehead. "Well, Grandma's right. You look beautiful in blue. And since you'll be carrying this everywhere, why not have it match your eyes?"

A few minutes later, another young clerk had wrapped a powder blue vanity case in sheets of yellow tissue paper and slid it into a cream-colored box. She noticed Ellie staring at the brass name plate pinned to her dress.

"Angela," the girl said, tapping her pin. "My mother thought she was giving birth to an angel. What a surprise I was."

Ellie laughed. "I know a woman named Angela."

The woman pushed the lid onto the box and slid it into a large, flat-bottomed bag with braided cotton handles. "Has she earned the name?"

Ellie thought about Brick's mother, and how his face softened whenever he talked about her. "I think her son would say so." The woman looked up from the receipt she was writing and smiled at Ellie. "Well, any man who loves his mother like that is a real catch."

Aunt Nessa moved a little closer to Ellie. "My niece has big plans," she said, taking the bag from the clerk. "Which is why she needs this." She handed it to Ellie. "Let's go up to lunch and talk about all that."

On the elevator, Ellie smiled at the male operator and

looped her arm through Aunt Nessa's. "I just can't believe how nice you are to me," Ellie said. "And how everyone knows you here and fusses over you."

Aunt Nessa laughed softly. "Never confuse customer service with kindness, honey. They hover because I've spent a lot of money here over the years."

They got off the elevator and started walking toward the restaurant. Ellie caught her reflection in a gilded mirror on the wall. Her cheeks were red, and her forehead was shiny from sweat. She set the shopping bag on the floor. "Aunt Nessa."

Her aunt turned around. "My word, Ellie," she said, walking toward her. "What's the matter?"

Ellie clasped her cheeks with her hands. "Aunt Nessa, I don't know." She glanced again at the frightened girl in the mirror. "I don't know what I'm going to do next." Nessa pointed to the shopping bag. "Pick that up, and follow me. We'll figure it all out over lunch."

Ellie took a deep breath as they walked into the restaurant. "I've never seen a place like this in all my life," she said, staring at the silver gazebo in the center of the room. It was wrapped in a trellis of silk vines and flowers, and overlooked a gurgling fountain.

Her aunt pointed to the raised platform parting the room full of linen-draped gold-and-silver tables for four. "They sometimes have fashion shows during lunch," she said. "It can be a bit much when you're trying to have a conversation, but a lot of the ladies love it." She nodded at the hostess approaching them. "Hello, Arlene," Nessa said, patting Ellie's back. "This is my niece, Ellie. She's never been here before." The hostess extended her arm toward the dining room. "Well, then, this is a special day for you, Miss Ellie. Welcome to the Silver Grille." She walked them to a table by the wall of windows.

"I've never heard of Indian chicken curry," Ellie said.

"It's got a bit of kick, but it's delicious," Aunt Nessa said.

"Sounds like it's calling to you. And wait until you taste their orange tea biscuits." She handed the menus to the waitress. "We'll take"—she looked at Ellie—"the butterscotch cream pie for dessert?"

Ellie clapped her hands together. "I've never had that, either."

Ellie opened the pocketbook on her lap and pulled out the receipt for her train case. "Miss Eleanor Fetters," she read aloud, tapping her name written in her aunt's hand at the bottom. "I feel so grown up." Aunt Nessa leaned back in her seat. "As you almost are." She lifted her cup and took a sip of tea. "Now, what's on your mind?"

Ellie spread her napkin across her lap. "What makes you think I've got anything on my mind?"

"You're almost eighteen, honey. On the brink of womanhood." She reached for a biscuit. "And I heard about Brick's scholarship."

Ellie slumped back in her seat. "Is there anyone who hasn't? You'd think he was just elected president or something."

Nessa split open the biscuit and handed half to Ellie. "Don't, honey. Nothing ages a woman faster than bitterness. Brick's gain is not your loss."

"Grandma and Grandpa don't like Brick. They don't approve of his father."

"Yes, well," Aunt Nessa said, "it's easier to judge the father you had no role in raising."

Ellie sat up straighter. "I never thought of it that way."

Her aunt waved her hand. "I don't mean to be harsh. We're complicated creatures, every last one of us."

"Aunt Nessa, can I ask you a question?"

"You may."

"Did you ever, I don't know." Her aunt was holding her teacup now with both hands. "Did you ever think you'd get married?"

Aunt Nessa set the cup down. "I did," she said. "Even knew the fellow I wanted to marry."

"You did?"

"Benjamin Whitmore. Sweetest boy. His father was a pharmacist, which was almost like being a doctor in our dinky little town. Nice man. His mother taught the piano."

"Why didn't you marry him?"

Ellie waited as her aunt took another sip of tea. She looked out the window for a moment before continuing. "Well, I thought about it. A lot. He proposed three times." She looked at Ellie. "Can you believe that? Three times, this handsome boy asked me to marry him. And three times I had to say no."

"Didn't you love him?"

Aunt Nessa looked away again. "I did love him. But I guess you could say I loved my freedom more. When I was your age, a woman couldn't be a teacher after she had a baby. She couldn't even be in the classroom once she started to show. I loved teaching. More to the point, I loved having a career. I didn't want to give that up."

Ellie waited for the waitress to set down their plates and leave before asking another question. "Do you ever regret that decision?"

"Ellie, we all make choices in life. I made mine, and I've never looked back. What you really want to know is what you should do with the rest of *your* life."

Ellie nodded, her eyes welling. "I just don't know what will happen to me if Brick goes away. I do want to be married."

"And you will be, someday. But what else do you want to be?"

"What else can I be? I have no money, and no scholarship. And Grandma and Grandpa won't even talk about me going to college."

Aunt Nessa reached across the table and grabbed Ellie's

hand. "My sister and her husband love you very much, but they don't know what's out there for a young girl these days."

"What do you mean?"

"What I mean is, you could go to nursing school." She scooped up a forkful of rice. "Your grades are excellent. You could get a full scholarship at St. Luke's Hospital in Cleveland. I've already been in touch with them. I've been sending girls to them for years. They'll train and board you for two years, and then they'll hire you." Nessa waved her hand in front of Ellie's stunned face. "Ellie, did you hear what I just said?"

"Why?" she whispered. "Why didn't anybody tell me this?"

Her aunt smiled. "I'm afraid Clayton Valley hasn't caught up with the rest of the world yet."

Ellie set her fork down, her appetite vanquished. She looked around the room, suddenly aware of the hum of conversations. For the first time, she imagined Brick playing basketball at Kent State and felt only happiness for him.

"I could go to nursing school," she said. "I could work as a nurse. And then when Brick graduates from college—"

"When Brick graduates, he can only hope you'll still be waiting for him," Aunt Nessa said, flagging the waitress. "Let's ask for dessert right now. Let's celebrate, and then let's start planning." She reached across the table and grabbed Ellie's hand again. "You have a big, bold adventure waiting for you, dear one. Don't be late for your own life."

CHAPTER

9

Brick looked at the full moon peeking through the sliver of his bedroom window and thought about his afternoon with Ellie. This was their third time, and just thinking about her got him ready for the fourth. She wanted him as bad as he wanted her, even if they always had to have the God talk first. Would God want them to be doing this? Would God punish them? Was God disappointed in them?

He was certain God didn't care what they did. If God was always hanging around, he sure played favorites, and neither he nor Ellie had made the list. How could God let Ellie be abandoned by her parents? And why did he stick Brick with Bull McGinty for a father? Ellie hated it whenever he asked such questions. "Everything happens for a reason, Brick. Sometimes we have to wait it out to see what God has planned."

He imagined her face flush with hope, and felt another round of guilt. What would happen to Ellie if he left? To his mom? Would God take care of them? He pulled the bedcovers tighter around his neck and scratched Patch's head as the dog groaned in his sleep. Brick looked at his alarm clock. 4:06. *Jesus.* He'd been awake all night. He pulled the wool blanket up to his nose and inhaled. The scent of Harry was long gone.

The blanket was the only thing of Harry's that Brick had wanted after his brother died in the war. He had been six years old when his brother's plane exploded over England, leaving the McGinty family in shards. He remembered every horrible moment of that summer afternoon in '44. The knock on the frame of the screen door. The creak of rusty hinges as his mother pushed it open. A man's low voice. His mother's scream. Brick's attempt to catch her as her knees buckled. She fell to the floor, pulling Brick down with her. "Too much," she wailed, rocking in his arms. "You ask too much of me."

Not long after Harry's funeral, Brick found his mother sitting on the kitchen floor, staring at a cardboard box stamped UNITED STATES NAVY. Her hands trembled when she sliced open the shipping tape. Brick tiptoed toward her as she slowly pulled out each of his brother's belongings and set them gently on the linoleum floor, as if she were setting an altar for communion.

After a few minutes of this, Brick bent down and leaned on his heels to get a better look. He ran his fingers along the grooves of Harry's hand-carved wooden box, the one he had made in high school. He echoed his mother's deep breath as she opened it to find his cigarette lighter and a bundle of letters from home, tied with twine, all of them written in her hand. She pulled out Harry's penknife and set it on the floor, next to a small brown envelope stuffed with his collection of palm-size picture postcards. She took out Harry's prized fountain pen, a gift from his oldest sister, Lillian. "He wrote all his letters with this," she said, holding it up to the window light. "Look," she said, pointing toward the nib. "You can see his fingerprint."

A folded olive-colored blanket lined the bottom of the box. Angie lifted it out with both hands and unfurled it across her lap. Brick slid next to her and held up a corner of the blanket to his face. He took a deep breath and exhaled. "Can I have it, Ma?"

Angie looked down at him, her eyes red and watery. "What?"

"Can I have the blanket?"

"Of all the things here, why this?"

Brick buried his face in it again and took another deep breath. "It smells like him, Ma. It smells like Harry." Angie lifted the blanket and inhaled, and started to sob. Brick jumped to his feet. "I'm sorry, Ma. I'm sorry." He ran out of the room wishing he'd never said a word.

A few months later, after Bull had unleashed another round of fury, Brick woke up to find Harry's blanket draped across the foot of his bed. He never mentioned it to his mother. As much as he feared his father's temper, he feared his mother's tears even more.

Brick looked at the clock again. 4:35. He stood up and wrapped the blanket around his shoulders while Patch rolled over onto his back, his legs splayed as he continued to snore. Brick smiled. "Lucky you, boy. At least you can sleep." He walked over to the window. The fat snowflakes looked so innocent as they steadily buried the town. His father's truck was parked next to his. A rare sight. Bull often left the house for days at a time now, but his mother had seemed to stop caring years ago. The week after Harry died, she'd cleared out her bureau drawers and moved into Harry's bedroom. She had slept there ever since.

Gone were the long nights when Brick used to lie in bed with a pillow over his head, trying to muffle the sounds of his father's drunken rage as they wafted through the floorboards. So many mornings, Brick would walk into the kitchen and hear his mother softly singing the same hymn, over and over.

There will be peace in the valley for me, someday
There will be peace in the valley for me, oh Lord I pray
There'll be no sadness, no sorrow
No trouble, trouble I see
There will be peace in the valley for me, for me.

She was fifty-four now, and looked ancient. Her hair was snow white and thinning, her face sliding away and pooling around her neck. The kindest woman he knew was surrendering to the dark cloud that had been trying to catch her for years. She walked more slowly, and he could no longer ignore how often she paused and pressed a palm against the small of her back. The more slowly she moved, the more Brick hovered. "What's wrong, Ma?" he'd ask, trying to nudge her into a chair. Her answer was always the same: "Nothing God won't fix down the road, Son." Even when he stood right next to her, his mother looked so alone.

Nine of the ten McGinty girls were married now, all of them living within ten miles of the house. Only Lillian had managed to get away, running off to Cleveland as soon as she graduated from high school to work as a live-in maid for a wealthy family on the city's east side. As soon as Bull found out the family was Jewish he declared Lillian dead to him and to the whole family. "You tell her to stay away from here," he yelled at Angie. "She is no longer a member of this family." Lillian hadn't been back for a visit since, but she was in constant touch with her mother. Every Saturday morning, Angie kept watch for the mailman. Lillian had learned to time her letters to arrive when Bull was reliably hungover and unlikely to snatch them out of Angie's hands and burn them over the stove.

Sometimes Brick thought about what it'd be like if his father were dead. Not murdered, just fall-in-the-mud dead, face-first, from a heart attack, maybe, or a stroke. Maybe drive into a telephone pole after a late-night binge in Erietown, taking his latest whore with him. Brick imagined his father's truck sliding out of control on the ice, the crunch of steel and glass as it slammed through the railing and soared into the night sky before dropping like a bomb into the black river below. His mother would finally be free. She could sell off the farm and all of its bad memories. Buy a little place near his sisters, and paint every room in her favorite colors of lavender and robin's egg blue.

Brick stood at the bedroom window and closed his eyes against the tears trying to break free. "I didn't pick him, God," he said. "You're the one who made him my father, and then where did you go?" He tossed the blanket onto Patch. "C'mon, old man," Brick said softly. "We're going for a ride."

He pulled on his jeans and sweatshirt and grabbed his letterman's jacket. He ran his fingers across the large felt letter— a green "J" for Jefferson High School—that his mother had stitched on the front. Twice, on two jackets, she'd done that for him. He fingered each blanket stitch as if he were working the beads of a rosary: 164 stitches. Every time he performed this ritual, he could see his mother sitting next to him in his truck, his first jacket draped across her lap as she hummed and pulled through one stitch after another.

Brick was the first freshman in the history of Jefferson High to letter in varsity basketball. The green "J" sat on his dresser for months because he couldn't afford the jacket. In early August before his sophomore year, he was about to leave to help bail the second cutting of hay at the BeBouts' farm when his mother pressed a wad of bills into his palm. "Get that jacket, Brick," she said, closing his fingers around the money. He handed it back to her. "That's a year's worth of your egg money," he said. "You know I earned money all summer working on three different farms. As soon as I help Tag McHenry finish his barn next week, I'll have enough money to buy it on my own."

Angie shook her head. "I don't want you missing August practices because you're helping Tag McHenry, and I want my son to wear that jacket he has earned."

"Ma, if Dad finds out he'll go crazy." Angie shoved the money back into his hand. "He has no idea how much I make on the eggs. Never has."

Twice, at her insistence, Brick drove his mother to Otis Outfitters in Erietown. First, to get measured for his jacket, then to pick it up. His mother had tucked needles and a spool of green thread into her purse so that she could stitch the letter onto his jacket on the drive home.

It had been nearly eighty degrees on the first day of school, but Brick wore the jacket anyway. His freckled face was sweaty and red as a radish as he walked through the halls, but it was worth every second of suffering. People treated Brick differently when he wore that jacket, from Pastor Culver at Sunday service to Mr. Simpson at the dry goods store. Best of all, Ellie swooned the first time she saw him in it. "You look even bigger, Brick," she said, and then leaned in and whispered, "Makes me feel things." He flexed his biceps and pulled her in closer.

The following summer, Brick grew four inches and his shoulders ballooned, fraying the seams of both of the good shirts he owned. It got to the point where he couldn't even raise his arms when he wore his jacket, but he refused to part with it and he couldn't replace it. The drinking was catching up with Bull, and every cent Brick made was going to his mother now. No one dared make fun of how Brick looked in his jacket, but he knew what everyone had to be thinking. His face burned whenever he walked past a gaggle of girls and heard them giggle. Maybe they were laughing at him, maybe they weren't, but once you think you're the butt of everyone's joke you see mocking in every smile.

In mid-October, Coach said, "Why don't you come by for dinner tomorrow night? I need to pick your brain a bit about Friday's game." Brick figured Coach was doing what he always did, which was to make sure he had a decent meal with no Bull-drama on the night before a game. This time, though, after Brick thanked Mrs. Bryant for dinner and backed away from the table to leave, Coach laid his hand on his shoulder and gently pushed Brick back down into his seat.

"Wait here just a minute," he said. "Got something for you." He walked out of the kitchen, and Mrs. Bryant set down a second slice of rhubarb pie in front of Brick. "It's a special occasion," she said, patting his back. Brick wolfed down the pie in six bites and stood up. "Thanks, Mrs. B.," he said, handing her the plate at the sink. "I've got to get home." He pulled his jacket off the back of his chair and had already tugged it on when Coach returned to the kitchen and tossed a new letterman's jacket to him.

"I—I can't accept this, Coach," Brick said, staring at the jacket in his hands. "I don't have the money to pay you back. I appreciate the thought, but no McGinty accepts charity."

"That's your father talking, Brick," Coach said. "He won't help you, and he doesn't want anyone else to help you, either."

"Sam, honey," Mrs. Bryant said, shaking her head. She draped the washrag over the faucet and untied her apron. "Excuse me, boys, but I'm in the middle of *The Story of My Life* and I want to finish it before it's due back at the library." She smiled at Brick. "It's Helen Keller's autobiography. She is blind and deaf, you know, but her teacher, Miss Annie Sullivan, helped her learn how to communicate with the world." She walked toward her husband and squeezed his shoulder. "Imagine," she said, pausing in the doorway. "Imagine how sad Helen Keller's life would be if she'd been unwilling to let that Miss Sullivan help her."

Coach waited until his wife left the room and then grinned at Brick. "My Loretta isn't the most subtle of women."

Brick nodded. "No, sir. But she sure is smart."

"Look, Brick. This isn't charity. Mrs. Bryant's going to remove your letter and we're going to give your old jacket to Curly Jackson. You know him. That little guy, the freshman running back. He doesn't have any jacket at all and winter's just around the corner. I guarantee you *he* won't let pride get in the way."

Brick stared down at the jacket and ran his hand along the back of it. "Tell you what," Coach said. "You take the jacket, and in return, you help me build a first-floor bathroom."

Brick looked at him and laughed. "I don't know the first thing about building bathrooms. And I sure don't know anything about plumbing."

"Guess it's time you learn," Coach said. "My father was in construction. He taught me how to build just about anything from scratch. As soon as the winter breaks, you're mine every weekend until we finish." He pointed toward the living room. "That way, Mrs. Bryant gets off my back about her precious powder room, and your delicate ego survives the injury of a good deed. Deal?"

Brick tried not to smile, but he couldn't help it.

"Go give Mrs. Bryant your old jacket so she can pull out the stitches on that letter. I've known your mother for more than twenty years. She's going to want to stitch it on your new jacket before you leave the house tomorrow."

Brick smiled again. "Yes, sir, she surely will."

Several weeks later, on the first weekend thaw, Brick was at the Bryants' door. Mrs. Bryant clapped her hands at the sight of him. "Thank you for this, Brick," she said. "I don't know how I would have gotten him to finally do this if it weren't for you."

For three months of weekends, Brick and Sam Bryant worked side by side. Brick learned how to pour concrete and lay tile, install plumbing and wire for electricity. He loved watching the room take shape, one task at a time, and spending time with Coach, who never raised his voice no matter how many mistakes Brick made. "I feel like I'm learning how a house works," he told Coach one day when they broke for lunch. "I understand what's going on behind the walls now. I can see its heart."

"Yep, that's the beauty of building with your own hands," Coach said, handing him a sandwich wrapped in wax paper. "You'll have that over the city boys for the rest of your life."

They finished before the cherry trees bloomed in late spring. Mrs. Bryant taped a strip of pink crepe paper across the doorway and made a show of handing the scissors to Brick instead of her husband. "I know who was the muscle behind the brains," she said. "Sam's been bragging about you like the son we never had."

Brick glanced at her and then looked at the floor. "I just want to say. I just want to thank you—"

Mrs. Bryant patted his arm. "Go 'head, honey. Cut the ribbon. Think of it as a christening."

"You're the only boy on my team that earned his jacket twice as an underclassman," Coach said. "I'm real proud of you."

Now, whenever Brick visits the Bryants, he washes his hands in the powder room and excuses himself at least once during dinner. Not to use the toilet. He just quietly lowers the seat and sits on it, remembering every piece of wood and tile he installed with his own two hands.

Just before school let out for the following summer, Coach handed Brick a business card for Blade Construction in Erietown. "Guy's a friend of mine. He's looking for top-notch workers, ones with muscle and experience, so I gave him your name. Give him a call." Brick earned more money in one summer of construction than his father had made all year as a mediocre mechanic. He planned to do it again this summer and sock away every cent before leaving for college.

Maybe.

Brick grabbed his keys off his bedside table. "C'mon, Patch." He tiptoed down the two flights of stairs with Patch behind him and eased open the kitchen door, slipping out into the darkness. They walked side by side, Brick and Patch, their breaths clouding around their heads as they made their way through the falling snow to Brick's truck. Harry's truck, Brick always called it, because as long as it was still Harry's, he wasn't really gone.

The day after Harry's funeral, Brick's brother-in-law Luke walked into the kitchen and asked Brick for the keys to Harry's truck. "Your brother planned to give it to you when you're old enough to drive," Luke told him. "We need to get it out of here before your father tries to sell it." Brick looked out the screen door and saw his sister Irene sitting behind the wheel of the truck. She locked eyes with him and nodded. Brick stood on tiptoes to grab the key ring off the hook by the door and tossed it to Luke. "It'll get better, little buddy," Luke said, hugging him. "One of these days, you're going to get in that truck and drive away from here for good, just like Harry wanted you to do."

For so many years now, Brick had clung to those words. *Like Harry wanted you to do.* Maybe that was who he should be praying to.

Brick scooped off the wet snow piling up on his front window and side mirrors. He slowly opened the driver's door, but it still creaked like hell. Brick looked up at his mother's window. No light. He scooped up Patch and slid him across the front seat before climbing in. The door creaked again when he pulled it shut. Still no light in his mother's window. He didn't worry about his father. He wouldn't wake up if the place were on fire. Brick shook his head free of the fantasy and turned the key.

Brick drove about forty minutes before hitting Erietown's city limits. He pulled into the empty parking lot at Erietown Plaza and cruised past the darkened stores. So many businesses, all in one place. Hills department store, Lawson's Dairy, Kroger,

Jerome's Paint Store. He couldn't remember the last time he'd driven his mother here. She used to love to put on one of her Sunday dresses and climb into his truck for an afternoon of shopping. Lately, though, she always begged off when he suggested they go into town. "Not up for the crowds, honey," she'd say, handing Brick her errand list. "You do it for me, will you?"

Brick pulled back onto Route 20, which became Erie Road once he hit town. He drove past Antonio's Pizza and Grant's Bakery, and the new burger joint that had opened just two months ago. He'd promised Ellie he'd never eat there until they could do it together.

He slowed down as he drove past the cluster of houses lining Erie Road a few blocks before the town square. They were all built right after World War II, each of them with a front porch and neat squares of yard in front and back. For some reason they always made Brick think of Harry. How, had he lived, he would have married Rachel Skidmore and they would have lived in one of these houses. Harry always talked about moving to Erietown one day, and how he and Rachel were going to buy a house big enough for his mom to come live with them. "Just you, Ma," he'd say, winking at Brick. "Maybe take this rascal with us, but only until he's old enough to buy his own house down the street." Living on the same street as his brother. Wouldn't that have been something. He pulled to a stop in front of Cecil's gas station and cut his headlights. A light was on in the house across the street. The snow had slowed enough for him to make out two shadowy figures moving in the kitchen, in the back of the house.

The woman wore a nightgown and was helping the man button his coat. He grabbed a lunch pail off the counter, then turned toward her, lifting her face for a kiss. They looked to be laughing, the way she tossed her hair and arched her back as he leaned in. From this distance, they could have been Harry and

Rachel. They seemed happy in each other's company. The woman turned the man around, patted his back, and pretended to shove him out the door.

Brick watched and waited. He could make out the woman's figure in the front window, waving as her husband pulled his car to a stop at the edge of the driveway and waved. It was a Buick Skylark. Even in the snowfall, Brick could tell by the sheen of its paint that the man took good care of it. A match flared in the driver's seat, and for an instant Brick could see the man's face as he lit his cigarette. "Shit, Patch," Brick said. "He doesn't look much older than me." Patch raised his head and inched closer to Brick's thigh.

Brick's fingers tightened around the steering wheel and he ducked from the beams of the man's headlights as he pulled onto the road. The Skylark headed east. Brick waited until it was a quarter mile away before flicking on his lights and easing his foot on the gas to follow.

The Buick turned at the intersection and headed north, toward the harbor. Three miles later, Brick guessed his destination. "EEI," he said softly. The man was a utility worker. First shift.

The Erie Electric Illuminating Company was a plant with three smokestacks on the shore of Lake Erie. Brick knew what it looked like because his sister Virginia's husband worked there, in maintenance. Brick followed the man until he pulled into the gravel driveway, and then he looked at his watch: 5:50 A.M. Just enough time to park and punch the clock by six. He turned in to the plant driveway and drove slowly past the guard shed. The guy in the window waved him through, and Brick pulled into the plant parking lot. The man he'd been following was getting out of his parked car with his lunch pail in his hand. He wore a yellow hard hat now, and he paused to cup his bare hands around his face to light another cigarette. He tilted his head to blow the smoke high above him, then leaned against the car door to slam it shut. He started to walk, joining a stream of men swinging lunch pails and blowing clouds of smoke until they reached the entrance. One after another, they tossed their cigarettes onto the gravel and disappeared behind the large metal doors.

"You're right, Harry," Brick said, staring at the plant. "It's time to get away from here."

CHAPTER

10

Wayne Fetters paused at the top of the stairs to listen to the debate in the kitchen. His granddaughter was lobbying Ada, but Ellie was no match for the household budget director.

"The fancier it is, the less use it will be to you after," Ada said. "Why spend money on a dress you'll never wear again?"

"But you don't know that, Grandma. Maybe I can wear it to my friends' weddings. Becca's marrying Johnny Whipple right after graduation."

"So I heard," Ada said, her voice flat. "How in the world did she manage to get that announcement in the *Erietown Times*?"

Wayne smiled. They only subscribed to the *Clayton Valley Gazette*. Becca's grandmother must have brought the *Times* in to show off for the Thursday busybody Bees.

"Her daddy went to school with the editor," Ellie said, sighing. "Celia Brownstone's getting married, too. She said she expects Alan Uitto to propose by Thanksgiving."

"She does, does she? Has anyone told Alan?"

"C'mon, Grandma. Please? Just this once?"

The stairs creaked under the weight of Wayne's feet as he walked down, triggering a sudden shuffle of paper and a "shhh" from Ada. By the time he entered the kitchen, Ada was at the stove and Ellie was sitting on her hands, eyes wide. "What's all the fuss about?" he said.

"Girl talk," Ada said, flipping sausage patties. "Nothing you need to bother yourself with."

Ellie was squirming in her seat. "What's that?" he said, pointing to the corner of the magazine sticking out from under her skirt.

"What's what, Grandpa?"

"Am I going to have to pull it out, or are you going to hand it to me?"

Ada tsk-tsked as she cracked eggs into the skillet. "I've already told her no, honey."

He pointed at Ellie's chair, and she rose just high enough for him to pull out the magazine. He sat down and flipped through the dog-eared pages full of makeup ads and girls in fancy pastel dresses. "So this is what you girls talk about."

"Grandpa, we were talking about prom dresses."

Ada set a bowl of home fries on the table. "And how we're not buying one of those getups when I'm fully capable of making one." She snatched the magazine from Wayne and handed it back to Ellie. "Put this away now, sweetie, and pour the juice. Time to eat."

"I don't know, Ada," Wayne said. "Maybe just this once, we should take Ellie shopping for a special dress."

Ellie set the glass jug of orange juice on the table and wrapped her arms around his neck. "Oh, Grandpa, do you mean it?" He laughed and pried her fingers off his neck. "Not if you're going to choke me to death."

He stood back up and walked over to his wife. "We're not going to argue about this, honey. This time, you aren't staying up past midnight at that sewing machine. A girl only gets one prom, and Ellie is going to look as pretty as her grandmother did at the annual Spring Delight."

Ada's shy smile surprised him.

"Look at you," he said, cupping her face with his hands, "looking as sweet as the day we met." She batted his hands away.

"Go sit down, Romeo. I'm not going to have everything I just cooked go cold."

That weekend Wayne drove Ellie and Ada to Brennan's department store in Erietown, all three of them dressed in Sunday clothes. Ellie walked through the double doors and squealed. "I can't believe I'm here."

"That makes two of us," Ada said, clutching the handle of her pocketbook with both hands as she looked up at the vaulted ceiling. Wayne touched her elbow and steered them toward the directory on the wall. "Let's find out where they hide those dresses, and then I'll leave you to it."

Ellie stood in front of the three-paneled mirror and tried to smile as her grandmother stood behind her. She was wearing the third of four dresses that Ada had selected, all of them high-collared and made of sensible cotton. "I don't think so, Grandma."

Ada tucked at her waist. "It's your size but it's a little snug. That's the problem when strangers mass-produce your clothes."

The size is definitely *not* the problem, Ellie wanted to say. Grandma was trying, she knew that, but ten minutes into their shopping, Ellie worried that her first step through the door at Brennan's department store was to be the highlight of this trip.

The saleslady named Polly walked up holding a sky blue

strapless dress. "Now, this is what the girls are wearing to prom," Polly said, looking past Ada as she approached Wayne. "Is this what you had in mind, sir?"

Ada turned to behold the guilty grin of her husband, standing by a rack of dresses with his hat in hands. "Wayne, I thought you were waiting in the car."

"I changed my mind," he said. "You've been up here almost an hour. Thought maybe I could be helpful."

Ellie took the dress from Polly and held it up, fluffing the layers of taffeta flaring out from the beaded bodice. "Oh, Grandma. Have you ever seen anything so beautiful?"

Ada flipped over the price tag and put her hand on her heart. "Ellie, I could make three dresses with this much money."

"Ada."

Ellie, Ada, and the saleswoman turned in unison to look at Wayne, their row of faces a palette of emotions, from hopeful to horrified. He was standing by the dressing room entrance, his arms crossed. "I don't care what the dress costs. Go try it on, Ellie."

In the dressing stall, Ellie stripped to her underwear and held the dress up in front of the mirror. "Oh, boy, Grandma," she whispered. She would have to ditch the bra. She unhooked her bra and carefully stepped into the dress.

Polly tapped on the doorframe. "Do you need any help with that zipper?" Ellie slid back the curtain just wide enough for her face. "I'm a little nervous," she whispered. "I'm not wearing a bra."

Polly slipped into the room and tugged the curtain closed behind her. "We've got the perfect undergarment for this kind of dress." She stepped behind Ellie. "Let's zip it up and see what you think."

Her grandparents' bickering ended the moment Ellie walked out of the dressing room. Wayne started fidgeting with the fedora in his hands. Ada clicked open her pocketbook and pulled out a hankie.

Ellie swirled in front of the mirror. "I don't recognize myself. I've never looked like this a day in my life." She turned a somber face toward Ada. "Grandma, I know this isn't the one you wanted."

"It's going to need hemming," Ada said. "All those layers."

Wayne walked over to his wife and put his hand on her back. "Go get dressed, Ellie. I think we've found your prom dress."

In the dressing room, Ellie held up her arms as the saleslady stood behind her and released the hook and eye at the top and unzipped. Ellie's hands flew up to cover her breasts as the dress dropped to the floor, the stiff taffeta landing in a cone around her legs.

"I'll go put this in a garment bag for you," Polly said, averting her eyes. "You're going to be the most beautiful girl at that prom."

"Thank you," Ellie said, cupping her breasts. Polly left with the dress, and Ellie dropped her hands and looked in the mirror. She'd worn that dress for less than ten minutes, but she looked different now, even naked. Aunt Nessa was right. Ellie wasn't just Brick's girlfriend. She was a woman now, with her own potential. She looked at her bare breasts and thought about how Brick's face changed whenever he touched them. She touched her hardening nipples and looked up at her face. She was a woman with desires, too.

She heard her grandfather's voice, and the spell broke. She quickly fastened her bra and pulled on the dress her grandmother had made for her. In the silence of the dressing room, she could hear them talking.

"She's all grown up, Wayne. Are we doing the right thing here? Letting her go to the prom with Brick. In that dress. If she still thinks she's going to marry that boy . . ."

"No need to work yourself up over that, Ada. It'll all be over soon. He'll be gone by August."

Ellie smiled as she buttoned up the front of her dress. She would be gone by August, too.

"Why yes, Doctor," she whispered as she combed her hair. "Draw the patient's blood? Right away, Doctor."

CHAPTER

11

Ellie sat down on the edge of her bed and clutched handfuls of quilt. "I promise, I promise, I promise," she whispered, rocking back and forth. "If you make it not so, dear God, I promise we'll never do it again until we're married. I promise, I promise."

Tears spilled down her cheeks as she rocked faster, kneading the quilt into folds. "Please, God. Don't do this to us. To me. To Brick."

She stopped rocking and covered her face with her hands. Her fingers were frigid against her cheeks. *Cold hands, warm heart,* her grandmother always said.

Grandma. Ellie started to cry.

She walked over to the window. The snow had been falling for hours, and the clouds were still thick and gray as steel wool. On the ground, the daffodils and hyacinths in full bloom two days ago were invisible now. She stretched her neck to look farther down the lawn and jumped back, wincing from the pain of her breasts pressing against the window. They'd been tender for the last week or so, and swollen. She could barely fasten her bra.

Five times. Five times she had given in to Brick. "No," she said out loud. "To me. I gave in to me."

Everybody—her grandmother; her gym teacher, Mrs. Stenback; her best friend, Becca Gilley—all of them talked about how a good girl waits, but no one mentioned how wonderful it feels when she doesn't. Ellie could not ignore the rising heat down there when she was alone with Brick, the bolt of lightning shooting up her spine. His breath became ragged and the only thing she wanted was him, all of him.

"I am my mother after all," she said, staring at the falling snow. "God help me."

She heard a light tap on her door and turned away from the window. "Ellie?" Ada said, opening the door just wide enough to peek in. "Oh, you are awake. Your light wasn't on, and I didn't hear any movement. I thought maybe you'd over-slept."

"I woke up too early, Grandma, and then I lost track of time."

Ada opened the door wider but stayed in the doorway. "You'll have to rush, honey," she said, her brow now knitted with concern. "The bus will be here in fifteen minutes." She closed the door softly, but nearly a minute passed before Ellie heard her grandmother walk away.

Ellie stood in the school doorway and held her books lightly against her chest, blind to the early-morning swirl of students around her. Each time another red-faced classmate pushed open the door, the cold wind fanned the pleats of Ellie's cheerleading skirt. She didn't feel a thing, or hear it. Every "Hi, Ellie!" as another student rushed past. The slam of lockers in the hallways. The first warning bell. All of it was lost on her. She just kept looking out the door's small square window, seeing nothing, barely breathing, as she mulled over last night's exchange with her grandmother.

"Well, what do we make of that?" Ada had said as she stood behind Ellie and tugged at the waistband of her freshly hemmed prom dress. "I wonder if that saleslady gave us the wrong dress. I remember thinking it was a little snug at the time, but not this tight. We can barely get your zipper up."

Ellie stood on the footstool in front of her grandmother's vanity mirror and tried to hide her panic. "I've been eating a lot lately, Grandma," she said, forcing a smile. "Maybe I'm just a little too happy these days, what with prom and other things."

Ada reached up and stuck two fingers into the side of Ellie's dress, under her arm. "This feels a little tight, too. Goodness, I don't remember that." She smiled at Ellie's reflection. "I must have been so stunned at the sight of you that I lost my seamstress head."

Ellie tugged on the top of the strapless dress, but it wouldn't budge. "The saleslady said I filled it out just right, Grandma. It's supposed to look like this."

Ellie stepped down from the step stool and took a deep breath to stave off another wave of nausea. "Thank you for hemming the dress, and trimming all the taffeta layers, Grandma. It fits perfectly. Really it does. Now I just have to wait two more weeks before I can wear it." She had walked swiftly out of the room, barely making it to the bathroom before vomiting again.

She turned around to look down the school's empty hallway. Nope. There would be no prom for Ellie Fetters. No nursing school, either. She pressed her back against the handlebar of the door and pushed it open. The snow swirled around her face, stinging her cheeks and bare legs. She squinted at the snow-covered cars in the parking lot. She didn't bother looking for Brick's truck. What did it matter now? "Please forgive me," she whispered.

She loosened the grip on her books, and they tumbled to the ground. She'd spent hours covering them in brown paper and decorating them. The ink on the hearts of ELLIE + BRICK was slowly bleeding out under the kisses of snowflakes. Ellie tightened the wool scarf around her neck and started to run.

She ran through the student parking lot, stopping at Brick's pickup, noting the Kent State ball cap sitting on the dash. He was the one with the future. He had always been the one who was meant to get away. All her years of praying, but God picked Brick.

Ellie ran toward the road. The snow was falling harder, and she could barely make out the berm. Her shoes were no match for the ice patches, and she fell on her bottom, her skirt fanning out like a parasol. She counted to ten to catch her breath, and stood up. She ran a few yards and fell again, this time landing on her knees. She stood up and started to cry. Her knees were bleeding. She patted them with her hands and felt nothing.

She ran past the Jamesons' house with the leaning shed that Grandpa kept saying should be torn down. The memory of his angry face, his certainty about right and wrong. "I'm sorry, Grandpa," she yelled. "I'm sorry, Grandma." She fell again in front of Clayton Valley Nazarene, where a lone man with a shovel waged a losing battle. She pulled off her glove to wipe her nose, then threw the glove in the snow. She started running again, but slowed at the sight of the drugstore. The inside of the shop glowed a warm yellow, casting a man in shadows as he stood by the window, a cup in his hand. She pulled up her collar, leaned into the wind, and kept going.

The snow was coming harder now, and she could barely see her own feet. She was shivering, but she no longer felt cold. She slowed down and sat on the side of the road. She reached up and patted her head. She'd lost her hat, and the peaks of icy curls crunched beneath her fingers. She bent her legs and wrapped her arms around them, pressing her face against her skirt as she rocked back and forth. "Sorry," she said. "Sorry, sorry, sorry . . ."

She didn't hear the truck screech to a stop, the creak of the door as it opened, the thud of boots barreling toward her. The only thing she heard was the faraway sound of Brick's voice calling her name.

CHAPTER

12

Ada walked into the empty sanctuary of Clayton Valley Methodist Church and sat down in the seat that had been hers for the last thirty years. Fifth pew from the front, center aisle.

She set her pocketbook beside her, folded her hands, and bowed her head. "Dear Lord . . ." she whispered. She sat in silence, waiting for the words to come. She was aware of her heart pounding under the gold cross of her necklace, the gentle heave of her bosom with every breath. She flexed her feet, cursing her decision to wear the tied oxfords rather than her more comfortable loafers. She shifted, straining the seams of the girdle that mocked her vanity. Why did she still bother with that thing?

She snapped open her pocketbook, pulled out a hankie, and dabbed her eyes.

Try again.

"Dear Lord . . ."

She unfolded her hands to grab the worn back of the bench in front of her and looked up at the crisscross beams of the ceiling. Dear Lord—what? What did she dare ask for?

Muffled laughter hummed through the floorboards beneath

her feet. She looked at her watch: 12:07. The Guild Bees were making lunch. She should be down in the kitchen warming her crispette squares for dessert. Not to mention the weekly gossip she was missing. She sat up straight and pressed her back against the hard wood. How her mind wandered lately, always to the wrong places.

Ada had been a member of the church's quilting guild for more than twenty years. For eight hours every Thursday, she joined nine other women around the large wooden frame. They arrived at eight and stitched until noon, when they broke for potluck. After dessert, they stitched for another four hours. The same ten women had gathered all those years, sitting in their chosen seats at the frame—Ada always at the northeast corner—and stitching quilts for the church's annual bazaar. Last year they'd lost Helen Beard, to cancer. The Bees voted not to replace her.

Wayne was right to tease her about the Bees' gossiping, as she had always been a willing participant in unraveling the missteps of other people's lives. *Vengeance is mine, saith the Lord.* It was only a matter of time before her Ellie would be fruit for the frame. Soon, everyone would know what she had already figured out about her granddaughter. They would never say anything directly to her, of course. That'd be a breach of Bee etiquette. Instead, they'd greet Ada with sad, knowing smiles, and grab her hand. "How *are* you, Ada?" "You look so *tired,* Ada." "Anything I can *do,* Ada?"

Ada had committed this same act of superior concern countless times over the years. There was something sinfully satisfying about being kind to a person who knew how lucky she was to be on the receiving end of one's good manners.

Ada looked up at the painting hanging high behind the altar and locked eyes with Jesus, knocking on the door. How many times in the last thirty years had she stared at that painting, searching his face for answers? "I am the light of the world," she whispered. "Whoever follows me will not walk in darkness, but will have the light of life."

What did Jesus know of this modern life? "Yes," she said, staring at the painting. "You let Mary Magdalene wash your feet with perfume. But how does that help my Ellie? How does that help her in the here and now?" She pressed her palm against her chest, her eyes filling with tears. She'd just compared her granddaughter to a prostitute. "Blessed are they that have not seen, and yet have believed," she whispered.

She squeezed her eyes shut, cataloging the evidence she could no longer ignore. The new box of Kotex under the sink, never opened. Ellie's retching behind the bathroom door. Her pale face and refusals to eat breakfast, even when Ada made her favorite hash and poached eggs.

"I'm not hungry, Grandma," Ellie had said just that morning, pushing away her plate. She'd grabbed her coat and flown out the door before Ada could even make eye contact with her. You forgot your boots, she wanted to say.

Ellie was seven weeks from graduating from high school. Ada counted on her fingers, calculating the possible due date. Her eyes welled up again at the thought of her granddaughter dropping out of school, so close to being finished, having a baby no one wanted.

And then what? Brick McGinty—he had to be the father—was leaving in August to play basketball for Kent State. She and Wayne had been so relieved when they first heard about Brick's scholarship. Finally, a way to get that boy out of Ellie's life. "So she can meet a decent boy who'll take care of her," Wayne had said to Ada in bed, the evening he found out about Brick's scholarship. "So she's got a chance at a better life." Ada had said nothing. Their granddaughter had been an acquiescent child, but she was headstrong when it came to Brick, and determined to prove them wrong.

Brick's father was a horrible man by any measure. Ada

knew Angie McGinty to be a kind and long-suffering woman. What had Brick learned from growing up in that family, that marriage? It was something you couldn't know about a husband until it was too late.

In recent weeks, Ada and Wayne had been quietly hopeful. Wayne spent many evenings in the barn, a single lantern glowing overhead as he built a hope chest for Ellie, carving a web of curly vines into the lid before staining and polishing the wood. While Wayne built, Ada sewed. She bought a bolt of pale blue linen to make sheets and matching pillowcases, a tablecloth and six napkins. It was the first time they'd ever put such effort into a gift for Ellie, and both of them were caught off guard by their own tears the morning Ellie came downstairs to the sight of her own hope chest sitting next to her chair in the kitchen.

Ada had taken quiet pleasure in watching Ellie add her own bits and pieces to the trove. The apron she'd worn as a little girl, made by Ada with scraps left over from a church dress; a set of cotton table coasters Ellie had stitched in Home Ec, and four place settings of the Harvest pattern of Lenox china, a gift from Widow Evans next door. "It was our wedding china," she told Ellie the day she brought the box over and set it on the kitchen table. "I have no children. Your grandma told me about your hope chest. It would do my heart good to see those dishes come to life again." Ellie gently unwrapped each shiny piece of china, thanking her neighbor each time. "I can't wait until I'm setting my own table."

Ada went to bed that evening with plans to call Bea Wilkins the next morning. "Just to let her know she should encourage her boy Keith to stop by soon," Ada whispered to Wayne. "He's always had a crush on Ellie."

Ada unsnapped her pocketbook and pulled out a hankie to dab at her eyes. "Who's going to want our Ellie now?"

Ellie would never give up any child of hers for adoption. Ada knew that without asking. She and Wayne had raised her as their own daughter, as best they could, but Ada always knew Ellie was haunted by questions with no good answers. How do you explain to a child why both of her parents had been willing to give her away? How could Ada answer that, when she never understood how her son was capable of such a thing?

Ada looked up again at Jesus. How could he have let this happen to Ellie? With all that suffering so early in her life, had she not earned his intervention? She tried to imagine telling her husband that Ellie was pregnant, and the anger bled out of her. Ada bowed her head, whispered again, "Dear God . . ."

She heard the sound of a man clearing his throat from the back of the room and turned around. "Pastor Woodruff."

"Hello, Ada." Peter Woodruff smiled as he stood at the far end of the pew and pointed to the spot next to her on the bench. "Mind if I join you?" Ada straightened her spine and patted her hair. "Of course not," she said, pulling her purse onto her lap. "Please."

Peter Woodruff was thirty years her junior, and looked even younger; a soft-spoken man, and a graceful one. His smile always made it to his eyes, and Ada trusted that in a person. He was in his mid-forties, and still single. Every young woman in Clayton Valley came to the church's annual Strawberry Festival, including some of the Catholic girls, to their mothers' horror.

He pointed to his Levi's as he sat down. "Sorry for the getup. It's snowing like crazy out there, and I wasn't sure I'd make it to the church and back home without having to push my car out of a snowdrift. Can you believe it? In April?"

"Wayne wouldn't let me walk. Dropped me off in the truck. Thought I was crazy for coming here today." She offered a weak smile. "This weather should be no surprise to you, Pastor. You've lived here how many years? How many white Easters have you preached?"

He grinned and shook his head. "Some things you never get used to, I guess. This will be my fourteenth Easter here. Half of them full of daffodils and tulips, the other half looking like Christmas."

"Right down to the packed pews," Ada said.

"Indeed."

She looked down at her lap and pressed her pocketbook against her stomach.

"What brings you upstairs, Ada?"

"Oh, I don't know, Pastor. Lot on my mind, I guess."

"Ellie, I'd imagine."

"What do you know about Ellie?"

"You've always worried about Ellie. Looks like you've been crying."

She shook her head. "I can't talk about it. I've got to keep myself together."

She pulled off her glasses and wiped her eyes. "Pastor, what do you say to a girl when she's . . . when she's not married and you've done everything you can to help her stay pure and . . ."

"Gus Campbell called me a little while ago," he said.

Ada looked at him and frowned. "I'm sorry?"

"Gus Campbell, over at the pharmacy?"

Ada sighed. Was there a man alive capable of talking about what's really on a woman's mind? "I know who Gus is, Pastor. I've been going to his store for all of my married life."

Pastor Woodruff nodded. "Of course, Ada. Didn't mean to offend you. I just wasn't sure you heard me, is all."

"What's Gus Campbell got to do with anything?"

"He called me. He saw Ellie this morning. Running in the snow, crying."

"What?" Ada said, her eyes wide. "That's impossible. Ellie's in school. She's never missed a day of school since she was eight years old. So, I'm sure it wasn't Ellie."

"Did she leave without her boots this morning?"

"Well, she . . ." Ada looked at her lap. "She was in a hurry."

"Gus heard a scream—'a wail,' is what he called it—and looked out the window. Ellie was lying on the ground, not even trying to get up. By the time he'd pulled on his boots and coat, she was getting into a truck. The McGinty boy's, he thought."

Ada's shoulders sagged. "Oh, Pastor, our girl is in so much trouble. As bad as you can imagine."

"Well," he said, "death is as bad as I can imagine, so I'm hopeful it's something less than that."

"But, Pastor, she's—" Ada started to cry.

"I'm sorry, Ada," he said. "But she's not the first girl, you know. She's a sweet, lonely girl who fell in love with the first boy who wanted her."

Ada looked up in horror. "She was never alone, Pastor. We have always been there for her. Wayne loves her as much as I do."

"I didn't say she was alone, Ada. I said she was lonely, through no fault of yours. She's always felt set apart, you know that. Never felt she really belonged anywhere. To anyone."

"Did she tell you that?"

He shook his head. "I don't tell your secrets, Ada, and I'm not about to share Ellie's. And I'm not telling you anything you don't know. She's never gotten over being abandoned by her parents."

"Her mother, yes," Ada said. "What a troubled woman."

"And her father, too," he said. "I'm sorry, Ada, but you know your son let her down, too. He let all of you down. I don't need to remind you about our long talks after Ellie first came to live with you." Ada said nothing, her face burning.

The pastor looked up at the ceiling. "Remember when you fell in love with Wayne? How different you felt, just because he loved you?"

"It's been a long time, Pastor. And I resisted temptation. Always."

He ran his fingers through his hair. "It was a different time. These kids have so many outside influences now. Fast cars. Hollywood. Take *Peyton Place.* Have you read that book? Main character is an unwed mother."

"Ellie has that library book on her bedside table," Ada said. "I never knew what it was about."

"The old days are gone, even here in Clayton Valley," he said. "All we can do is our best and hope their character grows strong."

"Pastor, my Ellie has plenty of character. She's the kindest child I know. I've never known a more generous soul. Everybody loves her."

Pastor Woodruff smiled again. "There you go. That's the Ada I know. Proud of her girl, and ready to let me know it, too. That's what she's going to need from you. That loyalty, that faith in all that's good in her. All that's still in her. She's a wonderful girl, and she's got a rough road ahead of her."

"I can't even imagine it."

"Yes you can, Ada," he said. "That's why you're here praying."

"Trying to pray, Pastor. So far, I can't find the words."

"Shall we pray together?"

Ada shook her head. "No, I appreciate the offer, but this one's between me and God."

He slapped his palms against his thighs. "I understand." He stood up. "Well, let me know how I can help. What are Ellie's plans?"

"I don't know," she said. "I haven't talked to her. She doesn't even know I know."

"How'd you—"

She looked up at him, and this time she was the one smiling. "I wasn't always an old woman, Pastor. There are some things a woman knows."

"Ada," he said. "I deserved that."

Ada folded her hands on her lap. "I'm not saying anything to Ellie until she's ready to talk."

He started to turn away, but then hesitated. "God loves all his children, Ada. Every last one of us, no matter how we come about or how we end up. He doesn't care if we're popular, doesn't even care if we're like everyone else. All he cares about is the content of our hearts."

She looked up at him. "Your predecessor, Pastor Quinn, would have dragged me up to that altar, pulled me down onto these rickety knees of mine, and prayed for Ellie's soul."

"Ah, Martin A. Quinn. He was quite the mighty avenger, I hear. Not my style. Not my story, either. You don't know this, but I was raised by a grandmother who loved me to death, too. Maybe that's why I can't do the fire-and-brimstone thing. My own beginnings are shrouded in second chances."

He smiled at Ada's look of surprise. "Sin was around long before Ellie met Brick McGinty," he said. "No one is a discard in God's eyes."

Ada stared at the back of the pastor's flannel shirt as he walked out toward the main hall. The things you don't know about a person. She turned to face the altar, bowed her head, and closed her eyes against the sound of footsteps climbing the basement stairs.

"Ada?"

Ada sighed.

"Ada, lunch is ready. You coming down?"

Ada pretended to push a few bobby pins into her hair. "I'll be right there, Lois," she said over her shoulder. "You girls start without me."

"Don't be silly, Ada. We're waiting to say grace until you get down here. Hurry, though. You know how dry Esther's tuna noodle gets if it sits too long in the oven."

Ada waited for the sound of Lois's footsteps on the stairs, and bowed her head to try one last time.

"Dear God . . ."

She squeezed her hankie and looked up.

"Help us. Please."

Women's laughter greeted her at the top of the stairs. She paused and took a deep breath before slowly descending. They didn't know anything yet. For one more day, at least, Ellie was the last thing on anybody else's mind.

CHAPTER

13

The heater in Brick's truck was on the brink of giving up, but it didn't matter. Every few minutes he felt another bead of sweat slide down the side of his face. He jammed his knees against the steering wheel to keep the truck on the road as he pulled off his sweatshirt and threw it on top of his jacket. He wrapped his fingers around the wheel again and started to gag. He pulled off the road and slammed on the brakes, kicking open the door just in time. Flakes of snow pricked the back of his neck as he leaned over the side of the truck and retched until there was nothing left in him.

He shut the door, collapsed against the back of the seat, and pulled his handkerchief out of the back pocket of his jeans to mop his face. "Jesus. Jesus, Pint."

After Ellie had finally calmed down, and after they both had stopped crying, they agreed to return to school and act like nothing was wrong. "I just need time to think," he said, pulling her into a hug. "I don't mean because I don't know what to do. I just have to figure out the best way for us to do it."

She pushed away from him, her face stunned. "I'm not doing anything illegal, Brick. If you don't want this baby—"

He grabbed her shoulders and shook her. "Of course I do, El. I want you"—he put his palm on her stomach—"and I want our baby. I want to marry you. Just give me a little time."

She wrapped her arms around his neck. "You said *our* baby," she whispered into his ear. "Our."

He drove her to the same door where, two hours earlier, she'd dropped her books in the snow and started running. Thank God for those books. How else would he have known she was in trouble? After first period, Becca Gilley had made a rare stop at Brick's locker to tell him that Ellie had never showed up for homeroom. "She never does that," Becca said. "Thought you might know where she is."

"How would I know?" he said, reopening his locker and squatting to pretend he was searching for something.

"Okay, then you probably don't want to know that Jerry Finkle saw her standing in front of your truck after the morning bell." He continued rummaging until Becca finally gave up and walked away. He pulled on his jacket and headed for the exit. As soon as he opened the door he saw the pile of Ellie's soggy books on the ground. He picked them up and headed for the truck.

The early-morning snow flurries had turned into a squall. It was like pushing through giant balls of cotton, his truck crawling because he couldn't see more than a few inches in front of him. He leaned over the wheel as he drove, squinting as his eyes darted from one side of the road to the other in search of Ellie. His head was pounding by the time he found her.

God. The sight of her there, a tiny heap on the left side of the road. He jerked the truck to the opposite lane and slammed on the brakes, kicked open the door and ran to her, yelling her name.

She didn't seem to recognize him as he scooped her into his

arms. "I'm sorry," she whispered, staring straight ahead. "I'm so sorry."

Her teeth chattered as he peeled off her wet coat and her soggy shoes and socks. He draped his jacket over her, wedged her bare feet between his thighs, and rubbed her hands and legs to get the blood flowing. It took nearly an hour before the blue disappeared from her lips. By then, she'd told him she was pregnant.

Now he was throwing up his guts. He pulled into the school parking lot and parked in his usual spot, between two cars buried in snow. He turned off the truck and slumped forward, wrapping his arms around the wheel, pressing his forehead against it. "Jesus, Pint." He could hear the distant laughter of classmates across the parking lot. He focused on the voices, and one of the girl's squeals tipped him off. His teammates were throwing snowballs at some of the cheerleaders.

Not a care in the world. When was the last time he'd felt that way? Brick squeezed his eyes shut, and thought about his brother, Harry. Never, not since Harry died, had he felt safe enough to just play around.

His classmates' laughter ended as quickly as it had started, leaving him alone in the silence. He opened his eyes. For the first time in months, Brick thought about his future and felt a sense of relief. The decision had been made for him. He pulled on his sweatshirt and his jacket and pushed open the door. His sneakers had barely hit the ground before he heard Coach Bryant's voice.

"Brick! Where the hell have you been?"

Brick whipped around. "Hey, Coach."

Sam Bryant walked toward him, his bald head a red and shiny beacon. "Principal Stanley is looking for you. Said he heard that you ran out this morning and left school grounds in your truck. You know the rules on game day." He shoved his hand under the snow on the truck's hood. "Engine's still warm. Looks like he's right."

Brick stared at the ground. "I had to get some cigarettes, Coach."

"Try again, Brick."

Brick took a step back.

"It's me, son. I can tell by the look on your face that something's wrong. You can trust me. You've got no reason to lie to me."

Brick stomped his feet to knock off the snow. "I've got a lot on my mind, Coach," he said, jamming his hands in his pockets. "A lot to figure out."

"Let's go," Coach said, pointing to the door. "Let's go solve whatever problem you think you have."

CHAPTER

14

For the next few weeks, Ellie plotted her crime.

That's how it felt, all the secret machinations, the guilt simmering in her gut. Slowly, one piece of clothing at a time, she packed the suitcase that belonged to Pastor Woodruff. "Don't fill it all at once," he'd said when he handed it to her. "Be discreet."

She had thought Pastor Woodruff might be the one person to help her, and she was right. Brick had dropped her off at the church last Friday morning, when she knew the minister would be in his office working on Sunday's sermon. As soon as she saw Pastor Woodruff's face, she started to cry. Within the hour, without judgment or lecture, he had arranged for Ellie and Brick to be married by a pastor friend of his in Cumberland, Maryland.

Sneaking the suitcase into the house had been a nightmare. First, she lied, telling her grandmother that cheerleading practice would be running late and Becca Gilley's dad would drive them home. Brick dropped her off at the end of the long driveway, so her grandparents wouldn't hear her arrival. She carried the suitcase to the side of the house and hid it behind the bushes under the awning, to keep it dry until she heard her grandparents' bedroom door close for the night. Her heart pounded as she ran outside in the frigid cold, then tiptoed as she carried the suitcase up the stairs and stashed it under her bed.

She started packing the following week. On Monday, she threw in two pairs of underwear. On Tuesday, she added a slip and two pairs of socks. By Friday, she had added three head-bands, two bows, and her favorite bra, the one with a single pink rose embroidered between the cups. One day, she hoped, it would fit again. Ellie filled her new train case, too, with things that mattered to her: a tiny blue bottle of Evening in Paris cologne, her church-school Bible, the small framed pho-tograph of her with her grandparents, taken the summer she came to live with them.

She'd been so excited the day Aunt Nessa bought the train case for her, for a future she was about to lose. She hadn't yet received the letter of admission from St. Luke's, and she tried not to think about it. After she had filled out the application and mailed it, she'd decided to keep it a secret from her grand-parents. "To surprise them," she had told Aunt Nessa. Now she lived in constant fear that her grandmother would see the St. Luke's letter before she did. No one would care about Ellie's broken dreams, and they would surely blame her for taking Brick down with her—and it wouldn't be long before they knew. She had to tug hard on the tabs of her skirts to button them now, and spent all day feeling like her stomach was being cut in half.

The day after she had spilled everything to Pastor Wood-ruff, it had occurred to Ellie that Grandma Ada might notice that she hadn't had her period. For the next five days Ellie took a handful of sanitary napkins from the box under the sink and tucked them into her coat pockets, then threw them away in the girls' bathroom at school. She'd complained about cramps at breakfast one morning, too, and was taken aback by her grandmother's sudden interest.

"Cramps?" Ada said, spinning around from the frying pan on the stove. Ellie was sure she'd seen her grandmother smile before adding in a somber voice, "Just part of being a woman, Ellie." Ellie had teared up and had to leave the room. What a life of lies she was building. What kind of girl did this so easily, so willingly?

Ellie opened the drawer to her bedside table and pulled out the small calendar with the puppy on the cover. *Happy New Year from Brennan's Department Store*. She opened it and started counting the days since she'd last pretended to have a period. Four more days to go before what would have been the start of her next one. She shoved the calendar back into the drawer and tapped her toe against the suitcase to make sure it was fully hidden under the bed before heading to the kitchen.

Her grandmother was up to her elbows in a mix of ground beef, eggs, and breadcrumbs, making meatloaf. She was humming "Rock of Ages," as she so often did when she thought no one was listening.

"Grandma?" The humming stopped. "I'm going to need more Kotex, please. Will you be going to Campbell's Pharmacy this week?" Her grandmother turned and looked at her from head to toe. Ellie slowly crossed her hands over her stomach.

"Grandpa can take me on Friday," Ada said, returning to the bowl to toss in a cup of diced onion. "I need some witch hazel and cotton balls." Her voice sounded flat to Ellie, and distant. Ada tipped the bowl and scooped the contents into the loaf pan. "'Less you need 'em tomorrow."

"No, Friday's fine, Grandma. Thank you." Ellie walked to the cabinet and pulled out three supper plates. Silently, they worked together in the kitchen, Ada sliding the loaf into the oven and setting the timer, Ellie setting the table. Ellie pointed to the metal bowl of potatoes on the counter. "Want me to peel these, Grandma?"

Ada shrugged her shoulders as she filled a pot with water. "If you want to."

Ellie tried to laugh. "Oh, Grandma. Of course I want to." She tied on one of the bibbed aprons hanging by the door and rummaged through the drawer for the peeler, silently calculating how many more suppers she'd have in the only real home she'd ever known.

Nine, twelve, fifteen . . . seventeen. Seventeen days.

Ellie set the potatoes on the table and placed the big yellow ceramic bowl next to them. She peeled the first potato in one continuous loop, held up the brown corkscrew of peel, and bounced it in the air. "I'm going to get all five of them this time, Grandma," she said, smiling. "Boing, boing, boing."

"I remember the first time you did that," Ada said, sitting down next to her. "You weren't more than ten, and you were so pleased with yourself." She smiled softly at Ellie. "You were such a little cutie."

Ellie had never heard her grandmother use such a term of endearment for her. "I remember, Grandma," she said, pointing to the window over the sink. "You hung it on the herb nail for a week."

Ada stood up. "Well, those dishes won't clean themselves, will they?"

Ellie watched Ada wash the bowl and thought about how Pastor Woodruff had spoken in such a gentle voice about her grandmother. "She will always love you, Ellie," he said, "no matter what. Your grandmother has known her share of sorrows, and she is a woman of faith. She knows the ultimate judge is God, not us, and all she's ever wanted for you was a life with a good man and your own family."

"Not like this, Pastor," Ellie said. "Not in this order, and definitely not with this man. My grandparents hate Brick."

"Don't underestimate your grandmother," he said, handing her a tissue. "She'd be the first to tell you she wasn't always an old woman. She remembers what it feels like to fall in love."

Ellie had been thinking about that ever since he'd said it. She'd known her grandmother only as a kind old woman who'd worn the same horn-rimmed glasses for as long as Ellie could remember and curled her hair with a Toni home perm every six weeks, like clockwork. Ellie had never imagined her grandmother at her age, her future sprawled out in front of her. Did she ever dream of being someone with a different life than the one God gave her?

Once, when Ellie was about eleven, she saw Grandpa pat Grandma's behind when he thought Ellie wasn't watching. Grandma had shooed him away, but she was smiling. They had four sons, after all.

Everybody changes, Ellie figured. Everybody starts out as one kind of person and ends up being somebody else. Life does that to you, just as a river has its way with a stone. Even when you don't notice it, life is rearranging you.

CHAPTER

15

Ada buttoned the collar of her cotton nightgown and reached for her robe. It was Wayne's poker night, and she was grateful for the chance to undress in the open, instead of huddling in their bedroom closet. Fifty-one years of marriage, and Wayne Fetters hadn't seen her naked since their first year together. Even then, she disrobed for him only in darkness.

He used to complain about that, in the early years of their marriage. "Ada, honey, nobody can see you but me," he whispered in the dark, but she couldn't bring herself to do it. The only thing her mother had ever told her about sex was that mystery kept a man hungry, and home. Finally, after five years or so of marriage, he stopped asking, and for the longest time Ada felt wounded by the absence of his entreaties. What a sad surprise, to find yourself mourning the loss of something you were always told you shouldn't want.

She walked over to her vanity by the window and sat down on the upholstered bench, her knees parting the opening in the table's faded skirt. She reached for the switch on the table lamp, glanced in the mirror, and thought better of it. The sun was taking its good old time tonight, and its golden glow softened her face.

She unscrewed the lid on the jar of cold cream and dipped her fingers into it, letting them rest there for a moment. Her hands were raw from scrubbing vegetables and canning today. When had she stopped rubbing Vaseline into her hands throughout the day? She used to keep her hands soft no matter how long a day of laundry or pulling weeds, and she felt a sense of pride every time Wayne pulled her fingers to his lips, kissing each tip. She frowned in her mirror. Every inch of her was giving up.

She scooped out a dollop of the cream, rubbed her hands together, and then kneaded the cream into her cheeks and forehead, and into the deepening folds of her neck, careful not to smudge the lace of her collar. She dipped her fingers back in the jar and rubbed a little more cream into the sharp lines of her cheekbones, a legacy of her mother. The older she got, the sharper they became.

Her thoughts turned to Wayne again, and how he had saved her all those years ago. Ada's father had died when she was eight. Her mother was already sick, but no one knew it yet. Ada and her sister, Nessa, did all they could to help their increasingly fragile mother, but no matter how hard they prayed, their mother got worse. "God always knows best," she told her daughters as they sat on the edge of her bed. "I need you to promise that you will never question God's judgment." Ada nodded, but Nessa was having none of it.

"Dad is already dead," she told Ada that night. "God can go pick on somebody else."

Three days after their mother's funeral, Nessa announced that she was moving out for good, and begged Ada to come with her to Erietown. "A new life, Ada. One where anything can happen."

Ada clutched her hands, in tears. "I love you so much, Nessa, but I'm not made for your life. I'm made to be someone's wife and mother, right here in Clayton Valley."

Two weeks later, Wayne Fetters, the tall, lanky boy she'd known all of her life but never thought about twice in a single day, knocked on the door and asked through the screen if she might step out for a moment to answer a question. Ada had barely shut the door behind her before Wayne dropped to one knee and reached for her hands. "Ada Travis, I'm not sure how you feel about me, but I know what I think of you. Would you ever marry me?"

So like Wayne to just get to the point. She nodded and that was that. Ada shoved her clothes into an empty feed bag and they married on a Friday morning at Clayton Valley Methodist, with just Nessa and Wayne's widowed aunt in attendance. They moved into the aunt's farmhouse until Wayne could finish building this house just a quarter mile away.

Ada's eyes drifted from the window to the old woman looking at her in the mirror. Where was all this coming from, all these memories? She turned on the light and leaned in for a closer look. Her eyes were still big and blue, each side accented with wrinkled slopes like parentheses that deepened when she smiled. Ellie loved that about her grandmother's face. "They're like stars, Grandma, sparkling right next to your eyes."

Every scenario she could imagine for Ellie filled her with dread. Ellie was at least three months pregnant, she was sure of it. Even Wayne had started asking questions. "What the hell's wrong with her?" he'd said just last night. "She hardly talks all of a sudden, and I can't remember the last time I heard her laugh." Ada said nothing, her only option to keep from lying to her husband.

What was Brick planning to do? Go to college and leave Ellie behind? Forget about college and marry her? Stay in Clayton Valley for the rest of their lives? The choices were all Brick's now. She pulled open the center drawer and looked again at the light blue business envelope addressed to Miss Eleanor Grace Fetters. She'd been hiding the letter for a week now, afraid to even mention it to Ellie.

Ada looked at the return address—*St. Luke's Hospital, School of Nursing*—and felt another wave of anger at her sister. What was Nessa thinking, filling Ellie's head full of big ideas? Ada held the opened envelope, weighing her options yet again. Which was worse? Never knowing that you'd been right to dream? Or finding out your dream came true only after you'd lost it? Ada slid the letter back into the drawer and closed it.

She picked up the hand mirror, a gift from her mother on Ada's fourteenth birthday. "Save it for your wedding day," she'd told her after Ada had peeled away the pink tissue paper and held it up to her face. Ada had run her fingers over the ivory inlay on the back of the mirror, tracing the edges of the large "A" scrimshawed in script in the middle. She had no idea how her mother had managed to order the mirror, or how she had paid for it. Her only income, beyond her late husband's small savings account, came from the piecework she did for the dry goods store after it started selling linens and women's clothing.

"Women and their mysteries," Ada whispered, flipping over the mirror. The glass was smoky and freckled with age. Every evening Ada cleaned it with the sleeve of her robe and followed her mother's advice. This time, she lifted the mirror to her face and gasped at the sight of Ellie's reflection behind her.

"Hi, Grandma."

Ada set the mirror on her lap and turned around. "Ellie? I didn't even hear you come in. You 'bout scared me to death."

Ellie was standing just inside the doorway, her shoulders hunched forward, her arms holding a sweater draped across her stomach. "I'm sorry, Grandma. I was just wondering if I could come in for a minute."

Ada slid to the edge of the bench and Ellie sat down, resting her head on her grandmother's shoulder. She lifted the mirror from Ada's lap and looked at her reflection. "Oh, Grandma," she said.

Ada worked her fingertips into Ellie's curls and breathed in the scent of her granddaughter. "What is it, Ellie?"

Ellie wrapped her arms around her grandmother's waist and said nothing.

"Ellie, I can't help you if you don't tell me what's wrong."

They sat entwined, each of them with her eyes closed. "Guess I just needed to feel you close for a while," Ellie finally said. Ada looked at her granddaughter's face in the dresser mirror. She was just a child still, her eyes so big and blue, and so afraid.

"Ellie, what's going on with you?"

Ellie sat up straighter, careful to keep the sweater draped across her stomach. "Nothing, Grandma. Just so much to do before graduation. Maybe it's getting to me. So much change." Ellie reached for the hand mirror on the table. "Grandma, could you tell me the story again? About what your mother said when she gave you this mirror?"

"It was so long ago," Ada said, stalling.

"She gave it to you wrapped in tissue," Ellie said. "You were sitting on the edge of her bed, facing a window."

Ada nodded. "She was already very sick."

"Which is why she gave it to you early."

Ada nodded again. "That's right. I didn't realize it at the time, but she knew she didn't have much time left."

" 'Every lady needs a good hand mirror.' That's what she told you."

Ada wrapped her arm around Ellie's shoulders. "She lifted the mirror to my face and said, 'You should always be able to feel proud of the girl you see in that mirror. If you don't like the face in the mirror, you know you've got to do something about it.' "

Ellie lowered the mirror and set it back on the table. "Do

you, Grandma? Do you always feel proud of the girl you see in the mirror?"

Ada kissed the top of Ellie's head. "It doesn't matter, Ellie, who we see in the mirror. What matters is who God sees. 'For the Lord does not see as mortals see; they look on the outward appearance, but the Lord looks on the heart.'"

Ellie leaned into her grandmother's bosom. "That might scare me more, Grandma."

Ada wrapped her arms around Ellie. "No sweeter heart exists than yours." She caught a glimpse of the worried old woman in the mirror, and looked away.

CHAPTER

16

Ellie's hands fumbled as she tried to coax the folds of the road map back into place. The seams were already frayed and on the verge of splitting, and the last thing she wanted to do was set Brick off again.

She had no idea how to make sense of the map's web of fine lines and emblems. She didn't even know how to drive. The more Brick had tried to explain it, the more flustered she had become.

"Jesus Christ, just forget it," he'd said, finally. "I'll pull over every time I need to check it." How she annoyed him. Finally, the map collapsed into its tidy rectangle. She turned on the flashlight again to read the script on the faded front. PURE TRIP MAP. *Compliments of Your Pure Oil Dealer.*

She flipped it over to look at the back. "Be sure with Pure!" She stared at the four red letters, P–U–R–E, and felt the sting of indictment. Everywhere, it seemed, she was finding signs of God's judgment. The broken latch on her borrowed suitcase. The blinding rain that had sidelined them minutes after they crossed the Ohio border into Pennsylvania. She shut off the flashlight. "Where did you get this map?" she said.

"What?"

She held up the map. "Where did you get this?"

"It was in my dad's truck," Brick said. He looked at her again and tightened his fingers around the wheel. "What's the matter now?"

"What's the *matter*? I'm pregnant, Brick. You're giving up your college scholarship, and I can't even get a high school diploma. We're sneaking away in the middle of the night to get married by a man we don't even know." She flicked the map with her finger. "And now I got this bright red 'pure' looking at me. Another sign that God is mad at me."

Brick sighed. "Ellie, God doesn't give a goddamn what you and me are doing. He doesn't care."

Ellie clutched at the tiny cross around her neck. "How can you say that, Brick? Do you want us to crash now?"

"Pint, I needed a map. I took the only one I could find. It was in my dad's car. God isn't going to use an asshole like him to send us a message. If God cared about what happened to us, he wouldn't have let you get pregnant."

Ellie lowered her head and stared at the ragged remains of her fingernails. She webbed her hands over her stomach and bowed her head, silently mouthing, "I'm sorry."

"Look, Pint, we agreed that the only way we could get married was to elope. If your grandfather knew you were pregnant, I'd already have a shovel in my head."

"Don't even say such a thing."

"It's true and you know it. He hates me already. This would make him want to kill me."

"He's going to find out about it eventually," Ellie said. "When we come home."

Brick shot her a look and grabbed her hand. "We can't go home, Ellie."

She whipped around to face him. "What? What do you mean we can't go home? Where else are we going to go?"

"We've got to get a fresh start, Ellie. We've got to get out of Clayton Valley. We've got to go somewhere where everybody doesn't already know us. For the sake of our kid, El."

"We got *started* by falling in love," Ellie said, relieved to be feeling something other than fear. "We made love because we were *in* love, because we felt something too strong for each other to fight it."

Brick shook his head, his eyes locked on the road. "Okay, Ellie. Whatever you say."

"Pull over."

"Knock it off, Ellie."

"I said pull over. I mean it. I want to get out."

"Pull over five miles out of Erie, Pennsylvania. Really. And then what? Don't be ridiculous, Ellie."

"If you're saying you don't love me, then I'm not marrying you, Brick. It's that simple. Pull over."

"I'm not stopping."

"Drive as long as you want, but I'm not marrying you."

"Pint."

"No. This is already too hard, Brick. I don't want either of us to start out feeling stuck with each other."

Brick slowed and pulled over on the side of the road. "Pint," he said, turning to look at her. He reached for her shoulder, but she pulled away and pressed against the door. "Ellie, listen to me. I'm nervous, is all. Things have happened really fast, and I'm trying to do the right thing here."

"The right thing? You mean, not what you wanted."

Brick shook his head. "Well, c'mon, Pint, this isn't exactly how we had planned things."

"We both had plans, Brick."

He nodded. "I know. And you would have been a great nurse." He reached for her hand, and this time she squeezed his.

"Do you really think so?"

"I do. You make everyone feel better. You make me feel like I can do anything. We just need a chance, is all. A fresh start. That's why we can't go back."

She squeezed his hand harder. "Then where are we going to go, Brick?"

He hesitated. "Well, we're going to get married, and then we're going to move into a house in Erietown. On Route 20, but it's in the city so it's called Erie Street. You're going to have a baby, and I'm going to work at the power plant."

"Are you telling me you already got a job?"

"My sister Katie's husband, Jack, got it for me. In maintenance. Not like a custodian maintenance. It means I'll learn how to fix everything in that plant. I'll be on probation for the first three months, but after that I'm in the union." He cupped her chin in his hand and turned her face toward his. "Union wages, Ellie. No farm life for us. We can rent a house. It'll be empty in three months, and Jack knows the landlord. He's gonna lend me the deposit and first month's rent. I start work next Wednesday."

Ellie looked at him like she had never seen him before. "What about graduation?"

Brick turned to face the windshield. "Coach will make sure Principal Stanley gives me my diploma anyway. I won't take finals, so my grades will be shit, but at least I'll have proof I graduated."

Ellie let go of his hand and looked down at her lap. "Well," she said, folding her hands. "That's great, Brick. Anyone knows you need a diploma to get a good job."

Brick sighed. "I'm sorry, El. It's not fair what they're doing to you. Don't you think I know that?" She nodded, silently staring at her lap. "You don't need to work. I'm going to take care of you."

"It's not just about that, Brick. I worked hard in school. I got way better grades than—"

"Go ahead and finish the sentence. Better grades than me, you mean."

Ellie shook her head. "I just don't understand why you're allowed to pick up your diploma and I can't even clean out my own locker."

"What difference does it make now?"

"It matters to me, Brick. I didn't expect to be able to go to graduation, but I've done all the work. I thought I'd be able to take the final tests and still get my diploma. How come I'm the only one being punished?"

"You think you're the only one—" The look on her face stopped him. "Pint," he said, grabbing her hand, "only one of us can be pregnant. That's God's plan, too, right?"

She lowered her head and nodded. "Yes, and I did that all by myself. I'm the Virgin Mary Eleanor Grace, carrying the Christ Child."

Brick tapped the tip of her nose. "Does this mean we have to name him Jesus?"

Ellie laughed. "I can't believe you just said that."

Brick looked at her and grinned. "Do you have any idea how great it is to see you smile?"

Her posture softened. "Why didn't you tell me any of this?" she said. "Why didn't you let me know all your plans?"

Brick sighed. "*Our* plans. And it was supposed to be a surprise. A nice surprise. I wanted you to know I had taken care of everything, that I'm a man who takes care of his family." He reached over and touched her cheek. "That's what a man does when he loves his wife."

Ellie slid toward him and buried her face in his shirt. "I'm so sorry, Brick. I'm so sorry this has happened to you."

He wrapped his arm around her, pulled her in tight. "I'm not. I'm not sorry one bit. Who knows what would have happened if I'd gone off to college? Like you said, you're the one with the grades. I could have flunked out the first month, for all we know."

"Brick, I didn't mean—"

He shook his head. "No, it's okay. This way I'm in charge of my own future. We're going to move to Erietown and stay there just until I save up enough money for us to move to Cleveland."

"Cleveland?" she said, smiling. "Let's not get ahead of ourselves. We've got a lot of years together. And wherever you go, I go, too."

He kissed the top of her head. "That's how it's gotta be, Ellie. I gotta be in charge here. And you gotta trust me."

"I do, Brick," she said, lifting her face for a kiss. "I do."

He kissed the tip of her nose. "We'd better get going," he said, unwrapping his arm. "We're supposed to be in Cumberland to meet Pastor Woodruff's friend by four o'clock."

She slid across the seat to the passenger side as he eased back onto the road. She cupped her cheeks with her hands and frowned. Her face had to be a wreck by now. She reached back for her vanity case and set it on her lap. She turned on the flashlight and lifted the lid, then gasped.

Brick looked over and laughed at the reflection of Ellie's shocked face as she held up her grandmother's hand mirror. "Yeah, you might want to clean up a little," he said. "You look like a raccoon after all that crying."

Ellie curled her fingers around the ivory handle and pressed the mirror against her chest.

"That's not it," Ellie said. "She knows."

"What?"

"My grandma. She already knows."

CHAPTER

17

Ellie pulled the bedspread taut and plumped the pillows before propping them against the headboard. She walked to
the foot of the bed and put her hands on her hips, surveying
her work. "Much better."

Brick sat in the room's one chair wedged in the corner, his
leg dangling over one of the arms as he read the *Baltimore Sun*.
He peered over the top of the newspaper and smiled at her.
"Ellie, it's a hotel. They have maids who do that."

"Not if we never let them in. Not if we keep that Do Not
Disturb sign on the door."

Brick's smile faded. "I'm sorry, Pint. I'm sorry we had to
wait until now to be in a bed. I'm sorry we didn't start out like
this."

Ellie pulled the newspaper out of his hands and tossed it on
the floor as she plopped onto his lap. "Don't, Brick," she said,
wrapping her arms around his neck. "Don't think it, don't say
it ever again. These have been the two best nights of my life,
and I've already forgotten what we left behind. I am so happy
to be Mrs. Brick McGinty. That's all that matters now."

He clasped her face in his hands and pulled her in for a

long, deep kiss. "I love you, Ellie. I can't believe how much I love you."

Two hours and forty-seven minutes later, they had the first fight of their marriage. Ellie would come to remember it that way, to the minute, stewing on it over the years. She saw it as a warning sign that she would never be enough for Brick McGinty.

Ellie was sitting on the closed lid of the toilet watching Brick shave, the foam on his face disappearing one stripe at a time as he pulled the razor down his cheeks. "Brick, we have one night left here."

He held the razor under the running water and pressed it against his upper lip. "Now, tell me something I don't know," he said, staring straight into the mirror.

"What I mean is what are we going to do after tomorrow? Where are we going to live? The people who live in the house you rented for us won't be moving out for another three months. We need a place to stay."

They had already agreed there was no point in either of them calling home. Ellie was too ashamed to face her grand-parents, to hear the disappointment in their voices. Brick's mother didn't even yet know why he was gone, and there was no way he was going to expose Ellie to his father's fits of rage.

"You should at least call your mother," Ellie said. "Think of what she's going through, worrying about where you are."

Brick rinsed off his razor and turned off the spigot. "This is something I have to tell my mom in person," he said, reaching for the hand towel in Ellie's lap and dragging it over his face. "Something I have to say to her face-to-face, and not when he's around."

What Brick didn't say was that he was sure his mother al-ready knew. He'd asked Coach to tell her.

He'd never seen Coach so angry as that afternoon when

he'd told him about Ellie. Didn't speak to him for the entire game and walked out of the locker room before the boys had even showered. By the next morning, though, he seemed resigned to Brick's plight.

"The missus says you're doing the right thing, and that we have to respect that," Coach said to him behind the closed door of his office. "I'm not saying we're not disappointed for you, Brick, but Ellie didn't get this way by herself. You've got to be a man now."

Brick fiddled with his ball cap as he spoke. "If my mom calls while we're gone, would you please tell her where we are? And why, Coach. Could you please tell her why?"

Coach sighed. "You let me know what night you're leaving, and I'll stop by and see her the next morning. I'll pick up your dog, too, and keep him until you return." Brick looked up, surprised that Coach had remembered. Coach was the only person besides his mother who knew about how Bull had once tried to kill Patch after he'd damaged the pup's eye.

"Coach, I don't expect—"

"Save it, son. You're going to need that dog, and your father will be out for revenge once he hears about that scholarship you're throwing away."

Brick scoffed. "He would have done everything he could to ruin my chance at that if he knew about it."

"I don't doubt that," Coach said, "but he still would have enjoyed bragging about his college boy once you were gone. I'm sorry, Brick, but there's no sugarcoating this one. Your father is going to take this personally, you running off and getting married, and he'll be looking for a way to make you pay."

Brick stood up and shook Coach's hand. "Thank you, Coach. I'll bring Patch over the night we leave. He's old, but he means everything to me. And thanks for talking to my mom."

Some things Brick hoped Coach had kept to himself when he visited his mother. The money he'd loaned them for gas, and to pay for three nights in the hotel. "Every man should give his wife a honeymoon," he told Brick as he stuffed the bills in Brick's coat pocket the night he dropped Patch off.

It would hurt his mother to know her son had turned to Coach instead of her, even if she didn't have the money to help.

"Brick," Ellie said, snapping him back to the tiny hotel bathroom. "Brick, what are we going to *do*?"

Brick threw the towel on the floor and turned to face her. "'What are we going to do, Brick?' '*Save* me, Brick.' '*Help* me, Brick.'" He leaned toward her and she stood up, grabbing the plastic shower curtain behind her for balance. "'It's all up to *you*, Brick,'" he said. "'Fix *every*thing, Brick.'"

Ellie was now grabbing the curtain with both hands, cowering with her eyes closed. Bracing herself, he realized, for him to hit her.

"Ellie," he said, reaching for her. He pulled her close and wrapped his arms around her. "I'm so sorry," he whispered.

She felt his grip soften as he kissed the top of her head. "I'm sorry, Pint," he said. "I don't know what came over me. I'm just getting used to everything, I guess." She pressed her hands against his chest, gently this time, and he stepped back far enough for them to look into each other's eyes.

"Promise," she said. "Promise you'll never touch me like that. Like your father did to you, and to your mother."

Brick's eyes filled with tears. "I promise," he said, grabbing her hands. "I promise to be better than my father. I will never raise my hand to you."

He pulled her onto his lap, and she rested her head on his shoulder. "I want to call Aunt Nessa," she said. "She will let us stay with her, I know it. And she likes you. She told me so last Christmas."

"She liked me before you were pregnant. Big difference. She's the one who talked you into applying to nursing school."

"She's not like that. She won't ask a lot of questions. She'll be on our side."

Brick got up from the bed and walked to the window, jingling his coins. "Do I have a choice, Ellie?"

"Do *we* have a choice, you mean? From now on it's we, not I. Us, not me. That's what it means to be married. It will only be for a few weeks. Just long enough for those people to get their butts out of our house."

Brick turned to look at her and smiled. "Such a dirty mouth on my wife."

Ellie stood up and looped her pocketbook over her wrist. "I'll be back in a minute."

"Where are you going?"

"To the lobby," she said. "I'll be back in five."

She walked across the open-air balcony, grateful for the cold air as she ran down the two flights of stairs and into the lobby. She walked to the telephone booth she'd noticed the night they arrived. She pulled the door shut and sat on the bench before reaching for the receiver. She gave the operator the number and felt instantly calmer at the sound of Aunt Nessa's voice.

"Yes, yes, of course, Operator," Nessa said. "I'll accept the call. Put her through this instant, please. Ellie? Ellie, are you there?"

"Hi, Aunt Nessa."

"Ellie! Where are you? Your grandmother is worried sick about you."

"I'm in Cumberland, Maryland, Aunt Nessa. At a Holiday Inn." She cleared her throat. "Brick and I got married, Aunt Nessa. I'm three months—"

"Shh. No need to broadcast your whole life to a bunch of snoopy strangers. I know all about it. How can I help?"

Of course, Grandma had told her sister, who was also her best friend. Ellie started to cry. "Aunt Nessa, I don't want you to think bad things about Brick. He wanted to marry me the minute he found out that I was—"

"Ellie, honey, I don't need the recipe, just tell me what's cooking. When are you coming home?"

Ellie sniffed and cleared her throat. "Well, that's the problem. We're leaving tomorrow, and Brick has rented a house for us in Erietown, but we can't move in for three months. And we can't go home, Aunt Nessa. Who knows what Grandpa would do, and Brick's father is such an awful man that I don't even know how bad that might—"

"Ellie, you and Brick pack up your things tomorrow morning and get yourselves to my house. This is your home for as long as you need it."

Ellie closed her eyes and whispered, "Thank you, Aunt Nessa. We'll help with groceries, and I'll clean every day that we're there. Make a list of chores you need Brick to do, too. He'll work on them in the evenings and on weekends when he's not working at the plant."

Ellie heard her aunt sigh. "So, Brick's got a job."

"Yeah."

"Which plant, honey?"

"The power plant, Aunt Nessa. He got himself a job at Erie Electric. A union job. It's only a couple miles from your house, right on the lake, by Lake Shore Park."

"I know where it is, Ellie." She paused, and Ellie could hear her slow, deep breath. "So," Aunt Nessa said more cheerfully. "A few changes in your lives."

"Big ones, Aunt Nessa."

"Well, buck up and enjoy the last day of that honeymoon of yours. The back bedroom will be waiting for you two when you get here."

"Oh, thank you, Aunt Nessa. Thank you so much."

"And it's your turn to send me a postcard. First time you've been out of Ohio. How exciting."

"Yes," Ellie said, smiling. "So exciting. I'll see you soon, Aunt Nessa."

Ellie walked over to the rack of postcards next to the reception desk. She spun it around slowly, examining every picture before settling on one of the Maryland state map. She slid it across the counter to the receptionist.

"Five cents," the woman said without looking up.

"Oh, wait," Ellie said. "Please, I mean." She returned to the rack and pulled out two cards: one with a picture of North Mechanic Street in downtown Cumberland, and another of a row of beach umbrellas in Ocean City. "I'll take these two, too."

CHAPTER

18

Angie McGinty clicked off the light switch in the kitchen and walked slowly through the house, stopping every few steps to let the pain move through her. She paused at the front window. Almost two in the morning, and still no Brick. Patch was gone, too.

She made her way upstairs, one slow step at a time. She stopped at the landing and waited for the pounding in her chest to settle down before heading to her bedroom at the end of the hall. She was no longer the Angie her girlfriends used to tease for having so much energy. It was a sin to be proud, but maybe God would understand since he'd made everything else about her so ordinary.

Angie pulled off her dress and slip, started to move toward the closet, then draped them on the chair instead. She was exhausted all the time now. She'd dropped nearly twenty pounds in the last couple of months, and yet her stomach just kept getting bigger and harder, like a boulder inching its way out from under her rib cage.

Her daughter Lillian, who lived in Cleveland, was the only one who knew what was wrong with Angie. The distance made it easier for Angie to tell her. If any one of her other nine daughters found out how sick she was, she'd be dealing with a house full of hysterical girls insisting they were taking her to Doc Brown.

She would have to tell them what Doc already knew, and what she'd told him after he urged her to go to Cleveland for chemotherapy. "What's the point of that now?" she'd said, and Doc didn't argue. They both knew she'd waited too long.

Angie McGinty had made a life of what God had dealt her. She was ready to play out this last hand.

"Just take care of my Brick," she whispered as she sat on the edge of the bed. "That's all I ask."

He wasn't coming back. She could feel it. He'd been more distant in recent weeks, avoiding eye contact and short-tempered with her in a way he'd never been before. Just yesterday, he'd snapped at her when she asked if he'd ordered his graduation gown. "I told ya, Ma, I don't want to wear a candy-ass gown with a stupid board on my head. I can graduate without looking like a fool." This was not her Brick.

She reached for the nightgown folded under her pillow and pulled it over her head, slowly stood to let the hem fall around her knees, then slipped under the covers. The moon was a bright sliver in her window tonight. She squeezed her eyes shut as she clasped her hands across the swell of her abdomen and started to pray.

"All I ask is that you keep him safe." She mouthed *amen,* then summoned her nightly travel back in time to shoo away the dark scenarios swirling in her head. She was young and lean and could outrun every boy she knew. She smiled as she twirled alone in the fields behind her house, the wind her only companion. No pain, no foreign object in her body squeezing the life out of her. She faded off to sleep as young Angie started to run, run, run, oblivious to the life that would catch up with her.

. . .

The next morning Angie had just sat down at the kitchen table for a second cup of coffee when she heard a knock at the door. Whoever it was had come to the kitchen door. Had to be a friend.

She grabbed the edge of the table and took a deep breath before pushing herself to her feet. She hobbled to the door and peeled back the curtain to come nose to nose with the grim face of Coach Bryant.

She yanked open the door and pushed back the screen. "Coach, what is it? Is my boy—?"

"He's fine, he's fine, Angie," Coach said, removing his hat. She opened the door wider and gestured toward the table. "Come on in. I have coffee on the stove."

He stepped inside and wiped his feet on the rag rug before closing the door. "Thank you, Angie. A cup of coffee would be nice right about now. I'm starting to think we're going to skip spring altogether this year."

"Oh, you know how it is here in Clayton Valley," she said, walking to the stove. "Our moody Lake Erie, always changing her mind."

He pulled off his jacket and draped it around the back of one of the chairs, set his hat on a corner of the table, and sat down. "Is your husband here, by any chance?"

Angie continued to face the stove as she poured the coffee. "No, Bull's not here right now." She smiled at his sigh of relief, grateful for the camaraderie. She set the coffeepot back on the burner and turned around to face him. "What brings you here?"

He rose to take the coffee from her with one hand, using his other hand to cup her elbow as she walked to the table. "Always a gentleman," she said.

His eyes fixed on hers as he tried to ignore the breathless framing of her words. "Angie, I'm here to tell you something about Brick. And I just want to say, I wish I weren't about to add to your troubles today."

She set down her coffee cup. "If you can tell me my boy's alive, Coach, I can handle anything else."

"Oh, God, Angie. Why even think—?" He held up his hands. "Dammit, Angie, I'm sorry. Of course." She looked down at her lap and said nothing.

"He was a good boy, your Harry. A great athlete, with a kind way about him. He had the biggest laugh. You'd hear him laughing and you'd start laughing, too."

Angie nodded. "Sometimes I see something that I know Harry would have thought was funny, and I can hear that laugh of his in my head."

Coach waited for a moment before continuing. "Angie, Brick asked me to stop by. To let you know what's going on." He cleared his throat. "Angie, Ellie Fetters is pregnant."

Silently, she nodded.

"Ellie's pregnant, and your son has done the right thing. He dropped Patch off at our house, and he and Ellie drove to Maryland and got married."

"Maryland? Why Maryland?"

"I don't know. Something about a shorter waiting period or how it's easier to get a marriage license there. I'm not clear on the details. The Fetterses' pastor set it up."

"Pastor Woodruff?"

Coach nodded. "He knew another minister in Cumberland who could marry them."

Angie folded her hands on the table. "So, a minister married them. That's good."

Coach took another sip of coffee. "I want to say something else, Angie. Your son is an honorable young man. He wanted to tell me himself, tell me in person, that he was going to have to turn down the scholarship."

"What scholarship?"

Coach pushed his chair back a bit. "The basketball scholarship?" he said slowly. "To Kent State?"

Angie took a shallow breath and exhaled slowly between pursed lips.

"Angie, I thought you—" She waved him silent and exhaled slowly again before looking at his face. "My Brick had a college scholarship, and he never told me?"

"Angie, I think maybe he—"

She waved him off again. "That poor boy. He must have been so scared."

Coach shifted in his chair. "Scared? Why would he be scared? This was the chance of a lifetime. I'm sorry that Ellie may have trapped him like this."

She narrowed her eyes at him. "Shame on you, Coach. You know that's not true. Ellie Fetters's only crime is thinking since the day they met in seventh grade that the sun rises and sets in my son. I've seen how she looks at Brick. I've watched the way his face changes every time he says her name to me. She believes in him. Always has. I don't need to tell you why that would matter to a boy like him, a boy who grew up in this house."

Coach shook his head as he whistled, long and soft. "I'm a little surprised to hear you defend that girl," he said. "Principal Stanley says she's ruined his life."

"Nonsense," Angie said. "She has *saved* his life. Do you have any idea the comfort I draw from knowing he'll have her by his side?" She narrowed her eyes. "Will he still graduate?"

Coach nodded. "Principal Stanley promised that he would."

"And Ellie?"

"Angie, you know a pregnant girl can't graduate."

"I know she can't walk in a cap and gown, but she can surely get her diploma. She's a bright girl, and you know it."

Coach shook his head. "Principal Stanley's pretty mad at her."

Angie gripped the edge of the table. "Do I need to go down to that school, or are you going to take care of this? You know he'll listen to you."

"Why do you care, Angie? After what's happened?"

"That's exactly why I do care," she said, releasing her fingers. "This is the kind of thing that can hang over a marriage. Is that what you want?"

"No," Coach said, shaking his head. "Although, I'll admit, I was real angry when Brick first told me."

"What changed?"

He stood up and pulled on his cap. "I told my wife. She set me straight. And if I didn't know better, I'd swear you and my Loretta had a little chat before I got here."

"Thank you, Coach."

He smiled sheepishly. "You know what Brick told me? If it's a boy?"

"I don't even need to guess," she said, returning his smile. "They're going to name him Sam."

CHAPTER

19

Ada frowned at the dangling mailbox cover. How many times had she asked the postman to slam it tight after he slid the mail into the box? She peered in and immediately recognized Ellie's small backhand script on the postcard sitting on top of the slender stack of mail. She looked around and slipped it into her apron pocket before walking up the driveway.

She set the rest of the mail on the kitchen table and walked to the window over the sink. She could barely make out the shadow of Wayne on the tractor. He'd be in the fields for at least another hour before coming in for lunch. She sat down in her rocker and slid the postcard out of her pocket.

Dear Grandma,

I found the mirror in my vanity case, so I guess you already know what's wrong with me. I'm so sorry I let you and Grandpa down. I cry every time I imagine what you must think of me now. Brick and I got married. He tells me he loves me every day, and I know he means it. He already got a job at EEI. I have wanted to be a mother all my life, but I'm a little scared about it right now. We will be at Aunt Nessa's until we move into our new house at 1225 Erie Street. I hope you'll call. I miss you, Grandma.

Love,
Ellie (Mrs. Brick McGinty)

P.S. Thank you for the mirror. I will cherish it. I hope I can look in it soon and feel proud of the girl looking back at me.

Ada tucked the card back into her pocket and thought about all the things Ellie needed right now. The hope chest Wayne had made for her at Christmas, of course. All the hankies and clothes she'd left behind, too. *To fool me,* Ada thought. *To keep her plans a secret.*

On washday, two days before they eloped, Ada had been pulling the fitted sheet off Ellie's bed when the toe of her shoe hit something hard, so she pulled up the bed skirt. As soon as she saw the suitcase engraved with Pastor Woodruff's initials, Ada had known what Ellie had planned. She'd been surprised by her sense of relief.

Wayne may have hated Brick McGinty, but Ada was glad the boy had done the right thing. She was grateful to Pastor Woodruff, too, even though it hurt that he had gone behind her back to help Ellie and Brick leave town.

"I know this isn't what you wanted for your Ellie," Pastor Woodruff had told Ada when he showed up at her door the day they left. "But I believe this is all part of God's plan."

"You could have told me you knew, Pastor," she said. "You could have let me know she was going to run away, and how I could help."

"Ada, I mean no disrespect. I told you before I wouldn't violate her trust, just as I've never betrayed yours. You love that girl with all your heart. She loves you, too, and wanted to save you the expense and embarrassment of a wedding in Clayton Valley."

Ada sighed. "The Bees will be busy with this one."

"The Bees are your friends, Ada. There's not a one of them who hasn't had to deal with life's disappointments. I know that even better than you."

Ada tried not to smile. "Well, that's none of my business, is it? I do appreciate the reminder."

"With a little time, you'll all forget how their marriage started," he said. "Time has a way of taking care of that. Time, and love."

Ada pulled out the postcard again and squinted at the postmark. Ten days had passed since Ellie had mailed it. She was already at Nessa's house. Ada couldn't deny that the two most helpful people in Ellie's life in recent weeks, Pastor Woodruff and Nessa, were also the two least judgmental people Ada had ever known. And two who never married.

She patted her pocket, infused with a new sense of certainty as she stood up. With or without Wayne, she was going to see Ellie.

Nessa answered the phone on the second ring. "Well, it's about time you called," she said, but Ada could tell from the sound of her voice that she was overjoyed to hear from her. "She needs you, Ada."

That was all Ada needed to hear. She would walk the fifteen miles to Erietown if Wayne refused to drive her. She walked to the kitchen and slid the chicken casserole into the oven, then went upstairs to the bedroom. She sat down at her vanity and reached for the bottle of White Shoulders that Wayne had bought her five birthdays ago. "Desperate times," she whispered at the mirror as she dabbed her neck and her wrists with the perfume.

Ada waited until Wayne had finished his lunch and was nibbling on one of the cinnamon rolls left over from breakfast. She refilled his coffee cup, set the percolator back on the stove, and sat down across from him. "I need to talk to you," she said.

He took a sip and lowered his cup so gently it barely registered a sound as it met the saucer. His eyes were red. Tired, Ada told herself, and for just a moment she questioned her timing until she remembered what Nessa had said.

She reached into her pocket and locked eyes with him as she slid the postcard across the table. Wayne looked down at the familiar handwriting and smiled as he reached into the chest pocket of his overalls. He pulled out a postcard and slid it across the table.

"You aren't the only one she loves, Grandma," he said, his eyes wet again as he smiled at his wife. "I got to the mail before you did. I say we make a trip to your sister Nessa's tomorrow. How's that sound to you?"

CHAPTER

20

Ellie handed Brick a bottle of Schlitz and then settled into the rocker next to his on Aunt Nessa's screened-in porch. "You're starting to look a little pregnant, Pint," he said, his face beaming. She placed her palm on her stomach. "I hope you're still going to love me when I can't see my feet anymore."

"I love you more every day, El," he said. "I can't wait until we're in our home and rocking that little guy to sleep each night."

"Honey, I hope you won't be disappointed if it's a girl."

He took a swig of beer and shook his head. "I'm going to love it no matter what it is. But I have a feelin' it's a boy."

"Well, we'll know for sure soon."

The newlyweds fell silent as they rocked, Brick slow and steady, Ellie moving in quick, short bursts. Their view was full of the sights and sounds of the rowdy softball practice on the field across the street. Grown men, all past their prime, drinking beer and slugging balls. *One of life's mysteries,* Ellie thought as Brick closed his eyes and fought the urge to join them.

They were far enough from the kitchen that they didn't hear the phone ring. For another thirty seconds, Ellie later thought, they still believed life was finally calming down. Brick was working at the plant, and they were only two weeks and three days away from moving into their own home.

Aunt Nessa stood ramrod straight at the phone as she listened. "I'm so sorry, Lillian," she said. "Hold on please and I'll go fetch him." She walked quickly through the dining room and toward the front door, pausing at the sight of Ellie and Brick. Two kids, still, holding hands across the doorway, rocking in unison.

"Brick. Your sister Lillian is on the phone."

"Lillian?" he said, springing out of his chair.

Ellie stood up. "What is it, Aunt Nessa?"

Nessa pressed her hand against Ellie's back. "Go be with him, sweetie. It's about his mother. He's going to need you."

"Hi, Lil!" Ellie heard him say as she walked to the kitchen. By the time she got there, he was slumped against the wall, both hands clasping the receiver. When he saw Ellie, he turned away. *Will it always be like this?* she wondered. *When my husband needs me most, he will turn his back to me?*

Brick squeezed his eyes shut as Lil talked, silent as he tried to absorb the news.

"Yeah. Yeah, Lil. I'm still here. How come she never told me?"

Ellie could hear snippets of her sister-in-law's voice.

Cancer.

Didn't want to worry you.

We thought she had a little more time.

Ellie walked up to Brick and laid her hand on his back. He started to sway.

This was not the plan.

Since their wedding day, Brick and Ellie had mapped the best time to visit Angie, and just yesterday they'd decided to go to Clayton Valley next Sunday. Ellie was starting to show, and she had wanted to wait to see her new mother-in-law until she could go into town and buy a decent maternity blouse. They'd had it all figured out. They'd drive Ellie to Brennan's department store on Saturday. Brick would sit in his parked truck and listen to the Indians game on the radio while Ellie bought her new blouse and stopped at the glass cases near the exit to pick up a half-dozen cream puffs at the store's bakery.

It would be such a nice surprise for his mother, seeing them walk in as husband and wife, Ellie carrying a Brennan's box tied with string that ended in a little bow in the center.

Brick stood up straight and rolled back his shoulders. "Yeah. Yeah, Lil." He turned and pulled Ellie close. "I'm—we're on our way," he said, his voice trembling now. "About an hour." He hung up the phone.

"Oh, Brick." The look on Ellie's face was his undoing.

"Ellie, my mom," he said, starting to cry. "She's dying."

Ellie wrapped her arms around his waist, and he buried his face in her hair. Brick breathed in the scent of his wife, the strength of her. He would always remember this day for the worst of reasons, but he would also never forget how safe he had felt in Ellie's arms. It was the closest he ever came to believing that God knew his name.

PART II

CHAPTER

21

Ellie stood at the dining room window and watched her daughter, Samantha, bark up orders to the Kleshinski boys. Lenny was her age, and Bobby was barely a year younger, but there they were, two lanky shadows against the setting sun, marching around the swing and hoping to win the approval of five-year-old Samantha McGinty.

Sam was clapping, and Ellie could tell even through the glass that she was chanting something. She pounded the window frame with her fists to loosen it and grunted as she heaved open the window. The cool breeze billowed her maternity blouse as goosebumps danced up and down her arms.

"Sam," Ellie yelled, leaning into the screen.

Sam took several steps toward the house. "Are you all right, Mommy?"

"I'm fine, honey," Ellie said, her arms draped across her swollen abdomen. "Be nice to Lenny and Bobby. You don't always need to be in charge."

The boys waved to Ellie. "Sam's helping us with our rhythm, Mrs. McGinty," Lenny shouted. "Next we're gonna learn the Twist."

The boys tried to mimic Sam, their skinny arms and legs flailing as they sang. "Come on, baby," they screeched, "and go like this."

"Okay, okay," Ellie said, laughing. She lowered the window but didn't close it. The evening sounds of children playing always soothed her. She walked back into the kitchen and plunged her hands into the gray water, thinking about how Brick had been right about Sam's big gift last Christmas. God, she loved that record player, just as he had predicted. It had become such a father-daughter thing for them, shopping for the latest forty-fives once a month at Hills department store, then sitting together cross-legged on the floor to listen to them.

Ellie loved to sing the church hymns of her youth, and she and Brick could dance up a storm at the union hall dances. But that was big band music, and with a purpose. For Ellie, popular music was something to put on in the background while she dusted or folded laundry. For Brick, the songs opened a window somewhere inside him. Ellie tried not to feel left out.

"You're always asking me to share my feelings," he told her once in the car after she wrinkled her nose at a song he said he liked on the radio. "Well, this tells you what I'm feeling."

"Really?" she said. "Patsy Cline's 'She's Got You' tells me what you're feeling? Jay and the Americans singing 'She Cried' after he broke up with her is about you?"

"That's not what I meant. It's not the exact words. It's how a song loosens you up to think about things you didn't even know were in your head."

"I'd love to hear about those things," she said.

"It's not like that," he said, and shut the radio off.

Sam couldn't get enough of her father's music, and she had a great memory for lyrics. She only had to hear a song twice before she could sing the whole thing as if she had lived it. The Four Seasons' "Walk Like a Man," Elvis's "Can't Help Falling in Love"—Ellie couldn't decide whether it was humorous or whether she should worry about how much Sam took the lyrics to heart.

"Look at her face, Pint," Brick had said recently as Sam sang along to Ray Charles's "You Don't Know Me." "She feels it in her bones."

Ellie pulled the plug to drain the sink. She could not deny the relief it still brought her to see how much Brick enjoyed having a daughter.

All through that pregnancy, they both had referred to the baby as "he" and "him." They'd started calling him Sam, too, for Coach Bryant. Ellie had readily agreed to the name, eager to keep Brick excited about becoming a father. Their baby's middle name would be the same as Brick's: Samuel Paull McGinty.

After thirty-six hours of labor, she was wheeled into the delivery room, where the last thing she remembered was someone putting a mask over her face. She awakened to the sound of a nurse asking if she'd like to hold her baby girl. She was so pink and perfect, her blue eyes as big as Ellie's. Ellie had been nervous about how Brick would react. When the nurse finally called him out of the waiting room, he rushed to Ellie's side and scooped the baby into his arms.

"Brick," she said, on the verge of tears. "It's a girl, you know. We have a daughter."

Brick laughed. "Oh, Ellie. I know that. I've known that for three whole hours already." He pushed back the edge of the blanket to get a better look at their daughter's face. "Oh, look at her," he said. "Look how beautiful she is. Look at those eyes. Her little cheeks." He touched one of the baby's hands, and Ellie could hear his throat tighten as the baby clutched his finger. "Look at those fingers," he said. "They're so long. Just like Ma's."

He clutched the baby to his chest and leaned in to kiss Ellie. "She's perfect. I love her. And I love you so much."

Remember this, she thought. "I'm so happy, Brick," she said, her voice quavering. "I guess we're going to have to come up with another name."

He laughed again. "I already figured that out. We can still call her Sam. Short for Samantha, right?"

It was her turn to laugh. "Really, Brick? Are you sure you don't want to wait for a son? You had your heart set on naming a boy after Coach."

Brick shook his head. "Nah, I don't want to wait for anything. I want to call her Sam. We'll pick a different name for our son."

"Okay then, she's Samantha," Ellie said. "Samantha Joy McGinty?"

Brick kissed the baby's forehead and handed her back to Ellie. "I like that. I like that middle name. What do they call it? Our bundle of joy. That's what she is."

She could never have imagined this life on that snowy day that Brick had found her collapsed on the side of the road. Her pregnancy had started out as the worst news of her life, and ended up being the reason for everything good in it now. Their marriage. The move to Erietown. This house. Ellie had been so excited to have her own stove, her own living room, her own everything. She didn't care that the front screen door had a hole in it the size of her fist, or that the linoleum in the dining room curled in two of the corners. For the first time, she felt in charge of at least a part of her own life.

She felt bad, though, about being nearly twenty miles away from her grandparents. It may as well have been two hundred miles, because she was still learning to drive. What an adventure that was turning out to be. She and Brick had agreed that he couldn't be the one to teach her. "I don't have the patience you need," he said.

"Talk about an understatement," she'd told her best friend,

Mardee Jepson, the next day. "Could you imagine Brick the first time I hit the brake too hard?"

"I'd want to sit in the backseat for that one," Mardee had said, laughing. "The thought of big ol' Brick McGinty at the mercy of his little wife."

At Brick's suggestion, Ellie asked Roger Kleshinski, the father of Sam's friend Lenny, and, more important, Brick's coworker at the plant. "A union brother," Brick had said, slapping Roger on the back the first time he showed up to ride with Ellie in his station wagon. "Only man I would trust to teach my wife how to drive."

It didn't take long for Ellie to realize that Roger was scared to death of her husband. "Every time I clip a corner or forget to signal, Roger waves his arms and says, 'Now, Ellie, I've got to get you home to Brick in one piece,'" she told Mardee. "At this rate, I won't have my license until I'm a grandmother."

Still, Ellie thanked God every day for her new life. When her grandparents had shown up at Aunt Nessa's house right after they were married, Ellie could barely look at them, she was so afraid of their disappointment. But her grandmother had wasted no time in pulling her in for a hug. If she was angry or hurt, Ada Fetters sure didn't show it. Grandpa Wayne had stood behind his wife, smiling shyly, as if he were just making his granddaughter's acquaintance.

Brick's face was somber when he came home from work and walked into the kitchen with his hand extended to Wayne. "Sir," he said.

"Hello, Son," Wayne said, rising from the table.

Son. Ellie had nearly burst into tears.

The two men just stood there, facing each other, but looking elsewhere. "There you are," Ada said, springing out of her chair to rescue Brick with a hug. "Welcome to the family, Brick." Brick patted Ada's back with both hands, his puzzled face a clear amusement to Aunt Nessa, who snickered behind her napkin.

"Aunt Nessa," Ellie whispered, tugging on the back of her skirt.

"My Lord," Nessa said. "He looks like he's trying to put out a campfire on Ada's back."

On moving day, two months later, Brick and his high school teammate Duke Jenkins had just finished carrying in the last of the furniture donated by Nessa when Ellie's grandparents pulled up. Ellie was standing on the front porch, barely breathing as she peered over the railing and into the bed of the truck. So many things from home. Her chest of drawers and bedside table, and open boxes teeming with signs of her earlier life: the framed scripture verse stitched in her grandmother's hand; a stack of Grandma's embroidered hankies, tied with ribbon, and the homemade rag doll Ada had had waiting for her the day she moved in with them.

Grandpa Wayne climbed out of the truck and walked over to Brick. Another handshake, another "sir."

"Like an Amish greeting at the dry goods store," her grandmother said, and Ellie couldn't help laughing. "Oh, Grandma. Really. Why must they act like this?"

"They're rivals, honey," her grandmother said, shaking her head. "One of them had you all to himself until the other one showed up and swept you away. They'll declare a truce eventually."

They ran out of time. Both of her grandparents were gone before Sam turned three. One cool autumn evening, Wayne was late coming in for supper—a first in their five decades of marriage. Ada pulled on her coat and walked out to the field. "At fifty feet, I thought he was working on the tractor," she said to Ellie in a flat voice over the phone. "He looked to be doing something with the engine. I yelled and yelled for him, and he wouldn't answer. It wasn't until I was almost on him that I realized he wasn't moving." Her voice broke, and she started to cry. "My Wayne," she said softly. "My sweet, sweet Wayne."

It was the first time Ellie had ever heard her grandmother sob. Six weeks later, Ada was canning the rest of Wayne's tomato crop that Brick had helped harvest when she collapsed on the kitchen floor. She never regained consciousness.

"She died peacefully," the nurse told Ellie as she stood in shock next to her grandmother's hospital bed, with Brick standing behind her. "Massive stroke. We see this a lot. When one goes, the other dies of a broken heart." Ellie leaned back into Brick, feeling faint as he wrapped his arms around her. As soon as they were in the car, he pulled her beside him. "I understand why she went," he said, his voice trembling. "I wouldn't want to live without you." She leaned into him, too raw with grief to speak.

A week later, Ellie found out she was pregnant again. After two miscarriages, she couldn't help but think that the timing would make this one different.

Now, she draped the washrag over the faucet and walked slowly to the dining room, collapsing into a chair. She leaned forward and pressed her fist into the small of her back. Sam would be in any minute now, and Ellie didn't want her to see her in pain. How that child hovered.

Brick was working so much overtime now that even when he was home he seemed to be somewhere else. Thank God for the new friends she had made in the neighborhood, most of them girls around her own age with husbands and kids and their own sets of problems. They got together in the morning several days a week. "To keep our heads above water," Mardee liked to say.

Ellie loved everything about being a hostess. Setting out the cups and saucers, folding the paper napkins into triangles, filling the dainty sugar bowl and cream pitcher that her friend

Becca Gilley, now Mrs. Martin Bowman, had given her as a wedding gift. She usually made the coffee cake recipe on the back of the Bisquick box. She liked the smell of cinnamon filling the house, and how the girls made a big deal over her whenever she served it warm. It made her feel important and refined.

"Even Jackie Kennedy would feel special at our table," she said once to Sam, who was helping wipe smudges off the spoons. "You and Caroline Kennedy were born just months apart. I wonder if Caroline ever helps her mommy around the house like you do."

Sometimes when she hosted, Ellie would sit quietly and take in the hum of voices. It gave her a deeper understanding of why her grandmother used to show up every week for the quilting bee. Marriage was often a lonely business, she was learning. Every wife needed her women friends to keep her strong.

The more Ellie settled into her life as a wife and mother, the more she thought about her own mother, who gave her up when she was eight. What if she'd had girlfriends gossiping in her kitchen, a husband who loved her? Ellie had never been able to imagine a woman giving up her child, but after she became a mother the truth got cloudier. Raising even one child was exhausting and isolating, but as long as she had these friends she felt less alone.

Ellie didn't want to know her mother, but she didn't want to hate her, either. She just wanted both of her parents to stay away. They would never get near enough to matter to Sam, especially now that Sam was old enough to ask her own questions.

In two weeks, Sam would start kindergarten. Ellie dreaded not having her constant companion with her in the mornings. Ellie never had anyone care as much as Sam seemed to about her, about her opinions, her moods. So often, at the slightest sound of her mother's discontent, Sam would stop everything and lock eyes with her mother to try to understand what was on Ellie's mind. "Mommy's little confidante," Ellie called her.

She pressed her fist into her back again, and reminded herself to be grateful for the message behind the pain. This baby was going to make it.

Her first miscarriage had been at eleven weeks, which had scared her, but didn't feel ominous. The second time was horrible, for her and for Sam, who'd already started patting her belly and saying, "Hi, Baby McGinty." She had been five months pregnant, clearly showing, when she woke up in the middle of the night in a pool of blood. Brick called Mrs. Kleshinski down the street to take Sam and then raced Ellie to the hospital. Within an hour, the doctor said he was sorry but it was clear she was going to lose that baby. Brick's face was ashen. He grabbed his coat and left, saying he had to get to work.

"He's just being a man," the attending nurse told Ellie, who had burst into tears. "They can't take the pain, the misery of it. They can't let themselves think about what they've lost, or what you're going through. Try not to let it bother you. He can't help who he is."

Ellie looked at the nurse's naked ring finger and felt a surge of resentment. So free with advice about a marriage. What did she know about what a husband, what *her* husband, felt? Later, lying alone in the dark, Ellie considered the unimaginable. Maybe Brick wasn't as big and brave as she'd always thought him to be. For a few hours, she forced herself to face the possibility that her husband might be a coward, or at least about some things. Maybe he was someone who ran away from trouble. When she had gotten pregnant with Sam, had he been running toward her, or away from his fear of failure at Kent State?

After a night's sleep, she woke up mortified that she'd

thought so little of her husband. For weeks after that, she prayed for forgiveness. A wife needed to believe in the man she trusted with her future, with her life. She had to have faith in Brick. It was as simple as that.

Despite her sadness, Ellie harbored a secret that renewed her hope. Two days after the miscarriage, she had asked to see the doctor. He arrived several hours later, looking important and bothered.

"I just want to know, Doctor," Ellie said, looking down at the stiff sheets tucked around her. "Could you tell if I was having a boy or a girl?"

His face softened as he sat on the side of the bed. "You had a boy growing inside you, Mrs. McGinty, and you can have a boy growing inside you again someday. But you have to give your body a rest. For six months, at least, use your diaphragm."

Ellie didn't hear a thing he said beyond the news that she had been carrying a boy. A son. She was determined to get pregnant again, as soon as possible. She owed Brick that. He'd been so patient, so sweet about Sam. He deserved a son.

It took so long for her to conceive again. Her body had needed time to recover, but Ellie couldn't pretend their marriage hadn't changed. It was as if a switch had tripped in Brick. Maybe it was the sight of all that blood on the sheet when she miscarried, or her tearfulness for weeks after. He no longer reached for her with that look of hunger in his eyes. Sometimes they went more than a week without having sex. Without even kissing hello or goodbye.

At first, she'd been relieved when Brick wasn't waking her up most mornings to have sex. She had needed time to get over what had happened, losing a baby that had already started moving inside her. By the time she started feeling better, though, Brick was absent even when he was home. In his place was a brooding man who often stopped at a bar after work, and drank more beer at home. Stroh's or Schlitz, whichever was cheaper that week, Ellie bought it by the case so that he could walk through the door, set his lunch pail on the counter, and pull out an ice-cold beer.

She patted her stomach. She was pinning all her hopes on this baby. If she could give Brick a son, he would be a happier, better husband. She was sure of it. "Be a boy," she whispered, rubbing herself with the palm of her hand. "We need you to be a boy."

CHAPTER

22

Brick yanked open the car door, threw his metal lunch pail across the front seat, and rolled down the window before climbing in. Christ, it was hot. Fresh out of the shower and he was already soaked with sweat.

He pulled the door shut and looked in the rearview mirror, raking his fingers through his wet hair. He looked at his watch. He'd been held up by a union matter, which meant he was already late getting home from work even without stopping at Flannery's on the way. Ellie would be pissed.

She had no idea what his days were like, and it bothered him sometimes: whenever she bitched at him to take out the trash, or complained about him falling asleep on the couch after dinner. Most of the time he was glad his wife never saw what he had to do for a living. Taking orders from assholes half his size, no matter what they told him to do. His skin turning black from the coal that fueled the plant, day in and day out.

She'd almost started an argument this morning over his leaving for work before dawn. "It only takes you seventeen minutes to get to the plant, but you always leave here an hour early. Why are you always in such a hurry to go? I miss you so much."

She'd worded it just right, making it about wanting him around longer, so he kept his temper. "Ellie, I can't let anything make me late. If I get a flat tire or have to wait for a train to pass, I still have time to get there and clock in by seven."

She had responded with the softest smile, grabbing his shoulders as she rose on tiptoes to kiss his cheek, her swollen belly bumping against his. He'd kissed her forehead, which was already damp with sweat. Summer was hot and humid in Erietown, but these last few days had been the worst he could remember. He wasn't sure if that was a reflection of the weather or of his mood. He was simmering all the time lately.

Sometimes Brick couldn't quite believe how much his life had changed in the last five years. In the first six months of his marriage, he'd buried his mother, rented his first house, and welcomed a baby into his life. Now he had another on the way. He also became a dues-paying member of Local 270 of the Utility Workers Union of America.

What did it say about him that he was most proud of his union card? It wasn't that he didn't love Ellie and Sam. Everything he did was for them. But all he had to do was look at every asshole around him at the plant to know it didn't take any talent to make a baby.

His job at the plant was different. He'd had to earn his union card during his first months on the job, and he'd had to earn every increase in his pay grade. He started at Level 1 like every new guy in maintenance, but by year five he'd left a lot of them behind. He was in line soon to be promoted to specialist, which came with options. He could become a lead worker, making him one of the few guys at the plant who could repair just about anything, or he could apply to help train new guys. The latter held no appeal. Just trying to teach Sam how to tie her shoes had revealed Brick to be a man of limited patience. He'd rather be known as the expert, the guy summoned after someone else had fucked up.

Brick pulled out of the plant parking lot and thought about his early days on the job. Competition was stiff for union jobs. If he hadn't worked in construction his last two summers of high school, he would never have gotten the chance, even with his brother-in-law's pull.

Coach's reference had to have helped. Using the names Sam Bryant and Brick McGinty in the same sentence had reminded the hiring supervisor of happier times. "Some of the best high school basketball I've seen in northeast Ohio," he had told Brick after glancing at his application. "I was a referee back then. You were top scorer in the state three years in a row, am I right?" Brick had nodded, his smile tight.

Brick had known so little about power plants when he started. Every day for the first year or so, it seemed, he was fucking up something. Just remembering to return the tools he checked out during the day was a constant source of irritation. He was used to his own tools in his own toolbox, the one Coach had helped him stock after he got the construction job. At the plant he had to use company-issued tools, which required a series of steps every time. He had to figure out which tools he needed for each job, then stand in line at the toolshed counter to check them out. So much wasted time, standing there listening to everyone's bullshit as he stared up at the dark green and white steel sign hanging overhead:

THE BEST SAFETY DEVICE
IS A
CAREFUL MAN

In his third week, he was standing in line in front of Carl Malone, a fifteen-year veteran of the plant and a union steward. "Isn't that the dumbest-ass thing you've ever seen?" Malone said.

Brick turned around and Malone pointed at the sign. "As if *our* being careful is the only problem in this shithole. Like it's Pete Keller's and Lenny Mulholland's fault that they can't breathe anymore, their lungs are so ruined. Or Johnny McHenry's fault that the company hadn't replaced that bent fuel shut-off valve on the power boiler. Blew him sky-high and took off his fuckin' arms. Because Johnny wasn't a careful man."

It wasn't long before armless Johnny McHenry started showing up in Brick's dreams. He had never met the guy, but he always woke up drenched in sweat after seeing the shadow of an armless man flailing at the plant entrance, banging his head against the doorframe as he laughed at Brick.

He'd made the mistake once of mentioning these nightmares to Ellie. Instead of comforting him she'd started to cry and begged him to quit. Better to keep the hazards of the job to himself.

In the beginning, Brick was terrified of injuries. The first time he accidentally splashed a drop of acid on his face he ran to the eye wash so fast that he tripped over the steel toes of his new boots and fell headfirst into a nearby pole. The two guys who saw him howled with laughter, and by the time he was in the showers everyone was calling him Bumble Brick.

He took it for almost two weeks, until it came out of the mouth of Ronnie Spinoza, another scrawny new guy who'd started on the same day as Brick. The locker room was full of men drying off and getting dressed when Spinoza yelled over his shoulder, "Hey, Bumble Brick, careful about tripping and bending over in the shower." Brick finished buckling his belt and planted a fist in the face of Spinoza, who fell against the wall and slid to the floor. Brick grabbed the front of Spinoza's shirt to yank him up, but three other guys pulled Brick back.

"I understand he pissed you off," Carl Malone said as he escorted Brick to his truck. "But Spinoza's in the union, and you don't punch a brother. You're lucky Prick Kennedy didn't see you."

He was referring to Dick Kennedy, the shift supervisor and a man who had the misfortune of reminding Brick of his father. Same small build, same way of sneering every time a word came out of his mouth. Brick hated him on sight after watching him scream at a secretary outside the front office, near the break room. She kept apologizing through sobs, but he wouldn't let up. "I said I'm sorry," she said.

"I'm sor-ry, I'm sor-ry," Kennedy said, mocking her in a high-pitched squeal. That's what tipped Brick off about Kennedy. He liked to beat up on people who had to take it, constantly reminding everyone that he was the boss. Brick had learned early from his feelings for his father that fear wasn't respect, and Brick wasn't afraid of anyone.

Brick started flexing his hands as he watched Kennedy go after the woman, and felt Malone suddenly standing next to him. "Watch yourself," Malone said softly. "He ain't worth losing your job."

Kennedy turned to look at Brick. "What are you staring at?"

Brick felt Malone squeeze his elbow, so he held out his hand to introduce himself. Kennedy waved it off. "Come to me when you've been here six months. If you can last that long."

Malone slapped Brick's shoulder. "Aaaand that's Prick Kennedy, your new boss. He gives you any trouble, you come to me."

Brick was everything Kennedy wasn't, and Kennedy knew it. Over the next five years, he circled Brick like a wolf on the prowl, but Brick remembered his mother's long-ago pleas, and trained himself to ignore the bully looking for a fight.

Brick had been at the plant for almost four years before he started joining the guys at the bar after work. He didn't want to do it until he no longer felt like a newbie, and by that time he had already moved from second to first shift and was one of the best troubleshooters. He'd cringed when he first heard his job was classified as maintenance, but he ended up liking the variety, and being needed. Wherever there was a problem, he was the guy to fix it. He liked the look of relief on the guys' faces when he showed up, and how they nodded their thanks after he'd finished.

One wintry afternoon, he'd just come in from a cigarette break, his face red and wind-burned, when Bobby McIntire came up to him and punched his arm. "Hey, how come you never stop with us after work?" he said.

"No reason, Mac. I just like to get home." He propped one of his boots on a pipe to tighten the lace and then adjusted his hard hat. "Ellie always has beer at the house for me. I like to see the kid before she gets cranky. You know how they get around bedtime."

"Do I," Mac said. "We have four boys, and Maggie's pregnant again. Jesus." He grinned. "And she wonders why I drink."

Brick smiled and tried not to hate him for his good luck. After all that blood in the bed following Ellie's second miscarriage, he had been half-afraid to touch her. He had thought she was going to die that night. Scared the shit out of him for months.

"You guys stopping tonight?" Brick said.

"Sure. Flannery's. Why don't you come? It'd be good for you, Brick. And I might have an ulterior motive."

Brick cocked his head. "Yeah. Like what?"

"We're going to talk about our roster for the softball team. I hear you're quite the athlete."

Brick shrugged. "I was better at basketball." Mac smiled,

and Brick answered the obvious question. "Right field. Pitcher in a pinch. Okay at the plate, I guess."

Mac slapped him on the back. "I heard you could hit that ball to Canada. We need you. Artie O'Connor says you've gotta be a power at the plate. We just don't know if a guy your size can run."

"If you hit it far enough, you don't have to run," Brick said, smiling as Mac laughed. "I'll be there. But when Ellie finds out, *you're* taking that call at the bar."

Playing softball with the guys made Brick feel younger, less tied down. None of the guys seemed to resent him for who he was or what he could do. They were just glad he was on their team. They saved his seat for him at the bar, and at games they shouted themselves hoarse whenever Brick rounded the bases and headed home. They were the closest he'd come to having brothers since Harry had died.

He loved the growing crowds, too, and the way they rose to their feet whenever he hit another homer or hurled a ball from right field to throw out a runner at home. "Brick, Brick, Brick," they'd cheer whenever he was at the plate. A sportswriter for the *Erietown Times* compared him to one of Brick's favorite movie characters.

Just like Shane, Brick McGinty is steady as he goes. Every time he hits another home run, he quietly trots off the field like it's just another day on the job. No slapping hands with other players, no verbal replays of his magnificence. He just nods his thanks to his fellow players and then reaches into his back pocket for a fresh strip of gum before he sits down on the bench.

"I read the story out loud to the girls at coffee this week," Ellie told him, gesturing to the large newsprint photo of Brick taped to the fridge. "They swooned."

Brick pretended to be embarrassed by the fuss, but he never corrected Ellie when she told Sam that he was the best softball player in Erietown. It was a good example for his daughter, he told himself. When you're good at something, you let others do the bragging.

CHAPTER

23

Ellie's eyelids fluttered as the nurse tapped on the back of her hand. "Mrs. McGinty. Mrs. McGinty."

She could feel tiny pricks of pain on her hand, but the effort required to raise her eyelids struck her as an impossible proposition.

Another tap, this time harder. "Mrs. McGinty, don't you want to see your new baby boy?"

Ellie floated to the surface and opened her eyes. "My what?"

The nurse lifted the blanketed bundle in her arms. "Congratulations. You have a son."

Ellie rose up on one elbow and pushed a damp curl from her eye. "I'm sorry," she said, squinting up at the nurse. "My manners. What is your name?"

"I'm Mrs. Bertha Drake. I assisted your delivery."

"Thank you," Ellie said. "May I hold my son, Mrs. Bertha Drake?"

The nurse lowered the baby into Ellie's arms. "Shall I go fetch your husband?" Ellie looked down at the sleeping baby and touched his chin. "Brick's here? I didn't know if anyone had been able to reach him."

Mrs. Drake slid a palm under Ellie's neck to raise her head just high enough to plump her pillow. "Your friend called the power plant. Mrs. Kelshinski, is it?"

Ellie smiled. "Ruby Kleshinski. She lives two houses down. I called her when my water broke."

The nurse eased Ellie's head back onto the pillow. "Well, she's a good friend to you. She took care of everything, let me tell you. Brought you here and held your little girl's hand until we wheeled you back, then called your husband at work. She called the desk later to make sure we told you your daughter could spend the next few nights with her."

Mrs. Drake's salt-and-pepper hair and horn-rimmed reading glasses dangling from the cord around her neck reminded Ellie of her grandmother. "Was it always like this?"

Mrs. Drake was tucking in the sheet at the foot of Ellie's bed. "Was what always like this?"

Ellie traced her son's tiny eyebrows with her finger. "Did we always depend on each other like this? On other women?"

Mrs. Drake stood up straight and pressed her fists into her hips. "Hmm. Now there's a question no one's ever asked me." She smiled at Ellie. "A woman's world has always revolved around children and other women. At least as long as I've been around, and I'm almost sixty." She smoothed the sheet draped across Ellie as she talked, tucking it in around the sides of her body like a cocoon.

"Don't get me wrong," she continued. "We love our men, and the *idea* of a husband is a good thing. What woman wouldn't want that?"

Ellie thought of her brave, independent Aunt Nessa, teaching until she was seventy and dying in her sleep on a train bound for New Mexico. She'd never wanted to marry, and she was the happiest woman Ellie had ever known.

Mrs. Drake plucked a tissue from the box on Ellie's nightstand and blew her nose. "Men need us more than we need them," she said, and then lowered her voice. "Including the doctors around here. They walk around acting like God, but you should see the panic when one of them has to buy a birthday present for his wife. They have no idea what women want."

She washed her hands in the small sink in the corner. "That's why we need our women friends. We're with each other from the beginning to the very end, and everything in between. We understand each other. It's instinctual."

She nodded toward the baby in Ellie's arms. "You don't have to worry about any of that right now. You have a daughter, and now you have a son. He's yours for a while, but she'll be your best friend for the rest of your life. Way of the world, I guess. Our boys grow up to become men who leave us."

Ellie wriggled to inch herself higher in the bed. "Would it be possible to see my husband now? Could someone please send him in?"

Mrs. Drake smiled. "Of course. Listen to me go on. If there's ever a time when your husband is all yours, it's right after you've given birth to his first son. I'll go fetch him."

Ellie didn't have a mirror, but she could easily imagine how bad she looked. If she could get to her purse, she could at least dab her nose with powder and put on a little lipstick. Her eyes scanned the room until she spotted it in the chair in the corner, on top of her folded clothes. She was trying to decide whether she could slide out of the bed with the baby in her arms when a nurse's aide walked into the room. Ellie was relieved to see that she looked to be about her age. Ellie smiled sheepishly as she pointed to the chair. "I'm sorry to ask, but would you mind bringing me my purse? I'd like to put on a little makeup before my husband walks in."

The aide grabbed the purse and handed it to Ellie. "I'm Lavelle. You're one of my patients for the evening."

Ellie nodded her thanks. "Hi, Lavelle. I'm Ellie." She looked down at her baby and then smiled at Lavelle.

"A boy, huh?" Lavelle said, peering into Ellie's arms. "Well, isn't he adorable."

"Our first son," Ellie said, kissing the tip of his nose. "Isn't that right, little man?" She held him tight in her left arm as she opened the handbag with her other hand and rummaged for her lipstick. Lavelle picked up the tissue box and held it for Ellie. "Thanks," Ellie said, plucking a tissue. She slid it between her lips and made popping sounds as she blotted the lipstick. "I feel so much better."

Ellie heard steps and looked past the aide, to the door. Her face lit up, and Lavelle turned around. "Brick," Lavelle said, dropping the tissue box onto the floor. She bent down to pick it up and took a step back.

Ellie looked back and forth at their faces, searching for clues. Lavelle grabbed Ellie's used tissue, avoiding eye contact as she crumpled it in her hand. "Congratulations to both of you," she said, rushing out the door with the tissue box in her hand.

Ellie pulled the baby closer against her swollen breasts. She turned to face the window as Brick walked to the side of her bed. "Ellie." She could feel his breath on her neck. "Who's that little guy in your arms?"

She shifted the baby slightly away from him. "Who was that woman, Brick? How did she know your name?"

"I don't know, Ellie. Maybe she saw my picture in the paper. Earlier today a guy in the waiting room—"

"No," Ellie said, slowly shaking her head. "I saw the look on your face. I saw the look on *her* face. She knew you."

Brick sat down on the edge of the bed. Ellie inched away

from him. "Ellie, don't do this. Please. I have no idea who she is. I don't care who she is." He looked down at the baby. "We've got a son, Ellie. We've got a boy. That's who we should be talking about."

He reached toward the baby. "Can I hold him?"

Ellie loosened her grip, and Brick lifted him out of her arms. "Wow," he said, "look at that hair."

"A redhead," she said. "Just like his daddy."

Brick exhaled slowly and looked at Ellie. "He's perfect."

Ellie continued to stare at the baby. "He needs a name," she said.

"I was thinking," Brick said. "I was wondering if we could name him Reilly. For Mom."

Ellie could feel her mood soften at the mention of Angie O'Reilly McGinty. She thought of Angie's final hours, how Brick had stayed by his mother's side until her heart finally stopped. Maybe Mrs. Drake was wrong about boys. Brick was a man, but he was always his mother's son. Even now, six years after her death.

"I like that," Ellie said. "Let's call him Reilly Paull. Paull-two-els. For your mother's only brother."

Brick lifted the baby higher to get a better look. "Thank you, Ellie." He tilted the baby so that she could see his face. "Thank you for giving me Reilly Paull McGinty."

Ellie nodded, silently noting the fear in his eyes.

Two hours later, after Mrs. Drake had shuttled Reilly off to the hospital nursery for the night, Ellie lay on her back in the dark, unable to sleep. She reached over to turn on the table lamp and blinked a few times as her eyes adjusted to the soft light, grateful that she didn't have a roommate.

The door opened slightly, and Lavelle peered in. "Do you need anything, Mrs. McGinty?"

Ellie motioned for the aide to come into the room. "I'd like to ask you something, if you don't mind."

Lavelle walked slowly toward her. Ellie patted the spot next to her on the bed, but Lavelle shook her head. "We aren't supposed to sit on patients' beds," she said. "I need this job. I don't want to get fired."

"Sorry," Ellie said. "I don't mean to get you in trouble. I just thought you might be tired from standing on your feet all day."

"I've had worse jobs," Lavelle said, picking up Ellie's water pitcher to refill her cup. "I like making patients feel a little better, a little more comfortable. It's a lot better than dodging dirty men's passes at your ass and watching people drink themselves into an early grave."

"Did you tend bar?"

"For almost five years," Lavelle said. "At Flannery's. I jumped at the chance when this job opened up." She picked up the pitcher again, looked at Ellie's full cup, and set it back down. "Do you need anything else?"

"I need to know how you know my husband."

Lavelle avoided looking at her. "Maybe I saw him at the bar a few times. You know, with the other guys. After they got off work." She pushed her hands into her pockets and shrugged. "I knew him a few years ago. But that was before he was married to you. He was kinda with my sister Kitty for a while."

Ellie's skin started to prick at the back of her neck. "Kitty," she said, trying to sound calm. "Oh, yeah, he told me about her. I think it was right before we started dating. What year was that?"

"Oh, God," Lavelle said, fanning her face with her hand. "I'm so glad I didn't tell you anything you didn't already know. Let's see, had to be at least two years ago. Maybe three, even."

Ellie clenched her jaw and took a deep breath. "So, nineteen sixty, maybe."

Lavelle nodded. "Sixty. Sixty-one, maybe. I don't remember for sure. When did you and Brick start dating?"

Ellie lay back on her pillow and closed her eyes. "High school," she said. "We married in nineteen fifty-seven."

Ellie silently counted to ten. When she opened her eyes, Lavelle was gone.

CHAPTER

24

Samantha sat on the edge of the sofa and kept her eyes on the clock.

"Daddy will be home when the little hand is on the four and the big hand is on the six," her mother had said. Sam knew this was true. Brick had been coming home at the same time from the day that baby Reilly came home. Made a fuss about it, too. "Four-thirty, Sam, and your daddy is home sweet home," he said almost every night.

In the months before Reilly was born, Sam had been a little nervous when her father was home. By the time her father asked her to bring him beer number four—she always counted because Mrs. Babcock said they should practice their arithmetic at home—her father was usually sad.

"Your grandma Angie would have loved you, I'll tell you that," he'd told Sam last Valentine's Day, after he started sipping beer number four. "You have her long fingers." He raised his hand so that Sam could press her palm against his. "My fingers will never be as big as yours, Daddy." He smiled, but it didn't mean she had made him happy. She could tell by his eyes.

Sometimes, Sam would say, "I love you, Daddy," and hold her breath for as long as she could so she wouldn't miss it if he finally whispered, "I love you, too." Mommy said Daddy loved Sam but that men just don't say that kind of thing out loud. Sam knew that wasn't true because Mary McCallister's daddy always said, "I love you, baby girl!" For no reason at all.

After baby Reilly came home, her father's mood changed, but she didn't trust it. He talked in his new voice, but his smile was frozen, like she was looking at a picture of him. Still, it was a nice change, she decided. As soon as she heard his car pull into the driveway, even if she was sitting in her little rocker and feeding Reilly, she'd stand up and carry her brother to the door to greet their father. She wondered why Mommy never did this, but she didn't ask why. She didn't want to upset her.

Her mother was different, too. One Mommy went to the hospital and another Mommy came home. Sam wondered if that's what happens when you have a boy. Maybe you have to give up something nice about yourself for God to give you a son. Maybe Mommy told God she'd never laugh really loud again and he said, "Okay, then I'll give you a boy." Sam wished she could ask someone about that who would give her a straight answer. Mommy no longer sat on the edge of Sam's bed to hear her prayers, so Sam kept slipping in the question before the amen. So far, God had nothing to say about it.

Sam looked at the blank TV screen. Daddy usually pulled into the driveway right after Barnaby said goodbye, but before Captain Penny told his first story. She loved Barnaby and Captain Penny. They never looked angry and they seemed to be talking right to her. Normally, Barnaby would be talking to her right now, but as Mommy had said, there was nothing normal about this day.

"You have a job to do, Sam," her mother told her as she bundled up Reilly. "You need to concentrate."

This was Sam's first time to be home alone. A special occasion, she decided, and walked upstairs to change into the blouse she knew was her father's favorite because two months ago he had leaned down to touch her face and told her the blue flowers embroidered on the collar matched her eyes just right. He said it again just four nights ago, but Sam knew habits had a way of stopping as fast as they started in their house. "Don't get used to it," she told herself whenever something new and good happened a few days in a row. Like when Daddy started giving her a Tootsie Roll after dinner. After three nights of that, Sam's mother snatched the candy out of Sam's hand. "Like we've got money for those dentist bills," Ellie said. Sam didn't cry. She had been ready for it to end.

She pulled her blouse out of the dirty clothes hamper in the hallway and tugged on it to smooth out the wrinkles. She tiptoed into her parents' room and held her mother's favorite hand mirror, running her fingers along the letter "A" on the back before she flipped it to make sure her face was clean. She dabbed a single drop of White Shoulders on the inside of her wrist and then rubbed her wrists together, just like her mother used to do before baby Reilly was born.

If Sam had known a baby boy could change a family so much, she wouldn't have prayed so hard for a brother. "Sorry, God," she said as she screwed the cap back onto the bottle. "But that's how it looks to me."

Sam walked back downstairs and thought about her mother's sudden exit this afternoon. The phone rang and Sam answered just as her mother had taught her to do. "McGinty residence. How may I help you?"

"Honey," the man said, "I need to speak to your mama." Sam called her mother to the phone.

"Today?" Ellie said. "Well, he won't be home until four-thirty."

Pause.

"I see. Yes, I agree. Better for everyone."

Her mother pressed her finger on the button in the cradle

of the phone and dialed. "Mardee? I'm sorry to ask this, but can you come get me, please? Yes, it's happening. Between four-thirty and five. I'm so—" Her mother glanced at Sam. "Well, you know." She hung up the phone and draped her apron over the back of her chair at the dining room table instead of the hook on the basement door.

Sam followed her mother around the house. Ellie picked up two clean diapers from the wicker basket on the floor and stuffed them in the bag she used for baby Reilly's stuff. She opened the refrigerator, pulled out a bottle of formula, and tossed it in the bag, too. She started walking up the stairs, paused on the third step, turned around, went back into the kitchen for another bottle, and crammed it into the bag.

After her mother went upstairs, Sam emptied the overflowing diaper bag so that she could put things where they belonged. When she was finished, she retrieved Reilly's stuffed Leo the lion from the playpen and buried her nose in its mane, inhaling the scent of her brother before setting it on top. Overhead, Reilly had started to wail, and moments later Mommy carried him downstairs.

Ellie glanced at the clock before she pulled open the closet door and grabbed her jacket.

"Hold your brother for a minute," she said, handing Sam the crying baby.

"There, there," Sam said, hoisting him over her shoulder and patting his back as she swayed. She started humming one of her made-up lullabies, and Reilly stopped crying. "You have the touch, Sammy," Mommy often said. But not today.

Her mother buttoned her jacket. "Sam, I need you to stay here and wait for Daddy."

"Where are you going? Why can't I go?"

Her mother took Reilly, and immediately, he started crying again. "Sam, I can't answer a lot of questions right now. There's a man who's going to come to the door, and he's going to have something for Daddy."

A car horn beeped outside, and Ellie opened the door. "He's going to have an envelope for Daddy. I want you to stay here and be with him."

"What should I eat for dinner?"

"You know how to make soup. You can make dinner for you and Daddy."

Sam nodded. "I guess so."

"That's my girl," her mother said. And then she was gone.

Sam now decided to stop looking at the clock and walked over to get a better look at the framed pictures hanging on either side of it. Jesus was on the left. President John F. Kennedy was on the right. The Jack-and-Jesus wall, Daddy called it. Before Reilly was born Mommy sometimes laughed when Daddy walked to the table for supper and yelled, "Hi, Jack! Hi, Jesus!" "Honestly, Brick," Mommy would say, but she was always smiling. Sam liked it when Daddy teased Mommy and Mommy pretended not to like it.

Sam sometimes wondered why, if Jesus was the son of God, he didn't look happier. Maybe he knew what was coming.

Most of her friends' houses had the same picture of Jesus. Long hair on his shoulders, eyes looking up. At God, she figured. The picture in Mary Beth Murphy's house was different. Jesus was bloody hanging on the cross, on the wall right over their TV. Sam burst into tears at the sight of him and ran all the way home.

"That's the problem with Catholics," her mother said at supper. "They spend too much time on the crucifixion, instead of the resurrection."

Brick laughed. "President Kennedy's Catholic."

"And we voted for him," Ellie said. "That's how openminded we Methodists can be."

Her mother's "we" had snapped Sam to attention. She couldn't remember a single time Daddy had walked into church with them, but she was relieved to know that God knew her father was a Methodist.

Sam looked at President Kennedy and wondered what it would be like to have a daddy who wore a suit and tie to work. She'd never seen her father in a tie, and she once heard him make fun of their neighbor Mr. McDonald for having to wear a "monkey suit" every day to his job at the People's Savings and Loan.

Daddy didn't seem to feel that way about the president, and neither did Mommy. When Mrs. Carlton from church said she was shocked to see a Catholic next to Jesus in the McGinty house, Sam's mother stopped pouring coffee into her cup. "Well, Gloria, God loves everyone. Even the bigots." Mrs. Carlton picked up her purse and left.

Daddy loved that story.

Sam heard the sound of her father's car tires crunch across the driveway cinders. She smoothed the front of her blouse and walked to the kitchen door. She smiled at Brick as soon as he pushed it open. "Hi, Daddy."

"Hi, sweetie," he said, ruffling her hair with his left hand as he set his lunch pail on the counter. He looked around. "Where's Mommy?"

"Mommy and Reilly—" She stopped at the sound of someone knocking on the front door.

"I'll get the door," she said, running to the front of the house. "It's probably the man with the envelope." She pulled open the front door and saw the gun resting at eye level in the man's holster.

The sheriff's deputy leaned down until his eyes met hers. "Is your daddy here, honey?"

Before she could say a word he stood up and extended his

hand over her head. "Mr. McGinty?" Sam felt her father's hands on her shoulders.

"What can I do for you, Bill?"

The deputy pulled his hand back. "I'm sorry, Brick, but I have to do this by the book." He reached into his back pocket and pulled out a blue envelope. "Richard Paull McGinty, you are hereby served by the Clayton County Sheriff's Department."

Brick snatched the envelope out of the man's hand and ripped it open. "What the——?" He threw the paper to the floor. "You like doing this for a living, Bill? Breaking up families?" He squeezed Sam's shoulder. "Ruining the lives of innocent children."

"It's not personal, Brick."

"Every second of this is personal. Get the hell off my porch before I throw you off."

The deputy started to lean down to say goodbye to Sam, but Brick yanked her back and slammed the door. He picked up the paper and walked into the kitchen. Sam picked up the envelope and climbed onto the couch to press her face against the window. The deputy was shooing away a handful of curious kids gathered around his cruiser. He turned to look back at the house, and Sam pulled the thin curtain across the window. She jumped off the couch and walked through the dining room just as her father started to cry.

"Ellie, my God."

He was standing in the far corner with his back to Sam, his face buried in his hands. "Ellie. Oh my God, Ellie."

Sam had never seen her father like this. She ran over to him and pressed her cheek against his back, wrapping her arms around his waist. He clutched her hands. "My sweet little Sam."

"Daddy," she said. "What's wrong?"

He turned around and hugged her. "Mommy doesn't want me living here. Mommy doesn't love me anymore."

Sam burrowed her face into his shirt. "Mommy loves you. I heard her tell Mrs. Jepson on the phone yesterday that she loves you."

She could feel his grip soften, and his chest stopped heaving. He let go of her and reached for the dishrag draped over the faucet. "You heard Mommy say that?" he said, wiping his face. "You *heard* Mommy?"

Sam nodded. "That's how she said it. *I still love Brick.*" She pointed to the can of Campbell's tomato soup on the counter. "I'll make dinner," she said. "I'll make us baloney sandwiches and soup, just like Mommy told me to."

He threw the rag into the sink. "Mommy thought of everything, didn't she?"

Sam opened the fridge and turned to look at him, but he did not return her smile.

CHAPTER

25

The lupines behind his mother's headstone were limp and brown. Brick felt a silent reprimand in their lifeless stalks shuddering in the wind, as if demanding to know, *Where have you been?*

He hadn't visited the cemetery since last fall, when he planted the row of seeds for his mother's favorite flower. He had planned to see them in full bloom, a blue and purple halo over her head, proof of his devotion. He'd let so much get away from him.

He crouched on the grave and stared at the headstone. Specks of dirt had settled into the grooves of his mother's name. Brick pulled a handkerchief from his back pocket and dug out the dirt in the letters.

ANGELA MCGINTY
OCTOBER 12, 1898—APRIL 20, 1957

Lillian had paid for the gravestone, but gave in to their father when he insisted she not include their mother's family name, O'Reilly. So like Bull McGinty, pissing to mark territory that wasn't his to claim.

Brick wiped the front of the stone from top to bottom, and shook his head at the blackened handkerchief. Ten older sisters, and not one of them could be bothered to tend their mother's grave. No wonder Ma was ready to die. Everyone she loved had let her down.

It had been an unusually warm day for November, but the setting sun was no match for the wind. He sat cross-legged on the grave and pulled up his collar around his ears. He looked around to make sure he was alone.

"Well, Ma, we have a boy now. I have a son. We named him Reilly, for you. His middle name is Paull-two-els. For your brother. His hair's red, just like yours and mine. You should see him." He looked up at the moon. "Well," he said, his voice less steady. "Maybe you do see him. I like to think that."

He reached out and traced the date of his mother's death. Less than three months after he married Ellie, Angie was gone. Seven years later he was still waking up in the middle of the night, drenched in sweat from the same dream. He's chasing his mother down a road. She is young, no older than Brick is now, but he knows it's her. She looks so happy, her feet barely touching the ground as her long red hair flies behind her. She glances back at him and laughs, always just beyond his reach as he calls out to her. "Ma! Ma!" So often, he wakes up with a jolt, his legs tangled in the soggy bedclothes, tears rolling into his ears.

About two months before Reilly was born, Ellie had shaken him awake from the dream, and tried to make him feel better about it. "Maybe your dream is your mother's way of letting you know she's happy now, and free. She's telling you we don't have to worry about her anymore." He was hungover, and still felt guilty about Kitty. He felt like shit every time Ellie made an effort to be nice to him.

God, he'd been an asshole that night. "You know what, El?

Life isn't a goddamn fairy tale, okay? And it doesn't always 'work out.' Not for people like us. Every mistake comes with a price tag, and we can't pay to fix it."

She had looked stunned, clutching her swollen belly. He'd later worried that she'd thought he was talking about her pregnancy. He'd been excited when she told him, but he was also heartsick to learn that she'd waited to tell him until she was almost five months along. "I didn't want to get your hopes up," she'd said, "in case something went wrong again." Had he known, he never would have laid hands on Kitty McKenzie.

He had thought Ellie was gaining weight. Letting herself go, he'd told himself. Going to bed earlier, too, leaving him alone with his beers and TV.

He touched his mother's tombstone. "My biggest mistake, Ma, grew out of that lie I told myself."

He'd started lingering longer at Flannery's, and Kitty was always there to greet him when he walked through the door. She worked in the front office at the rubber plant up the road, and she'd always had an eye for Brick. Rushing up to give him a hug and then swirling around to yell at the back table of girl-friends. "I'll be back in a minute, girls. Just saying hi to my boyfriend here."

At first, he'd pry her hands from around his neck. "You know I'm married, Kitty," he'd say or "C'mon, that's enough." But he was the kind of guy who loved the attention, and she was the kind of woman who knew it.

Once night he came home from work and Ellie started bitching at him, first thing, about how she needed more money for groceries. How maybe if he spent less money on beer and bars she could afford to make something other than fried Spam and hamburger goulash every second and fourth week of the month.

"Goddammit," he yelled, slamming his lunch pail on the counter. "Like I'm not working my ass off, day after day. While you're sitting here at home." He heard a whimper and turned around to see Sam hovering in the doorway, staring at him— blue eyes wide, chin quivering.

"Now look what you've done," he said, glaring at Ellie as he pointed at Sam. He grabbed his car keys off the counter and left.

As usual, Kitty ran up to him when he walked into Flannery's, but this time he pulled her in for a hug and buried his face in her hair. "How 'bout we get out of here?" he whispered. She stepped back slowly and studied his face. "Go sit at the bar," she said.

He sat down on his usual stool. A few minutes later Kitty slid up behind him and slipped him a folded paper napkin. He waited until she walked away to read her note.

1801 Stone Road, Apt. #3

That's how it started.

It helped that Kitty didn't look anything like Ellie. Kitty was a good six inches taller, with a waist so small he could circle it with his hands. He liked the way her breath fluttered at his touch, and how she writhed under him, arching her back and calling him the dirty names that Ellie would never say. Kitty let him shower at her place after, too, without saying a word about why. Finding Ellie asleep in bed when he got home was all the evidence he needed that she didn't care.

The morning Ellie told him she was pregnant, she apologized for how tired she'd been, how "chunky" she'd gotten. "You must have thought I was getting fat on you," she'd said with a nervous laugh. Brick rushed to her and held her tight, afraid to let Ellie see his face.

He broke it off with Kitty that evening, during a quick stop at the bar after work. "We always said we were just having a little fun," he said as they stood in the back parking lot.

"Did we? You prick."

Brick looked around the lot. "Don't make a scene, Kitty."

She screwed up her face and started talking in a whining voice. "Poor, pitiful Brick. 'My wife ignores me.' 'You make me feel like a *real* man.' And now I find out you've been screwing both of us all along. So what if your wife's pregnant? You think I'm just going to fade away?"

"Don't do something you're going to regret," he said, slowly.

"You mean that *you'll* regret."

"No," he said, leaning in. "I definitely mean *you*."

She stepped back. "Fine," she said. "You're a loser, anyway."

Two days later, the hang-up calls started coming to the house at suppertime.

Sam answered the first two nights. Brick winced at the sound of her innocent voice. "McGinty residence. May I help you?" Pause. "Hello? Hello?" Each time Ellie smiled at her and shrugged. "Just hang up the phone, sweetie. It's obviously a wrong number."

On the third night, Sam answered again, but this time she turned to Ellie and said, "Mommy, I can hear breathing, but the person won't say anything." Brick started to push away from the table, but Ellie beat him to it. She grabbed the receiver. "Pervert!" she yelled, and slammed it down. She looked at Brick. "When did you start wanting to answer the phone?"

From then on, Ellie answered the phone every time it rang during supper. Every time, she slammed it down. "Who the hell is doing this to us?" she said after the sixth night.

That evening, Brick opened the fridge as Ellie washed the dishes. "I'm going to make a beer run," he said. Ellie looked at him. "We've got at least six bottles in there."

"It's all Stroh's," Brick said, shutting the door and reaching for his jacket. "I feel like Schlitz tonight."

Ellie started scrubbing a pot. "I always buy what's on sale."

Brick drove first to Flannery's. When he found that Kitty

wasn't there, he drove to her apartment. "Go to hell, Brick," she yelled from behind the door.

He looked around to make sure no one was in the stairwell and pressed his forehead against the door. "You call my house one more time, and I will tell your boss that you've been stealing from petty cash. He'll believe me, too. I've known Freddy since grade school. That cheap bastard will have you arrested." He didn't wait for a response. On the way home, he stopped at Cal's Corner and bought a six-pack of Schlitz.

The calls at suppertime stopped, but the damage was done. Brick was too nervous at dinner, too edgy. He started volunteering for overtime most weeknights and worked a few weekends, too. "I'm going to have another mouth to feed," he told Ellie when she complained that he was never home. "We're going to need the money."

On the day Reilly was born, Brick walked into Ellie's hospital room and saw Kitty's sister Lavelle in that nurse's aide uniform. The look on Ellie's face told him he was about to pay for what he'd done.

He'd been prepared for Ellie to hate him for a while, and that she might even take the kids and stay with a friend for a few days. Never did he think she would see a divorce lawyer and send a deputy to the house. Brick spent that first night away at the Wigwam, but returned home the next evening to talk to Ellie.

"You don't have grounds," he told her. "You can't get a divorce without grounds. And you can't even afford a lawyer."

Ellie was eerily calm, her voice empty of emotion. "I've got proof of your adultery," she said. "Lavelle and Kitty said they'll testify against you. And my lawyer says the judge will make you pay my legal bills."

He packed two paper bags full of clothes and left that night; now he was staying in the basement at his sister Gloria's house, across town. "I'm still in shock, Ma," he said. "Ellie always said most people were inherently good, despite the evidence. I've never seen her give up on anyone. Until now."

Brick had lost almost twenty pounds in the last five weeks. His work clothes hung on him. Whenever one of the guys asked why, he tried to make a joke of it. "Getting ready for next season," he'd say, patting his shrinking gut.

Some of the guys had to know about the divorce papers. Three of them were married to women in Ellie's coffee klatch, and Jack Connelly's wife sang in the choir with her at church. Even if she hadn't told anyone, take one look at Ellie and you knew something was wrong. She'd lost a lot of weight, too, way beyond the baby pounds. Her face was gaunt, and her big blue eyes were rimmed with dark circles. Last time he'd picked up Sam after supper to take her for ice cream, Ellie stood in the doorway like a tiny ghost, avoiding his gaze. He felt like his chest was going to explode.

He had to talk to somebody. It couldn't be Coach. If he told Sam Bryant that Ellie wanted a divorce, he'd also have to tell him why, and the thought of that made Brick's gut roil. He surely couldn't talk to anyone at work. To confide a weakness would compromise his image as a tough shop steward for the union. You lose your power as soon as people find a reason to pity you.

And so here he was, talking to the one person who had never judged him. He looked up at the darkening sky and blinked back tears. "Patch is gone, Ma. Did I ever tell you? Died a year ago in his sleep, right before Christmas. He had a good, long life, thanks to you." He wiped his eyes with the dirty handkerchief. "You should have seen him with our Sam, hovering like a cattle dog. God, I miss him."

He shivered and pulled his collar tighter. "I've screwed up, Ma. I don't know what I'm going to do if Ellie goes through with this. I don't want to live without her. Without the kids. I've been so hateful, Ma. I get so angry. I'm afraid I'm—" He buried his face in his hands and started to sob. "I'm afraid I'm just like him."

He rocked back and forth for a while, his forehead against his knees until he could stop crying. He touched her name. "I love you, Ma. I wish I'd told you that more when you were still around." He shivered and waited for another gust of wind to pass. "I know you'd say I should be asking God for help, but I think he gave up on me a long time ago. Maybe you could put in a good word for me? I'll bet he listens to you."

Another memory bubbled up, from the day his mother died. Before Brick and Ellie walked into the house, Lil had pointed up to their mother's window and said, "There's nothing we can do but keep her comfortable. She's in God's hands now."

Brick spit on the ground. "Here we go again. God, God, God. Where's God been all this time? Why didn't God help her when she needed it? Why's God taking *her* instead of that maggot she married?"

Ellie grabbed his arm, but he yanked it free. "No. No, I won't treat her nice because it's what God wants. I'll be nice to Ma because she deserves a better life than the one your God gave her."

Brick touched his mother's headstone again. "I'm sorry I said that, Ma." He leaned in and flattened his palms against the stone. "I just didn't want you to die." He stood up and brushed off the seat of his pants, and walked to his car.

That night, for the first time in months, he slept through the night. Once again, he dreamed of his mother. She was still young and happy, still laughing as she ran in front of him as he yelled, "Ma! Ma!" This time, though, she stopped, her face turned away from him as she held out her hand and waited for him to catch up. "Ma," he said, grabbing her hand. When she turned to look at him, it was Ellie who returned his smile.

CHAPTER

26

NOVEMBER 22,
1963

Mrs. Babcock closed the door and dragged the piano bench to the front of the classroom.

"Children," she said, her voice trembling. "I want you to put down your crayons and pay attention, please."

Sam had already stopped coloring the moment she saw Mrs. Babcock sit down on the bench. Her teacher had never done that in the middle of the day before, and Sam had a sense of things. When grown-ups do something you've never seen them do before, it's because something's wrong.

She slipped the Forest Green crayon into her new box of Crayolas and eased the lid closed. Her father had bought the crayons for her three days after he moved out of their house. *Six days after the deputy knocked on our door* was how she thought about it, and she thought about it every day. Five weeks and two days later, Sam still had no idea why Daddy wasn't living at home, and her mother just cried whenever she asked. If Mommy didn't know why Daddy was gone, they were really in trouble. Every night, Sam asked God to please help Mommy figure it out.

Sometimes Sam woke in the middle of the night to the sounds of her mother crying. Sam knew what she had to do.

She'd tiptoe past Reilly's crib in her parents' bedroom and crawl into the space on the bed where Daddy used to sleep. Mommy still slept only on her side of the bed, facing the wall. Sam would cling to the curve of her back and hold on to her until she fell asleep. In the morning, Mommy always acted surprised to find Sam lying next to her. Sam never reminded her why. She just got ready for school, which was the only place where life still felt normal.

Until this afternoon. Now Mrs. Babcock was sitting on the bench with her head in her hands. Sam loved Mrs. Babcock. She had been extra nice to Sam ever since Day Eleven, when Sam started crying for no reason and Mrs. Babcock asked her to stay behind during recess "so that we can have a little chat." As soon as Sam told Mrs. Babcock about the deputy at the door, Mrs. Babcock had pulled her into the longest hug in Sam's six years of life.

"You poor, poor child," Mrs. Babcock said. "You deserve so much better." It was the nicest thing anyone had said to her since her father moved out.

Sam hated to see Mrs. Babcock so unhappy. She glanced around the room and raised her hand. Her teacher looked at her with damp, red eyes. "Yes, Sam?"

"You can talk now, Mrs. Babcock. Everybody's paying attention."

"Thank you, Sam." Mrs. Babcock crossed her arms over her bright green sweater and leaned slightly forward. "Children, I have very sad news."

Sam sat up straighter and resolved to be strong, no matter what. As long as the bad news had nothing to do with Mommy or Daddy, she could be brave. "Or Reilly," she whispered, and silently apologized to God for forgetting him.

"Children, an awful thing has happened today," Mrs. Babcock said. "A horrible man has shot"—she clutched the single strand of pearls around her neck—"has killed our president." She pulled a hankie out of the sleeve of her sweater and dabbed at her eyes. "President John F. Kennedy is now with our Lord and Savior."

Several of Sam's classmates gasped. Sam was silent, thinking of President Kennedy's picture in their house, and how Jesus was always looking at him on the wall. Maybe he knew something like this was coming.

Mrs. Babcock waved her hankie. "I know this is a shock." Sam blinked a few times, thinking of her father as she nodded her head. "Principal Ryan asked all of us teachers to tell you now because we don't want you to hear this news from strangers on the way home. Our country is in shock, just like you. You may see Mr. Sawicki looking upset in his barbershop, or Miss Dunham crying behind the counter at the newsstand. Your parents might cry today, too. Give them hugs, and be extra good tonight."

Silently, the children collected their artwork and crayons and opened their desktops to stash them inside. They waited, staring at Mrs. Babcock, who had run out of words. Sam looked around the room. Her classroom was divided equally between black and white students, and she was not surprised to see her black friends so upset, too. If only Daddy could see how sad they were about President Kennedy. Maybe he would change his mind about black people. She would tell him. Might make him feel a little better, knowing how much everyone loved President Kennedy.

The children watched Mrs. Babcock for a sign of what they should do, but she was still sitting on the piano bench with her face in her hands. Sam thought about what she would do if that were her mother sitting there, looking so sad and alone. She stood up, and when Mrs. Babcock didn't tell her to sit down, she walked up to her teacher and stood behind her so that she could wrap her arms around her back and lay her head on her shoulder. Mrs. Babcock pressed her cheek against Sam's hand.

Leroy Riley was next. He was wearing his Cub Scouts uniform, which made him look serious even when he wasn't. He sat down on the bench and scooted up against Mrs. Babcock, taking her hand in his. "Leroy," she said, softly.

Patty Hairston was the first black girl to walk up. She stood next to Sam, draped her left arm over Mrs. Babcock's shoulder, and placed her right hand on top of Sam's.

The room filled with the screech of chairs against the wooden floor. One by one, the children gathered, building a hive around their teacher. They waited, silent and warm, until the last bell of the day sent them into a world that would never be the same.

Ellie and Mardee stood in front of the television with their arms wrapped around each other, waiting. Less than an hour ago, Walter Cronkite's faceless voice had interrupted *As the World Turns* to announce that three shots had been fired at President Kennedy's motorcade in Dallas, Texas. "The first reports say that President Kennedy has been seriously wounded by this shooting," he said.

"Who can watch this now?" Mardee said, pointing to the soap opera. "When are they going to let us know?"

Cronkite reappeared on the screen a few minutes later, surrounded by phones and the sound of clicking wire machines. He held up a grainy photo and described it as a picture of the president's motorcade. "From Dallas, Texas, the flash apparently official," he said, removing his glasses. "President Kennedy died at one P.M. Central Standard Time—two o'clock Eastern Standard Time—some thirty-eight minutes ago."

Ellie and Mardee gasped in unison as Cronkite slowly put on his glasses.

"He's stalling," Ellie said, her voice trembling. "He's trying not to cry." She walked over to the television and turned off the volume. "I can't," she said, tears streaming down her face. "I can't listen to another word. Not now."

Mardee pulled her into a hug. "My God, El." Ellie pulled her hankie out of her pocket and frowned at the soggy, crumpled wad. "I've got to get another hankie. You want one?" Mardee nodded.

Ellie walked up the stairs and stopped at Reilly's crib to pull his blanket over his shoulders. So much had changed in the hour and a half that he'd been sleeping. When she'd put Reilly down for his nap, Caroline and John-John still had a father.

She walked over to her dresser and pulled out the top drawer, tearing up again at the sight of her grandmother's embroidered hankies. Grandma was the only person who could have helped her see God's plan in this. In all of it, in everything that had happened in the last six weeks.

Ellie snatched several hankies and tiptoed back downstairs. She handed one to Mardee, who ran her fingers along the faded lavender French knots clustered to look like lilacs. "Your grandmother?"

Ellie nodded. "I wish she were here."

Mardee wrapped her arm around Ellie and pulled her close. "I know you do, El. I wish I'd known her. She sounds like such a strong and kind woman."

"Oh, boy, was she," Ellie said. "Better on both counts than I am, particularly the tough part."

"Oh, I don't know. I think you've been real tough lately, giving Brick the boot."

Ellie laid her head on Mardee's shoulder as they stared at the silent screen. Walter Cronkite was talking again, but neither of them wanted to hear what he had to say.

"I keep telling myself this was the right thing for me to do, Mar, but I miss him so much. I'm either crying or trying hard not to. If I'd been stronger, maybe I could have seen another way through this. I just couldn't take it. I couldn't take knowing he'd been with another woman."

"Let's sit down," Mardee said. Ellie slumped down beside her on the sofa.

"El, it was awful what Brick did. I know he broke your heart. But he's a man, and he made a man's mistake. God knows he regrets it. Remember how happy he was the day Reilly was born?"

Ellie nodded. "He was. But he was scared, too, after seeing that nurse's aide in the room. Sometimes I'm glad she told me, but a lot of the time I hate her for ruining my life."

Mardee patted Ellie's thigh. "She's as bad as her sister, if you ask me. You lying in that bed, just hours after delivering that enormous baby, and she's telling you your husband had an affair."

"I tricked her into telling me."

"You can only trick someone who has a secret she wants to tell," Mardee said. "It was a hateful thing she did."

Ellie leaned forward and started rifling through the stack of *Life* magazines on the coffee table. She pulled out the March ninth issue and held it up for Mardee. "Did you see this one?"

Mardee nodded. "Who didn't? Astronaut John Glenn is ours, Ohio born and raised."

Ellie pointed to the photo of his wife sitting next to him in the open convertible. "Annie is, too." She reached back into the stack and pulled out the March second issue, which also had John Glenn on the cover. "Look at this," she said, pointing to the top right-hand corner. She read the headline aloud: "The Glenn Story Nobody Saw. At home with Annie and the kids while John orbited the earth." She turned to the dog-eared page. "This is a whole story about what Annie went through, waiting for him to circle the earth and return to her back on earth. Imagine that."

"I guess I never thought about how hard it was for her," Mardee said. "All that worry. I'd be scared out of my mind."

"She was so strong," Ellie said. "Look at her here." She pointed to a black-and-white photo of Annie Glenn sitting at a desk with a stopwatch and her finger on a map. "She tracked his entire flight. She had to be as brave as her husband—and with her two kids sitting there, and a magazine guy photographing her every move."

She closed the magazine and set it back on the table. "I think about her a lot, especially lately," she said. "Makes me feel a little braver. If Annie Glenn could keep her cool while her husband was way up there in space, I can keep it together with Brick living at his sister's." She took a deep breath and glanced at Mardee. "You probably think I'm crazy."

"Nope. I think you admire Annie Glenn," Mardee said, sliding her hand across Ellie's back. "And I think you miss your husband."

Ellie stood up and walked into the dining room to look at the framed portrait of the president. The Jack-and-Jesus wall. Ellie usually pretended to be annoyed at Brick for calling it that, but secretly she was amused. When did she stop feeling that way? she wondered. When did she become so irritated with her husband?

Even after Sam was born, she got that fluttery feeling in her stomach in the hour before he came home. Brushing her hair, refreshing her lipstick, changing her blouse—when had she stopped doing all that? Long before Reilly was born. She searched her memory for an incident, a moment, when Brick's arrival was no longer the highlight of her day. She couldn't name any one thing he'd done that had flipped the switch. Whatever had changed had happened inside her, in increments. Something had chipped away at the initial freedom she'd felt to have her own life, her own house, a husband to call her own.

Early in their marriage, Ellie used to walk around her house after Brick left for work and name out loud her possessions. "My table." "My couch." "My living room rug." Now they were just stuff she had to clean. Her new beginning had turned into work that never ended, every minute of her life, it seemed, spent taking care of somebody else or some other thing. Where was the freedom in that?

Ellie looked again at the president's face and winced. What was wrong with her? How could she stand in front of this important man, who looked so tanned and intelligent, still so very much alive, and feel sorry for herself?

Ellie traced the outline of his face with her finger. Jackie would never see him again, never hear his laugh, never feel him lying beside her. She dropped her hand and grabbed the back of Brick's chair at the table.

Mardee walked up beside her. "El, honey? You all right?"

Ellie stared at Jesus' soft brown eyes for a moment before answering. "Yes. I will be."

Brick pulled into the parking lot at Sardelli's and turned off the ignition. The lot was as empty as the roads. Everybody he knew just wanted to be home right now. Home with their families.

Brick had stopped at Sardelli's only twice before, preferring Flannery's, where he wasn't the only mick in the joint. But he had stopped going there after he broke it off with Kitty.

He still hadn't heard from any lawyer, which made him think Ellie might be having second thoughts about the divorce. Maybe she just needed some time. Or maybe she had wanted to scare him. She sure as hell had. He'd learned something about his wife the day that deputy came to the door. Ellie had her limits.

He leaned his head back and closed his eyes. John F. Kennedy was dead. Some fucker had shot him. Carl Malone, the shop steward, had waited until the guys were in the locker room before telling them. Several of the guys had slumped down on the benches, their faces twisting in disbelief as they held their hard hats in their hands and listened. Brick had frozen in place, staring at the floor as Malone told them what he knew. Brick remembered only phrases.

Shot in the head.

A convertible.

Jackie next to him.

Dallas. Fucking Dallas.

They had been stone silent after that, the locker room echoing only with the sounds of running water and slamming lockers. After his shower, Brick reached for his Brylcreem and walked over to the mirror. Christ, he looked ancient. He raked the comb through his wet hair and decided to skip the Brylcreem. Fuck it. What did it matter how he looked? Jack Kennedy was dead.

Did Ellie know yet? God, she loved the Kennedys—as much as he did. Loved everything about them. The way they all played touch football, how they stuck together as a family. She worshipped Jackie. She wore little white gloves to church, and got her thick, curly hair teased into a bouffant to look like Jackie's.

How many times had he heard Ellie tell Sam, "You and Caroline Kennedy are the same age. Born the same year, less than four months apart." Sam always grinned, as if her mommy and the First Lady had planned it that way.

Sam.

He lowered his head against the steering wheel, his chest

heaving. What's it like to be a six-year-old kid hearing that somebody shot your president?

Brick noticed some movement on the restaurant's roof. A man was standing in the center of the flat roof, pulling on a cord to lower the American flag to half-mast. After he'd finished and refastened the cord, he pulled off his ball cap and placed it over his heart for a moment.

Brick looked at his watch. Almost five. He'd been sitting in his car for nearly an hour. The man on the roof was gone, and the sun had set.

Brick started the car. It was time to go home.

PART III

CHAPTER

27

1957

Rosie Russo walked out of the school and stopped at the sight of them. Jesus, there they were. Next year's whole goddamn homecoming court for William Jennings Bryant High School. What were they doing walking her way home? None of them lived anywhere near her.

She walked slowly, keeping her eyes on the gaggle of girls as they rounded the corner of Briar Road, their chorus of voices undulating between low hums of gossip and bursts of laughter. Rosie rattled off their names in her head: Laurie Kornemann, Mary Dawn Slack, Gail Kruckberg, Beverly Sewell, and Laurene Edmond. Every last one of them with a mother who volunteered at the school. Two of them, Laurene and Mary Dawn, had dads who helped coach, football and basketball respectively. On assembly days, they showed up at school in suits and ties.

These were the special girls, with their fair skin and light hair that flickered in wisps around their faces. So pretty and perfect. So not like Rosie. She reached up and unleashed her thick black hair from its ponytail, ruffling it with both hands to shake off where her mind was going with that. "Bitches," she whispered.

She kept walking behind them, certain of her invisibility. If Rosie were hit by a car right this minute and lay dying in the street, not one of them would be able to say her name to console her in the last moments of her life. Not that they would try.

Not hard to imagine that tombstone:

HERE LIES ROSEMARY RUSSO
UNKNOWN BY MOST
IGNORED BY ALL

They were born lucky and never alone, the kinds of girls who held court in the middle of any room as their fans gathered around them. Only Mary Dawn had ever spoken to Rosie on purpose, and that was the second worst day of Rosemary's life, rivaled only by the day her father left.

Rosie had been in Home Ec with all of them, seated alone at the foot of the long oak table. Mrs. Shepherd stood at the head of the table as she delivered her annual tutorial on "foods of the world." This was Italy Day, and when Mrs. Shepherd said something about the "pungent power of Mediterranean spices," Mary Dawn leaned toward Rosie and wrinkled her nose.

"Your people like garlic, right?" she said.

Rosie couldn't believe she was talking to her. "Yeah," she said, sliding her elbows off the table and sitting up straighter. "For sauce, mostly."

"Uh-huh," Mary Dawn said, her voice growing louder. "My mother refuses to cook with it. Says garlic has a way of staying with you. Seeps out of your pores." She flashed an exaggerated frown of sympathy as the girls started exchanging glances. "It must be so embarrassing to smell like your mother's kitchen all the time." All of them started flapping their hands in front of their noses, pretending to wave away the stink.

Rosie stared straight ahead. *I will not cry. I will not cry.*

"Okay, girls," Mrs. Shepherd finally said. "Quiet down."

No defense of Rosie. No detention for them.

Why couldn't her mother cook ring around the chicken or Boston baked beans like the other mothers? Why didn't she ever use Crisco, like they did in class, instead of smelly olive oil? At the sound of the bell, she dashed out of the room.

Now, she squinted her eyes at the girls as they rounded the corner onto Matthew Avenue. She was not going to walk another inch behind those witches. She crossed the street and headed south on Route 41, which would add at least a half hour to her walk. She was fine with that. Nothing but trouble was waiting for her at home.

On her walk to school that day, she'd had one encounter too many with Alan Fletcher. Her fist had landed squarely in his right eye, but her joy was short-lived. His squeals had summoned Greta Marino to her kitchen window, robbing Rosie of her victory.

Mrs. Marino was widowed and loved to commiserate with Rosie's mother in their mutual loneliness. "So young to be without our men, Lucia. So unfair."

Mrs. Marino also enjoyed raising the stakes of Lucia Russo's suffering. "And poor you, Lucia. Your husband runs off and sticks you with raising that handful of a girl all by yourself. I'm sorry you don't have a son like my Salvatore to take care of you. You have it so much harder than I do."

Rosie always looked at her mother and rolled her eyes. If Sal Marino was the best his mother could count on to take care of her, she'd better plan to work the rest of her life and learn karate. Laziest boy in the school, and scrawny as a street dog.

"I could take him," Rosie had once bragged to her mother. "I could wrestle Sal to the ground and use him for a lawn chair."

She had expected her mother to laugh in solidarity, but nope. "How are you ever going to get a husband, talking like that? A boy wants someone who's soft, Rosie. Who makes him feel like a man."

Her mother was a pile of contradictions. For months, Rosie had been begging her mother to let her bleach the fuzz on her upper lip, and to lighten her hair. "To make me look prettier, Mama. Like the other girls."

Every time, her mother refused. "Those girls will be invisible by the time they're thirty, they're so pale," she'd said last weekend. "You're exotic, Rosie. Men like that. You're like Sophia Loren."

Rosie shook her head and sighed. "Nobody knows who she is, Mama."

"*Scandal in Sorrento*?" Lucia said, shimmying from the kitchen to the sink. "*Lucky to Be a Woman*? You watch, Rosie. Everyone is going to know who Sophia Loren is."

Rosie imitated her mother's dance as she made her way to her across the room. "Okay, Mama," she said, wrapping her arms around her waist. "If you say so."

Her mother was going to be furious with Rosie for punching Alan Fletcher, and Rosie had no doubt she already knew about it. Mrs. Marino would have taken care of that.

Telling her mother the truth wouldn't help. If Rosie explained that Alan had gawked at her breasts and said, "Nice titties, Rosie," her mother would blame her for her neckline. If she told her mother that Alan had poked a finger into her bra, she'd blame Rosie for that, too. "Why'd you get close enough to give him the chance, Rosie?"

What she would never tell her mother, what she could

barely admit to herself, was how much she had liked that kind of attention. She wasn't offended by Alan's finger slowly circling her nipple. How could a girl object to that bolt of lightning? It was Alan's lack of permission, and that stupid-ass grin of his as he made her weak in the knees. That's why she'd slugged Alan Fletcher.

She slowed her walk along the busy road, clouds of dust billowing around her sneakers in the dry dirt. It was only the middle of May, but it was already so hot and humid that the people in Blackford County had settled into their August moods. Smacking their children in public. Barking at cashiers for prices that weren't their fault. Yells piercing the air from second-floor windows opened wide to windless nights.

Rosie shaded her eyes as she walked. Not a cloud in the sky. Even the weather wasn't on her side. She wished for a button she could press, a lever to pull, to force the sky to match her mood. She was tired of feeling mocked by sunny days.

Two more weeks until school let out, and then another endless season of helping her mother do other people's laundry, from early morning until dinnertime. "You don't need to get a job at the Burger Chef," her mother said when Rosie came home with the application. "How you gonna get there, Rosie? How you gonna get home? How you gonna buy the uniform? We take in twice the laundry in the summer months because you're here to help. It's our time to *make* money, not spend it."

Lucia Russo always had her list of reasons for how life could never work out. They were the wrong kind of people for dreams. "You're born, you work, you die," her mother was fond of saying as she made the sign of the cross. "We offer up our suffering to God, and one day he welcomes us home."

Rosie couldn't work up any enthusiasm for a God that expected people to thank him every day for a lifetime of misery just so they could earn a place in his house once the living was done. As her father had long ago proved, you could find that kind of man right here on earth.

She walked around the corner and stopped under the shade of the willow tree. It was tall and ancient, and took up most of the Parkers' front yard.

What if?

She looked around to make sure no one had just heard her big idea busting loose.

What if this was the time to leave? To go far away and move in with Aunt Lizzie?

She looked around again. The branches fluttered and waved, as if egging her on.

Rosie sat down on the edge of the lawn and pulled her knees to her chest, wrapping her arms around them. There was nothing but bad memories for her here in Foxglove. Her mother loved her, but Aunt Lizzie believed Rosie deserved a better life.

Aunt Lizzie was her father's younger sister. She grew up in Foxglove, but as soon as she graduated from high school she moved to the northeast corner of the state, to Erietown. "Named for one of the Great Lakes, Rosie," Aunt Lizzie had told her on her last visit. "An entire town right on Lake Erie. Cool breezes in the evening no matter how hot the day."

Her real name was Isabella, but she'd changed it to Lizzie as soon as she left town. "Isabella's too formal," she'd told Rosie. "A girl needs to sound friendly." She wore shorts with sailboats and anchors on them, and bandannas and straw hats to protect her hair, which she streaked with blond highlights every summer to show off her tan. From June through August, Aunt Lizzie smelled like Coppertone lotion. Rosie loved to imagine her aunt hopping into her Ford Thunderbird and scattering seagulls as she hit the gas for her four-hour drive south to Foxglove.

Not that she visited anymore. Aunt Lizzie hated Rosie's mother. "She doesn't just push my buttons," Aunt Lizzie once told Rosie, "she *installed* them."

Lizzie blamed Lucia for her brother's sudden exit four years ago. "He's so afraid of you he won't even let any of us know where he went," Lizzie screamed at Lucia in their kitchen.

"Coward, your brother," Lucia said, pretending to spit on the linoleum. "What kind of man leaves his wife and his child, leaves us with nothing? *Nothing.* He's in hiding because he doesn't want to help support his own daughter. He's with that horrible woman. I know it and you know it, and now my poor Rosie knows it, too."

Rosie sat at the table, her eyes wide with the discovery of just how much had already gone wrong in her life. The two women froze, staring at her.

"I'm outta here," Lizzie finally said, pointing at Lucia. "You're a sick woman. You poison everything—poison every*one*—you touch." She gestured toward Rosie. "Poor Rosie. What's to become of her?"

Rosie ran after Aunt Lizzie as she walked toward her car. Aunt Lizzie left her with a promise. "You know where I live, honey," her aunt said as Rosie leaned into the open window. "When you decide you want to be something more than the lonely Italian girl in Foxglove, you catch a Greyhound and come up north. Come live with me in Erietown. I'll give you a chance for a new life."

"Aunt Lizzie, please don't stay away. Mom doesn't mean that."

Aunt Lizzie scribbled something on a small piece of paper, folded it into a square, and pressed it into Rosie's palm. "You tuck this away someplace private," she said. "Someplace where you can always find it."

Rosie stuck it in the pocket of her jeans shorts and stepped back, covering her face with her hands as her aunt revved the engine and peeled away in a cloud of dust. It was the last time she would ever see Lizzie Russo in Foxglove, Ohio.

Rosie didn't read her aunt's note until bedtime, and then immediately folded it into a tinier square. She crawled into the back of her bedroom closet and wedged it between the floorboards in the corner.

That had been three years ago. She hadn't looked at it since, out of loyalty to her mother, but she never forgot it was there. Lizzie's home address, and the address for the Greyhound bus station in nearby Marietta. It was the tiniest shred of hope in Rosie's otherwise pointless life.

Now, as Rosie thought about it, her heart started to pound. She tipped her face toward the sky and closed her eyes. Maybe it was time. Maybe it was time for her to go somewhere else, where she could be someone else. The thought of leaving her mother brought tears to her eyes. She loved her, but Lucia Russo would spend the rest of her life as the abandoned wife, waiting for God.

She could leave Rosie behind. She could get on that Greyhound bus and become eye-turning, take-no-bullshit Rosemary, the most popular girl in Erietown.

A breeze kissed her damp neck and stray strands of hair danced across her face, applauding the first big idea she'd ever had.

She heard it. She was sure of it.

Go, Rosie, the wind whispered. *Go while you still can.*

CHAPTER

28

The woman behind the ticket counter pulled off her reading glasses to get a better look at the scared young thing standing in front of her. "You got no one pickin' you up? Child, have you ever *been* to Erietown?"

Rosie couldn't see why she should be answering a Negro woman's questions about anything, but after a long and lonely ride on a Greyhound bus she was oddly comforted to be on the receiving end of this stranger's concern. "No," she said. "I mean, no, ma'am. No one knows I'm here yet. Ma'am."

The woman's face softened. "What is your name?"

"Rosie. I mean, Rosemary. Rosemary Russo."

"Well, Rosemary, the last city bus for the day just left. You can't just be wandering the streets." She looked down again at the slip of paper Rosie had slid across the counter to her. "Do you have a phone number for this address?"

Rosie shook her head again. The woman pulled out a phone book from under the counter. "Okay, what is this person's name?"

A young black man standing behind Rosie shouted over her head. "Some of us here need to get a ticket," he said. "Today."

The woman scowled at him. "And you've got three other windows you can use," she said. "I don't need any mouth from you, Leonard Moore." He held up his hands and started walking over to the line on their right. "Sorry, Mrs. Colbert."

"You don't know sorry till I talk to your mother," she said. "Usin' that tone of voice with me." She looked back at Rosie. "What's her name, honey?"

"Lizzie. Lizzie Russo. But her real name is Isabella." Mrs. Colbert flipped open the phone book and ran her finger down a column of names. "Same last name. She a relation?"

Rosie nodded. "Yes, ma'am. She's my aunt."

"Hmm. I don't see any woman listed here under Russo. Is that her married name?"

"No. I—I—" She set her suitcase on the floor. "I don't know if she's married."

Don't panic, Rosie told herself. She had gotten this far by herself. She wasn't going to give up now.

Nearly twenty-four hours had passed since she'd sneaked out in the middle of the night and walked to the edge of her long driveway where that awful Alan Fletcher was waiting for her in his brother's car. She'd talked him into driving her the thirty miles to the Marietta Greyhound station. He was so shocked at how nice she was being to him that he walked her into the bus terminal and insisted on waiting with her until the bus to Erietown rolled in four hours later, at sunrise.

"Rosie," he said as they sat on the bench. "You sure you know what you're doing?"

"I've never been so sure of anything in my life," she said. "I have to get out of here if I'm ever going to be who I'm supposed to be." She could tell by the look on his face that he had no idea what she was talking about. His confusion made her feel sorry for him, but it also affirmed her decision.

In the six hours since, she'd seen so much of Ohio that she'd never known existed. Miles of flat farmland, and so many colored people in the cities. After the bus stop in Canton, almost half of her fellow passengers were colored. She sat ramrod straight and afraid for her life, refusing to get off the next three bus stops for food or even a bathroom break. Now here she was talking to the first person who bothered to be nice to her, and she was colored, too.

All she had to do was find Aunt Lizzie's house.

Mrs. Colbert waved her hand and frowned. "Helloooo?"

"I'm sorry," Rosie said. "I was just thinking. Maybe she doesn't have a phone. Or maybe she doesn't want anyone to have her number."

The woman closed the phone book and folded her hands on the cover. "Anyone in this town with a phone number is in this book. Don't you have phone books where you're from?"

Rosie tried to remember ever seeing one in her house. She shook her head. "I don't think so. Not in Foxglove."

The woman sighed. "Foxglove? You from the hills?"

"Between them," Rosie said. "But I don't live there anymore."

Mrs. Colbert smiled. "If you're from Foxglove, you must be pretty surprised to see me sitting here behind this counter."

Rosie blushed. "No, ma'am."

"Oh, sweetie," Mrs. Colbert said, chuckling. "Your eyes give you away. Now, listen, this address you've got here is in the harbor."

"No, I know for sure that she lives in Erietown."

"The harbor is part of Erietown. It's on Lake Erie, where the ports are. You're on the south side of town right now. You have to cross the bridge and go down the hill to get to where your aunt lives. There are two neighborhoods there. One's for the Italians, the other's for the Finns."

"We're Italian," Rosie said.

The woman nodded and stared at her for a moment. "How old are you?"

"Twenty-three."

The woman frowned. "What a coincidence. I'm just a year older. You sure we ain't Irish twins?"

Rosie sighed. "Seventeen," she lied again. "But I'll be eighteen in two more months. You aren't going to turn me in, are you?"

The woman shook her head. "I figure if you got yourself on that bus to come all this way to find your aunt, you got your reasons. No business of mine." She looked around to make sure no one was eavesdropping before leaning over the counter. "All right, listen," she said, softly. "If you want to wait another hour and"—she glanced at the clock on the wall— "and thirteen minutes, I can drive you part of the way to that address."

For the first time, Rosie smiled. "Oh, thank you Mrs.— Mrs. Colbert?"

"Mmm-hmm," the woman said. "I can take you as far as the end of the bridge, to Sardelli's. I can't be driving alone in that part of town. Your aunt's Italian. If she's still living here, someone at Sardelli's will know her."

Rosie tilted her head. "I don't understand why you are . . ." She hesitated and decided not to ask. "I'm so grateful. Ma'am." Mrs. Colbert pointed to the row of benches closest to the ticket counter. "You sit over there. Don't wander off, and don't let any of those men hanging out by the entrance start talking to you. Anyone starts messing with you, you come right back to this window."

Rosie nodded and picked up her suitcase. "Yes, Mrs. Colbert. Thank you so much." Mrs. Colbert waved her off and yelled, "Next."

Rosie sat down in a spot that allowed her to keep an eye on her first friend in Erietown. Mrs. Colbert wasn't anything like her mother always said about colored women. She pulled out a small notepad from her purse and started her list.

Things Mom was wrong about:

1. "All colored people (not her word but I'm never going to use that word again) hate white people."
2. "Nice girls don't shave their legs." (I shaved my legs last night and the only thing different about me is my legs.)
3. "Only Catholics will go to Heaven." (I've already met one nice person headed for Heaven and I'm pretty sure she's not Catholic. Mrs. C. at bus station. God, you know who I mean.)

Rosie tucked the notepad back into her purse and thought about the letter to her mother she'd left on her pillow.

Dear Mama,

I'm sorry, but I had to go. Remember when Father Mark said at Easter mass that we never run out of chances to be somebody else better? Well I decided that I had to leave my old self behind so that I can meet the new Rosie waiting somewhere else. I'm sorry to sneak off but I know you would never have let me go on my own like this. I promise to write to you as soon as I get to Erietown. That's where I'm going to live. When I get a job, I'll start sending you money.

I love you, Mama. This isn't your fault.

xoxoxo
Rosie

P.S. I'm going to be Rosemary from now on, so don't be confused when you see that name in the return address on my envelope.

Maybe her first letter now that she was away from home would be about Mrs. Colbert. To make it clear how she was different now.

. . .

One hour and seventeen minutes later, Rosie was in the passenger seat of Mrs. Colbert's car. "This is a pretty car. What kind is it?"

"Nineteen fifty-five Ford Fairlane," Mrs. Colbert said as she pulled out of the parking lot. "My husband, Fred, works at the Ford plant, so he got the employee discount. Part of their union contract. First new car we've ever owned."

Rosie ran her fingers along a seam of the seat's fabric. "I've never been in a new car. It's so clean."

"Oh, my car is always clean, no matter how old." Mrs. Colbert turned to look at Rosie. "So, now you're Rosemary."

"People back home call me Rosie, but I was thinking I'd start going by my full name."

Mrs. Colbert nodded. "Rosemary. I like the sound of that. More mature. And if you're starting out fresh, why not start out with a name you want everyone to call you?"

Rosie smiled. "That's what I thought, too. I just have to get used to thinking like a Rosemary."

"How is a Rosemary different from a Rosie?"

Rosie looked out her open window. "I guess mostly I don't want to be who I was in Foxglove."

Mrs. Colbert glanced at her. "And who were you in Foxglove?"

"I dunno. *Rosie* has never fit in anywhere. She has to hide entire parts of herself because people will hate her if she's just herself." She shook her head. "I don't know if any of that makes sense."

"More than you know," Mrs. Colbert said. "People take one look at you and think they have you all figured out. Is that what you mean?"

Rosie turned to face her. "Exactly. Like how you look tells them everything about you. About what's going on inside you."

Mrs. Colbert slowed suddenly and leaned across Rosie to yell out the open window. "I'll be there in a little bit. Just got an errand to run." Rosie could tell by the look on the two black women's faces that Mrs. Colbert didn't usually drive through town with a white girl in her car. She started paying more attention to the neighborhood. It was all colored people, sitting on porches, checking mailboxes, yelling at little children riding tricycles or running through sprinklers in the yards.

"What part of Erietown is this?" Rosie said.

"Not your part of town," Mrs. Colbert said, but she was smiling. "This is my neighborhood. The west end."

"You mean I'm not allowed to live here? Because I'm not colored?"

"We prefer 'black,'" Mrs. Colbert said.

Rosemary blushed. "I'm sorry. I didn't know."

"Now you do," Mrs. Colbert said, patting her hand on the seat. "And yeah, you're white—and Italian. It's not that we don't want you here. It just isn't done. Your people and my people, we don't mingle."

"Is that why you can't take me to my aunt's house?"

"It's not a good idea," Mrs. Colbert said. "Let's leave it at that."

They rode in silence as the neighborhood turned into a series of factories and plants before they crossed a bridge and pulled into a parking lot. "Well, here we are," Mrs. Colbert said, pointing to the neon sign. "You go in and ask for Vinny Sardelli. He'll be in the kitchen. You tell him or anyone else working at Sardelli's—they're all related—that your name is Russo, and somebody will help you."

Rosie turned around to reach in the backseat for her suitcase. She noticed Mrs. Colbert anxiously checking her rearview mirror, no longer smiling or making small talk.

"Thank you, Mrs. Colbert, for helping me. I hope we see each other again."

"You're a nice girl, Rosemary. Don't let anyone tell you anything else." She opened the pocketbook sitting next to her on the seat and pulled out a piece of paper and three one-dollar bills. "Now, this is in case of an emergency," she said, handing Rosie the money. "And this"—she waved the piece of paper—"is my phone number at work and at home, and my home address. My house is right off West Avenue, the street where you saw those women waving at me. We're all church ladies, and Jesus doesn't see color."

Rosie slipped the paper into her shirt pocket. "It doesn't feel right taking any money from you, Mrs. Colbert. You don't even know me."

Mrs. Colbert chuckled. "I know you now. I hope you'll remember that the first person you met in Erietown was a black lady who wanted to make sure you were safe."

"I'll never forget that. I promise." Mrs. Colbert looked again in her rearview mirror. Rosie turned around to look. Five men were huddled at the entrance of the restaurant, smoking and staring at Mrs. Colbert's car. Rosie stepped out with her suitcase and closed the door. She leaned into the open window and whispered, "You go home now, Mrs. Colbert. I'll be fine."

Mrs. Colbert stared straight ahead and nodded. She lifted her chin just a tiny bit higher, Rosie noted, and took her good old time turning the car around before she pulled onto the road and headed home.

CHAPTER

29

1962

"Rosemary! Rosemary, goddammit, your aunt is here."
Rosemary Russo scowled at Vinny Sardelli as she pulled off the hair net and untied her apron. "Jesus, Vinny, is that any way to talk about my aunt? She's not deaf, you know."

"I'm sorry, your highness. I keep forgetting we now have royalty working here at Sardelli's."

She fluffed her long blond hair with her fingers as she walked over to Vinny's brother Mike, who was cooking at the grill. "You okay without me for a few minutes?" He nodded. "Sure, honey. Go see her."

She pushed through the swinging doors that separated the sweltering kitchen from the air-conditioned dining room. "Out of my way," she said, pressing her palms against Vinny's chest. He stepped aside with a bow and ushered her through with a sweep of his arm. "By all means, your majesty. Don't let work get in the way of your family reunion."

Rosemary glanced at her wristwatch. Not even noon, and Aunt Lizzie sitting in the corner, already sipping a gin and tonic. She leaned over the side of the bar. "How long has she been here?" Tony DeGrazia tapped the bottle of gin and looked up at the ceiling as he started counting his fingers. "One, two, three." Rosemary's eyes widened. "Three whole minutes," he said, laughing.

"Asshole."

"Don't worry, Sister Rosemary. She just got here. She's fine. Now go over and be a good niece."

Rosemary smiled at her aunt as she walked toward her. "Aunt Lizzie! When did you get outta jail?" Several heads turned to look at the tanned, middle-aged woman burying her face in her hands.

"Honestly, Rosemary, why do you do that?" Lizzie said, grinning. "Embarrassing your aunt like that. Your aunt who took you in—"

"When I was a desperate, tearstained teenager roaming your neighborhood, calling out, 'Aunt Lizzieeeeee. Aunt Lizzieeeeee.'"

They both laughed. "Seriously, Aunt Lizzie. You make me sound like such a loser with that story."

"You were lost, honey, but you have never been a loser."

Rosemary leaned over and kissed her cheek. "Why are you here at lunchtime? And where's Uncle Danny?"

"So many questions," Lizzie said, taking another sip of gin. "He got called to Youngstown early this morning. Another Saturday, can you believe it? Problem with a furnace in one of the mills." She poked her fingertip at the ice cubes in her drink. "I know he's been fixing these things for thirty years, but I still worry about him. Maggie Petrelli's boy Alfie was burned so bad no one would even recognize him now. Won't leave the house. Poor Mags."

"Uncle Danny knows what he's doing," Rosemary said. "It's why they send him. He's a pro. You know that."

"My head knows, but in my heart . . ." Lizzie started fidgeting with the crucifix hanging from her neck. "I get this feeling, this lump, in my heart." She shook her head. "Don't wait as long as I did to marry, honey. You spend your entire marriage wondering why couldn't you have met each other sooner. You're always thinking about how time is running out."

Rosemary watched her aunt as she lifted her glass and took a big swallow. That would explain the drink this early in the day. When she was younger and still lived in Foxglove, Rosemary had had no idea Aunt Lizzie was such a worrier. She seemed so carefree, so confrontational, especially on Lizzie's final visit to Foxglove, when she had peeled out of their driveway after screaming at Rosemary's mother.

Almost five years had passed since the day Rosemary had shown up at the Greyhound bus station and that black lady dropped her off at Sardelli's. Mrs. Colbert, she silently remembered, who had been right about Vinny Sardelli. As soon as Rosemary described Lizzie Russo to him—"tall and probably tanned already, maybe a little loud"—he knew who she was, and where she lived.

"She's Lizzie Martinelli now. Danny's wife. Married three years ago. We catered the reception."

When he found out she'd just arrived from Foxglove on a Greyhound bus, he told her to wait right there and called for his mother in the kitchen. Mrs. Sardelli grabbed Rosemary's hand and led her to a small table in the back. She gave her a Coke and a lecture about showing up in a bar by herself, then brought a heaping plate of ziti and a heel of crusty Italian bread. In the time it took Rosemary to scarf it down Vinny had called Aunt Lizzie and arranged for his brother Carlo, who also worked at the restaurant, to take Rosemary over to the house. On the drive there, Carlo asked her if she needed a job. Three days later, she was busing tables at Sardelli's.

Rosemary reached across the table for her aunt's hand. "Aunt Lizzie, how late is Uncle Danny going to be?"

"Late late. Every minute of it overtime. At least there's that."

"Okay. Then why don't you go do a little shopping, and come back and get me at six? We could go to a movie maybe.

We could go see *A Raisin in the Sun*. Everybody's talking about that one."

Her aunt shook her head. "Nah. I'm not watching a movie about a bunch of black people."

Rosemary sighed. "But Sidney Poitier is in it. He's dreamy. And it's based on a poem by Langston Hughes, who lived for a while in Cleveland."

"How would you know that?"

"I read the play. Got it at the library."

"Well, fancy you." Lizzie shook her head again. "Yeah, okay. Still not going. Everybody wants us to feel responsible now. Like it's my problem what's happening to blacks."

Rosemary took a deep breath. She owed everything to her aunt. She wasn't going to sit here arguing with her about a damn movie.

"*The Apartment* is finally playing at a theater downtown."

"Oh, I love Shirley MacLaine," her aunt said, waving to the waitress and mouthing "check." "She reminds me of you a little, with those long legs of hers and that sassy smile."

Rosemary smiled. "Only you think that, Aunt Lizzie. *The Apartment* it is. Come by at six and we'll eat some chicken parm, then head over to the Shea."

Lizzie pulled out her wallet. Rosemary grabbed it and shoved it back into her purse. "I've got this, Aunt Lizzie. You know your money's no good as long as I'm working here."

"Thanks, sweetie," Lizzie said, snapping her purse shut. "How you like working in the kitchen?"

"Fewer assholes, more calories." They both laughed. "I liked the tips when I was waiting tables," Rosemary said, "but I make better wages working in the back. And Mrs. Sardelli and Mikey are teaching me how to cook. I like that. I like making people happy with my food."

"Still, with your good looks and personality, it's a shame they don't have you on the floor anymore."

"I wanted this, Aunt Lizzie. Soon I'll learn how to tend bar. Vinny's already agreed. That's where the biggest money is."

"Biggest assholes, too," Lizzie said. "Wait'll you see what happens when they're drinking with no food in their stomachs and no wife giving them the stink eye across the table."

Rosemary laughed. "That's why I wanted to learn the kitchen really well first. I told Vinny I'd make up a few dishes for the late-night crowd and talk them into eating at the bar. Vinny gets the bigger bar tab, I get the bigger tip."

Lizzie slid back her chair and stood up. "You got it all figured out, kid. But working nights? You really want to give up your whole social life?"

Rosemary stood up and hugged her. "Oh, right. Because I'm dating so much these days."

"Two different boys want to marry you. Nice boys. Both of 'em with good jobs, one at the mill, one at the docks. But they aren't good enough for you. You waiting for a doctor? A lawyer, maybe."

Rosemary grabbed her aunt's hand and led her toward the exit. "I'm waiting for love, Aunt Lizzie." She stopped at the door and turned around to face her aunt. "I'm waiting to feel it here," she said, pointing to her chest, "when you know you just can't live without him."

Lizzie hugged her again. "Oh, honey. If you're looking for that kind of love, maybe you shouldn't have gotten off the bus in Erietown."

CHAPTER

30

NOVEMBER 22,
1963

Rosemary walked into the bathroom and started pulling out the large pink rollers from her hair. She was still exhausted from last night. Two of the girls had called in with the flu, and on the same night Paul Anka was singing in Cleveland. "Sure, the flu," she said, yanking out the last roller. "I'm *that* stupid." She was stuck waiting tables and tending bar.

She dragged herself to the kitchen, made a tuna sandwich, and ate half of it. She looked at her watch and decided to take a quick bath before going downstairs.

The phone rang three separate times while she was soaking. She had no idea who it was, and she didn't care. She'd had it with pretty much every guy she knew. She hadn't worked her way up to being Sardelli's best paid bartender to end up with a loser who thought popcorn and sex at a drive-in movie were the height of adventure.

Aunt Lizzie had warned her. If she was looking for excitement, she had picked the wrong town. "Same clowns, just more of them, Rosie," she said. Her aunt was the only person in Erietown who called her Rosie. Everyone else knew her as tall, blond, take-no-prisoners Rosemary Russo. She enjoyed trading insults with the regulars, and felt a sense of victory every time she made a row of men at the bar howl with laughter. So many of them had trusted her over time with their secrets, their worries and disappointments. Made her feel important.

"You can't tend bar for the rest of your life, honey," Aunt Lizzie had said last week. "At some point, don't you want to settle down? Get married? Have a few babies?"

Rosemary understood the origins of her aunt's lobbying. Lizzie had married too late to have children, and she longed for a baby in her life. A part of Rosemary—a big part of her, really—wanted to give her one.

"Aunt Lizzie, I have to meet the right guy first."

"I see men fawn over you all the time. Look how many of them come to the bar just to see you."

"And two-thirds of them are married."

Her aunt nodded. "You're a good girl for telling them to hit the road. You don't want that mess. If they'll cheat on their wives, they'll cheat on you. That's in the Bible."

Rosemary smiled. "Sure it is."

She stepped out of the tub and toweled off. She wiped the steam off the mirror and frowned. Her roots were starting to show again. She tied on her chenille robe and walked into the kitchen to add Miss Clairol to the grocery list stuck to the refrigerator door.

The phone on the kitchen table started to wail again. She sighed and answered on the third ring. "Rosie, oh my God. I've been trying to call you for hours. Isn't this just awful?" Her aunt started to cry.

"What's the matter, Aunt Lizzie? Did something happen to Uncle Danny?"

"Jesus, Mary, and Joseph. You don't know?"

As Aunt Lizzie started to talk, Rosie slowly lowered herself into the chair. Who shoots a president? She looked out the window as her aunt continued to talk. She liked her bird's-eye view from upstairs. You could tell what kind of night it was going to be by the mood in the parking lot. If a bunch of guys showed up at once, after a shift at the plant or one of their games, they'd tip better than average because most men don't want to look cheap in front of their buddies. If a couple was arguing when they got out of the car, you could pretty much ignore them except to refill their drinks because they were in no mood to be nice to anybody. Her tips depended on her knowing who wanted to play and who wanted to be left alone.

CHAPTER

31

APRIL 1964

Ellie wiped down the kitchen counter and tossed the rag into the dishwater. "I'm sorry I haven't been any fun lately," she told her best friend, Mardee. "It's just so hard. Listening to everyone talk about their happy marriages right now."

Mardee handed her the stack of dessert plates. "Oh, please. That story of Irene's?"

Ellie laughed softly. "That was too much. Bragging about how her Carl, a two-hundred-and-eight-pound pipe fitter, picked up Kotex for her at the Revco." She cocked her head and spoke in a high-pitched voice: "'He stood right there in line and paid for it.' Good Lord."

"Imagine putting your husband through that," Mardee said. "And then bragging about it."

Ellie was relieved to laugh, but the respite was short-lived. After Mardee had finished helping her clean up and left, Ellie was back to thinking about how much everything had changed since Brick's affair last year. She used to feel so sorry for women like her. Only a few months ago she'd been telling Brick how shocked she was that Dee Bradley had taken her husband back.

One night in February, Dee had answered the phone after midnight and had to listen to a woman describe the star-shaped mole on her husband's ass. Duane wasn't home at the time, and as Dee told Ellie the next day, she didn't need to be an engineer to do *that* math. Dee slammed down the phone and woke up all four kids, herding them into the station wagon and driving them to her mother-in-law's house.

"Didn't even call ahead," Ellie told Brick. "Handed the baby to her mother-in-law and told her, 'I'm going to the Wigwam motel to retrieve that lyin', cheatin' son of yours.'"

As the *Erietown Times* later reported, Dee banged on the motel door until Duane finally answered it wearing nothing but a pillow over his business. The night manager called the police after Dee screamed that she had a gun in her purse. She didn't, of course, but the story didn't mention that until the seventh paragraph.

"And now," Ellie had told Brick, "after all that, Dee is taking Duane back." Brick had been so quiet as Ellie went on about how she couldn't imagine doing such a thing.

No one in the coffee club talked about Brick in front of her these days, except for Mardee, who was the only friend she trusted now. All the girls knew what had happened, of course, because all of Erietown knew. For the first time in her life, she could see the appeal of living somewhere like New York City, surrounded by strangers.

She had forgiven Brick, but she couldn't forget. That's what she prayed for now. To wipe away all those awful memories, including her own bad behavior.

When she had told Brick that both Kitty and her sister Lavelle, the nurse's aide, had agreed to testify against him, she was lying. She didn't want to know what Kitty even looked like, let alone talk to her. The look of shock on Brick's face told her all she needed to know about his guilt.

"Pack up your clothes and get out of here," she had told him.

He had stopped crying and got angry. "This is what you

want to do, is it?" he said, stepping toward her. She walked backward until she was standing by the window, her hands pressed against the cold glass.

"You haven't thought this through, Ellie. You don't even know how to pay a bill. And suddenly you're going to be divorced? No man is going to want you."

Ellie narrowed her eyes and felt a sudden sense of calm. "Oh, I know you," she said, raising her left hand. "I wear the ring of your mother, who wanted to die because it was the only way to be free of a man like you."

He took another step, and she could feel his breath on her face. "Go ahead," she said, covering her face with her hands. She closed her eyes, bracing for the blow.

"Jesus, Ellie."

She heard the bedsprings squeak and opened her eyes. Brick sat slumped on the bed, his hands at his side.

"I'll never be like him," he said. "I promised you. I promised you that."

She dropped her hands. "You promised a lot of things, Brick." She walked down the hall to Sam's room and sat on the edge of her bed until Brick left. At the sound of his car engine, Ellie started to cry.

For a few days, Ellie thought she could go through with the divorce. How could she not? Even if she could find a way to forgive him, how would she ever stop imagining him with that other woman? His big hands touching the private places of someone else. His red hair threaded with another woman's fingers, as they lay there, sweaty and skin to skin.

Then she started noticing changes in Sam. The way she hovered over Ellie, offering to bring her food, to run a bath for her. How she kept checking on her, gauging her mother's mood.

Ellie looked into her six-year-old daughter's eyes and recognized the same fear of abandonment that had choked off her
own childhood.

It had been a mistake to leave Sam alone, waiting for Brick
that day. It had never occurred to her that Sam would answer
the door to the deputy. That Brick would fall apart right in
front of their daughter.

Twice, Sam's teacher had sent a note home expressing concern. In the first one, Mrs. Babcock asked if there was anything that might have changed in Sam's day-to-day life. Ellie
had responded with a terse note assuring her that Sam was fine
and just adjusting to sharing her mother with the new baby.

The second note, mailed rather than delivered by Sam, was
more direct.

Dear Mrs. McGinty,

*I understand that Mr. McGinty is currently not living at your
house. This has upset Sam a great deal, and understandably
so. She worries that her father may go away for good, and that
she will never see him again. Perhaps you and her father could
sit down with her and reassure her. Your little girl is such a
sensitive child, and she is very sad. We should do all that we
can for this child in this difficult time.*

Sincerely,
Patricia Babcock

Ellie slammed the letter down on the dining room table and
called for Sam, who was making Reilly giggle in his playpen.

"What do you think you're doing, telling your teacher
about our private business?"

Sam's chin started to quiver. "She asked, Mommy. She
asked me why I was sad."

Ellie pulled Sam onto her lap. "What happens in this family stays in this family. Is that clear?"

Sam nodded, biting her lip to keep from crying. Ellie reached for her daughter's hand. "Sam, honey," she said, her voice softer, "you're only six. The world can be very confusing to a little girl. But I'm a lot older than you."

"You're twenty-three," Sam said.

"That's right," Ellie said. "I'm sorry you've had to learn so early that you can't depend on the men in your life. They'll disappoint you."

"You mean Daddy."

"What I mean, honey, is that men just don't have it in them to be everything they promise to be."

The sad look on Sam's face made Ellie wish, for the first time, that she'd had only sons. God made the world for men. Women were an afterthought, just like Eve. No matter what she did, Ellie would never be able to save her daughter from that heartache waiting to ambush her.

That night, Sam woke up again to her mother's sobs and crawled into bed with her, as usual. Feeling her daughter's warmth against her back, her little arm draped across her shoulder, stirred such guilt in Ellie. She had to fix this. She wiped her face with the edge of the sheet and turned to face Sam, stroking her cheek until Sam closed her eyes. Maybe she wasn't cut out for this new life of hers.

Who was she if she wasn't Brick McGinty's wife? She had no idea, and with an alarming clarity, she realized that she had no interest in finding out. Her train case, the gift from Aunt Nessa, was on the top shelf of her closet, wrapped in tissue and packed away with the high school dreams of Ellie Fetters. She was Ellie McGinty now, the mother of two children who needed her—and their father.

The next day Walter Cronkite interrupted regular programming and Ellie's life. When she heard the car door slam in the driveway that evening, she ran to the back door and into Brick's arms, breathing in the scent of her husband.

That had been months ago. She had not kept her promise to God, to make the most of this second chance. She had to start by making things right with Sam.

That evening, Ellie stayed in Sam's room long enough to pull the covers taut and wedge them under her armpits. Sam beamed, lifting her arms as Ellie tucked, and then lowering them to clasp her hands over her chest for her bedtime prayer.

"Dear God, now I lay me down to sleep . . ."

"Sam, honey."

Sam opened her eyes. Ellie smoothed her daughter's bangs from her forehead. "Remember when I said men will always disappoint us?"

Sam nodded.

"Well, I forgot to tell you something else about that." Ellie turned to look at the empty doorway before continuing. "I forgot to tell you that a woman's greatest power is forgiveness. If we can find it in our hearts to forgive the men, the people, who hurt us, it will all be okay."

Ellie stepped out of her housecoat as she walked into her bedroom. She opened the bottom drawer of the dresser and pulled out the filmy black negligee Brick had given her three Christmases ago. She stood in front of the mirror and held it up against her naked body. Her face looked shy, and hopeful.

Someday, Ellie vowed, she'd tell her daughter about this power, too.

PART IV

CHAPTER

32

NOVEMBER 1965

Brick walked into the house and heard the sound of his daughter's voice as the dining room filled with light.

"Thank you, Daddy."

He shot a curious look at Ellie, who was stirring a pot of beef stew at the stove. "What exactly did I do?"

Ellie raised her cheek for his kiss and nodded toward their daughter, who was standing by the light switch, holding Reilly's hand. Brick set his lunch pail on the counter and walked into the dining room, simultaneously cupping their heads and mussing their hair. "What are you thanking me for, Sammy?"

She turned around and grabbed his hand. "For the light."

"Come again?"

"Mommy says every time we turn on a light we should thank you. 'Cause you're making it for us. You're making the electricity."

"And just how do you think I make electricity?"

Sam shook her head with impatience. "You already know. You throw a big bolt of lightning high into the sky"—she raised her arm and sliced the air—"and it flies straight to our house." She pointed to the switch plate on the wall. "This plastic keeps us from getting electrocuted."

"Like this!" Reilly said, making shooting sounds as he thrust his arm into the air. "With a big boom."

Brick laughed and picked up Reilly. "It's a little more complicated than that, Sammy. But I'm glad that you think your daddy can harness lightning."

"You mean that's not how you do it?"

Brick looked over his shoulder at Ellie. "El, you have a pen?"

"On the telephone stand," she said, leaning away from the stove just far enough to see them.

He grabbed a ballpoint pen imprinted with Reddy Kilowatt, the Erietown Electric mascot. The jagged caricature was supposed to resemble a current of electricity, but Brick could see how Sam saw it as lightning. He walked to the dining room table and sat down, propping Reilly on his knee as he pulled a paper napkin out of the plastic holder. He clicked the pen and looked at Sam. "Do you want to learn how Daddy really makes electricity?"

Sam sidled up next to Brick as he spread the napkin open on the table. "Okay, this is what Daddy does all day to make sure you have electricity."

"And a paycheck."

"That's right. A paycheck."

"Every other Thursday."

"Yep."

Sam propped her elbows on the table. "We celebrate with Jones' chips and Lawson's French onion dip on Fridays."

He laughed. "Okay, let's talk about electricity." He drew a square in the left-hand corner. "You know what coal is, right?"

"It's black, and dirty," Sam said. "It's what Great-Aunt Nessa used to put in her furnace with a shovel."

"That's right, Sammy. Coal is fuel, and we use big machines to unload tons and tons of it every day out of railroad cars that roll right into the plant."

"You have trains at your work?"

"Yep." Brick pried Reilly's hands off the pen and tapped the bottom of the square. "There's a giant furnace there. Big as this house."

"Wow."

"Wow," Reilly echoed.

Brick grinned. "That's where the coal, the fuel, is burned to give us lots of energy."

"You mean like the energy we get when we get a good night's sleep?"

"Well, sort of," Brick said, unaware that Ellie was now standing in the doorway with her arms folded, watching. "Except we're talking about an energy out there that's much stronger than all of us."

"Like God."

"Okay, yeah," Brick said, smiling at Sam. "Like God. Think of it as God's energy."

"That's big," Sam said.

"Weally, weally big," Reilly said, spreading his arms wide.

"That's right, buddy." Brick drew an arrow from the bottom of the box to the top. "Now, see these?" he said, tapping the pen on the napkin. "These are pipes above the furnace, and they are full of cold water. The heat boils that water." He looked at Sam. "What happens when Mommy boils a pot of water on the stove?"

"Clouds!"

"Right. We call those clouds 'steam.'" He drew a circle and filled it with a series of slashes.

"That looks like a flower, Daddy."

"It's called a turbine. It's full of these blades, and it spins really fast."

"Does the electricity come out of that?"

"Not yet." He drew three long cones that stood close together. "You know those towers at the plant you saw when

Mommy brought you to the park on the lake?" Ellie stood up straighter. Brick had remembered that story.

Sam shot her hand in the air. "We waved at you and yelled, 'Hi, Daddy!' But Mommy said you probably couldn't see us."

Brick leaned down to grab one of Sam's hands, and one of Reilly's hands, too, and pressed their palms against his chest. "I felt you here. In my heart."

Brick tapped his pen again on the napkin. "Well, those are called cooling towers. And there's a generator, too. It's connected to that turbine, to that windmill, by something called an axle. The generator spins around the blades of the windmill, and the energy from that—it's called kinetic energy—makes the electricity."

Sam leaned into him. "Daddy, you are so smart."

"Not smart, Sam. Just used to doing the same job, over and over. For the rest of my life."

"That's forever, Daddy."

"It sure feels that way," he said. "But you and Reilly? You're never gonna carry a lunch pail to work, I promise you that. You two are going to college."

"I don't want to move to college," Sam said. "I want to stay right here, in Erietown."

He kissed her cheek and laughed. "Don't worry. It's a good thing, Sammy. It's where dreams come true."

"All right, you guys," Ellie said. "Dinner's ready."

Brick turned to smile at her, but she was gone.

CHAPTER

33

Rosemary Russo looked out the diner window to the sight of Aunt Lizzie trying to wedge her red Cadillac between two pickups. Bursts of male laughter erupted inside the diner as Lizzie repeatedly lunged forward and then plowed in reverse.

"Hey, Rosemary," Glenn Fisher yelled. "Someone should go out there and tell your aunt those trucks ain't moving, even for her." More laughter.

Lizzie finally gave up and parked the car with a foot and a half of its rear sticking out. She pried herself out and inched her way along the narrow path between her car and the pickup on her driver's side, tossing her half-smoked cigarette into the truck's flatbed on the way.

"Goddamn," Frank Mericka said, his nose pressed against the window. "That's my truck."

Lizzie smoothed her skirt with both hands and hobbled on high heels across the gravel lot.

Rosemary stood up and waved to her. "Over here, Aunt Lizzie."

"Woman, you are a danger to the civilized world," Frank said to Lizzie.

She flipped him the finger, and the men laughed again as

she plopped down in the seat opposite Rosemary. "I swear Louie keeps making those parking spaces smaller and smaller. He's got that whole back lot full of weeds, but he's too god-damn cheap to pave it."

"And good morning to you, too, dear auntie." Rosemary grabbed one of Lizzie's hands and kissed the back of it. "Maybe you should think about getting a smaller car. Uncle Danny says he's had to repair your front bumper twice already. Says you don't 'comprehend the length of your front end.'"

"That's a boob joke, sweetie." She turned toward the counter and waved. "Hey, Louie, you got anyone serving coffee in this joint?"

The burly man standing behind the counter grabbed the pot off the burner. "Aw, Lizzie Martinelli is in the building." He looked up at the ceiling. "Why, God? What did I do now?" He walked over and turned her coffee cup upright in its saucer. "For you, your highness. Marjorie's having a smoke. She'll be back in a minute."

"Those things'll kill your wife, Louie," Lizzie said. She pointed to Rosemary's plate. "I'll have that. Eggs over easy and some toast."

She reached for the front section of Rosemary's *Erietown Times*. "Anything happening in this town?"

"Dear Abby says you should always give up your bed for your mother-in-law when she comes for a visit."

"And leave your husband in it, or does mama's boy get to sleep with his poor wife?" Lizzie jabbed her finger at the newspaper. "See? Right there. That's why her and her sister don't get along. When you got a sister getting paid to give so much dumb-ass advice, it's embarrassing. You know what I mean, with that crazy mother of yours."

Rosemary lifted the sports section to hide her face. Lizzie reached across the table and pulled down the corner far enough to see her niece's eyes. "I'm sorry, sweetie. That wasn't nice of me. I shouldn't say bad things about your mother. She loved you a lot. She just never got over your father leaving her. If I'd known then—if *any* of us had known—that she had that cancer growing in her, things would have been different."

Rosemary nodded. "I think about her a lot. How she cried when I first called her from Erietown. How she said she always knew I'd leave."

"She knew you had to, honey."

Rosemary wiped her eyes with her napkin. "Aunt Lizzie, I can't stand to think about what I'd be like now if I hadn't gotten away. I owe everything to you and Uncle Danny." She smiled. "And that black lady, Mrs. Colbert. The one who drove me to Sardelli's."

"Pretty gutsy of a black woman back then," Lizzie said, picking up the front section and leafing through it. "It'd still be gutsy. The only black people down here in the harbor work in the plants. Danny said they stick to themselves. Do everything together. They walk in and out of the plant together. Sing their own songs. Sounds to me like they don't like us any better than we like them."

Rosemary shrugged. "Maybe they're afraid of us. Look at what's happening to those blacks at the lunch counters down south. In *this* decade. Police hosing down women and children. Just because they want to vote. And those Ku Klux Klan goons. They killed those three northern boys in Mississippi. And bombed that church in Alabama. Killed four little girls. Everybody knows it was the Klan. If I was black, I wouldn't trust white people either, no matter where I lived."

Lizzie shook her head to hush Rosemary as Marjorie set down the plate of eggs and toast. "You girls need anything else?" she said, looking only at Lizzie.

"Not from you, Marjorie."

Rosemary smiled as Marjorie stomped away. "I thought you didn't agree with me. About black people."

Lizzie flipped open a napkin and spread it across her lap. "Those little girls," her aunt said. "I'll never forget Walter Cronkite reading that white guy's column about how it was white people's fault."

"No, that's not what he meant," Rosemary said. "He was talking about white people in the South, and about how they weren't doing anything to stop the Klan. How all of them were holding that little girl's shoe. Flew right off her foot in the explosion."

"Imagine being her mother finding that." Lizzie waved her fork in the air. "Look, maybe they are scared, those black guys at Danny's plant. So they don't mingle. So what?"

Rosemary looked down at the open newspaper and tapped the half-page picture before sliding it toward Lizzie. "I've seen this guy before."

Lizzie looked at the picture of the man in the softball uniform and laughed. "Honey, everybody's seen him before. That's Brick McGinty. Hell, even Danny and I have seen him play ball. In the tournament last fall."

Rosemary pushed away her plate and leaned forward on her elbows. "What's he like?"

"I don't know," Lizzie said. "I didn't meet him. I just watched him play softball. He's got that red hair, and even from a distance you can see he's covered in freckles."

Rosemary picked up the picture of him. "I think he looks handsome. I've seen him in Sardelli's. Looks like he has a soft side to him, too."

Lizzie took a sip of coffee. "Well, all I know is he can really hit a ball, and he's married to a cute little thing with a big beehive. Everyone seems to like her."

Rosemary leaned back against her seat. "How do you know she's his wife?"

"The way everyone went over to tell her what a great ballplayer her husband was, how they hugged her. She's got a great laugh, I recall. After the game"—she tapped her finger on the picture of Brick—"she ran over to him and he picked her up and swirled her around."

Rosemary cradled her coffee cup and looked out the window. "You don't need to be so specific."

"Apparently I do."

Rosemary turned to look at her. "Why do you look so angry, Aunt Lizzie?"

"I'm not angry, honey. I'm smart. Is he at the bar a lot?"

"No."

"Your answer should have been, 'I don't know.' Sounds like you've been on the lookout for this guy. This *married* guy."

Rosemary wadded up her napkin and threw it on her plate. "Well, I'm not. I'm just observant. And to be honest, Aunt Lizzie, I'm not crazy about your tone of voice."

"Good, because I'd hate for there to be any doubt about how I feel about you going after someone else's husband. Nothing but heartache for everyone involved, Rosemary. You remember that."

Rosemary tried to reach for Lizzie's hand, but she pulled it away. "Listen to me, honey. Coming here to Erietown was your one big chance. You've been here eight years now, and you've built quite a life for yourself. You've got your own place, your own car. You're blond and beautiful, and you're in charge of your own life. You don't want to lose the most important thing a woman has, and that's your self-respect."

Rosemary sighed. "Aunt Lizzie, you're overreacting."

"I know that look on your face. I've seen it on every woman who has convinced herself that she's entitled to something she knows she shouldn't have. He's married, Rosie."

"It's Rosemary."

"Not if you act like you never left Foxglove. Show some class, honey."

"You sure are assuming a lot. All I said was he was handsome."

Lizzie leaned toward Rosemary. "I know you, honey. You lose interest in a man as soon as you know he's all yours. You want the guy you can't have. I blame your miserable excuse for a father for that."

Rosemary pushed her hand away. "This has nothing to do with my father. I haven't seen him since I was nine years old."

"I know that. He was the most important man in your life, and he abandoned you. You've been trying to replace him ever since."

"That's sick," Rosemary said. "That makes it sound like I want to marry my father."

Lizzie touched her cheek. "Oh, sweetie, we all do. Why do you think we're all so fucked up?"

The Grandin family lived only three houses down from Sam's house, but they were a world away. They had the first dishwasher in the neighborhood and two TVs. The second one was in the kitchen, and Mrs. Grandin almost always turned it on in the last hour before Mr. Grandin came home. Sam liked watching the vertical groove between Mrs. Grandin's eyebrows slowly disappear as she sat at the table and sipped on her crystal glass of ice and "mommy juice."

The Grandins owned Speedy Dry Cleaners, and even though it was just down the street, Mrs. Grandin liked to drive her convertible there when she dropped off Mr. Grandin's lunch. Sam liked the convertible but agreed with her mother that Mrs. Grandin went overboard when she named the car Miss Daisy Mae. Proof positive, Sam's father said, that Mrs. Grandin was "Miss Daisy-crazy."

Mr. Grandin wore a suit and tie every day. "That's how you know he doesn't work for a living," Sam's dad said. On top of that, he was a boss, which in the McGinty family was as bad as voting for Nixon. Brick said the word "boss" was just code for Republican, but Ellie insisted that wasn't always true.

"Mr. Baylor put a Kennedy sign in his bakery window in nineteen sixty," she said. "For all the world to see."

"And how dumb-ass was that?" Brick said. "Republicans boycotted the bakery for two whole months. Every man in our local had to take a turn driving across town to buy six-dozen donuts from Baylor's every morning until Election Day to keep him in business. You aren't taking a stand if everyone else has to hold you up."

Sam loved the Grandins' driveway. It was paved, instead of the black cinders in the McGinty drive. Perfect for jumping rope and better for hopscotch, too. For this, Sam was willing to put up with the Grandins' only child, Jenny, who never ran out of reasons for why she was sorry Sam's life wasn't as good as hers.

"I'm sorry your television is smaller than ours, Sam."

"I'm sorry your sheets don't match your bedspread, Sam."

"I'm sorry you have that hole in the toe of your sneaker, Sam."

Sam didn't blame Jenny for bragging. If she had a canopy bed and her own bathroom she'd probably have a hard time keeping it to herself, too. Sometimes Sam watched Jenny's lips move as she yakked on and on, and Sam had to picture Jesus to stop thinking about punching Jenny in the mouth. This was new for Sam. Even when her brother, Reilly, popped the head off her Bubble Cut Barbie, it never occurred to her even to pinch him, let alone smack him.

No matter how mad she got at Reilly, when she looked him in the face she saw their mother's eyes looking back at her and their father's red hair standing straight up on the top of his head. Whenever Sam and Reilly sat down side by side on the porch swing, the knobs of their knees were perfectly matched, like four little acorns from the same tree. Reilly was five years younger and all boy, but he was a part of her.

Sam tried to remind herself it wasn't really Jenny's fault that she was spoiled and rich. For that, she blamed Jenny's father. A suit and tie changes a man. Every time Sam saw Mr. Grandin, she thought of Mary Agnes Lane's dad, and what had happened that day a year ago.

Mr. Lane worked at the People's Savings and Loan. He'd seemed nice enough the first and only time he saw Sam standing in their kitchen. He set down his briefcase, leaned toward Sam, and said, "Hi there. And what's your name?" Wanted to know where she lived, what her favorite subject was at school. He asked for her father's name, too, and asked where he worked. As soon as Sam told him about her dad's job at Erie Electric, he stood up and smiled at Sam again, but it felt different. He walked into the dining room, where Mrs. Lane was setting the table. Didn't even whisper. "Let's not make this a habit," he said.

Sam looked over at Mary Agnes's face and watched her invitation for dinner evaporate. "Maybe tonight's not—" Mary Agnes didn't bother to apologize.

Sam's mother had already given her permission to eat dinner at the Lanes'. She'd know something was up if Sam came home early. So Sam walked around for a while to give her face time to stop burning. The longer she walked, the easier it was to forgive Mary Agnes. It wasn't her fault. Their fathers hated different people, but their daughters' shame was the same. Sam prayed every night that her black friends at school would never know what her father said about them, but she still worried that someday he'd say the wrong thing at the precise moment when God was distracted and not available to rescue her.

Sam was determined to keep to herself what had happened at the Lanes' house. A doomed plan in Ellie McGinty's house. Two nervous weeks had passed when Sam was doing home-

work at the dining room table and her mother stopped kneading the meatloaf mix just long enough to say, "Why haven't
you invited Mary Agnes Lane over to reciprocate the invitation?"

"She says she can't, Mom."

"Can't what?"

"Can't come over."

"Why not? She's been here plenty of times."

Sam really didn't want to get into it, as her mother liked to
say whenever it was Sam who had all the questions. But she
could tell by the look on her mother's face that avoidance was
a failed strategy. She laid down her pencil as her mother washed
her hands. "Maybe it has something to do with her dad saying
not to make it a habit."

Her mother wiped her hands on her apron as she walked
toward Sam. "Not make *what* a habit?"

Sam sighed. "Me, I guess."

Ellie sat down next to Sam and folded her hands on the
table. With every answered question, Ellie's knuckles grew
whiter.

"When did he say that?"

Sam lowered her head. "After he asked where Daddy
worked."

"And what did you tell him?"

"I said he worked in maintenance at Erie Electric."

"Oh, Sam. That makes him sound like a janitor. He's a
maintenance *mechanic*. Your father can fix anything in that entire plant. Only a handful of men in this whole county can do
his job."

Sam looked up at her. "Mom, I think what Mr. Lane cares
about is where Daddy works, not what he does there."

"Well," Ellie said, pushing away from the table, "we'll see
about that."

Her parents had a loud and spirited conversation in the

driveway before dinner, and after saying grace Brick told Sam that she was to have nothing more to do with Mary Agnes Lane.

"Act like you can't even see her," Brick said. "Treat her like she's the white trash she is, Sam. We'll see how her asshole of a father likes that."

Sam had a few things she wanted to say to her father. Mary Agnes's father was never at school, so how was he going to notice if Sam ignored his daughter? Also, all of Mary Agnes Lane's clothes came from Brennan's department store. Unlike Sam, whose clothes came from the JCPenney and Hills department stores. Mary Agnes Lane was not white trash.

The immediate problem was Mary Agnes's proximity. She sat right next to Sam in class, all day long. Not only would Sam pretending she couldn't see Mary Agnes be impossible, it would be un-Christian, if her mother's frequent lectures on the topic were true.

The more pressing problem was Brick McGinty's growing list of friends Sam was supposed to avoid. Until Mary Agnes, their only crime had been skin color, and that was no crime at all. Every time Brick slammed his palm on the dinner table and shouted that horrible word about black people, she saw the faces of Valerie Jackson and Philomena Dyer and Gary Colbert. This made her want to cry. They were her best friends, and they were nicer to her than any of the white kids whose fathers wore ties to work. Two of her black friends' fathers wore suits all the time, and even they liked her.

Sam knew from experience that saying any of this to her father would ignite his temper faster than a match to a cat's tail, so after talking it over with God for a few weeks and getting no answer as usual, she decided to ignore her father's orders. Every bad thing he said about black people made no sense to her. So she ignored him.

She had a feeling God approved.

. . .

Four months after Sam was disinvited to dinner at the Lanes' house, Jenny Grandin's name was added to Brick's list of banned friends.

Mr. Grandin had always nodded hello to Brick when both of them were out mowing their lawns, but that was about it for exchanges. Her parents never visited the Grandins, but Sam didn't think much about that because the McGintys seldom invited anyone for dinner.

"Daddy works hard and wants to relax when he's home," her mother said whenever Sam brought it up. That didn't stop Sam from wondering why they never had any relatives over. As far as she knew, Sam had only one living grandparent, and Brick hadn't spoken to his father since before she was born. The only time Sam worked up the nerve to ask her mother, Ellie jumped back like she'd been hit by lightning. "That man put your grandma Angie into an early grave."

Sam was six at the time, and she had no idea if that meant he'd shot her grandmother or buried her alive, but it relieved her of any desire to meet the man.

The only outside people who came into the McGinty house were the neighbor ladies who came for coffee after Brick left for work. The coffee club, her mother called it. They were the same women in her monthly canasta club, and Sam had known them all of her life. Last month it was Ellie's turn to host the card club, but she had to ask Eloise Bender if she could swap months because the strike at the plant "made things tight."

Sam didn't know much about the strike, except that her father and his friends did all the real work and the bosses wanted to cheat them out of the money they had earned. Local 270 had finally had enough of that bullshit—that's how Brick always said it and so Sam said it, too, in her head—and one morning at 11:00, right after the coal train had arrived, they threw down their shovels and tools and walked off the job. Sam looked at the picture of the picketing workers on the front page of the *Erietown Times* and asked her father if that meant their lights would stop working.

"The scabs will keep the lights on, Sam. They always do." Sam had no idea how the stuff of scraped knees had anything to do with making electricity, but she could tell her father was in no mood for the question.

For nearly three months, Brick drove to the plant and took his turn with the men on the picket line, singing labor songs and shouting swear words at anyone walking into the plant. Sometimes on weekends Sam and Reilly went with him. It was the closest Sam had ever gotten to the monster of the building that took her father away from them so many days and nights. She liked the way her father sometimes wrapped his giant hand around hers as they walked and sang the same songs he used to sing to her at bedtime. "Which Side Are You On," "Union Maid," "This Land Is Your Land"—Sam knew them all. She loved how all the men looked up to her dad, just like she did. Whenever someone called him "Brother Brick," she pretended she'd just found another uncle.

Sam's mother mostly worried during the strike. "I don't know how many more ways I can serve Spam for dinner," she told Sam as they lined the baking sheet with pineapple slices. "We'll never make back the money we've lost on this strike."

Brick heard and walked over to Ellie and squeezed her shoulders. "We can't think about it that way, El. This is the only way to get better pay and work conditions. This is about the future."

One Saturday evening, on day twenty-seven of the strike, Sam walked to the Grandins' to play with Jenny. Minutes later, she returned home. Ellie was standing at the counter, hovering over her red-plaid *Better Homes and Gardens* cookbook. She held her finger in place on the page and looked at Sam. "What are you doing back already?"

Sam took a deep breath and decided to just get it over with. "Jenny's dad said he didn't want me over there as long as Dad's strike is going on."

Ellie raised her finger to her lips to shush Sam, but it was too late. Brick was sitting at the dining room table. He looked up from the stack of bills. "What did you say, Sam?"

"Go outside," Ellie said, turning Sam to face the door. "Go find Reilly and play some catch."

"Samantha Joy," Brick said. "Get in here."

Ellie sighed and patted Sam's back. "Do what your father says."

Sam walked into the dining room. "Hi, Daddy."

"What did you say about Bill Grandin?"

"Nothing. Just that I can't play at their house until your strike is over. I don't care. Really, I don't. Jenny brags too much."

Brick tipped his chair back onto its hind legs and webbed his fingers behind his head. "He did, did he? Did he tell you that himself?"

"No, Jenny told me. But I could see her dad standing behind her in the kitchen."

"What a coward," Brick said, slamming the front legs of the chair onto the floor. "Making his daughter do his dirty work." He looked at Ellie, who was standing in the doorway, and then back at Sam. "You know why, don't you?"

Ellie walked up behind Sam and wrapped her arms around her. Sam looped her fingers around her mother's clasped hands and shrugged her shoulders. "I don't know, Daddy. 'Cause he hates workers?"

"It's about money, Sammy. He's got a cleaning contract with the plant. As long as we don't have a contract, he doesn't have one. This is all about lining his own goddamn pockets."

"Brick."

"How could he be that way?" Sam said. "I'm one of Jenny's best friends."

"No, Sam, you're Jenny's backup friend."

"Brick, don't."

"Ellie, she should know how these people think. Sam, you're Jenny's friend because you're always available, any time, any day." His voice grew louder. "You're around when her real friends, her *rich* friends, are on vacation in Florida or in Canada or back in the *Old Country* in It-a-ly. Their real name is Grandinetti. Did your little friend ever tell you that? Her father changed his name so that he could do business on our side of town. Ashamed of his own name. Damn dago."

Sam's heart started to pound. "Daddy, I don't think Jenny knows about her dad cleaning your clothes."

Brick looked at his daughter, his eyes narrowing. "Don't kid yourself, Sam. They probably laugh about it over dinner." He stood up. "Well, you know what? He's not going to clean my clothes ever again. After this strike is over, Ellie, I'm going to bring my work clothes home."

Ellie sighed. "Brick. All that white dust you'll bring home."

"What have you got to do all day anyway? It's not like you have a job. It's all on me to support this family."

Ellie stepped back, and Sam reached for her mother's hand. "Fine," Ellie said, batting Sam's hand away. "Fine, Brick. And when is that going to happen, do you think? When are you going to start supporting this family again?"

Brick stood up, his fists flexing at his sides. "You know we're striking for money. For safer work conditions, too. You know that, El."

He turned to look out the window, plunging his hands into his pockets. "And Sam?" he said, jingling his change. "I don't want you going anywhere near that Grandin girl again. Strike or no strike, she doesn't deserve you."

Sam started blinking back tears. "But, Daddy, she's the only girl who lives near me who isn't already on the list."

"What list? What the hell are you talking about?"

"The list of friends I'm not allowed to talk to anymore. Georgie, Philomena, Mary Agnes . . ."

Brick turned and slammed his fist on the table. "Family, Sam," he said, staring at the table. "Family comes first. In the end, it's all you got."

He looked at Ellie as he tucked his faded cotton shirt tighter into his belt. "I don't ever want our kids to think that money buys class." She nodded. "I know, Brick." She reached for his hand.

Sam's shoulders relaxed. She knew what she had to do.

After dinner, she helped with the dishes and waited until her parents sat down on the porch swing before slipping out the back door. She walked three houses down and knocked on the kitchen door, forcing a smile at the sight of Lenny Kleshinski.

He tapped the bridge of his glasses to push them up on his nose. "Sam," he said, easing open the screen door. "What are you doing here?"

"I'm here to see you, Lenny. I figure it's time we became best friends."

He stepped outside and closed the door. "I thought you and Jenny Grandin were best friends."

Sam shook her head. "We gotta stick with our kind. Your dad and my dad work at the same plant. We go to the same Christmas party, and our mothers belong to the same coffee club." She shrugged. "There's nothing in the Bible that says a boy and a girl can't be best friends."

"I'm Catholic."

"So was President Kennedy." She looked up at the darkening sky and pointed to the moon. "It's getting late. Let's meet here tomorrow, after church. I'll bring my bike."

"Okay," Lenny said, pushing up his glasses again. He opened the door and stepped back into the house.

Sam was halfway down the driveway when she heard him shouting something through the screen door. She turned to look at him. "What did you say?"

"I said you're pretty smart."

"Why?"

"There's no way your dad will say you can't be friends with a union brother's kid, even if I'm a boy."

"Lenny," she said. "That's not why—"

"It's okay, Sam," he interrupted, smiling. "I need a best friend, too."

CHAPTER
35

It took a while for Brick to comprehend what he and Ellie had lost. They could rebuild a marriage, but he would never again see that earlier version of himself in Ellie's eyes. Even after Sam was born, Ellie sometimes looked at him as if she couldn't believe her luck. So random, the way she'd suddenly stop in her tracks to watch him, pressing her palm against her bosom as if she had just stumbled upon a mirage.

"You're my dream come true," she'd whisper in his ear, after rising on tiptoes and holding on to his shoulder. God, how he had loved that.

After she found out about Kitty, Ellie never said that to him again. Every once in a while he would still catch her staring at him. He'd get his hopes up, holding his breath as he waited for her to tilt her head with that shy smile of hers. Every time, she startled and looked away.

What can I do? he wanted to know. *What can I do to win you back?* He was too afraid to ask. "There are some things you can't take back," she'd told him after she found out about Kitty, her face contorted in disbelief. "You were inside her. *Inside* her."

He had promised he would never step foot in Flannery's again, and he kept his word. He started coming home every night after work, too, and for more than a year he refused to join the other guys at Mickey's unless Ellie went with him. Whenever she did, Ellie didn't think twice about leaving Reilly in Sam's care.

"That girl was born old," she said.

Brick wasn't so sure of that. Around Ellie, sure, Sam was a little mother. But when his daughter was alone with him she still seemed like a little girl, eager to hold his hand and peppering him with questions about the smallest things. "How does the radio station know when you've picked them to listen to?" she asked one day when they were driving to Cal's Corner to pick up sandwich meat and beer. The last time they went to Dairy Queen, Sam held up the waffle cone and said, "Look, Daddy, it's like a tiny brick wall all around the bottom. How do they do that?" She was such a curious kid.

One thing Brick wouldn't give up was softball. "I need it, Ellie," he said. "I need it to work off all the bullshit at the plant." She didn't argue. Less than a year after the strike, three guys had been injured at the plant, and she knew all of their wives. One of the men, Herman Pinkard, was almost killed, and by the end of that workday Ellie was waiting for Brick on the porch. "Here," she said, holding out a bottle of Schlitz. "Thought maybe you needed this sooner today." She'd been crying, he could tell. She still cared.

Brick was now a senior shop steward for the union, and it was a second full-time job holding management accountable. After Pinkard was injured, Brick backed Prick Kennedy into a corner and jabbed his finger just an inch from his chest. "Danger is incremental," he said. "One shoddy shortcut leads to another and then another, until one of our men is dead." Last month, Brick had been introduced as "Erietown's hero" at a statewide meeting at a union hall in Columbus, to wild applause. For the first time since high school, he felt like a point guard again, the brains of the team.

He loved this new role, but he needed the release of hitting that softball, and Ellie seemed to understand. She came to Brick's games, and sometimes tagged along with him to join the other players and their wives at Mickey's. That worked for a few months, until one night on the way home Ellie announced that she was done.

"I'm sick of watching you flirt with the waitresses," she said in a flat voice, staring straight ahead as they drove home. "It's humiliating. It makes you look ridiculous, and makes me look like a fool."

"Ellie, you've had three beers and you're imagining things."

"Yes, that's your problem. *My* drinking."

Only then did it occur to him how much Ellie had changed. She didn't need him in the same way she used to. She was volunteering at the front desk at Erietown General two days a week, answering phones and giving people cheerful directions. She joined the Women's Guild at church, too, and was in charge of its annual rummage sale, which required a few evening meetings.

The third time, after Ellie didn't come home until after ten, he accused her of neglecting Sam. "She's eight, and you've got her in charge of dinner and Reilly's bedtime," he said. "She's too young for all that responsibility."

Ellie just laughed. "It makes Sam feel good to be in charge," she said. "I cook before I go, so all she's doing is serving and cleaning up. And she's been giving Reilly a bath since she was six."

"That's not the point."

"I've got a brain, Brick, and I plan to use it. Besides, it's nice to be appreciated once in a while."

"What's that supposed to mean?"

"If you don't know by now," she said, turning off the dresser light, "I'm done trying to explain."

If he hadn't been drinking, he told himself later, he would

never have raised his hand. He was bone tired, his head pounding, his shirt drenched in the humid July night. That new look on Ellie's face, as if she thought he was too stupid to understand, triggered something old and familiar deep inside him. His hand froze in midair, but Ellie had already backed up and fallen against the open window. He leapt and grabbed her waist, terrified that she was about to fall to the ground.

They collapsed on the floor, both of them in tears. Brick grabbed her face with both hands. "I'm sorry, Pint, I'm so sorry." He kissed her cheek. "Tell me the name of one husband who doesn't sometimes lose his temper. Tell me one husband who's perfect."

She cupped his hands with hers, tears running down her cheeks. "Not a single one. Not one of you." He pulled her into his chest, taking fragile comfort in her concession.

The following morning, Brick grabbed his lunch pail, which Ellie had packed, as always, and paused at the door. "I'm sorry, Ellie. I promised I'd never hit you. And I never will. That was the booze last night."

She set the coffeepot on the burner and turned to look at him. "That was your father last night, Brick. That was Bull McGinty. He's been dead for three years now. Let's leave him buried in that pauper's grave, where he belongs." She walked over to him and surprised him with a kiss.

Work that day was worse than usual. He had to break up a fight that a new union hire, Johnny Wilcox, started with a supervisor, who had a broken nose before Brick could pry them apart. "I don't care how mad you were," he yelled at Wilcox in the locker room, "you don't throw a punch at a manager. We're going to have to fight like hell to keep your job." Instead of thanking Brick, Wilcox took a swing at him. Two guys had to pull Brick off of him, and Wilcox was sent home.

Three hours later, Brick's head still throbbed from the whack. On the drive home, he thought about what Ellie had said to him the night she accused him of flirting at the bar. "I'm never enough for you," she'd said. "Those waitresses, with their pink lipstick and their long bleached hair. Did it ever occur to you that the reason they're working in a bar is because they're too selfish to take care of anyone else? Look at them, our age and trying to look like teenagers. Of course they're going to laugh at your stupid jokes. They aren't raising your kids and scrubbing grass stains out of your softball pants."

He started picturing those girls' friendly faces. No good could come from stopping at the same bar where he took Ellie.

He looked at his watch. Four-fifteen. "Why not," he said, tossing what was left of his cigarette out the open window. He turned right and headed into the biggest regret of his life.

Brick loved the smells of Sardelli's. He was a meat and potatoes man, accustomed to coming home to the same bland blend of aromas that had been in his childhood home. He'd never thought twice about it until he walked into Sardelli's. The garlic of marinara, the capers and lemon of chicken piccata—so many foods not afraid to announce themselves. He liked to walk in and see how many of the night's specials he could figure out by the smells from the kitchen.

Brick hoped Ellie would be willing to try a meal there soon. She always said feeding her family was one of her most important jobs as a wife and mother, which was why cooking made her so miserable. "I'm just no good at it, Brick," she said so often after dinner. "Nothing about it comes naturally to me."

He thought she cooked just fine, but once he went back to working a lot of overtime he thought it'd be fun to take her and the kids out to dinner once in a while. Neither he nor Ellie had ever eaten in a restaurant when they were kids. Brick saw it as a sign of their rising station in life. He took them to

Bob's Big Boy or Sweeney's Café and felt a surge of pride watching his wife eat off dishes she didn't have to serve or clean. He liked how the waitresses fussed over the kids, too. In one of their few conversations about parenting, Ellie and Brick had agreed that their kids' clothes would always be clean and pressed, and that their manners would be good enough to cause them to be mistaken for the richest kids in Cleveland.

"Just because we don't have as much money as those people doesn't mean we have to look or act like it," Ellie said. Brick liked that about her, the way she raised her chin in the air and insisted on their rightful place in the world. "That's right," he said. "Money can't buy class."

Brick pulled into Sardelli's parking lot and tried to remember the last time they'd eaten out as a family. It'd been months. Why'd he stop offering? His mood lifted as he parked. He'd go in for one drink and then get Ellie and the kids and bring them back for dinner.

He walked in and his shoulders relaxed. The dinner crowd hadn't arrived yet. He sat down at the far end of the bar and reached for the menu of the day.

"Now, there's the face of a hungry man."

He looked up and returned the barmaid's smile. "Am I that obvious?"

She laughed and tossed back her blond mane of hair. "It's my job to notice. And with that gorgeous red hair of yours, that sure is an easy thing to do."

Brick laid the menu on the bar. "Well, thanks. Guess I'm not your usual clientele."

She nodded. "You're Brick McGinty."

Brick leaned back on the stool. "How did you know that?"

"I read the stories just like everybody else. But those black-and-white newspaper pictures don't do your hair justice. Or your blue eyes."

"So, you know my name, but I don't know yours." She

leaned toward him, her breasts inches from his fingertips as she held out her hand. "I'm Rosemary."

"Well, hello, Rosemary," he said, clasping her hand. "What's good around here?"

"You mean on the menu?" she said. Brick laughed and she stood up, releasing his hand. "The lasagna just came out of the oven."

"Okay," he said. "Give me that. And a salad."

She walked to the kitchen door, swung it open, and yelled out his order, then walked back over to him and pointed to the tap. "What'ya having?"

"Schlitz."

"Schlitz it is." She returned with his beer, then crossed her arms on the bar and leaned forward again. "So, what are you doing here all alone on a Wednesday evening?"

"Technically, it's not evening yet."

"Technically, you're not alone either."

Brick laughed again. "How long have you worked here?"

"Since I was seventeen. Started in the dining room, then learned how to cook everything on the menu. I switched to bartending four years ago. More money. And I like the conversations."

"I can see that. More variety, too."

She shrugged her shoulders. "I don't know about that. But you're definitely a change of scenery."

Brick looked across the bar. "Don't worry," she said. "I'm not talking loud."

Brick shook his head. "So, you're a mind reader, too?"

She smiled. "Not really. As a matter of fact, I was just trying to figure out what you do for a living, and I'm comin' up blank."

"Erietown Electric."

"The power plant."

"Right. I make electricity."

"And how do you do that?"

Brick smiled. "I won't be boring you with that story."

She leaned in closer. He could make out the dusting of powder on her breasts, the smell of something exotic on her neck.

"I want to know," she said.

He studied her face for a moment. "You got a pen and a napkin?"

She reached under the bar top and set a stack of white paper napkins in front of him, then reached into the back pocket of her pants and pulled out a pen.

Brick pulled a napkin off the stack and drew a large square. "This is a furnace," he said. "It's bigger than this bar."

CHAPTER

36

Ellie felt Sam's breath on her arm and elbowed her away. "Sam, for God's sake, I'm standing at a hot stove. Announce yourself when you walk in the room."

Sam swept her arms out at her sides and bowed. "Mother, it's your daughter, Samantha Joy McGinty. I have arrived."

Ellie laughed and waved her spoon over the pot. "Let me finish filling these stuffed peppers. Go fetch the potatoes."

Sam dipped her finger in the sauce and tasted. "Mmm, good batch. What did you do different?"

"I added a little Worcestershire." She tapped the tattered cookbook with her free hand. "Mardee's idea. She says this book's good for basic recipes, but it lacks imagination. We need a little more spice in life."

Sam picked up the cookbook and read aloud the title on the faded green cover: *"The Betty Furness Westinghouse Cook Book."* She continued in a high-pitched, clipped voice, "Prepared under the direction of Julia Kiene."

"Very funny," Ellie said. "It wouldn't hurt you to crack that book open on occasion."

"I hate to cook."

Ellie scoffed. "As if that were ever the point. Welcome to every day of a woman's life."

Sam opened the book and read aloud her mother's handwritten inscription: "A gift to me from Julia Williams when I worked for her during my summer vacation before I entered my senior year. Eleanor Grace Fetters, 1956." Sam closed the book and set it on the counter. "Why do you always write who gives you a book?"

Ellie picked up the pot and carried it to the sink. "Because every time I see it, I remember the kindness of the person who gave it to me. The lady who gave me that book, for example. She took over Williams Appliances after her husband died, and I helped her that first summer. She taught me how to use the cash register and how to make total strangers feel as if they'd just walked into our home."

Ellie looked out the window as she kept talking. "I admired her. She was one strong lady. My first day on the job, she said, 'Ellie, life must go on. God doesn't give us anything we can't handle.'" Ellie looked at Sam. "Not sure what she'd make of me now."

"You could ask her."

Ellie shook her head and shooed Sam away from the oven door to open it. "She died. Not even two years after her husband died, she had a heart attack and she was gone. I remember Grandma saying maybe life was just too hard for Julia without her George." She slammed the oven door shut and looked at Sam. "That's what she always called him," she said, her voice softer. "'My George.' They spent every hour of every day together."

"You okay, Mom?"

Ellie wiped her hands on her apron. "Of course. Just telling a story." She pointed to the pot in the sink. "Fill that with water, and set the table. Daddy's working overtime again, so don't set a place for him. We'll do up a plate and leave it on the counter for when he gets home."

Sam reached for the bottle of Joy and, aware that her mother was watching, squeezed and counted aloud: "One drop, two drops, three drops. To quote the esteemed Eleanor Grace Fetters McGinty, 'We're not washing the Kleshinskis' Oldsmobile.'"

"Very funny," Ellie said. "Fill it with water and put enough Joy in there to wash the silverware after dinner."

Sam turned on the tap. "Why is Daddy working so much overtime? He hasn't been home for dinner in weeks."

"Don't exaggerate, Sam. He had dinner with us twice last week. He's giving up all those evenings with us to make enough money to buy a house."

"How much money?"

"I never have to worry about that," Ellie said. "Daddy takes care of all that. Deposits his checks, pays the bills. That's how a marriage works."

"We already have a house, Mom."

"It's not ours, Sam. We rent it from somebody else."

Sam pulled out her mother's footstool and sat on the top step. "I like this house just fine. It's got paneling in the living room, and the linoleum looks like bricks. Lenny says it looks classy."

"Lenny," Ellie said, wiping the countertop. "That boy is from another time, I swear. Acts like an old English man trapped in a skinny boy's body in Erietown, Ohio."

Sam laughed. "Still, he's my best friend."

"Clever you," Ellie said, tossing the dishrag into the sudsy bowl. "I knew exactly what you were doing when you decided on that one."

Sam shrugged and smiled. "Worked, too. We've been friends for two and a half years now, and Daddy hasn't said a bad thing about him."

"Uh-huh," Ellie said, shooing her off the stool. "And Daddy still likes his father. Funny how that goes. Like I said, Sam: Clever you."

Sam shoved the stool back under the counter. "Lenny understands me like nobody else. He likes books as much as I do, and he likes black people, too. Says we don't have to hate somebody just because our dads do."

Ellie frowned. "I'd keep that to myself when Daddy is home, if I were you."

Sam shoved her hands into her pockets. "If we move, I'll miss Lenny. A lot."

Ellie handed her three plates and pointed to the dining room. "Men aren't like us, Sam. Your father needs to feel bigger and stronger, and part of that means living in a house that is all his. It's part of taking care of his family." She smiled and reached up to smooth Sam's hair back from her forehead. "He loves us, which is why he's wearing himself out for us."

"Fine," Sam said, walking into the dining room. "I'll make Daddy a card, a Sam McGinty original, and stick it in his lunch pail."

"That's my girl," Ellie said.

CHAPTER

37

For the rest of his life, Brick would relive in his mind the chain of events that killed off the Brick McGinty he used to be. One bad decision rolled into another and another until the whole damn thing was too big to stop. Click–click–click, like the kids' dominoes falling. Ellie's God flicked his finger, and their family, the life they had built together, came tumbling down. Why does it take hurting someone to understand how much they used to love you?

He'd been bored, and he got reckless. He stopped after work at Sardelli's, and there she was, waiting for him. "I knew we were going to meet," Rosemary had told him that first night. "I just didn't know when."

He had loved all of her questions, and the way she cooed every time he added another napkin to show her how a guy as ordinary as Brick McGinty made electricity that lit up all of Clayton County. For the slightest moment, her enthusiasm reminded him of Sam and Reilly huddling around him as he drew on those napkins. How fast that guilt lost its power to the scent of her long naked neck.

She wouldn't let him wad up the napkins after he finished drawing. "I don't want to lose these," she said, plucking each square of napkin as if she were lifting a piece of art. "I'm going to hang these on my bedroom wall, to remind me of the power of Brick McGinty."

By the third beer, he knew he wasn't going home early to fetch Ellie and the kids. By the fifth, he knew he wasn't going home at all. "Double time if I stay," he told Ellie as he hunched over the pay phone outside the men's room.

"You do what you have to do, honey," Ellie said. "Sam and I will put your plate in the fridge." *Honey.* She hadn't called him that in such a long time. He'd hesitated only long enough to talk himself into resenting how goddamn long he'd had to wait for that.

If Rosemary hadn't lived above the bar, would he have let her grab his hand and lead him away that night? He used to wonder about that, before Ellie found out. "It doesn't matter where she lived," Ellie said. "What matters is that we weren't enough for you, Brick. That you've always wanted more. Why weren't we enough for you? Why wasn't I?"

The truth was messier, but he couldn't tell her that. He had wanted the young Ellie, his Pint, the girl who believed he was the best thing that had ever happened to her. She had made him feel like he could do anything in the world. The way her face lit up at the sight of him, so hungry for him. She protested the first time they made love, in his truck, but not much, really. By the third time she was wrapping her legs around him and whispering in his ear, "Fill me up." After Kitty, she never said that again.

Rosemary rekindled something in him. When her eyes widened at the sight of him he felt like that teenager again, his stomach tightening, the front of his pants swelling even as he approached the bar. The first time he was with her, he was too fast, barely sliding inside her before exploding. "I'm better than that, I promise," he said, lying on his back as they shared a cigarette. She took a long drag on it and stretched across him to rub it out in the ashtray on the bedside table. "Yeah?" she said, pulling him on top of her. "Show me."

Afterward, Rosemary rolled out of bed and started taping his napkin drawings in a row across the wall. She was naked, her ass framed by moonlight as she swayed her hips and hummed "Go Where You Wanna Go," by the Mamas and the Papas.

He stared at the drawings and felt a rising sense of panic as he tried to will his daughter's voice out of his head. *You throw a big bolt of lightning high into the sky and it flies straight to our house.*

Brick sat up and reached for his underwear on the floor. "I have to go."

"Go where?"

Brick looked up at her. "Are you kidding? I'm married, you know that. I have to get home."

"What are you going to tell Ellie?"

He stood up to pull on his pants. "Don't ever do that."

"Don't ever do what?"

"Don't ever say my wife's name," he said, tucking in his shirt. "She has nothing to do with this."

Rosemary sat down on the bed and draped the edge of the sheet across her lap. "And what is *this*? Us, I mean?"

He stood motionless at the side of the bed as she reached for the buckle on his belt. "What are *we*, Brick?" she said, slowly unzipping. He didn't even try to fight her.

Nights turned into weeks that became months of sliding out of Rosemary's bed and into the one he shared with his wife. Ellie was asleep, but she always left out a wrapped plate of dinner on the counter. "You're working so many extra hours for us," she'd told him after his sixth night with Rosemary. "The least I can do is make sure you eat."

He'd just hit the three-month mark of Rosemary overtime when he found Sam's card in his lunch pail. Slowly, he opened it.

Dear Daddy,

I miss you, but Mom says that's how it has to go right now because you're working a lot of over time to save money to buy a house. If you get too tired, you should come home because this house is every thing I ever wanted anyway.

I love you. Don't worry, I know you can't say it back, but Mom says how hard you work says the same thing.

Your Sam

His hands trembled and he folded the card into fourths and tucked it into his shirt pocket. He closed his lunch pail and stood up. Howie Lobdell had been watching. "Not eating, Brick?"

"Nah. Not in the mood for meatloaf again." What a shitty thing to say. Ellie didn't deserve that. He felt shorter with each step toward the exit, cowering from Ellie's God.

CHAPTER

38

Brick grabbed the end of the dining room table with both hands and leaned in. "I'm gonna catch you. You can't escape."

Sam and Reilly dropped their forks in unison and stared at their mother, who was gripping the other end of the table. "You just try," she said, her face flushed as she laughed. She took two steps to her right to trick Brick, and then darted to the left.

"You can't keep this up," Brick said. "You know you can't." Ellie put her hands on her hips and wiggled, waiting for his next move. He faked to the right and whirled around, grabbing her wrists. "Gotcha."

"No!" she screamed. The children clapped as he scooped her into his arms. "You're fast, Daddy," Reilly yelled. Brick started tickling Ellie in the ribs with both hands. "No, no," she said, laughing. "Brick. Stop! You win!"

Brick planted a kiss on her mouth. "Damn straight I win. Every time." He blew up at the wisps of his hair plastered against his sweaty forehead. "Look at what you did to me, woman. I look like I've played nine innings."

Ellie's eyes glistened. "Nice to know I can still get you worked up."

Sam's cheeks started to burn. She couldn't remember the last time she'd seen her mom and dad so playful with each other. She was grateful for the reprieve from the usual dinner-time gloom, but she was nervous about it, too. Didn't trust it. One fight and everything could go dark again.

"Live in the moment," her mother liked to say now that she was spending so much time at church. "You can't change the past and the future is in God's hands." As far as Sam could tell, God didn't spend much time with the McGintys.

After dinner, Sam stood at the sink washing dishes while her parents sat on the porch swing. She could hear her father singing his medley of Dean Martin songs. It'd been months since he'd done that.

She finished the dishes and pulled up the sink stopper, then walked slowly toward the front door. The empty swing was slowing to a stop. She heard the click of the lock on her parents' bedroom door, followed by her mother's laugh. She walked out the back door, where Reilly was sitting on one of the swings. He was swaying as he dragged the toe of his sneaker in the dirt, and as she got closer she could hear his soft voice singing the same line over and over, like a prayer. *Everybody loves somebody sometime . . .*

Brick stretched his free arm over the side of the bed to grab the cigarette pack on the table, moving slowly to avoid waking Ellie, who was nestled into his other shoulder. He slid out a cigarette and picked up the Bic lighter. He still hadn't found Ellie's lighter, and it bothered him more than he admitted. He was just about to strike a flame when he looked at Ellie's bee-hive blooming over his shoulder. With all that hairspray it'd

probably catch on fire. He smiled, surprised by his lack of an-
noyance. They were rounding a corner. He could feel it. The
way she'd smiled at him as he chased her around the dining
room table. God, he loved that, and the looks on the kids'
faces. He couldn't remember the last time all four of them had
been in the same room laughing.

She'd grabbed his hand on the porch swing and guided him
to their bedroom. She hadn't done that since his affair with
Kitty. He closed his eyes. His mistake with Kitty was nothing
compared to what he was doing now.

Ellie stirred and rolled over on her stomach. "Oh, my," she
said, looking up at him. "I must have fallen asleep."

He reached over and stroked her cheek. "Guess I wore you
out."

She lifted her face higher. "What's wrong?"

The skin on the back of his neck tightened. "Nothing." He
slid his arm out from under her and inched up against the
headboard. "I'm still amazed at what just happened here, in
broad daylight."

Ellie sat up, tugging on the sheet to cover her breasts before
turning to look at him again. "I love you, Brick."

Brick exhaled slowly. "I love you, too, El."

"No, I mean it, Brick. I really do love you. Even now. Even
after everything."

He nodded slowly, unsure of where this was going. "I've
never stopped loving you, Ellie. Not for a minute."

She pressed her lips together into a thin line and nodded
twice. "I wanted to believe that was true," she said. "But I went
a long time thinking you didn't, Brick. Thinking I wasn't
enough for you. But I do now. Look how hard you're working
to get us our own home. That's about a future. *Our* future.
That's love."

He could barely breathe.

"Brick," she said, cupping his face. "My Brick." He wrapped his arms around her and pulled her in, squeezing his eyes shut.

She pressed her ear against his chest. "Your heart," she said. "I can feel it pounding."

CHAPTER

39

Rosemary pulled herself up from her knees at the toilet and turned on the cold water. She splashed her face and looked in the mirror. "Jesus God. No, no, no." She held out her fingers and counted the weeks since her last period. "He's gonna kill me. He's gonna wish I was dead."

She walked into the kitchen and glanced at the clock on the wall. She wasn't due at work for another hour and a half. She lifted the window shade and looked down at the parking lot. Four cars, not one of them his. She had no idea if he was planning to stop after work. She never did, not once, in these last nine months.

She picked up the pack of Kents and pulled out the metal lighter she kept wedged in the middle of the stack of paper napkins. She flipped it over and felt the familiar burn as she read the inscription: LOVE, PINT. Rosemary had slipped the lighter out of his pocket two weeks ago, when he was in the shower. It was a test. How long before he'd ask her if she'd seen it? How long before he admitted he missed it?

Stupid games, but as of today, she was winning. She had something Ellie McGinty would never have. She was carrying Brick's third child, the one that doctors said his wife could never give him. The baby Brick desperately wanted. He'd never said it quite like that, but he had his ways of letting his hopes slip out.

Rosemary had once picked up his wallet on the table and thumbed through the pictures of his family. She'd been so upset by the photo booth picture of him with Ellie—"Our wedding day!" he had written on the back—that she didn't hide her snooping when he walked out of the bathroom with a towel wrapped around his waist.

She had expected his usual blowup at the proof of her prying, but he didn't yell. Didn't even look angry. He just said, slowly, "What are you doing, Roe?"

"I was just wondering why you left one of the picture sleeves empty," she said, fanning out the photos. "You told me you take pictures of the kids all the time, but you've got an empty one here."

Brick stepped back into the steamy bathroom. "I do," he said, looking into the mirror as he ran a comb through his hair. "Maybe I'm still not sure we won't have another one. Another boy, maybe. Despite the damn doctors. So, I keep that one empty. So I don't jinx it."

She deserved that sucker punch, she'd told herself at the time. She was getting into his business, as he always put it, and that never turned out well. They weren't supposed to talk about his wife and kids. Not ever.

She had overplayed her hand in the beginning, giving him the wrong impression about her. That first night at the bar she had played to win. She knew from years of customer confessions that marriages got tired after a while, and most husbands longed to believe there was more to them than an hourly wage job, and a wife and kids who always needed more than they could give them. Rosemary wanted to introduce Brick to the part of himself that he'd lost, and with her edgy banter and sympathetic smiles, she was sure she could do it. By the time

Brick McGinty sat down at her bar, she'd had years of practice on how to make a man feel shiny and new.

Their first few weeks were everything she'd hoped they would be. Sometimes they didn't get any farther than inside the door before she was naked and soon writhing underneath him. After three months or so, though, she started to wonder if there was anything else about her that interested him. He never asked her about her day, and except for quizzing her a little about her hometown of Foxglove, he seemed to lack any curiosity about her life before he'd met her. He didn't want to talk about anything from early in his life, and his wife and kids were off-limits.

He was always looking at his watch, too. "You know, you're not punching a clock here," she said to him recently, after they'd made love twice and he rolled out of bed.

"You know what you signed up for," he said. "You know I'm married." He walked into the bathroom and slammed the door. That's when she took his lighter.

There was that one time, though, when he said he wanted another child. She'd sat at the table as he finished his ritual for departure. Buckling his belt. Propping a foot on the toilet seat to tie his shoe. Unwrapping a stick of peppermint gum and popping it into his mouth, his square jaw flexing as he chewed.

He had smiled at her when he walked back out of the bathroom. Didn't seem the least bit angry about her sneaking through his wallet. Even kissed her goodbye.

She had talked herself into thinking maybe he was giving her a hint that day. Ellie couldn't have any more children. That's what he'd told her.

Rosemary sat down at the kitchen table and started writing on the notepad there.

Dear Brick,

She stared at his name, took another draw on the cigarette.

I'm writing this because I'm scared. I want to tell you we got a problem, and I don't want you yelling before I can finish explaining.

She set down the pen and balanced her cigarette on the edge of the ashtray. Brick had bought it for her in Niagara Falls, when he was with Ellie and the kids, of course. "You never take me anywhere," she had said to him when he handed it to her. "I make you feel like a man, but she still gets to be the woman in your life."

That argument had ended like all their other fights because she could not say no to Brick McGinty. All he had to do was reach into her blouse and nibble on her ear, and the heat rose in her like steam.

When was the last time he'd done that?

As you know—It was your idea for me to use the diaphragm because you said using a rubber was like taking a shower with a raincoat on. She paused. She'd driven alone to the doctor's office for that appointment, and lied to everyone—the receptionist, then the nurse, then Dr. Harris—about how she was secretly getting married in a month to a man in her hometown of Foxglove. "He's not Catholic," she'd whispered to each of them. "Mama needs more time to get used to the idea, but we don't want to wait."

Rosemary ground out her cigarette. "Jesus Christ," she said, remembering the first time she didn't use the diaphragm. "What the hell was I thinking?"

She heard a car pull up in the lot and glanced out the window.

"Shit."

Rosemary stood up quickly and felt another wave of nausea, so she sat back down. She could hear Aunt Lizzie's heels echoing in the stairwell. The door was unlocked. There was no stopping this.

Aunt Lizzie tapped on the door. "Rosie?" She turned the doorknob and frowned at the sight of her niece at the table. "You're as white as a ghost." She closed the door and sat down at the table. She felt Rosemary's forehead. "Your head's a little warm. How are you feeling?"

Rosemary stood up from the table and ran into the bathroom, barely making it to the toilet. She retched as her aunt stood in the doorway. She pulled on the lever to flush, and ripped off a piece of toilet paper to wipe her mouth.

"How far along are you?"

Rosemary dropped the wad of paper into the toilet. "I'm not sure," she said, speaking into the bowl. "Two months maybe."

"Je. Sus. Christ."

Rosemary closed her eyes and exhaled slowly. "Aunt Lizzie, I'd appreciate it if you'd save me the lecture. I already know how screwed I am."

"Who did this to you, Rosie?"

"Aunt Lizzie, nobody did anything to me. I was a willing participant."

"Wash your face," Lizzie said. "I'll wait for you in the kitchen."

Rosemary splashed cold water on her face and brushed her teeth, and sat down across from Aunt Lizzie.

"It's not one of the Sardelli boys, is it?"

"I'm pregnant, not insane." She covered her face with her hands. "I'm in trouble, Aunt Lizzie. Big trouble."

"So, you finally met Brick McGinty."

Rosemary started to sob. "What am I going to do?"

Lizzie lit a cigarette with Brick's lighter. "Didn't I tell you to stay away from him? How the hell did you meet him?"

"He started coming to the bar more often. I know you don't believe it, and I can see why you wouldn't, after I talked about how I wanted to meet him. But I didn't do anything before he became a regular at the bar. What am I going to do?"

"Well, you're going to have a baby, I guess. Unless you—"

"Never."

"Women do it now. There are doctors in New York."

"This is *my* baby. My chance to do something good in the world."

"Rosie."

"I'm having the baby."

"Not here, you're not," Lizzie said. "We could send you away. To family."

Rosemary shook her head. "I'm never going back to Foxglove. You can't make me go back there."

"Who are you talking to here?" Lizzie said. "I'm the one who saved you from Foxglove, remember? Danny's sister lives in Scranton, about five and a half hours from here. She's married, they have two kids. You can have the baby there."

"And then what?"

"And then you let Danny and me adopt it." Rosemary yanked her hand away, and Lizzie's voice grew louder. "You know how much I've always wanted a baby. Danny never wanted to adopt a stranger's baby. But this. This is family. And you." Lizzie shook her head, blinking back tears. "And you could move away and start over. Nobody would ever have to know."

Rosemary crossed her arms as she leaned against the back of her chair. "You're serious."

"You got a better plan, Rosie? Brick McGinty is never going to marry you. He'll deny the child is his. Your baby will grow up a bastard child."

"Aunt Lizzie, how could you say that?"

"It's not what *I* think, Rosie. It's what everyone else will think. And how are you going to support it? Take care of it?"

"Him."

"Sorry?"

"You keep calling the baby 'it.'"

"Well, you don't know if it's a boy or a girl."

"I know," Rosemary said, placing her hand on her abdomen. "I can feel him."

Lizzie scrunched her cigarette in the ashtray. "You think he's going to *want* this baby. That you're going to tell him you're pregnant and presto chango he's going to leave his wife and children so that he can marry you."

"I don't care if Brick ever lays eyes on this child."

"Lie to yourself if you want, honey, but don't lie to me. I know you. You think everything changes when he finds out you tricked him and got pregnant."

"Aunt Lizzie, I did not trick him. We had been fighting. And drinking. We made up. I got caught up in the moment."

"Make sure you're standing in a crowded room when you tell him that."

"This baby is mine," Rosemary said, more softly. "I'm sorry, Aunt Lizzie, but it would kill me to have my child not know I was his mommy."

"Oh, Rosie, you have no idea," Lizzie said, dabbing her eyes with a paper napkin. "You have no idea how hard this is going to be."

"I know, Aunt Lizzie. But you won't leave me alone in this, will you? You'll be the best aunt ever."

"I'll help you," Lizzie said, her voice resigned. "But you do have to decide what you're going to do about Brick McGinty. We have to talk about what comes next."

"Why does he need to know?" A car door slammed and they both startled. Rosemary squeezed her aunt's hand. "That could be him." Rosemary picked up the lighter and slipped it into the pocket of her robe before looking out the window.

Five cars in the parking lot. Not one of them was his.

CHAPTER

40

Ellie stood at the kitchen window and watched Sam cup her hands under the apple tree to yell up at Reilly. "No, no, to your right. See them? There must be seven right there. Throw 'em down one at a time."

Sam covered her head with her arms and ducked as an apple landed inches from her feet. "Not *throw*." Ellie could hear Reilly's high-pitch protest. "Okay, okay," Sam yelled. "I should have said *drop*. Just drop them down to me." She caught three in a row, laughing as she tossed each one into the basket. "There you go. We're on a roll, Reill."

Ellie walked away from the window wondering yet again how short, squat Ellie McGinty could have produced this tall, willowy girl. Not yet a teenager, but by last fall she had shot up taller than her mother and was all limbs, arms and legs flapping about like those of a marionette. Over the summer, Sam had sprouted breasts and an attitude.

"Mouthy and oblivious," she'd described her to Mardee. "Glides into a room like she owns it, completely unaware of the perverts gawking at her." Mardee just laughed and patted Ellie on the back. "Oh, boy. Here we go."

Ellie missed her little girl, and how she used to hang on her mother's every word. Now, whenever Ellie tried to confide in Sam she noticed a subtle shift in her daughter's demeanor. As if she'd heard enough, Ellie thought. As if it were no longer special to know her mother's secrets.

Ellie's eyes stung as she recalled last night's exchange. Sam had been finishing the dishes as Ellie wiped the stove top and mentioned how she missed Brick, who was working overtime again. Sam sighed, loudly, and looked away.

"Something wrong, Sam?"

"Nothing that isn't always wrong," Sam said, draining the sink. "I mean, there's always something, right, Mom?"

Ellie threw the rag onto the counter and walked out of the room. Two hours later, she was still sitting on the couch alone while Sam blasted Motown in her bedroom, guaranteeing Brick's bad mood when he finally walked through the door.

Ellie was tired of refereeing between those two. Brick didn't like Sam's music, and he didn't like most of her friends for the same reason. "She's going to date black boys, that one," Brick said. "I'll be damned if that's going to happen in my house."

Two weeks later, on the hottest night in July, Brick pulled into the driveway just as Gary Colbert strolled by the house and smiled at Sam on the porch swing. Brick insisted to Ellie he would have let it go if he hadn't seen Sam giggle and wave at the boy with a look he'd never seen before on his daughter's face. "Like she had a crush on him or something," he said. "Our Sam."

Brick yanked Sam off the swing so hard she had a big bruise on her upper arm the next day. "It was an accident," he told Ellie just as Sam was walking into the kitchen for breakfast. "I said I was sorry."

Sam's face was defiant. "No, you said you didn't mean it. You never apologized."

"Jee-zuz Christ."

"You can't make me hate black people just because you do,"

Sam said, glaring at Brick. "And you can't stop me from loving who I want. My body, my heart."

That did it. Brick grounded Sam on the spot, for two weeks. "I hear you as much as mention that boy's name, and I'll lock you in your room until school starts."

"Fine," Sam yelled as she marched upstairs to her room and slammed the door. Minutes later, Stevie Wonder was belting out "I Was Made to Love Her" and Sam was grounded for the rest of the summer.

"You had to blast the Motown," Ellie said to her tearful daughter the next morning. "You knew that would set him off." Sam wiped her eyes on her sleeve. "I'm not going to be like you, Mom. I'm not going to put up with him acting like my opinions never matter."

What was she teaching her daughter? She'd been asking herself that ever since, trying to see herself through Sam's eyes. What did Sam make of Ellie's life? Ellie was vice president of the Women's Guild at church now, and PTA president at Reilly's school. She read the *Erietown Times* every day now, too, before Brick got home, so that Sam could hear both of her parents discussing the evening news. Did Sam even notice?

Ellie looked out the kitchen window again. The kids' basket was almost full of apples, and the sight of it reminded Ellie of the other basket in the living room, full of Brick's work clothes waiting to be ironed. She'd been washing them for nearly three years now after his temper tantrum about Bill Grandin during the strike. Not because she wanted to, but because he had told her that was how it was going to be. "What have you got to do all day anyway?" he'd said. "It's not like you have a job."

She made a decision to do more at church the very next week. She needed to be with people who saw her as someone other than Brick McGinty's wife, or Sam and Reilly's mother. At Erietown Presbyterian, she was Ellie McGinty. Soprano in the choir. Devotions leader at the Women's Guild weekly luncheons. Organizer of the after-church coffee and cake in the fellowship hall. "There's talk that you should be Guild president next year," Donna Dickerson had told her last fall after choir rehearsal. "I'm going to nominate you, if Laurie Madison doesn't beat me to it."

Ellie turned to look at her. "I had no idea anyone would want me."

Laurie patted the gold cross hanging around Ellie's neck. "We joke that your nickname is 'Call Ellie.' Need to wrangle a new coffeepot out of Pastor Shiflet? Call Ellie. Need a cleanup crew for the annual Father's Day dinner? Call Ellie."

When Ellie shared that conversation with Sam, her daughter had actually looked pleased. "President of the Guild?" Sam said. "You mean, like in charge of everything?"

"Well, I guess I would be running things," Ellie said, smiling shyly.

"Pretty cool, Mom. It's not a career, but it's something."

Someday Ellie might tell Sam how that had made her feel. Maybe.

Ellie glanced up at the clock. Only four o'clock. Another long evening without her husband, who was working overtime again. She looked at the full dish rack. Why didn't they have a dishwasher by now? All that extra money he was making, and she couldn't name one new thing in their house. Her allowance hadn't moved up by a dime.

She thought again about the basket of clothes in the living room. Every week, she had done exactly as she was told, washing another load of his filthy work clothes, and then ironing them because that's how he wanted them before he got them filthy again. She reached under the sink to pull out a paper bag from Kroger, and walked to the living room. She grabbed a handful of the clothes and heard Sam's approaching footsteps as she started shoving them into the bag.

"You want me to iron those, Mom?"

"Nope." Ellie picked up another handful and crammed them into the bag.

Sam spoke more slowly. "Would you like me to help fold them before you do that?"

"Nope." Ellie crammed the last two shirts into the bag and handed it to Sam. "Put this on the back porch."

Sam took the bag, but didn't move. "You sure you want Dad to see his clothes like this?"

Ellie picked up the empty basket and started walking back into the kitchen. "I've never been so sure of anything in my life. If your father wants his work clothes cleaned and pressed, he can get them laundered by Bill Grandin, just like everybody else at the plant."

"Cool," Sam said, hugging the bag to her chest as she followed her mother. "Hope I'm here when you tell him."

CHAPTER

41

As soon as she saw his car, Rosemary knew something was wrong.

Ever since their first night together, Brick had parked behind the bar, next to her old Thunderbird, and waited for her upstairs in her apartment. This time—the last time, she would always remember—his car was parked on the side of the building, next to her apartment stairwell. His engine purred, the exhaust pipe puffing clouds of vapor into the night as he sat behind the wheel, blowing smoke through the window that was barely cracked open.

His eyes narrowed as she approached him. Ah, she was getting this Brick tonight. Angry Brick. Victim-of-the-World Brick. She knew him well. "Hello, stranger," she said. "I was beginning to think you'd left town."

He rolled up the window and cut the engine. She turned and walked toward the stairwell. She heard his car door open and his left shoe land on the gravel. She turned to face him and leaned against the doorjamb. He closed the car door with a soft thud and shoved his keys into his back pocket.

She raised her face toward the night sky and started softly counting aloud. "Ten, eleven, twelve, thirteen." She put her hand on her hip and forced a smile. "Seventeen. Seventeen days since you've been here."

Brick said nothing as he approached. She nodded toward the stairwell. "I've got some hamburger upstairs. And that pepper jack you like. Want me to make you a cheeseburger?"

He threw his cigarette on the ground. "Can't stay."

She looked down at the ground and watched the cigarette's ember flicker. *Stay calm,* she told herself. She shifted and threw her hair back before meeting his eyes. "Is that any way to treat your girlfriend?"

"Keep it down."

Rosemary took a step toward him. "Brick, I—"

He held out his arms and pressed his palms against her shoulders. "No. Don't."

"Don't what?"

He took a step back. "We have to talk."

"Of course we do," she said, reaching out to touch his face. He took another step back.

"Dammit. I said don't."

Her arm fell at her side. "Brick, what's the matter? Where have you been? I've been worried sick about you. And I have—"

He plunged his hand into his pants pocket and started jingling his coins. Rosemary clenched her jaw. This was not how this was supposed to go. Not here. Not like this.

"Brick, I have to tell you something."

He shook his head and looked at the ground. "I can't."

"What?"

He shook his head again, his fingers working the coins. "I can't do this anymore. It's wrong."

"Brick, wait." She shivered and folded her arms across her chest. "You don't know what I have to tell you."

"Doesn't matter," he said. "This isn't working." He looked around before continuing. "Look, I've been doing a lot of thinking. She didn't deserve this. Ellie. Ellie didn't do anything to deserve this. And Ellie needs me."

The sound of Ellie's name on his lips emboldened her.

"Oh, we're saying her name now, are we? The woman you said I was never allowed to mention? Ellie? *Ellie* needs you?"

The outdoor lights on the bar flicked off, casting them in darkness. "Vinny's closing up," she said. "He'll be out here any minute. Let's go upstairs and talk, where no one can hear us."

Her eyes slowly adjusted to the dark. His face came into focus, and she took a step back. "Why are you looking at me like that?"

"It's over," he said. "You and me and this, this thing we did. It's over." He held out his clenched hand and she clasped it with both of hers. "Brick, I—" He forced open her hands with his fingers and dropped the apartment key into her palm.

"You said I was the one who made you happy," she said, her voice trembling. "You said one day we were going to be together. That we would have a family."

"I never said any of that shit."

"In so many words, you did. I would never have—"

The front door of the bar slammed shut. They fell silent, waiting as Vinny Sardelli turned the key in the lock. Rosemary took a quiet step toward Brick and laid her hand on his arm as they waited for Vinny to walk to his car on the other side of the lot. At the sound of the engine turning, Brick stepped past Rosemary and hid behind her in the doorway. She closed her eyes and turned toward him, breathing in the smell of him. "Brick," she whispered.

He reached for her arm and yanked her in just before Vinny's headlights swept over the spot where they had been standing. She leaned into Brick and pressed her palms against his chest. As soon as they heard Vinny's car pull onto the road, he shoved her away and stepped out of the doorway. "I gotta go."

"You can't leave like this," she said. "You can't just go and pretend this never happened. That *we* never happened. I love you, Brick."

He reached into his jacket and pulled out a cigarette and a pack of matches. "Well, I love Ellie," he said.

Rosemary couldn't swallow. "You can't leave me, Brick. Not now."

He yanked open the car door. "You're beating a dead horse, Roe," he said, his voice low and flat. "I'm already gone."

Brick's chest was pounding. Where was the relief, the calm he thought he'd feel? He had laid it out for her. He was staying with Ellie and getting on with his life. He had expected her to cry. Maybe even scream at him. But she just stood there, speechless in the dark as he pulled out of the parking lot with his headlights off so he couldn't see her face.

He was not the bad guy here. He'd made a mistake, and now he had fixed it. Where was the peace his mother said always comes when you do the right thing?

He pressed his foot on the gas. He couldn't go home yet. He had called Ellie in the afternoon to tell her he was working a full eight hours of overtime. She wouldn't expect him for another hour or so.

He turned on the radio and winced at the sound of Diana Ross's voice. He looked at the dial, pissed that it was set to CKLW, and then he remembered why. Sam had been in the car with him yesterday while he ran errands, and for the first time she had worked up the nerve to ask if she could switch the station. "Dad, can we please listen to my music?"

My music. Not even a teenager, and she already had her radio station, her favorite songs. He used to love buying forty-fives and rushing home to play them for Sam on her record player from Santa. They'd sit together on the floor and sing along to everything from Neil Diamond and Petula Clark to the Beatles, when they were still mopheads. Now Sam was using babysitting money to buy her own records, and none of the music was his. Even when she was humming, it was Motown.

But when she asked if she could change the station on his car radio, he agreed. He missed sharing music with her, and sang along when Sam started belting out the Temptations' "Ain't Too Proud to Beg." The look on her face. It was everything.

He shut off the radio and turned onto State Route 11, toward Clayton Valley, and thought about Ellie. She sure had been in a mood lately. Jesus, that bag of his clothes waiting for him on the back porch. His stomach had lurched at the sight of it. He thought Ellie had found out about Rosemary and was kicking him out of the house. What a relief to see that smirk on Sam's face as she leaned against the fridge. "Mom thinks you should get your clothes washed at the plant like everyone else," she said. "I think she's right, Daddy. It's 1967. We women have better things to do." *We women*. Brick knew where that was coming from. That damn Emma Dunham down at the newsstand, filling Sam's head with women's lib shit. Another reason to move.

He rolled down the window and breathed in the smell of farmland stretching out around him. He knew by heart every curve in the road, the name of every family farming the land. The world that was turning his wife against him and every union meeting into a Martin Luther King rally hadn't touched Clayton Valley. Here, it was still 1955.

When he was a teenager he'd been so desperate to leave this hick town. Now he kept coming back looking for signs of who he used to be, when he was Clayton Valley's basketball star with big plans. He was going to go to college and Ellie would wait for him because he would graduate and be a coach at one of those big high schools in Cleveland. And then one snowy day in their senior year he found Ellie collapsed on the side of the road.

He grabbed the rolled-up towel in the passenger seat and wedged it into the small of his back. He was barely thirty, but too often he felt like an old man with his stiff back, the aching shoulder. His knees were crackling now every time he bent down to pick up something heavy. Christ.

Brick turned right onto the road that sometimes showed up in his dreams. He flicked off his brights and slowed to a stop at lot 52. He ground out his cigarette in the ashtray before pushing open the door.

The wind had picked up, as it often did when he visited his mother. That had always been her way, raising the energy around him. The grass was crunchy with frost, and when he sat down on the grave the wind threw a smattering of leaves across the gravestone. He shivered and buried his face into his collar to blow a hot breath down his chest. "I'm sorry, Ma. I'm sorry it's been so long since I visited."

He pressed his palm on her name. "I've been ashamed. I haven't told anyone else that, but I'm telling you. I'm ashamed of what I've been doing." He squeezed his eyes shut. "I did it, Ma. I did what you'd want me to do. I can feel I'm turning a corner."

He paused. This was the only place on earth where he never worried about sounding like an idiot. "I've made a lot of mistakes, Ma, but I hope you were right that if we ask God to forgive us, he will."

He sat for more than an hour, silent until he couldn't take the cold a minute longer. He patted the gravestone and stood up. "I'm going home, Ma. To Ellie and the kids, where I belong. I just wanted to let you know. Tell Harry I said hi."

He walked slowly back to the car, his shoulders bowed under the restlessness that wasn't done with him yet.

PART V

1969

CHAPTER

42

She heard Brick's voice before she saw him.

Okay, Son, now try this glove on. Don't worry about how stiff it is. I'll oil it for you when we get home. Just see if it feels right.

"How much?" the clerk said to Rosemary.

Rosemary looked at her. "What?"

"How much do you want to pay on your layaway today?"

"Umm."

The clerk looked at Rosemary. "You okay, ma'am?"

"Yes," Rosemary said. "I'm sorry. Five. I want to pay five dollars." She snapped open the wallet in her hand, pulled out a wad of singles, and slid them across the counter.

"That looks like more than five."

Now see, I know that feels a little too heavy right now, but you'll grow into that one. And this way, you'll build up your muscles.

Rosemary looked at the clerk. "What?"

The clerk fanned the dollar bills on the counter. "You gave me more than five."

Rosemary stared at the money.

You want to stand with your feet apart a little wider. Just like we talked about last weekend, remember?

Rosemary counted out five dollars and tried to smile.

"There," she said. "Five. Can I have a receipt, please?" She grabbed the counter with both hands and lowered her head. *Breathe*, she told herself. *Just keep breathing.*

That's it. All the way to the floor. See? That's how you snag a grounder. Now, spread your ankles apart and I'll roll it a little faster to you.

The clerk waved the paper under Rosemary's chin. "I said, here's your receipt."

"Thanks," Rosemary said. She shoved it into her pocket and started to walk away. "Ma'am," the clerk said, waving Rosemary's wallet. "You want this?"

The four women in line stared at Rosemary as she walked back to the counter. "Thanks." She stepped away slowly, weighing her options. If she walked to the right she could weave through women's lingerie to the exit and he'd never know she was there.

Yep, bat and glove. You need both to play baseball.

She pulled out the receipt and studied it. At this rate, she wouldn't be able to pay off the balance for Paull's tricycle in time for his second birthday.

She turned left.

Past the gardening tools. The folding chairs. The pet food. She hesitated at the first aisle of the toy department, the Barbie section. How many aisles did she have to pass before she hit sporting goods? Three? Or was it two?

Think, Rosemary.

She walked to the second aisle, paused, and grabbed onto a shelf to breathe. What will he do? How will he react? She looked at the row of diecast cars above her hand. Paull loved those little cars. She felt the usual pang, imagining his face if she could ever walk through the door with a whole set of them.

When we get home, we're going to oil this glove and stick your ball in it and you'll sleep with it under your pillow.

"Like you do, Daddy," a boy said.

Rosemary scooped up three of the cars and walked toward the sound of their voices in the next aisle.

"Now see, that's a catcher's mitt. See how it's round and padded? You're not going to be a catcher. You're going to play right—"

Brick dropped the glove on the floor.

"Okay, Daddy," the boy said, bending to pick up the glove and shoving it back on the shelf. He pulled out another glove. "Look how big this one is, Daddy." He turned to look up at his father.

"Hello, Brick."

She watched his fingers curl around the shoulder of his son.

The little boy looked at Rosemary and leaned into his father. "Who's that, Daddy?" he asked in a stage whisper.

Brick plunged his left hand into his pants pocket. "You know what, buddy? How 'bout you go get us some popcorn?"

"By myself?"

"Sure," Brick said. "You're six years old. You can do this." He quickly gave up trying to count and put all the change into Reilly's open hand. "Take all of this. The lady at the popcorn counter will take what she needs."

Reilly smiled at Rosemary. He had large blue eyes, with long eyelashes as red as his hair. "I've never done this before," he said. "Go all by myself to buy popcorn." He shook his head. "Wait'll I tell Mommy."

"Okay, pal," Brick said, his eyes on Rosemary. "Go on now."

Reilly pointed to the cars in her hand. "I have that one."

Rosemary looked down at the three cars. "Which one?"

"The Johnny Lightning Chevy Camaro. It's the only one I have with stripes."

Rosemary smiled at the boy. "Well, then, you just helped me decide. That's what I came over to ask: Which car would a little boy like you pick out?" She continued to look at Reilly as Brick inhaled. "Thank you," she said. "You've helped me make our son very happy."

Brick reached out and placed his hand on top of Reilly's head. "Okay, Son, go get the popcorn."

"He's adorable," Rosemary said.

Brick turned and watched Reilly until he was out of sight. "What are you doing here?"

"Shopping, just like you. For my son."

"Your son."

"Yes, that's right. My son. He's almost two."

His eyes narrowed; she looked down at the floor.

"Let me save you the trouble of all that math, Brick. I'm shopping for our son. Yours and mine."

"That's impossible."

"I can tell by the look on your face that you know it's not."

He stared at her.

"I know the feeling," Rosemary said. "That's how I felt when I heard you talking about all the nice stuff you were buying your boy. Your other son."

Sweat was beading on his brow. "I'm going to walk away from here," he said, "and I don't want you following me."

She took a step toward him. "Two years. Two years without a word from you. I never bothered you once, Brick. And you think you're giving me orders? Fuck you."

He looked around and ran his hand across his brow. "He's not my son."

"Really," she said. "Let me show you something."

Rosemary set the diecast cars on the shelf and pulled out her wallet. She opened it and thrust the first picture inches from Brick's face: "Meet Paull. Paull-two-els. Same freckles. Same red hair. Same smile, as you can see in this picture here."

Brick's face softened as he stared at the picture. She'd imagined this moment so many times, but she'd never dared hope for this reaction.

"Why, Roe? Why didn't you tell me?"

"When would I have told you? The only time I tried, you told me I was beating a dead horse. You never gave me the chance."

Brick shoved his hand into his pocket and scowled.

"No more coins to jingle, Brick. You gave them all to your son, remember? The one who gets to call you Daddy."

He pinched the bridge of his nose. "How old is he?"

"I told you. He's almost two."

Brick looked at the floor and nodded. "Two."

"He's a beautiful boy. Looks so much like you that sometimes I can barely stand it. Same soft red hair. He's covered in freckles. When he smiles, grown women accuse him of flirting."

He held out his palm. "Stop, Roe."

She pressed her palm against his. "It's been so long since I've heard you say my name."

He hesitated. Before dropping his hand, he hesitated. She was sure of it.

He looked at her. "Can I see him?"

"We live with my aunt now," she said. "I'm still working there. Not exactly what I had planned." Rosemary reached into her purse and pulled out a pen and the layaway receipt. "Here," she said, setting the paper on the shelf so that she could write. "This is the phone number at the bar. I'm there from five o'clock to one. Call me. If I don't answer, hang up. We'll set up a time for you to meet Paull." She handed him the receipt and smiled past his shoulder.

"Daddy, look!" Reilly grinned as he held up the red-and-white-striped bag. Rosemary and Brick stepped farther apart as he walked toward them. "I ate two inches of it already."

Brick roughed up his hair. "You sure did. You going to save any for me?"

The boy held up the bag. "Better take some now."

Rosemary held up the striped car. "Thanks for the advice, Reilly." She smiled at Brick. "You two have a wonderful day together." She set the other two cars on the shelf of baseballs and walked away.

"Okay, buddy," Brick said, scooping up the two cars Rosemary had left behind and wedging them into the glove. "Let's pay for this stuff so we can go home and hit some balls."

CHAPTER

43

Sam walked into the kitchen and frowned at her mother. "Why doesn't Dad ever pack his own lunch?"

Ellie tore off three squares of wax paper and lined them up across the counter. "Why should he do that?" she said, dropping a slice of Wonder bread on each square of paper. "Do you have any idea how hard your father works?"

"You work hard, too. Nobody's making your lunch."

Ellie slapped two slices of bologna on each slice of bread. "I see you've been reading more of *The Feminine Mystery*. Why does Emma stock that horrible thing?"

"Feminine *Mystique,* you mean," Sam said. "It's French."

Ellie pointed to the napkin holder. "Hand me three of those, pronto," she said. "That's Spanish."

"You should read it, Mom," Sam said, folding the napkins into triangles. "It's opening my mind. Aunt Emma says I have a lot of options in the world, and it's important to know about them. Says not every girl who grows up in Erietown has to spend all her life in Erietown. She also thinks it's important not to marry the first man who comes along."

"Uh-huh," Ellie said, picking up a butter knife and smearing yellow mustard on the circles of bologna. "Emma is forty-three and never married. Exactly what man is she waiting for?"

Sam peeled the plastic off a slice of American cheese and nibbled a corner. "She likes being independent. She has her own newsstand, and she never has to cook for anyone but herself unless she wants to. She's a modern woman."

"Give me that," Ellie said, grabbing the cheese. "I have just enough for your father's sandwiches."

Sam finished each sandwich with a slice of bread and wrapped them in the paper. "Dad eats the same thing every day. A little variety would be nice."

Ellie stacked the wrapped sandwiches in the lunch pail. "His *variety* is the Hostess fruit pie. Now go down to Emma Jane's and get him one. You got him cherry yesterday, so maybe apple."

"Aunt Emma says she's never seen Dad buy pie for his own lunch. That's not right, Mom."

Ellie reached into the pocket of her apron and slid a quarter and a dime across the counter. "Just go get the pie, Sam. And don't take forever this time. It's already after seven, and I need you to help Reilly with his spelling list."

"He hates spelling."

"Which is why you're going to help him practice." Ellie reached up and, with both hands, pushed Sam's hair away from her face. "My smart girl," she said. "Best speller in the class. Just like your mom used to be."

Sam took a step back. "I'm the only almost-thirteen-year-old girl I know who has to help her runt of a little brother with his homework." She shoved the change into her jeans pocket and walked out the door.

Ellie walked out behind her and pretended to deadhead the withering daffodils as she watched her daughter make her way down Route 20. A trucker honked his horn and catcalled at Sam, but she just raised her head higher and kept walking.

"Good for you, Sam," Ellie said. She'd never felt that confident a day in her life.

She thought of what she'd said to Sam about Emma Dunham and immediately felt guilty. She was good for Sam, and God knows Emma hadn't had an easy time of it. Emma was only sixteen when she inherited the West End News, after her father dropped dead at work. Danny Dunham's last morning had begun like every other morning. He unlocked the store door at 5:45 A.M., picked up the two stacks of morning newspapers tied with twine, and started sliding them into the front racks.

Dean Gayley, the barber next door, said he walked into the store to buy a paper. "Hey, Dean," Danny said, and collapsed on the floor. By the time the ambulance arrived, Danny was as gray as the newspapers scattered all around him.

Emma's mother never stepped foot in the store again, blaming it for his death. Emma was their only child, and she couldn't bear the thought of selling the place her father had called their second home. She dropped out of school to keep the store running. Twenty-seven years later, it was still the most popular newsstand in Erietown.

Ellie seldom visited the store, but Sam stopped in every day, even when Brick had a day off and didn't need a pie for his lunch pail. "We just talk, Mom," Sam explained. "About life and all. And she lets me read her books for free."

"Well, that's good, Sam," Ellie said. "I'm glad you've found a woman who knows about life."

"That's not what I mean, Mom. Aunt Emma has a job. She's in charge of things. Like I want to be someday."

Who do you think keeps this house running? Ellie wanted to say. *Who changes your sheets every week, and makes sure you always have clean underwear in your drawers? When you walk in after school and say the house smells so pretty, who do you think does that?* All of it unpaid work, which would not impress her daughter.

Whenever Sam talked about her future, Ellie heard: *I don't want to be my mother.* "Can't blame you for that, kid," Ellie said as she strolled back up the driveway. "I'm tired of being me, too."

She walked back into the house and thought about how she'd been raised to believe the Catholics got it wrong, praying to the Virgin Mary. "A sacrilege," Grandma explained. "We pray to God and his Holy Son." Ellie had accepted that without question when she was young, but it was harder now. She had far more in common with Mary, the unwed mother. "What she went through," Ellie once said to Mardee, a fellow Presbyterian. "She didn't have to deal with just shame, like I did. She had to flee to save the life of her son." In her own life, it was women who sustained her. All those coffee hours, the camaraderie of canasta, the support she got at church. She still prayed to God and talked to Jesus, but Mary knew her heart.

Ellie reached under the sofa cushion and pulled out the folded newspaper section. Every Thursday, she checked the list of want ads under "Female." She did not know how to type, so secretary was out. Mrs. Williams had taught her years ago how to work a cash register, but she didn't want Sam to make the obvious contrast between store owner Emma Dunham and her mother the cashier.

"It's out there," she said, sliding her finger slowly down the column of job listings. "One of these days, Mary and I will find the perfect job for Ellie Fetters McGinty."

CHAPTER

44

Rosemary was pushing Paull in the swing when she noticed another shadow beside hers in the sand.

"Weee," she said, ignoring Brick.

"Weee," Paull shouted as the swing moved forward.

"Roe."

She pressed her fingers against Paull's back and pushed again. "Hey, Brick," she said, still looking straight ahead. "I didn't know you were here."

"Pooosh," Paull said, kicking his feet in the air. "Pooosh, Mama."

She stopped the swing and pulled him out, propping him on her hip before turning to face Brick. "Pooh-bear, this is—" She raised her eyebrows and cocked her head at Brick.

"Brick," he said, staring at the boy.

"Bik," Paull said, curling into his mother.

Rosemary stroked his hair as she looked at Brick. "That's right, Paullie. Brick."

Brick studied the boy's face. He could have been Reilly at that age. "And what's your name, little man?"

"Paw," the boy said softly, glancing at him before burrowing into his mother's neck.

"Do you want to hold him?" Paull's fingers dug into Rosemary's T-shirt. "It's okay, sweetie," she said, uncurling his hands. "He won't hurt you."

"No, that's okay. I don't need to—"

"Yeah, you do," she said. "You do need to hold him." She pried Paull off her and tried to hand him to Brick. Paull wriggled to face her. "Nooo," he wailed.

"Roe, he doesn't—"

"Paullie, it's okay. He's a nice man."

"No, Mama." Paull started to cry, his arms clinging to her. "Mama. Mama."

"Oh, for God's sake," she said, wrapping her arms around him. "You're not making a very good first impression, Pooh."

Paull wrapped his arms around his mother's neck and stopped crying as quickly as he'd started. "It might help if you smile," Rosemary said to Brick.

"Roe, this is a lot to take in."

She kissed Paull's cheek and said nothing. Brick reached into his pocket and pulled out a Matchbox car. Rosemary recognized it immediately. It was one of the cars she'd left behind on the shelf the day she ran into Brick and Reilly in the toy department. Paull was suddenly riveted.

"Here," Brick said, handing him the mustard-yellow sedan. "This is a 1966 Opel Diplomat."

"Car," Paull said, reaching for it. "Car."

Brick smiled for the first time. "That's right." He looked at Rosemary. "He was never a mistake, was he?"

She lowered Paull to the ground. "You want to play in the sandbox, Pooh?" He ran toward it, shouting, "San! San!"

She looked at Brick. "What were you saying?"

"You getting pregnant. That wasn't a mistake. You meant to."

"I'm not going to stand here and have you accuse me of—"

"I'm not accusing you. I'm just acknowledging what we both know."

"What does it matter?" she said, pointing to Paull, who was picking up handfuls of sand and letting it run through his fingers. "He's here. He's perfect."

"I didn't know," he said, watching Paull. "I didn't know he existed. If I had, I would have helped out sooner." Rosemary reached for his hand. "No," he said, pushing it away. "I'm not going back to that. I'm here to let you know what I'll do for him."

"What does that mean?"

"I get paid three hundred and sixty-seven dollars and twenty cents every two weeks. I'll give you fifty dollars every other Friday."

"Fifty?"

Brick nodded. "I'll stick it in an envelope and—" He looked at the parking lot and squinted. "You're driving that Fairlane now?"

She nodded. "It was Vinny Sardelli's. He sold it to me when he bought a new car."

"Leave it unlocked at Sardelli's, in the back. I'll stick the money under the driver's seat every other Friday after work."

"You could just come in and—"

"No," he said. "I'm never going into Sardelli's again. I don't do that anymore."

"Sounds like you've made a lot of promises to Ellie," she said. "Does this mean you don't want to get to know your son?"

"Bik!" Paull yelled, waving his Matchbox car. "Bik, car! Car!"

Brick waved at him. "He's a cute boy."

"That's not what I asked."

He reached into his pocket and pulled out the other diecast car that Rosemary had left behind in the store that day. "This is for him," he said, handing it to her. "We've got some savings. I've got it, I mean. In the bank. For the kids' college . . ." His voice trailed off, and for a moment Rosemary thought he was about to change his mind.

"I'll withdraw some of it," he said. "I'll give you five hundred dollars so you've got an emergency fund." He nodded toward Paull. "For him. Just in case."

"What about *him*?" she said, pointing to Paull. "What do I tell him about his father? He's going to ask, you know. He's going to want to know his daddy."

Brick pulled out his keys from his other pocket. "Well, then, I suggest you go find him one."

CHAPTER

45

Brick pulled on his softball pants and smiled at Ellie, who was standing on the other side of the bed. "I'm so glad you and the kids are coming," he said. "If we win this one, we go to state."

Ellie walked over to the dresser and picked up the can of Aqua Net. "The kids are excited. I heard Reilly tell Sam at breakfast that 'Daddy is going to hit a home run.'"

"Hah," Brick said, lacing up his sneakers. "Pressure." He walked up behind her and wrapped his arms around her waist. "Thanks, Pint," he said, kissing her neck. "Thanks for coming."

They looked at their entwined reflection in the mirror. "Twelve years of marriage already," Ellie said, patting his arms. "And two kids, one of them about to become a teenager. Hard to believe, isn't it?"

Brick kissed her neck. "If she's anything like her mother was at her age, we'll have to lock her up until she goes to college."

Ellie reached behind her and cupped Brick's groin. "If she's anything like her mother now, you mean." He caught his breath, and she smiled, obviously pleased with herself. "C'mon, you. We have to get going if you want to warm up before the game."

Sam and Reilly were already sitting in the backseat, bubbling with nonstop chatter. "Daddy," Reilly said, "I told Billy Kleshinski that you're going to hit three home runs tonight."

Brick laughed and looked at Ellie. "Whoa, buddy. I thought it was one home run."

"I changed my mind."

The softball game was down in the harbor, at Smitty Field. They were playing Flannery's. "Mick versus mick," Murph had joked at practice last week. "All of us in dago town, not a dago in sight."

Brick pulled into the parking lot and looked in his rearview mirror. "All right, you two. Keep an eye on your mother."

"Daaaad," Sam said, rolling her eyes. He winked at her and stepped out of the car to get his cleats from the trunk. He sat on the side of the driver's seat to lace them, and when he stood up, Sam grabbed his sneakers out of his hand.

"Don't do anything different, Dad," she said, raising the sneakers over her head. "It's bad luck. I do this." She walked to the trunk, threw the sneakers into his duffel, and pulled out two packs of Wrigley's spearmint gum. "One stick per inning," she said, waving them at him. "Don't forget to change out before you run back into right field."

Brick swiped the packs out of her hands and stuck them in his back pocket. "Yes, ma'am."

Sam pointed to the field. "You have to walk in front of us. We'll be on our usual bench in the stands."

"Okay, boss," he said, walking backward and winking at Ellie. "See you at the game."

It was the seventh inning. Brick was at bat, digging the toe of his back foot into the dirt as he prepared to hit that third home run for Reilly. He was sweaty and on fire, feeling none of the usual fatigue that made his joints throb this late in the game.

The first pitch hit the plate.

"Ball!"

"Jesus, Jimmy," Brick growled over his shoulder to the ump. "You don't have to scream in my ear."

"Touchy, touchy," Jimmy Kelly said. "Just keep your eye on the ball, Brickie."

Brick swung.

"Strike!"

Flannery's fans cheered.

"C'mon, Pop!" Sam yelled. "Yeah, Pop!" Reilly echoed.

He heard a few laughs from the bench. "You heard 'em, Pop," Benny Walsh yelled. "Blow it out of here, Brick."

That's when he heard it.

"Bik!" the little boy yelled. "Bik!"

He turned to look.

"Strike two!"

She was sitting two rows behind his family, with Paull on her lap. Sitting there shading her eyes with a smile on her face, the breeze blowing her hair back as she whispered into Paull's ear. She was encouraging him to yell.

Their eyes met just long enough to wipe that smile off her face. He felt the ball sail past his face.

"Steeee-rike three!"

"What the fuck, Brick?" Benny Walsh yelled from the bench. Brick marched straight for Benny, his right hand clenching the bat. Murph jumped up and pressed his palms against Brick's chest. "He's just kidding, Brick. You've got two homers. We're two up, and Slattery's next. We're good. We're good."

Brick's temples were throbbing, his hand still gripping the bat.

"Brick."

He turned to look at Ellie, who was standing by the bench, her smile nervous. "The kids, honey."

"Bik! Bik! Car! Car!"

Ellie turned to look at the little boy waving the car in the air. "Isn't that cute? I think he's calling your name."

Brick dropped the bat. "El, maybe you should go. Take the kids and just go. I let Reilly down."

She looked at him and laughed. "Are you nuts? Have you seen the look on your son's face? He can't stop smiling. He's yelled himself hoarse cheering for you." She stopped smiling. "Brick? What is it?"

Suddenly, the Mickey's fans were on their feet. Slattery had just hit a line drive. Ellie pointed at the fans. "See what I mean? Look at him. Reilly's face."

Brick pulled the brim of his hat lower over his eyes and looked up at the stands. Rosemary was gone.

CHAPTER

46

Rosemary pulled down the tab on the Stroh's, her back to the bar as she shouted at Vinny Sardelli. "I heard you the first time," she said, staring at the foam as it rose in the tilted glass. "There's somebody who wants to see me. Tell him to pull up a stool."

When Vinny didn't respond, she turned to look at him. "What the hell's the matter with you? You look like you've seen a ghost."

He nodded sideways, toward the front door. "I think he means business, Rosie. Wouldn't even shake my hand."

Rosemary set the beer in front of the customer and looked at the exit. "Brick."

Vinny moved closer to her. "He hasn't been here in ages."

She turned to look at Vinny. "What?"

"I said, he hasn't been here in years. Just saw his picture in the paper. His softball team won the tournament. Flannery's."

"Mickey's," she said.

"What?"

She untied the apron around her waist. "He plays for Mickey's."

"Oh," Vinny said, staring at her. "Sure. Mickey's."

"I'll be back in a little bit," she said, smoothing her blouse.

Vinny put his hand on her shoulder. "You need any help?"

"No," she said, running her fingers through her hair. "I'm fine." She nodded toward the back door, and Brick walked out.

Rosemary stopped at the door and took a deep breath before pushing it open. He was standing by his car, smoking a cigarette.

"Hey," she said, as she walked toward him. "What brings you here for all the world to see?"

He walked toward her and grabbed her arm. She tried to pull away. "Ow, let go of me."

"Why were you there?"

She tried again to yank her arm away. "I said, let go of me. That hurts."

He dropped her arm. "Sorry," he said, stepping away. "Why were you at the game?"

"Wow," she said, rubbing her arm. "Look what it takes to get an apology from Brick McGinty." She shook her hair from her face and put her hand on her hip. "I read about it in the paper. About the game. I knew it was a big one. And I told you I wanted our son to know his father."

"And I told you that was never happening."

"Well, maybe you aren't calling all the shots anymore."

He moved toward her again and raised his hand. Rosemary tilted her head back and pointed to her chin. "Go ahead, Brick. Hit me."

He shook his head and lowered his hand. "I promised Ellie."

She shook her head. "More promises for poor Ellie." Her eyes widened. "Wait a minute. You promised Ellie what? Something about me? She knows?"

Brick thrust his hands into his pockets. "I promised her I'd never be like my father."

She lowered her chin. "Brick, do you have any idea how

hard it's going to be for Paullie after he starts school? He'll be the only kid in his class without a father. I grew up without a father. You never stop thinking there's something wrong with you."

Brick started jingling the coins in his pocket. "I've been giving you a hundred bucks a month for him, for months now. I gave you five hundred dollars of my kids' college money. And then you show up and practically sit right next to them. I'm done."

She crossed her arms against her chest. "You're done? What if I'm not? What if Paullie and I keep showing up until you agree to be a father to him, too? Maybe it's time Paullie met his brother. His sister. Poor Paullie. He was just as excited as they were at your game. He was cheering for his daddy, too."

"You stay away from my family."

"I know where you live," she said, her face defiant. "On Route Twenty. Erie Street. I've driven past your house a dozen times. You have a porch swing. And one of those netted backstops on the side of your house. For your other son."

Brick stepped close enough for her to smell the cigarette on his breath. "If you ever come anywhere near my family again, you'll never get another cent from me."

"Fuck your money, Brick," she said. "Fuck you and your perfect family that has no idea what you've been up to."

She walked back to the bar entrance and turned to look at him. He was wiping his forehead with his handkerchief. She waited until he had stuffed it into his back pocket and pulled open his car door.

"Hey, Brick," she yelled. "See you soon." She slammed the bar door and pressed her back against it as she slid to the floor.

CHAPTER

47

Rosemary opened her car door and rummaged under the front seat.

No envelope. Sixth week in a row.

She climbed into the car and pulled the door shut. "So that's that," she said in the darkness. She wrapped her arms around the steering wheel and laid her head on the backs of her hands. "Oh, God, Paullie."

The savings Brick had given her was gone. She had spent all of it on Paull. His first pair of real shoes, a winter jacket and boots, and two bags of clothes from size 2 to 6. She got him fun stuff, too, in a single shopping spree. A Matchbox carrying case and a dozen cars. An Etch-A-Sketch. A two-wheel bike for the future. A baseball glove and bat like the ones she'd seen Brick pick out for Reilly.

"Honey, he's a little young for some of this stuff," Aunt Lizzie had said after Rosemary rolled the bike into the garage. "Couldn't some of this have waited?"

"He's going to be bigger before we know it," Rosemary said, grinning as Paull kicked the tire. "I want him to have the same things that other little boys his age have. Like his brother has."

It was a mistake to take Paull to Brick's game. What was she thinking? And why did she tell Aunt Lizzie about it? "I hate him," Rosemary had told her that night. "I never want to see him again, ever."

"Oh, Rosie," Aunt Lizzie had said, "I wish I could believe you, but you are obsessed with this man. You're skin and bones, your eyes are sunken in, and your hair's falling out. When's the last time you even had a full night's sleep?"

"Aunt Lizzie, I'm barely holding it together here. Please don't add to this. Please don't make me feel worse than I do."

Rosemary reached up to adjust the rearview mirror and look at her face. Aunt Lizzie was right. She was a ghost, as hollowed out inside as she looked on the outside. "You can't keep living like this," Rosemary said to the mirror. "You're almost thirty. You're all used up. You need a plan."

She reached into her purse and pulled out her wallet. Every photo sleeve held pictures of Paull. She flipped through them slowly, pausing at the photo on his first birthday. She traced her finger along the top of his head, as if trying to push back the lock of hair in his eye. That bright red hair.

She knew what it was like to grow up without a father. The longing. All the guilt. Jesus, the guilt, that if she'd only been a better daughter, her father would have stayed. She could never give her son the family he deserved. She flipped to the photo of Paull with Aunt Lizzie and Uncle Danny. He was sandwiched between them on their porch glider, their arms entwined behind him. Lizzie's other hand rested on Paullie's thigh. She looked so proud of him, and so possessive.

Rosemary had appreciated her aunt's willingness to help take care of Paullie from day one, but lately Rosemary was feeling more jealous than grateful. He spent more time with Aunt Lizzie, who, unlike Rosemary, didn't have to work, and their daily rhythm of camaraderie made Rosemary feel increasingly unnecessary. Recently, Aunt Lizzie had developed a habit of correcting Rosemary in her interactions with Paull, always ending with the word "now," which felt like code for "while you were gone." Paullie wants his hot dog split length-wise *now*. Paullie likes to pour the Mr. Bubble himself for his bath *now*. Paullie prefers his red sneakers *now*.

Paullie preferred Aunt Lizzie for comfort, too. Rosemary thought about how he'd fallen down in the driveway last Saturday and scraped his knees. "Oh, Paullie," Rosemary had said, opening her arms wide as she walked toward him. He'd run past her, into Aunt Lizzie's arms.

"You are his family," she said to the photo of her aunt and uncle with Paullie, "but you are not his parents." She stared at her son's face and tried to imagine him at age four, age eight, age ten. The older Paullie grew, the more he would need a father in his life. It had been hard enough for her, a girl, to grow up fatherless. Being fatherless could ruin Paullie. How would he learn to be a man?

She tucked the wallet into her purse and started the car. She knew what she had to do.

Tomorrow. She'd do it tomorrow.

CHAPTER

48

Sam had just started to doze on the sofa when she heard the banging on their door.

"I know you're in there!"

Sam jumped off the couch, disoriented.

Bam. Bam. Bam. "Answer the door!"

Someone was knocking at the wrong door.

Sam stood up and walked to the window. The woman, unaware of her, ran her fingers through her bleached hair, revealing a canal of dark roots. A little boy straddled her left hip, his legs locked around her as he fidgeted with a small toy. The woman hoisted him higher and pounded her fist again, louder this time, her arm chopping the air like an ax as she rattled the screen door's aluminum frame.

Bam. Bam. Bam.

Sam stepped away to face the archway of the dining room. She watched the woman's shadow bob across the fake bricks of the linoleum floor. Only bad news came to the front door. Cops. Mailmen with registered letters. Army chaplains with frozen faces that made Mrs. Rosario and Mrs. Davis scream for Jesus.

No friend knocked on the McGintys' front door.

Bam. Bam. Bam.

"All *right*," Sam yelled. She pushed back sweaty bangs from her forehead and walked over to the TV set flickering in the corner. Lucy Ricardo was locked in the walk-in freezer, her hair a ridge of icicles as she wailed through the tiny, frosted window. Sam shook her head. How could one woman get in so much trouble? Ricky would be furious again. And Lucy would be scared of him, as always. Was there a single wife in America who wasn't afraid of her husband? That's what Sam wanted to know.

She looked over her shoulder and turned up the volume on the TV to let the stranger understand the magnitude of her intrusion before shutting it off. She walked into the dining room and smiled through the screen at the little boy.

"Hi," she said to the child.

The boy squealed and burrowed his face into his mother's shoulder. He was two, two and a half tops, she figured. Sam McGinty was the most popular babysitter in the neighborhood. She knew ages.

"Shh," the woman said, jostling him a little higher on her hip. She combed her fingers through his red hair, which was sticky from the heat. He peeked out at Sam, and she tried not to giggle at how his hair stood straight up, like an exclamation mark on the top of his head.

Sam narrowed her eyes and looked at him harder. He was sucking on the rear wheels of a diecast car. Green with white stripes. A Johnny Lightning Chevy Camaro, just like Reilly's.

The woman cleared her throat. "Is your mother home?"

Sam nodded.

"Well, would you *get* her?"

Sam raised her chin an inch, and waited for the "please."

"Now?"

"Oh. Sure," Sam said, acting as if the thought had never occurred to her. She flashed an adolescent's smile of victory. She had made her ask twice.

Sam pushed open the screen door. "Come on in."

The woman brushed past Sam and stopped in front of the square floor fan humming on high. The breeze parted the hem of her wrap dress, exposing her long pale thighs. She made no effort to smooth her skirt back into place. Her eyes darted around the walls, landing on the column of photos hanging to the right of the front door. Sam's seventh-grade portrait was on top, hanging over the family picture taken four years ago at the union Christmas party. Reilly's kindergarten picture was on the bottom. His picture was larger than Sam's, and bigger than the family portrait, too, if you counted the frame, which Sam always did.

The woman took a step closer and studied the McGinty family picture, which gave Sam time to study her. She was taller than Sam. At least five feet eight, she guessed, even in her flat, strappy sandals. Big boobs, too, which Sam immediately told herself nobody could blame her for noticing since the woman's blouse was cut just south of Nashville, as her mother was bound to note later.

Sam looked down at the woman's red toenails and curled her own dusty toes into the beds of her flip-flops. "I'll go get Mom," she said. "She's out back hanging laundry." Sam started to walk to the kitchen, but paused to look again at the woman. "What's your name, by the way?"

The stranger raised her eyebrows and shifted the child higher on her hip. "None of your business," she said, but then she smiled. "Rosemary. You tell your mother Rosemary is here." She cupped her son's face with her hand and kissed the boy's cheek. "Rosemary and Paull. Paull-two-els."

"Paull-two-els," Sam said, noticing now that the woman's hand was trembling. "Wow. That's just like my dad's middle name."

"Yeah," the woman said. "I know."

Sam had never heard her mother talk about any Rosemary, and her mother talked about everybody to Sam, but she decided not to press her luck with Miss None of Your Business and ask for a last name. She backed out of the room and into the sweltering kitchen filling with the smell of stuffed peppers bubbling in the oven. She pushed open the screen door and let it slam behind her.

It took a moment for Sam to spot her mother's scuffed Keds under the white sheets billowing on the line. Ellie was standing on tiptoe, clipping her husband's softball uniform to the clothesline. Sam cleared her throat as she approached her mother. "Mom."

Ellie held up Brick's softball pants. "Look at these knees," she said. "No matter what I do, I can't get these stains out anymore."

"He's just gonna get 'em dirty again anyway," Sam said. "It's post-tournament play. What difference does it make?"

Her mother pegged the pants to the line. "Every person who sees your father's pants on that field is thinking, *What kind of wife can't get grass stains out of her husband's knees?*"

Sam thought that sounded a lot more like her dad than any fan at a ball game, but she kept that to herself. Ever since her father had come home six weeks ago and announced they were moving, only her mother was allowed to criticize Brick McGinty.

"Mom. There's someone here to see you."

"What?" Ellie said, leaning over the clothes basket to pull out a wad of wet socks. "Who is it? It's practically suppertime."

"Some lady named Rosemary. She's got a little boy with her, too."

The socks fell to the ground. Ellie looked down at the grass but didn't move to retrieve them. Sam scooped them up and held them out to her mother. Ellie dug her fingers into her hips and moved her feet apart, as if bracing for a blow. "*Who did you say?*"

"Rosemary," Sam said, reaching into the clothespin bag and pinning the socks to the line. "And a little boy she called Paull."

Ellie blinked rapidly as she looked at her daughter. She reached up to her beehive and started pushing at bobby pins. Sam noticed that her mother's hands were shaking. She held her breath, and waited.

Ellie locked eyes with Sam. "Well, I'd better go in and talk to this Rosemary." She headed for the side door, untying her apron as she walked. "Here," she said, tossing it over her shoulder. Sam caught the apron and followed her mother to the side of the house. She stayed in the driveway as Ellie walked up the stairs and paused at the top, slowly pulling open the door.

"You stay out here, Sam," Ellie said. "If Reilly comes back, keep him out here, too."

Ellie stepped inside. Her eyes locked with Sam's as she eased the door shut.

CHAPTER

49

Brick threw his lunch pail through the open window of his car and looked up at the sky. A few clouds, a soft breeze. His favorite kind of evening. Almost made him wish the tournament wasn't over.

His team had finished second in the state, losing to Rosetti's Bar and Grill in Youngstown. He blamed himself for that. He'd hit only one home run in that game. Too much shit on his mind. He'd talked Ellie into staying home with the kids. That had thrown him off. He missed hearing the kids' voices in the stands cheering for "Pop-o," but he'd been on constant lookout for another visit from Rosemary. Her last words to him made his stomach roil every time he thought of them: "See you soon."

Tonight, though, on the drive home, he was feeling a sense of relief. The tournament was over, and now they just played for fun. One of the guys had bragged in the locker room last week that he was dating the blonde at the bar at Sardelli's. He was in the clear. Everybody was moving on.

He should never have paid that money to Rosemary. She had no proof that kid was his, and Brick McGinty was hardly the only mick with red hair in Erietown. He was still paying for his stupidity, working so much overtime his body ached in places he didn't know he had.

He drove past Lawson's and did a double take at the blinking Schlitz sign. Hell, why not? Why should Ellie always have to pick it up? He made a U-turn and pulled into the parking lot.

He didn't notice the cashier until she started chirping about what he was buying. "Chips and dip? Havin' a party, Brick?"

His scowl evaporated at the sight of their old neighbor. "Margie? When did you start working here?"

Margie Grandin smiled as she stuffed the bag of Ruffles and Lawson's onion dip into a bag. "After Bill died, we moved, as you know. Sold the dry cleaners two years ago. I've got too much time on my hands."

He searched his mind for the name of her daughter, the one he'd ordered Sam to drop as a friend. "How's your girl?" he said.

"Jenny?" she said. "Mouthy as her father used to be, that one. We spoiled her too much."

"It's the age, Margie. Our Sam is driving her mother crazy."

She held up another bag. "You want your six-packs in here?" He shook his head. "Nah. I got 'em." The chips and dip were a bribe, really, for Reilly. Maybe he'd sit and watch a little bit of the Indians game with his old man. Brick promised himself to be more patient this time with his son. What boy doesn't like baseball?

He took his time driving home. The evening breeze was getting cooler, and the cicadas were back, crooning in the night. It wouldn't be long before Ellie's favorite season was here. *Let's plan a drive to Pennsylvania when the leaves change,* he'd tell her tonight. She'll love that.

He turned on the radio and listened to Herb Score talk about the Indians' lineup. He turned onto Erie Street and shook his head at the sight of so many semitrucks still making their way east. God, he hated living on Route 20. Pretty soon, they'd have enough money to move. Another wave of relief loosened his grip on the wheel. He was keeping track in the little notebook in his duffel. Five more Saturdays would replace all the money he had taken out of the kids' college account. Ellie would never know.

He approached the Kleshinskis' house, which was four doors away from the McGintys'. Lenny was sitting on the porch steps reading a book. That was one boy he'd never have to worry about with Sam. They were more like siblings. Ruby, a tall and ample woman, stood behind her son, yelled through cupped hands at the two younger boys wrestling in the yard. He heard her shout "dammit to hell" and laughed.

He returned her wave, then looked straight ahead as life fell apart in slow motion.

His fingers went numb on the wheel as his head filled with the *woomph-woomph, woomph-woomph* of his pounding heart. He couldn't breathe.

He slowed his car to a crawl and paused at the lip of their driveway.

Her Fairlane was parked in front of their home, and she wasn't in it.

CHAPTER

50

S am heard the sound of crunching cinders in the driveway and waved to her father as she stepped out of the way. He didn't look at her when he pulled to a stop.

This was weird, her father's car stopping here next to the steps. He always drove straight to the back of the house after work. Brick's eyes were glued to the rearview mirror. She followed his gaze to the blue car parked in front of their house.

She rubbed her bare arms as she walked to her father's open window. "Hi, Dad."

Brick turned off the car. The engine clacked and clattered, getting in the last word before falling silent. She stepped back as he opened the door and slowly dropped one foot to the ground, then reached up to grab the roof to pull himself out. He was fresh from the shower at work. His hair was combed into shiny grooves, and he smelled like he always did at 4:30 in the afternoon. Sam breathed in the potion of Dial, Brylcreem, and Old Spice.

"Where's your mother?" he said, facing the street.

"Inside," she said. "We got company. Rosemary and Paull." *With-two-els,* she thought she should add, but the look in his eyes warned her off.

Brick turned to look at her. "How do you know her name?"

"I answered the door and let her in. Mom was in the back hanging laundry."

"She talked to you?"

Sam shrugged. "Not much, really. She isn't very friendly."

Brick inhaled deeply, and started rocking on his heels. "Where's your brother?" he said, shoving his hand into his pocket.

"He's at the Kleshinskis'," she said. "He's having supper there. Mom told him to be home by dark."

Brick looked out at the car in front of their house again, and then over at Sam. He pulled his hand out of his pocket and slid a single finger across her forehead, brushing a wisp of hair from her eyes. "You stay out here," he said. "Keep your brother out here, too, if he comes home."

Sam nodded, and her father climbed the stairs and pushed through the screen door. "Dad," she said, "who is Ro—" He slammed the big door behind him. Sam stared at the peeling strips of gunmetal gray paint. They never closed the big door in summer.

She sat down on the bottom step and picked the dirt out from between her toes. It had never occurred to her to paint her toenails. She stretched out her tanned legs and heard her mother's regular refrain in her head: *What I wouldn't give for those long legs.* Her mom was always imagining her new and improved life with body parts from her daughter. What she "wouldn't give" for Sam's hair, Sam's waist, Sam's five feet, seven inches. Sam looked in the mirror and saw nothing but problems. Ellie looked at her daughter and saw God's second thoughts.

She rubbed her arms again, and for the first time in years thought about that other knock on their front door. She had been a little girl then, sitting on their couch alone and waiting for her father to come home. "A man's going to have an envelope for Daddy," her mother had told Sam before she left with Reilly. "I want you to stay here and be with him."

Sam remembered sitting nervously on the sofa, staring at the clock as she counted down the minutes until her father came home. The man at the door was a deputy. Her father stood in the kitchen crying, telling Sam, "Mommy doesn't love me anymore."

She had been Reilly's age when her mother left her alone to wait for her father, to hold him as he sobbed. Maybe that was why she had always felt so protective of Reilly. Who does that to a little kid?

She walked around to the front porch, tiptoed up the steps, and sat cross-legged next to the screen door. She leaned in to hear over the din of traffic. "Ellie," she heard her father say. "Ellie. She doesn't know what she's talking about."

Rosemary was yelling. "A man's got responsibilities. He's as much your son as that boy on that wall."

The screen door rattled with a loud thump. Sam jumped up and ran down the stairs before turning around to look. The little boy's face was pressed against the screen, his hands spread like bat wings as he howled, "Bik. Bik."

Sam stared at Paull. *Pick him up,* she thought. *Somebody, pick him up.* She tried counting to ten, but by six she couldn't wait any longer. She went up the stairs and opened the door just wide enough to pick him up. She reached back and pulled the big door shut.

"C'mon, Paull-two-els," she said as she carried him toward the stairs. He was whimpering, instead of crying, and he wrapped his arms and legs around her. "You're a little monkey," she said, cupping her hand around his sweaty head and sitting down on the top step. She started rocking as she sang a made-up song about little boy Paull on a pony named Peter. The third time she sang it, he hummed along through sniffles. By the fourth time, he was sound asleep, straddling her chest.

She kissed the top of his head. "Oh, Paull-two-els," she whispered. "Try to remember this part of today, instead." She leaned against the banister, her hand still on his head as she closed her eyes and attempted to focus on the slowing buzz of evening traffic. Her shirt was soaked with sweat, but she didn't dare move him. She started to time her breaths to the heave of the boy's back under her hand, her eyes drooping.

The streetlights had clicked on by the time the door opened and Rosemary shook Sam awake. "Give me my boy," she said, pulling Paull out of Sam's arms. Sam felt a rush of cold air against her damp chest. She blinked and looked up. The woman's hair was a wild cloud around her face, which was pale with black circles of mascara pooling under her eyes. *Like a ghost,* Sam thought.

Paull started to cry as Rosemary marched with him to her car. "Shhh, shhh," she said, patting his back. "Mommy's here."

"You're *welcome,*" Sam shouted.

Rosemary opened the passenger side of her car and leaned in to drop Paull into the seat. She walked around the front of the car and yanked open the driver's door with a force that made her drop her purse.

"God*damm*it," she yelled.

Sam saw her start grabbing the scattered contents from the street. Normally, she would jump up to help, but she'd already picked sides.

The woman slid behind the wheel and slammed her door shut. The engine growled, and stopped. Paull started to cry. Rosemary turned the key again. Nothing. "Come *on,*" she yelled, turning the key in the ignition again. Nothing.

Sam was about to cock her head and smile until she saw the look on Rosemary's face. She was terrified. Sam looked away.

Rosemary turned the key again. This time, the engine caught and Rosemary peeled off into the night.

Sam counted to a hundred before she stood up. She looked

back at the screen door. The house was dark, and silent. She walked to the curb and spotted something metal gleaming under the streetlight. She wrapped her fingers around a silver lighter. She flipped it over in her palm and read the inscription: LOVE, PINT.

Sam looked at the house. Still dark. She tucked the lighter into her shirt pocket and tried not to think about what it meant. She had just started to stand when her knees buckled from a sudden force against her back.

"Gotcha!" her brother said.

"Reilly," she yelled, jumping back onto the curb. "You scared the shit out of me."

He laughed again. "Why's the back door locked?"

Sam grabbed him and spun him around so that his back pressed against her stomach. She pulled him in tight and slapped her hand over his mouth.

"Shut up, Reilly," she said, wrapping her arms around him. "Just this once. Shut. Up."

CHAPTER

51

If her husband hadn't looked so afraid, maybe Ellie could have told herself for a little while longer that the red-haired boy in the arms of the woman standing in her dining room was not Brick's child.

As soon as Brick walked into the room, though, Ellie knew.

"Ellie," he said, softly, walking toward her.

She held up her hand. "No."

"Ellie," he said, more loudly.

"No, Brick." She closed her eyes and shook her head. "No. *No.*"

The little boy started to cry. Rosemary shifted him on her hip. "Not now, Paullie," she said. "Please, not now." Paull cried louder and tried to wriggle out of her arms. He started to fall, and Ellie rushed forward, catching him.

"There you go, sweetie," Ellie said, lowering him to the floor.

She looked up at Rosemary. "Oh," Ellie said, as if she'd forgotten Rosemary was there. She looked at Brick. His eyes were wide with terror. She'd seen that face only once before, after he'd almost hit her.

"El."

She felt suddenly calm, as if someone had flipped a switch and turned off something inside her. Brick pulled out his handkerchief and handed it to her. "Here, honey," he said. "For your nose." Ellie unfolded it, dragged it across her face, and threw it to the floor.

Paull was standing at Rosemary's feet, whimpering. Ellie watched as he walked toward the door and pressed his hands against the screen, wailing.

"Oh, Brick," Ellie said. "Look what you've done."

Rosemary cleared her throat. "I just wanted to ask—"

"Shut up, Roe," Brick said.

"No, Brick," Ellie said. "Let her finish. Let *Roe* finish."

"I wouldn't have come," Rosemary said. "I would have stayed away if he hadn't stopped helping me with Paull."

Ellie started blinking. "What? What do you mean?" She looked at Brick. "Have you been living with them, too?"

"No. Absolutely not."

"What does she mean, then?"

"What I mean," Rosemary said, "is that he stopped giving me money to help raise our son."

Ellie stared at her. "Oh my God. All that overtime." She looked at Brick. "For our new house, you said. To give our kids a better life. It was all a lie."

"Ellie," Brick said, his voice breaking. "Ellie. She doesn't know what she's talking about."

Rosemary tossed back her hair. "A man's got responsibilities," she said, pointing toward the door. "He's as much your son as that boy on that wall."

Ellie looked at the boy again, and then at Rosemary. "I remember you," Ellie said.

Rosemary nodded. "At the Hills depart—"

"No," Ellie interrupted. "You were at Brick's game. I saw

you. I heard your boy say Brick's name." Ellie looked at Brick. "It all makes sense now. Why you didn't want the kids and me to come to any more games. You were afraid I'd figure it out."

"She never came to another game."

Ellie rolled her eyes. "That night when I told you I still loved you? When I said I believed you loved me, too? You were already with her." She counted on her fingers. "And she was pregnant with your baby."

"Ellie, I didn't—"

"He didn't know," Rosemary said.

Ellie looked at her. "What?"

"He didn't know I was pregnant. When he ended it with me, I didn't tell him. He didn't know about Paull until a few months ago."

Ellie shook her head and looked at the floor. "Why are you telling me this?"

Rosemary started to cry. "I don't want you to feel worse than you already do, I guess. And I'm not here to break you up. That's not it at all."

Ellie turned to look at the door. Paull was gone. She looked out the window and saw Sam sitting on the porch steps, holding Paull in her arms.

Ellie turned back to Rosemary. "Why are you here in my home?" Ellie said. "What could you possibly want from me?"

CHAPTER

52

On the drive home, Rosemary kept looking down at her sleeping son. "I'm out of options, Paullie," she said. "I'm all played out."

What had she been thinking? Of course Brick and Ellie McGinty would not raise him, and not because of Ellie. She had surprised Rosemary, the way she'd been with Paullie, so tender and concerned. "Brick, though," she said.

Paullie was a reminder of the worst thing Brick had ever done, and she could see now that he wasn't the type of man who took responsibility for his mistakes.

Rosemary felt a new camaraderie with Ellie McGinty. They were both victims of Brick McGinty.

Initially, Brick had made Rosemary feel like the woman she'd always wanted to be, beautiful and confident, and desired by a man who was willing to risk it all to have her. She was so sure Brick's lust for her would evolve into love, and that getting pregnant with Paullie would seal the deal.

Meanwhile, Ellie was doing what good wives do, trusting her husband to manage the money and believing his promises to take care of her for the rest of her life. She had believed Brick when he said he was working all that overtime for her and the kids. What must it be like right now to know that her husband had spent all of those nights in Rosemary's arms?

Rosemary could tell by how Ellie was with Paullie that she was a good mother, and capable of separating the child from the crime. Rosemary would never be able to do that. Just looking at their family photos on the wall had filled her with rage, and blinded her to the harm she was about to inflict on Ellie.

We gave up so much of ourselves for the same man, Rosemary wanted to say to Ellie now. *Were we naïve, or just needy?*

"I'm sorry, Ellie," Rosemary said as she drove. "I should never have put you through this."

She drove back to the harbor, where she had lived in Erietown all of her adult life. Across the bridge and into "the land of her people," Aunt Lizzie liked to say. So ridiculous, really. Why shouldn't the Italians live with the Irish, and the blacks and Puerto Ricans, for that matter? The men worked together, and sometimes drank in the same bars. They all cheated on their wives, too, and the women kept putting up with them no matter how you pronounced their last names.

For the first time in years, Rosemary thought of Mrs. Colbert, the black woman at the Greyhound bus station who had driven her to Sardelli's the day she arrived. "You're a nice girl, Rosemary," she had told her. "Don't let anyone tell you anything else." Rosemary had clung to those words in the early days here in Erietown. It was one thing to have your aunt say you're wonderful. It was something else to have a complete stranger see the good in you.

Mrs. Colbert had been wrong. Rosemary wasn't a nice girl. She had come to Erietown pretending to be someone else, but she'd ended up being exactly what Aunt Lizzie had tried to prevent: an unwed mother working at a bar and flirting with men to make more than minimum wage.

Those tips were getting lighter, too. There was a new girl

working the bar with her. Cindy. Blonder than Rosemary, and almost a decade younger. Rosemary was no fool. She noticed the regulars now called over to her rival when they sat their fat asses down on those stools. Her best years were behind her, and her little boy deserved so much more.

She reached down and smoothed Paull's damp face. The one thing she had done right tonight was to let him slip out that front door when she saw Brick's daughter reaching for him.

"That was your sister, holding you tight," she said as she drove. "She sang to you and she rocked you to sleep."

She kissed the tip of her finger and touched his cheek. "Remember that, Paullie."

PART VI
1975

CHAPTER

53

Rita Taylor elbowed Sam as she snatched her time card out of the rack and punched it in the clock. "Better get out there, Sammy girl," she said, slipping her card back into the rack. "The dining room is filling up and Bert's already yelling for you."

Sam rolled her eyes and punched her time card. "Bert can kiss my ass."

Rita tucked a pencil in her hair. "Still mad at him for last night?"

Sam put her hands on her hips. "As you should be, too. It's a ridiculous policy."

"You knew when you started here at Otto's Tavern that we get charged for any dish we break," Rita said, tugging on her sneakers. "What do you care about pol-i-cy? Three more weeks, you're gone."

Sam plunked down beside her. "It's not about me, Rita. This is a workers' rights issue."

"Listen to you," Rita said, laughing. "Sam McGinty, union organizer. Your dad put you up to this?"

"My dad doesn't even know about this."

"Good thing. He's expecting you to leave for college in September, not stick around here and organize a union."

Sam stood up and tied her apron. "What hurts one of us, hurts all of us. The owner of this restaurant deducts the cost of dishes we break from our puny wages. As if we mean to. As if we're throwing them across the room for the fun of it."

"Calm down, princess. This is your summer job, that's all it is. Soon, you'll leave."

"That doesn't mean I'm going to forget all of you." She pointed at Rita's sneakers. "Sexy."

"Turn fifty-five and get back to me. You can laugh at my bargain alley Adidas all you want, but at least I'm not limping home."

"Bert hates them."

"Well, to quote a famous waitress I know, 'Bert can kiss my ass.' Get out of this town. Go to college, and don't ever come back."

"Couldn't you act just a tiny bit sorry to see me go?"

"I've known a lot of girls your age," Rita said. "They walk in here for a summer job with all their big plans and end up working as a cashier or waitress. It's 1975, Sam. A different world, but it's not here in Erietown." Rita started walking toward the dining room. "Let's go. Our fans await."

"When you were my age, what did you want to do?"

Rita kept walking. "Doesn't matter, Sammy girl. There's nothing more boring than a story about a dream that died on the grill."

Sam was busing tables at the back of the dining room when Jeanine, the hostess, walked up to her and said, "The lady and her grandson at table seven asked for you."

Sam set down the stack of plates and turned to look. The woman was wearing high heels and a skirt she didn't bother trying to tug to her knees after sitting down. The boy had bright red hair and was swinging his long, lanky legs. Ten years old, Sam figured. She studied his face for a moment. "I don't know them," she said. "I don't think they've ever been here before."

"They stopped here last Sunday," Jeanine said. "She walked in and asked if you were working. When I told her you were off she grabbed her boy's hand and said she just remembered she had an appointment. An *appointment*. On a Sunday night."

"She knows my name?" Sam turned to look at them again. "Huh." She pulled out her order pad. "I'm on it."

She walked over and greeted them with a smile. "Hi, I'm Sam." The little boy glanced at the woman before returning Sam's smile. "I'm Paull."

"Well, hi there, Paul. How old are you?"

"Eight and three-quarters."

"Wow. You're tall for your age. I thought you were almost in high school." He giggled.

"He'd like a grilled cheese," the woman said. She looked at Sam, but didn't smile. "And a glass of milk. I'll have the chicken in mushroom sauce." She smiled at the boy. "Please. And a Coke."

Sam scratched down their orders. "Coming right up. Paul. Would you like me to bring over our box of crayons? You could draw on the back of your place mat."

He looked at the woman, who nodded her approval. "Yes, please."

Sam dropped off the order at the grill and grabbed a box of crayons from the hostess stand. "Here you go," she said, ceremoniously depositing the box in front of him. "You look to me like you might be an artist."

He smiled. "I kind of am, don't you think, Aunt Lizzie?"

The woman leaned against the back of her chair and crossed her arms. "Well, now that I think about it, you just might be.

Your mommy was an artist, you know. She used to doodle pictures of butterflies all the time. On the backs of napkins."

"Do you like to draw?" Paull asked Sam.

"Oh, sure," she said. "Funny, too. I doodle butterflies, like your mommy does."

"Did," the woman said. "She used to. He lost his mother six years ago."

Sam squatted so that her face was level with his. "I'm so sorry, Paul. I didn't know that. I'm sorry you lost your mommy."

He reached for the box and pulled out a crayon. "That's okay. I'm used to it. I don't really remember her." Sam glanced at the woman. She was staring at Sam.

"Would you draw a butterfly before you go?"

Sam looked around the room and saw Jeanine waving her over to a table of six. "Sure, but I have to be quick, so you'll have to be my assistant." She used the black crayon to sketch a butterfly hovering over a daisy. "Yellow, please," she said. He reached in and pulled out the crayon. "Thank *you*," she said, coloring in the petals. "Orange and green, please." He pulled out the two crayons.

She quickly filled in the wings. "Okay, one more color." She tapped her temple. "Hmm. Blue, please."

"I already have that one in my hand!" She smiled at him. "How 'bout that?" She wrote in block letters above the butterfly, ARTWORK BY SAM, and stood up. "Now," she said, patting his head, "I expect to see your butterfly before I leave. And you have to sign it, too, okay?"

The rest of the night was a blur. Sam delivered meals to the woman and Paull, but quickly dashed off to wait on four other tables. She returned to refill their water and check if they wanted dessert, but Jeanine ended up delivering their bill and cashing them out.

After she had finished her side jobs that night, Sam was

heading out the back door when Jeanine called to her. "Sam," she said, reaching under the hostess stand. "I was told to give this to you." She handed her a place mat. "That lady with the little boy said she thought you'd like this."

Sam smiled at the purple butterfly drawn in a child's hand next to hers. "Aw," she said, reaching for it.

She froze. *Butrflys by Sam and Paull.*

"Sam? What's the matter?"

"Nothing," she said, folding the place mat into a small square. "Nothing's wrong." She tucked it into her apron pocket and walked out the front door.

CHAPTER

54

Ellie groaned as she lowered herself to her knees in front of her hope chest at the foot of her bed. She shifted her weight, trying to find the sweet spot that allowed her to pretend that working forty hours a week on her feet wasn't taking its toll. She rummaged under the stack of her grandmother's unused linens until she felt the hard edges of the book. She pulled it out and stared for a moment at the gray-and-white cover.

"*Love, Marriage and the Family,*" she read aloud. "By Kenneth Walker." The book had been a wedding gift from Mrs. Archer, one of Aunt Nessa's neighbors. "Thank God that boy married you," Mrs. Archer said to Ellie, patting her stomach after arriving unannounced. Aunt Nessa slammed down the pot of freshly brewed coffee and escorted the visitor out the door.

Ellie turned to the page she had bookmarked, and read the circled passage:

> In the first place, it can be said that desire in men is more generally uniform than it is in women. Another way of putting this would be to say that women are the extremists and

men are the moderates with regard both to sex and to the emotions. The truth is reflected in such old sayings as: "the best angels in heaven and the worst devils in hell are all feminine." Whilst marked variations are found in the intensity of the sexual drive amongst men, the differences are much less marked amongst men than amongst women. In other words, many more cases of excessive passion or nymphomania and of complete indifference to sexuality, or frigidity, are to be found amongst women than amongst men.

Ellie's shoulders slumped as she recalled the flutter of shame she had felt the first time she read that. She had been so excited to be married, to share the same bed each night with Brick, but the permission she'd felt to explore that part of their lives evaporated with Kenneth Walker's withering judgment. Her swelling belly was not proof of their love, but evidence of her wantonness. She was a teenage girl so eager to touch, and be touched. For that, she was a freak.

"Thanks for nothing, Ken." She threw the book across the room and lay down on her back, clasping her hands across her stomach. Her daughter would mock Kenneth Walker and his disdain for women, of that she was sure.

They'd had a fight yesterday, after Sam told her about Val Murphy.

"You're so judgmental," Sam had yelled at her. "It's the seventies, Mom. Girls have sex."

"What girls? Are you having sex?"

Sam rolled her eyes. "That's not what I'm saying, Mom. It's just unfair for you to say Val's ruined her life because she did. She's pregnant, not dying."

"She was planning to go to college, Sam. Now she can't."

"You didn't go to college," Sam said, narrowing her eyes. "Is your life ruined?"

That's when it hit her. Ellie had been Sam's age when she

became pregnant. When her dream of becoming a nurse evaporated. "I should have told you sooner," Ellie said, fumbling with the buttons on her blouse. "I should have told the truth, that I had to get married."

Sam's eyes grew with each revelation. "What do you mean you had to?" Sam said.

"I was pregnant with you."

"So, you didn't marry the year before I was born? How could you have lied to me like that? And all those lectures about how nice girls don't have sex before marriage. God, Mom."

"I didn't want you to make the same mistake."

"So, I'm a mistake?"

"That's not what I mean."

Sam's eyes welled up. "I'm sorry your life is so miserable because of me."

"Listen, you," Ellie said, pointing at Sam. "I have loved being your mother." Her voice started to quaver. "I have loved it even when you've hated being my daughter."

"Mom, I don't—"

"I just want you to have more choices than I did," Ellie said. "I want you to become a mother when you want to. I don't want you fooling around in a car."

Sam sniffed and smiled. "I was conceived in a car?"

"Stop it, Sam."

"So, I'm just another tramp of hearts?"

"What?"

"A Springsteen joke. 'Backstreets'?"

Ellie tried not to smile. "It's not a joke if you have to explain it."

"I'm not Val, Mom. I'm not even dating anyone, and if I did Lenny would talk him to death anyway. So you can stop worrying about me. Clearly, I'm headed for life as a spinster with a cat named Aretha. Bruce if it's a boy."

Sam's face brightened. "Hey. At least I'd finally have a pet. God, why is Dad like that?" She lowered her voice an octave to imitate her father's voice: "No other dog could ever be as good as my Patch."

"Be nice, Sam. You don't know the whole story about Patch. It broke his heart when that dog died."

Sam put her hands on her hips again. "Mom. Is this about sex or dogs? Because I know what I'd rather talk about."

"Knock it off, Sam. I just want you to be careful."

Sam held up her hand and said, "I solemnly swear that my teen years have been, and will continue to be, far more boring than yours."

Ellie laughed. "You're terrible."

Sam walked to the door and stopped in the doorway. "I have to go to work. And, Mom, remember this: In two weeks, I'm going to be the first person in our family to go to college. I'm not going to do anything stupid."

Sam's vow was little comfort for Ellie. She grabbed the edge of the hope chest to pull herself to her feet, then walked across the room to pick up the book and toss it in the trash. "This ends with me," she said out loud. She walked downstairs to the kitchen and dialed the wall phone. "Mardee? What are you doing on Saturday? You up for a drive?"

Mardee held up the large paperback book and waved it toward Ellie. "My God, have you seen this thing? Look at this. Three pictures of a naked couple. Three different positions of sex, all about the clit-*oh*-ris."

Ellie glanced at the page. The car lurched, and they both shrieked. "I can't look at those while I'm driving," Ellie said. "They're drawings, not pictures."

"Oh, okay. Did you notice where the drawing of his hand is?"

Ellie raised her chin, her eyes on the road. "On her *clit*-o-ris, I imagine." She glanced again at Mardee. "I'm a nurse's aide. I know how to pronounce it."

They both started laughing. "Jesus Christ, El. I've never seen anything like this. Are you sure you want to give this to Sam?"

Ellie flicked on her turn signal. "I could never have made this trip without you. Thanks, Mardee."

Mardee laughed again. "Why did we have to go all the way to Cleveland to buy this? I'm sure Maggie at Lakeside Books could have ordered it for you."

"And told everyone in town about it," Ellie said. "You know how she is. Remember when Lois Ross talked about that *True Confessions* story about a woman being in love with a priest and everyone thought she was having an affair with that Father Mark? Maggie started that rumor."

"Oh, yeah," Mardee said. "Lois almost became a Presbyterian just to stop the gossip." She started thumbing through the book again. "Oh my God, listen to this: 'Orgasm may start with a spastic muscle contraction of two to four seconds' duration. Orgasm is three to fifteen rhythmic contractions of the muscles around the outer third of the vagina at point-eight-second intervals'—sweet Jesus, El. Who needs to know all this?"

"Pretty much every man on planet Earth."

Mardee slammed the book shut and set it on her lap. "Where did you get the idea that this book"—she pointed at it—"this *Our Bodies, Ourselves*"—is the thing Sam should be reading?"

"Phil Donahue."

"What?"

"Phil Donahue talked about it on his show, on one of my days off. About how times have changed, and women should be able to get what they need, too, out of sex."

"I thought you wanted to make sure Sam didn't get pregnant. What does orgasm have to do with that?"

"Mardee, you've been my best friend for seventeen years. We tell each other everything."

Mardee nodded. "Everything."

"Except we've never talked about sex."

"Why on earth would we do that?"

"Because. If we did, maybe we wouldn't feel so lonely about it. About what's happening. And what isn't happening, for that matter."

"Oh, for God's sake."

"I just mean that maybe that book is right. Maybe it helps if we can talk about it, at least with our friends."

Mardee picked up the book and started fanning the pages again. "Okay, fine. Let's talk about hymens. Here's a drawing of all the versions of hymens. I had no idea there were so many types." She flipped a few pages. "Or, no," she said, poking a picture with her finger. "Maybe we should start here. For our next canasta club, we can all bring our mirrors so that we can look at our vaginas."

"That's going a bit far." Ellie sighed. "Mardee, when we were Sam's age, we wanted to have sex, remember?"

"Barely."

"I still do."

"And Brick McGinty should drop to his knees every night and thank you and God for that miracle."

"That's long ago, Mar. It's behind us."

"I know, El. I'm sorry. And I'm glad you still like sex."

Ellie smiled at her. "Well, I do, and all of my life, I've felt that meant there was something wrong with me. I don't want Sam to feel that way. I want her to know it's normal, and I want her to protect herself, too."

"Well, look at you, Ms. Betty Friedan."

"I'm thinking more Gloria Steinem."

"Huh," Mardee said, closing the book. "So far, she's never married."

Ellie pulled the car onto the exit ramp. "Yeah, well. Some girls have all the luck."

Sam looked around the diner as she snatched the book and slipped it under the table and onto her lap. "Thank you, Mom." Her face was crimson.

Ellie reached under the table and tried to grab it. "I thought maybe we could talk about a couple of sections."

"No. Mom," Sam said, pulling the book closer.

Ellie tugged on it again. "Just. Give it." She yanked harder. "To. Me."

"Fine," Sam said, releasing both hands, which sent Ellie tipping the back of her chair into the elderly woman sitting at the table behind them. "Oh, my goodness," Ellie said, clasping the book to her chest as she turned to face the woman. "I'm so sorry."

The woman and her equally old companion were staring at the book's cover, speechless. Ellie looked down and flipped the book. She spun around, her eyes wide.

Sam grinned. "Well, their lives will never be the same."

Ellie set the book facedown on the table. "All I'm trying to say is that whatever you're feeling is normal. And I could help you understand a few things."

Sam waved her hands in front of her face. "Mom, if I were to make a list of what no teenage daughter wants to hear from her mother, ever, it would start and end with s-e-x."

Ellie flicked her napkin and spread it across her lap. "I'm a nurse's aide. I've seen everything. And I care more about your safety than your embarrassment." She picked up the menu and held it in front of her face. "I think we should go to Planned

Parenthood." Ellie lowered her menu. "*You,* I mean. I'll sit in the car. I want you to get on the Pill."

Sam's neck bloomed with blotches. "Mom, stop."

Ellie picked up the book and turned to one of the pages she had bookmarked. "Look, it's right here, starting on page 186. It even has pictures of different types of birth control pills."

Sam glanced at the page. "If I tell you I'll read this later, would you put the book away? It's our last lunch at Brennan's, Mom, before I leave for Kent State."

Ellie gently closed the book and slid it toward her daughter. "That's all I'm asking. I want you to feel better about yourself than I did at your age. And I want you to be safe."

"Not pregnant, you mean," Sam said. She returned the book to her lap and covered it with her napkin.

"Yes," Ellie said. "But it's more than that."

"What else could there be?"

"Well, there's venereal disease. He should always wear a condom."

"Ohhh-kay. Done."

Ellie raised her menu. "Let's make that appointment."

Sam leaned across the table. "You're not coming in with me."

"Got it."

"So bring a book."

Ellie smiled. "I have a book," she said, pointing at Sam's lap.

Later that evening, Ellie stood on the footstool and wrote on that day's square of the wall calendar: "Hi, Sam. On this day, Mom had the last word."

Sam squatted in front of her clothes closet and reached back for her record case holding all of her old forty-fives. She unlatched it and flicked through the alphabetized folders until she came to "P." She pulled out a loosely wrapped wad of tissue paper and shook it open. The lighter fell into her lap. A silver Dunhill, engraved on one side.

Sam ran her fingers across the inscription: LOVE, PINT.

For six years, she had tried to figure out a way to return it to her father. The contents of that woman's purse had spilled into the street on that awful day, and she was in such a rush to leave that she had missed this one thing. Sam had picked it up and recognized it as her father's lighter, a gift from her mother before they married.

For months, her father had been searching for it, repeatedly wondering aloud what had happened to it. Sam had found it all right, but she didn't want to reveal how.

She stood up and tucked the lighter into the front pocket of her jeans and walked over to her bed. Her mother's train case was sitting open on the bedspread, packed almost to the brim. Sam sat down next to it and tipped it upside down. Two folded squares of paper dropped on top of the pile.

She unfolded the yellowed newspaper clippings first. That woman, Rosemary, had showed up at their house the day before, and by the next morning Sam's father had moved out and her mother looked like a zombie from *Night of the Living Dead*.

The aftershock of the previous day's earthquake landed with the thud of the afternoon paper at their front door.

Ellie had been quietly warming up leftovers in the kitchen. Sam had opened the front screen door and picked up the latest edition of the *Erietown Times,* just as she always did.

There was only one headline on the front page, a double-decker in giant letters:

MOTHER DRIVES THROUGH BRIDGE RAILING, PLUMMETS TO HER DEATH

Sam had stared at the large, black-and-white photo of the Fairlane dangling off the hook of a giant truck on the edge of the Clayton County River. Two police officers were pointing at the car's collapsed roof. The driver's door dangled from its hinges.

She had run up to her bedroom and sat on the floor against the closed door before reading the story. Six years later, it felt only sadder to Sam.

A local woman, a longtime bartender at Sardelli's Restaurant, lost control of her car around 2:00 A.M. on Sunday, crashing through the north railing of the Clayton County Bridge and plummeting to her death in the river. Police Chief Walter Casey said the tragedy that claimed the life of Rosemary Russo appeared to be an accident, and one that could have been avoided.

"We've been saying for months now that the city needs to reinforce those rails," said the Chief. "It was only a matter of time before this kind of thing was going to happen."

Mrs. Russo was 29 years old and lived with her 2-year-old son and her aunt and uncle, Elizabeth and Daniel Martinelli. Mr. Martinelli said in a telephone interview that they were "heartbroken," and would raise the boy. "Family takes care of family," he said.

According to Mr. Martinelli, Mrs. Russo was preceded in death by her husband, Anthony Russo, of Scranton, Pennsylvania, who died in 1967 in Vietnam. "He never made it back to see his son," he said. "Rosemary never talked about that. She tried to stay positive for her son." Mr. Martinelli stressed that Mrs. Russo never drank, and that fatigue led to her death.

"She was out late because she worked a longer shift at the bar to make extra money for her son," he said. "She was exhausted. We're sure she fell asleep at the wheel."

Funeral services for Mrs. Russo will be private.

Mayor Frank De Luca expressed his sympathy to the Martinelli family and called on City Council to close the bridge and fix the railing before another innocent person is killed. "What does it take to make city council do its job and

(Story continued, page 8A.)

Sam picked up the second clipping and felt a chill crawl up her spine. In the bottom right corner of the page, there was Rosemary Russo. She was smiling, holding baby Paull—two-els in her arms.

The boy in Otto's, she thought. Table seven. She had recognized him, but he was leaner than the chubby little boy she had rocked to sleep on their porch that day.

In the photo, Paull was wearing a cone-shaped party hat, his cheeks smeared with cake. *Rosemary Russo with her son Paul, in 1968,* the caption read. *Photo courtesy of Elizabeth Martinelli.* They had spelled it wrong, Sam had noted that day.

She set down the clippings and unfolded the place mat. She ran her fingers again along the boy's crayoned letters. BUTRFLYS BY SAM AND PAULL.

The only time Sam had dared to ask her mother about Paull, two years after Rosemary's death, her mother had pulled over the car and grabbed her arm. "That boy was not your father's," Ellie said. "That woman was just trying to get your father's money."

"But, how could she do that if Dad hadn't—"

Ellie squeezed her arm harder. "Every man makes mistakes. He had a weak moment. Just one. She slept around with everybody and tried to pin it on your dad."

"You're hurting me, Mom."

Ellie loosened her grip and rubbed Sam's arm. "Let's never talk about this again."

Sam picked up the front page and stared at the yellowing photo of Rosemary Russo. She had long ago stopped trying to forget that day. Sometimes even as something is happening you know it's going to change you for the rest of your life.

She could see it all, those last hours of her childhood. That little boy with the same hair, same Johnny Lightning car as her brother's. The white sheets billowing on the line. Her mother dropping her father's wet socks on the ground. Her father's face when he pulled into the drive, looking in the rearview mirror at Rosemary's car parked in front of the house. And the boy, Paull, asleep in her arms.

Over the next year, so much had changed.

Two days after Sam's father moved out, he was back, with no explanation. That night, the four of them sat down to dinner. Just as Ellie was serving canned peach slices for dessert, Brick reached under the table and pulled out a box from Brennan's department store.

Sam studied her mother's face as she peeled back the layers of tissue paper and held up the lavender silk blouse. "Oh,

Brick, it's beautiful." She smiled at Reilly. "Did you help pick this out?" Reilly nodded, beaming. "I told Daddy your favorite color was purple."

Sam watched in disbelief. "Are you kidding me?" she wanted to yell at her parents. "We're just going to act like none of this happened?" She was disgusted with both of them, and asked to be excused from the table.

Within months, Brick and Ellie told the kids they were moving to a new house, one that they would own. Ellie got a job as a nurse's aide at Erietown General Hospital. A few months after she started working, Brick surprised Ellie with a used Dodge Dart for their anniversary. "So you can drive yourself to work," he said.

With each big change, Sam felt her parents leaving her further behind. For the first time, she had been glad that Lenny was her only close friend. "You're my only friend who knows about Paull-two-els," she said to him on their last night together in the same neighborhood. "What would I have done if everyone had known what Dad did?"

"Don't spend any more time on that, Sam," Lenny said. "We're getting out of here and going to college. We're leaving all that behind."

She refolded the newspaper clippings and Paull's drawing and pressed them against the bottom of the case. Lenny was wrong. You can leave, but some things follow you. Some things will never let you go.

She waited until her mother was sitting on the couch working on a crossword puzzle book, her nightly ritual. Sam opened the closet door in the front hallway and started riffling through the jackets.

"It's eighty-two degrees, Sam," her mother said. "You're not going to need a coat anytime soon."

Sam pulled out her winter parka and dropped it to the floor. "I'm not coming home until Thanksgiving, Mom. It could snow before then." She stepped deeper into the closet before pulling the lighter out of her pants pocket. She grabbed her father's old softball windbreaker in the back and pulled it off the hanger.

"Hey," Sam said, pulling it on and shoving her hands into the pockets. "Dad hasn't worn this in years. Do you think he might let me have it?"

"That's huge on you, Sam," Ellie said, rolling her eyes. "And, no, I don't think your father is going to be willing to part with that jacket. He's had it for twenty years. You know how he is about stuff like that."

Sam pretended to fumble with something in the right pocket. "Oh, my gosh," she said, holding up the lighter with a shocked look on her face as she approached her mother. "Look what I found."

Ellie set down the book and held out her hand. "Let me see that."

Sam dropped it into Ellie's palm. "This is the one Dad's been looking for, right? The one you gave him all those years ago."

"Yes," Ellie said, running her thumb across the inscription. "Yes, this is the one."

Sam walked back to the closet to hang up her father's jacket. "I'll bet Dad gives me the jacket now," she said, closing the door.

Ellie watched Sam climb the stairs to her bedroom and waited for the sounds of her stereo before rising from the couch and walking to the kitchen. She pulled out the box of aluminum foil and ripped off a sheet of it. She walked to the window over the sink and turned on the overhead light to get a better look at the lighter. So many tiny scratches after years of use, but the inscription was still vivid: LOVE, PINT. She had saved six months of babysitting money in her junior year to buy it for Brick that Christmas. It came in a special box, which she had wrapped in a remnant of fabric, instead of paper, and tied with a piece of Grandma's leftover bric-a-brac trim. Green, she remembered. He got a kick out of that, seeing the box stitched shut with three large loops of embroidery thread.

"How do you think of these things, Pint?" he asked, kissing her as she sat next to him in his truck. "I don't want to open it, it looks so nice."

It was the nicest thing anyone had ever given him, he told her that night. He would cherish it for the rest of his life, he said.

She had believed him, even after Rosemary. All those months he begged her to forgive him. Swore that little boy couldn't possibly have been his. She finally gave in, willing herself to believe him.

She clutched the lighter. Unlike her daughter, she would not pretend.

Ellie had stood at the front porch window that night, and seen it all. Rosemary marching across the grass with that boy in her arms. Spilling the contents of her purse all over the street. Trying again and again to start her car. Ellie had watched all of that, waiting for Rosemary to leave. When she finally pulled off, Ellie had taken a deep breath and started to turn away, but stopped when she saw Sam walk to the street.

Sam had bent down and run her hands across the pavement. Then she'd stood and held something up to the streetlight. She'd looked back at the house before sticking it into her pocket.

For six years Ellie had wondered what her daughter had discovered in the street that night. Now she knew. You don't get a man's lighter from a one-night stand.

Ellie picked up the sheet of foil and bunched it around the lighter. She walked over to the metal trash can and pressed her foot on the lever to open the lid. She tossed in the ball of foil and stared at it for a moment.

"Too bad for you," she said, slamming the lid shut. "Pint doesn't live here anymore."

PART VII

CHAPTER
56

1978

"M iss McGinty!"

Sam ignored the guy's voice and kept walking.

"Mizzzzzz McGinty! Wait up."

She slowed, but didn't turn around.

"Mizzzzzz McGinty, who is in my mandatory Ohio History class!" he yelled. "Wait up for a fellow inmate, *please*."

She stopped and slowly turned. "Could you be more obnoxious?" she said.

"Absolutely," he said, panting.

"How do you know my name?"

He laughed. "Everyone in the lecture hall knows your name. You're the only one arguing with Professor Dixon, week after week. Nice touch calling him Professor Nixon today, by the way."

"It was a mistake," Sam said. "I apologized."

"Okay," he said. "If you say so."

Her scowl deepened. "This is a stupid course required by this stupid university because we were stupid enough to be born in Ohio."

"Stupidity runs rampant, apparently."

"Who cares," Sam said. "Who cares that eight U.S. presidents lived, at some point, in Ohio? Harrison was a southerner and Whig, and the other seven were all Republicans."

"Ah, you don't like Republicans," he said. "I would never have guessed that from this morning's tirade about Nixon and the invasion of Cambodia."

Sam shifted her books from her right hip to her left. "Would you have called it a tirade if a guy had said it?"

He squeezed his eyes shut. "Let me think on that." He opened his eyes. "You're right. I would have called it a blovia- tion. Which, by the way, President Warren G. Harding—from Ohio—once defined as 'the art of speaking for as long as the occasion warrants, and saying nothing.' I would never accuse you of such a thing."

Sam refused to smile. "It was a necessary clarification of history, of the horrible cost of war. He spent an entire period on"—she raised her right hand and made air quotes with two fingers—"'Ohio at war,' and never talked about how many boys from our state died in Vietnam."

"It's still a touchy subject."

"You don't know anyone who had to go, do you?"

"That doesn't mean I don't care."

"It means it's not personal for you," Sam said. "People like you can pretend it never happened."

"That's a little harsh," he said. "And who are these *people like me*? That sounds biased."

Sam tilted her head and said nothing.

"You know," he said, "not everything that happens in the world happens to you personally."

"Ah, quoting Hubbell Gardner," Sam said. "Your hero."

He snapped his fingers. "Damn. I should have known you'd seen *The Way We Were*."

"I'm sorry war is a joke to you." She turned and started walking again toward the first-floor exit.

"Oh, c'mon," he said, catching up to her.

Sam stopped walking. "How can you not be offended that no one mentioned the students who were killed here?" He leaned back as she flung out her arm and pointed to the wall of windows. "Right there, on our campus, protesting the Vietnam War. Four dead, nine wounded."

"Somebody did mention it, as I recall," he said. "Somebody who was very loud about it and, now that I think about it, looked a lot like you."

"Where I come from, we can't pretend the war didn't happen," Sam said. "We lost so many of our boys over there. So many others came back so different."

"I'm sorry," he said, his voice softer. "It's a touchy subject here, is all I mean. All those outsiders agitating, as they say."

"They weren't outsiders," she said, her voice rising. "They were students here. And they weren't even all protesters. Sandy Scheuer was walking to class. Bill Schroeder was in ROTC, a bystander."

"You're right. That's awful."

She stopped and turned to face him. "Who *are* you?"

"Henry." He lifted an imaginary hat off his head and bowed. "Henry Wade."

"Does anyone call you Hank?"

He shook his head in mock outrage. "Never."

"Too bad," she said.

"It gets worse," he said. "I'm Henry Wade the Third."

"Of course, you are. Daddy's the second, I presume?"

"Indeed."

"What happened to junior?"

Henry slapped his palm against his chest. "We're not coal miners."

"We've had coal miners in our family," Sam said, "and their manners were a lot better than yours."

He tried to pull open the door, but she beat him to it. "I can manage this myself, thank you." He winced as the bottom of the door slammed against the toe of his sneaker. "Ow. Man, independence sure is painful."

She shoved past him. "See you next time," she shouted over her shoulder.

He kept pace beside her. "We're headed to the same place."

Sam glanced at him. "You're not in my honors American literature class."

"No, but I'm right next door, in the dishonorable American literature class."

She stopped and frowned. "I sounded really full of myself just then, didn't I?"

He shook his head. "Nah, that was when you were lecturing me about May fourth."

"Why don't you want to talk about what happened here?"

"Why don't you want to talk about anything else?"

"That isn't true," she said.

"Prove it," he said, pointing toward the student center. "We have forty minutes before class. Let me buy you lunch."

"I can afford my own lunch. I *work* for my money. Thirty hours a week, waiting tables."

He smiled, and Sam noticed how his blue eyes crinkled at the corners. "I wasn't offering to pay your tuition. I was thinking a hamburger."

"I prefer cheeseburgers."

"Well, okay," he said, guiding her toward the student center. "If you're sure that slice of American cheese won't cancel out your right to vote."

"So sarcastic, Henry the Third," Sam said, looking straight ahead.

"So suddenly lucky," he said, looking straight at Sam.

CHAPTER

57

Ellie pressed the open book against her chest and considered throwing it at her husband's head. He was sleeping in his recliner. He'd never see it coming.

Sam had given her Marilyn French's *The Women's Room* about a month ago. This was a hardback for a change, with eleven handwritten signatures on the inside cover. "Each of us girls in the dorm signed it after reading it," Sam said. "It's a manifesto."

Sam had given her the book during her final Thanksgiving break at Kent State, where she was apparently learning that her mother had done everything wrong. "It'll change your life, Mom," Sam had said after dinner. "At the very least, you'll finally understand what you've been putting up with all these years."

"Oh, good," Ellie said, peering over her reading glasses at Sam. "What happened to all of your JCPenney bras? Did you burn them?"

"Total myth, Mom. Women never did that, but who could blame them if they had?" Sam smiled at her mother's frown. "Carly Simon doesn't wear bras. You can see her nipples on the cover of her *No Secrets* album."

"Shhhh," Ellie said. "The last thing we need is your father hearing that. Especially now that you're dating that boy from Shaker Heights. What is his name?"

Sam looped the strap of her purse over her shoulder. "Henry. And he's not a boy, Mom. He's a man, and I'm a woman."

"Mmm-hmm. When are we going to meet this 'man'?"

"Soon, I promise. I'm meeting Lenny for a Coke." She pointed to the book in Ellie's hand. "I'll bet you see yourself in *The Women's Room*."

"Is there a nurse's aide with a know-it-all daughter in it? Does it have the part where she tells her mother that Jesus wasn't white?"

"C'mon," Sam said, pointing to the framed picture on the wall. "Jesus was Middle Eastern. He had brown skin."

"And you were *there*."

Sam laughed. "Mom. Honestly."

That had been barely a week ago. Now, Ellie couldn't wait to come home from work each day to read another chapter or two of *The Women's Room*. She pulled out a folded piece of stationery marking her place and opened it to reread the two sentences that had taken up residence in her head: *I've known for a long time that hypocrisy is the secret of sanity. You mustn't let them know you know.*

"My life," she'd told Mardee over coffee last Saturday, pointing to the page after reading it out loud to her. "I hate to admit that Sam was right, but it's like Marilyn French was writing about me."

"You're not a hypocrite, El," Mardee said, pouring another cup of coffee from the carafe Ellie had bought years ago with her first paycheck as a nurse's aide. "You're private. Nothing wrong with that. Nobody needs to know all your business."

"This isn't about what other people know," Ellie said. "It's about what I've had to ignore. All the stuff Brick has done, I mean. And it's never really gone away. Remember when that nurse's aide Lavelle trained me? The sister of Brick's *first* affair?"

"You handled that with such class."

"It was humiliating. And I couldn't even tell Brick, because then it would be all about how upset he was. Instead of him saying, 'Geez, Ellie, I'm sorry you had to go through that,' I'd be trying to make *him* feel better. Nothing is ever his fault. Even when Rosemary showed up."

Mardee reached for her hand. "Nobody knows about all that."

"Oh, please," Ellie said, pulling back her hand. "Everyone knows about her. And then she had to go drive off that bridge and die, so people just felt sorry for her."

"You don't think she did that on purpose?"

"I don't know. I hope not," Ellie said. "It does make me wonder if things would have turned out differently. If we had agreed to raise her son, like I bet she'd wanted us to."

"You've got to be kidding."

"I've thought about it a lot over the years. I was so upset that day. But when I found out she had died, I couldn't stop thinking about that little boy, and how she'd kept saying she didn't want him to grow up without a father."

"You sound as if maybe you do think he was Brick's."

Ellie picked up the tiny pitcher of milk and poured some into her cup. "I think I've spent my whole life pretending things are different from what they are. Even when I was a little girl, I wanted to make everyone think I was happy. So no one else would leave me, I guess."

Ellie stirred her coffee. "Do you ever think about how much difference money makes?"

"You mean, buying a bigger house? Owning a brand-new car, instead of a used one? Sure. Who doesn't?"

"I don't mean that stuff," Ellie said. "I mean the kind of money that lets you solve the big problems. Like that little boy.

If we had been rich, Brick could have paid her a lot of money to go away, and I would never have known about it."

"Oh, *that* kind of money," Mardee said. "Like the Kennedys."

"Or the Rockefellers."

"And movie stars," Mardee said. "You just know they're getting women pregnant all the time, but we never read about it."

"Same mistakes as us," Ellie said. "Same problems."

"Well, maybe," Mardee said, "but I don't think anyone's going to be comparing our husbands to Frank Sinatra anytime soon."

Ellie looked at her. "I know people think I'm a fool for sticking it out with Brick all these years. I just pretend I don't see that. I pretend I don't see any of it. That's how I keep all this going."

"No one's marriage is perfect, El. I give you a lot of credit for never pretending yours was. You never bragged about your marriage or your kids to make other people feel bad about their lives. That's why so many people like you. Life is already so damn hard. No one could ever accuse you of making another person feel even worse."

Ellie sat in silence for a moment, twisting her paper napkin as she took in the words from her oldest friend. "I never thought of myself that way," she said finally. "I've never thought I was someone who made anyone feel better."

"Well, you do. All the time. I've lost count of the number of our friends who've said something over the years about how you got them through something awful in their lives.

"And you know what else? Nobody feels sorry for you. You didn't get bitter, you got busy. You got a job, you got this new house." Mardee grabbed Ellie's hand. "You have never been a quitter, Ellie McGinty."

That evening, long after Mardee had left, Ellie picked up *The Women's Room* and wrote another passage inside the folded piece of stationery:

You have never been a quitter, Ellie McGinty.
Mardee Jepson
December 3, 1978

CHAPTER
58

1979

Henry pulled the blanket off Sam's head. "C'mon, I know you heard me."

"Hey," she said, pulling it up to her chin. "I'm naked here."

Henry sat on the edge of the bed. "Yes, I know. Just as you were ten minutes ago when we—"

Sam leaned across the bed to pick up her T-shirt and pulled it over her head. "Why do we have to talk about this right now?"

"You never want to talk about it. We've been together eight months. We're practically living together."

She sat up straighter. "Number one: We are not living together. I stay at your apartment because you have only one roommate, and I have forty."

"Four, you mean."

"It feels like forty, with all the guys sleeping over."

"And number two?"

Sam raked her hand through her hair. "There's no predicting how my father is going to react to you. Why ruin a good thing?"

Henry stood up and pulled on his jeans. "What's the worst he could do?"

"Oh, Henry, what you don't know."

Henry crawled onto the bed and sat facing her. "Sam, you've already met my dad."

"Well, after a point it was just going to look rude for me to not join the crowd gathering around his Mercedes-Benz."

"It's a Porsche."

"Whatever it is, it looks like a cartoon baby buggy with big eyes."

"Insulting my father. Nice."

"Why would any man think I'm insulting him if I make fun of his car?"

"Oh, Sam," he said. "What you don't know."

Sam kicked him from under the covers. "Why does it matter so much to you? Meeting my parents."

"It's the next step."

"To what?"

"Seriously?"

Her face softened. "I love you, too, Henry the Third."

"We graduate in June. We've got to start planning what comes next. You've applied to three elementary schools in Shaker Heights. You still want to teach there, right?"

"Well, are you still planning to move back to Shaker Heights?"

"You know I am," he said. "Dad wants me to clerk at his firm over the summer before I start law school in the fall at Case, which is a fifteen-minute drive."

"Then, yes," Sam said, reaching over and mussing his hair. "I want to teach in Shaker. Your high school classmate Beverly Wilson and I are going to share an apartment on Winslow Road with a ridiculously low rent payment. Like all good Shaker parents, hers own the building."

"That's not fair, Sam. How many times have I told you not everyone in Shaker Heights is rich?"

"You mention it every time you brag about how *deliberately integrated* it is. As opposed to Erietown, where we were all accidentally thrown together."

"You're a working-class snob."

"You don't think about class because you've never had to."

Henry reached for Sam's hand and smiled at her scowling face. "Have you told your parents that you're moving to Shaker?"

"Nope."

"What are you waiting for?"

"I was thinking maybe a tornado could lift them up and transport them to Oz. Or somewhere in Oregon."

"I'm serious. Why haven't you told them?"

"This is going to be hard for my mom," she said. "She has always thought I would move back home to Erietown."

"Well, that's hardly fair. When are you supposed to have your own life?"

Sam threw off the covers and stood up. "Henry, I wish you'd quit pushing me," she said, tugging on her jeans. "Why can't you be happy with what we have right now?"

"I am happy," he said. "I'm so happy I want to spend the rest of my life with you."

Sam reached for her hairbrush and bent at the waist to flip her hair. "We have to take it slow, Henry," she said, brushing in long strokes. "It's too soon to be talking like this."

When he didn't say anything, she stood up and pushed her hair from her face. "What is it?" She sat on the bed and pulled him down next to her. "Why do you look so sad?"

"It's because I'm your first, isn't it?"

"My first what?"

He sat up straighter and folded his arms across his chest. "It's because I'm your first boyfriend. You think there's got to be someone better out there."

She bumped up against him. "You are not my first boyfriend. You know that."

"Three guys—all dumped within a month. That's hardly a relationship."

"Henry, I am the first in my family to get the chance to go to college. I wasn't going to waste my time sleeping around and getting drunk all the time. I didn't want to be distracted."

"So that's what I am?" he said. "A distraction?"

She got up off the bed. "Obviously not. It's just, you don't know as much about me as you think you do. About my life, before I knew you. Before I ever got here to Kent State."

"Then tell me. Tell me what I don't know."

"You don't know what you're asking."

"There's nothing you can tell me that will change how I see you."

She walked over to the window. A handful of girls were laughing and clapping as three guys played Frisbee. "Must be nice." Sam looked at her watch. "I have to be at work soon."

"Sam? Look at me, please. What haven't you told me?"

"She knocked on the wrong door," she said softly.

"What?"

Sam slowly turned and looked at him, her eyes already glistening. "In August 1969, a woman came to our house. She knocked on the front door. Her name was Rosemary. I was twelve years old."

"Who was—?"

"She had a baby on her hip."

"Sam," Henry said softly. "Come here."

"He looked like Reilly."

He climbed off the bed. "Sam," he said, reaching for her.

"He looked just like my dad."

Henry raised his empty glass over the stack of books in front of him. "More, please," he mouthed. Sam picked up the pitcher of Coke and strolled to his table. "This is your sixth glass," she said as she poured. "You're never going to sleep tonight."

"Have I never mentioned that I'm Clark Kent? Superman is caffeinated for the night."

"You in tights," she said. "There's a picture."

"Calm yourself," he said.

"Henry, you didn't have to stay here the whole time. I'm fine."

"I never said you weren't. I just wanted to be near you. After everything you told me. It helped me see why you always act so tough."

"I am tough."

"You're strong, Sam. I don't know how you got through that time."

She stuck her finger in his hair and coiled a curl around it. "I had to keep it together. For Mom. One Saturday morning, weeks after, I woke up and it was pouring rain. It was October, and cold outside. I knew Dad and Reilly were at the diner, but I couldn't find Mom. I ran through the house, calling her name. I was panicked."

"Where was she?"

Sam released his curl of hair and sat down next to him. "Standing in the middle of the yard. No umbrella, no jacket. Her hair getting completely soaked. She had never done that before."

"What did you do?"

"I went out and tried to talk her into coming back in. She kept talking about Jackie Kennedy, and how lucky she was that her husband had died a hero."

"Jesus."

"She didn't come into the house until Dad pulled into the driveway. I'll never forget the look on his face. How he wrapped his jacket around her and led her up the stairs like a little girl."

She leaned back and crossed her arms. "You know what they don't tell you about these big, bad things that happen in your life? They're like tornados that pick you up in one place and drop you off somewhere else. And there's no turning back, no undoing it. You aren't who you used to be because the most important people in your life are not who you thought they were. And they can't help you figure out who you're going to be."

"You don't always have to go it alone, Sam."

"Maybe," she said, "but it's always good to know how."

He closed his book. "Ready to go?"

"Bruiser said he'd close for me," she said. "He thought I looked 'stressed.'"

Henry grabbed his stack of books and slid out of the chair. She kissed his cheek and whispered, "Easter."

Henry leaned back to look at her. "Is this code for something?"

"Easter weekend," she said. "On that Friday, come meet my parents."

"Ah, Good Friday," he said. He held out his hand for an imaginary handshake. "Hello, Mr. and Mrs. McGinty. I'm Henry, and I'm here to take your daughter away."

Sam patted his back. "Maybe work on that."

Sam held up a blouse covered in giant red poppies and
waved it in the air. "How about this one?"

Ellie blanched and shaded her eyes. "Something less mem-
orable, maybe."

"What's wrong with it?"

"Sam, I am four feet eleven"—she looked around and lowered her voice—"with a forty-DD bra. I'd look ridiculous. It's
all everyone would talk about for the next six months."

"Who's everyone?"

"Every woman I know who wouldn't be caught dead in
that, which is every woman I know." She tugged on the sleeve.
"My head on top of all those flowers? I'd look like a corpse
popping out of a fresh grave. Like *Night of the Grateful Dead.*"

Sam laughed. "*Living Dead*, Mom. *Night of the Living Dead.*
Or have you dumped Engelbert Humperdinck and become a
Dead Head?"

Ellie stared at her daughter. "I have no idea what you're
talking about."

Sam slid the blouse back onto the rack and pulled out another one. "This is cute."

"Horizontal stripes? Are you out of your mind? That's for a convict who gave the neighbor a poisoned rum cake."

"Which neighbor? I vote for Mrs. Ballsy."

"It's Halsey, and Virginia can't help it that she has to yell at Vern. He's practically deaf and refuses to get hearing aids."

"Like Dad, you mean."

"You father is not deaf, Sam. He's just stopped listening."

Sam returned the striped blouse to the rack. "Mom, the whole idea is to get you something new and different."

"Anything new will be different, Sam," Ellie said. "I haven't had a new top in ages." She pulled out a bright blue blouse and held it against her chest. "Like this." She raised it higher to her face. "Blue makes my eyes pop."

"And then what happens?"

Ellie ignored her and looked at the price tag. Sam grabbed the blouse out of her mother's hands. "Lady, know your place. I told you, this one's on me."

Ellie smiled. "You sounded like Arnie. Remember him?"

Sam nodded. "Your old hairdresser. I loved him. He used to give me all of his *New Yorker*s after he was done with them. Back then, I never understood the cartoons. Now I realize I've been living them."

"Right, Sam," Ellie said, smiling as she shook her head, "our life is just like *The New Yorker,* right here in Erietown."

Ellie pulled on the new blouse and stood in front of the mirror as she started buttoning it. Brick stood behind her and smiled at her reflection. "That's a pretty color. Is it new?"

"An early birthday gift from your daughter. You wouldn't believe our conversation this afternoon. Did you know Sam thinks we're practically New Yorkers?"

Brick combed his wet hair and patted the sides in place.

"Dressing you for the big occasion, huh? Sounds like our daughter's nervous for us to meet Henry the Turd."

Ellie frowned at him in the mirror. "Brick, you have to stop calling him that."

Brick grinned and tossed the comb onto the dresser. "No, I don't."

Ellie turned to look at him. "What if you slip and say it when he's here?"

"You know how hoity-toity he's going to be. We can't even call him Hank. What Henry doesn't want to be called Hank?"

"Out of my way." She shooed him aside and opened the closet door.

He sat on the bed, watching her. "I doubt you need that girdle for this," he said.

"This is not a girdle," she said, sliding one hanger of pants after another. "These are control-top pantyhose. No panty lines. And why am I explaining this?" She pulled out a pair of black polyester slacks and held them up to the window's light. "Toss me the lint roller, will you?"

He picked it up off the bedside table and lobbed it gently to his wife. "So, what did our daughter say that has you so worked up?"

"Who said I was worked up?"

"I can tell by your voice. What did she say?"

Ellie pulled on the pants and tucked in her blouse. "Did she tell you where she's planning to live after graduation?"

"That's months away. First she has to get a job."

Ellie zipped up her pants. "She has one. She's going to be a teacher in Shaker Heights. She's going to live in an apartment with that Beverly girl she's always talking about." Ellie turned to look at him. "She's moving away, Brick."

"El, we knew this could happen."

She sat down in front of her makeup mirror and flicked the

setting from "day" to "evening." "We'll never see her if she moves away."

"Sam will always be close to us. To you, especially."

She picked up the pencil and started filling in her brows. "And Reilly? He's going to move to Cleveland, and he's not going to college first. You'd better get used to it, Brick. As soon as they graduate from high school, Reill and Craig Kleshinski are going to work at that steel plant where Craig's brother Ronnie works."

Brick walked over to the chest of drawers and pulled on his watch and wedding ring. "The hell he is. We've got college savings for both of our kids, and both of our kids are going to be college graduates. I didn't work all that overtime so that my son could carry a lunch pail."

Ellie looked up into the dresser mirror. "Honey, I don't think you need to wear a tie tonight."

"His father, Henry the Second, is a partner at the largest law firm in Cleveland," he said, holding up his two ties. "This kid already thinks he's better than us. We owe it to Sam to make a good impression."

Ellie set down her tube of mascara. "Brick McGinty, you have always told our children that money is not the measure of a man, and that no one is better than they are. You have nothing to prove to this twenty-one-year-old boy from Shaker Heights."

"Blue then," he said, tossing the red tie on the bed.

CHAPTER

60

Sam and Lenny sat back to back in the dark on the Kleshin-skis' porch floor, their knees pulled up to their chests. "Man," he said, "Good Friday sure lived up to its name this year."

Sam sniffled and dug her hand into the cloud of wadded-up tissues on the floor beside her. "I just didn't see this coming," she said, squeezing the tip of her nose with a tissue. "I never thought Henry would be like this."

"Sam, I don't think it's fair to blame Henry for everything. He meant well. You seem so much bigger than Erietown to him. He wasn't expecting this. This town, this life."

Sam flipped around and caught Lenny as he teetered back-ward. "I walked three miles to your house because I needed to look into the eyes of the only person who understands me." The moonlight softened her face, but it couldn't hide the damage. Her eyes were red and puffy, her nose rubbed raw.

"I came home to meet him," he said. "That's the only reason I'm here."

"I know."

"And because of you, I am now going to have to go to Easter mass with Mom."

She looked down at the floor and said nothing.

"Okay, bad joke," he said. "Sam, I've known you all of my life. You're like a sister to me. Henry has known you for less than a year, and he wants to spend the rest of his life with you."

"Not anymore," Sam said.

"That's not true, Sam. You're the one who's changed your mind."

"Lenny, you had to be there. Mom and Dad, walking onto the porch all dressed up. Mom was wearing the new blouse I got her, and Dad was in a tie. A *tie*, Lenny. When's the last time you saw Brick McGinty in a tie?"

"Well, there was the funeral for Scotty McGuire," he said. "After he was killed in Vietnam. All of us union families went to that one. Even us boys wore ties."

"Nineteen sixty-eight," Sam said, pulling her knees to her chest again. "We were eleven." She looked at him, her eyes welling again. "Henry doesn't know a single person who served in Vietnam."

"He can't help where he grew up, Sam."

"I know. But it was one of those things that should have warned me. He doesn't understand who we are. Your girlfriend—Linda, right?—she grew up in a mill town. You don't have to explain things to her. Henry's never even thought about people like us. He's never had to."

"He's thought a lot about you."

"He knows the *college* Sam. But that's only part of me, and college will never change who I am. Kent State was my chance of a lifetime. For him, it was slumming. It was his big act of defiance, refusing to go to Harvard, his father's alma mater."

"How did he explain what happened today?"

Sam stretched her legs in front of her and leaned back on her hands. "Oh, you know," she said, imitating an Appalachian accent. "He was just trying to be like us plain folk. His exact words: 'I was trying to fit in.'"

"It's not like he showed up in a tank and cutoffs."

"He wore a T-shirt and jeans to fit in with my parents *in their own home*. The arrogance of that. And the look on Henry's face when he walked into our house. He kept looking around like he was inspecting a crime scene, and I started seeing our house the way he was seeing it. The ancient linoleum in the kitchen. The afghan with the big hole in the middle on the couch. That ridiculous cat clock with its ticking tail."

"You love Kit-Cat."

"When I was six. Henry just stood and stared at it."

"I find it calming," Lenny said. "Maybe he does, too."

"So, you think this is funny."

"What do you like about Henry?"

"Let's not do this."

"No, really, Sam. What is it that you liked about him, before he drove to Erietown?"

"His sense of humor," she said. "He always makes me laugh. And his confidence. He never seems to doubt his place in the world."

"Not like us," Lenny said. "We're people in transition, no matter where we are. We go to college, and our dorms look nicer than the houses we grew up in. I was amazed at how the showers always worked and the dresser drawers never got stuck."

"I could always tell the wealthier students by how they treated the housekeepers in our dorm, as if they were invisible," Sam said. "And all that complaining about the littlest things, like having to do their own laundry. You would not believe how many people I've had to teach how to use fabric softener."

She turned to look at him. "Are we ever going to fit in, Lenny?"

"Where?"

"Anywhere. I've always felt different. When I was growing up, all the other white girls wanted to play with Barbies and grow up to be Laura Petrie. I wanted to read books and be Emma Peel."

"And then there was your white-girl Afro phase in seventh grade," Lenny said. "My mom still talks about that."

"My one and only Toni home perm," Sam said, wincing. "I looked like a human Q-tip."

Lenny laughed. "You and I got out of Erietown, but only sort of. Every time we come home we see the reasons we wanted to leave, and then we feel guilty about it."

They sat in silence for a moment as two semitrucks rumbled past. "What about your parents?" Lenny said. "What did they have to say about all this?"

"Mom worked hard to be polite. Dad barely said a word through the entire dinner. As soon as we finished dessert he stood up, shook Henry's hand, and said, 'Lot of trucks on I-Ninety at night, so be careful driving back to Shaker.' Then he walked out the back door and that was that."

"He would do that to any guy dating his daughter," Lenny said. "You and Henry will talk more when you get back to campus. Things can work out."

"No," she said softly. "I realize now I'd have to change too much to be with him. He'd never say that, but over time I'd squash a big part of myself to keep him happy, to fit in with his friends. My mother never got to be who she wanted to be. I don't want that to happen to me."

"So, what will you do?"

"I'm not moving to Shaker Heights," she said, standing up. "In three months I graduate, and I'll come back here to Erietown."

"Sam, there are more places to live than Erietown. It's not your only option."

"I'm not a big-city girl."

"You don't know that," Lenny said. "You're tougher than anyone else I know."

"I'm strong," Sam said, standing up. "Not tough. Why doesn't anyone understand the difference?"

She hugged him and stepped back. "Look at you, Lenny Kleshinski. Contact lenses. A steady girl from Maine who wants to marry you. And now you're starting law school in the fall."

"At Ohio State. Just three hours away."

She nodded. "I love you like a brother. I always will. But you cannot be here for me. You are already gone."

CHAPTER

61

Sam hesitated at the end of the driveway and looked down at her watch. Nearly midnight, but the dining room light was still on.

It had all been too much. Her nervousness before Henry's arrival, watching her mother check every tabletop for dust, her father fiddling with the vase of daffodils he'd picked from his garden. The look on their faces as Henry stepped out of the car looking like he'd just spent the day at the beach. His smiling face morphing into a look of horror as Sam approached him.

"Sam," he'd said, louder than he intended. "I had no idea your dad would be wearing a tie."

"You're right," she said. "You have no idea."

Her mother had tried to rescue him. "What a relief," she'd chirped from the porch. "Now we can get out of these silly clothes and get comfortable."

Sam had known her father's first impression from the sound of jingling coins in his pocket. She gave Henry credit for this: One look at her father's face, and he knew he'd already blown it.

She stared at her parents' front door. This was not her home. She'd lived in it only a year or so before leaving for college, where she'd spent most of the last four years. Three hours ago, she'd thought she was moving away. This felt too familiar, this sudden unraveling of a life outside her parents' front door.

She squinted at the light in the window. The last thing she wanted to do right now was sit through one of her mother's heart-to-hearts. She started to walk backward in the driveway, but stopped when she heard the front door open. "Shit," she whispered.

"Sam?"

"Hi, Dad."

She heard him shut the door quietly behind him and walk across the porch. The streetlight brought his face into focus as he grabbed the railing and groaned when he lowered himself onto the top step. He patted the space next to him. "Give those feet of yours a rest."

She walked slowly up the stairs and sat down next to him. "Dad, I'm so sorry about what—"

He knocked the side of his knee against hers. "You don't owe anyone an apology, Sam."

"I don't know why he did that, Dad," she said, unbuckling her sandals. "Why Henry acted so weird."

"I think maybe you do," he said.

"I broke up with him."

"You sure you want to do that? Over a pair of blue jeans?"

"It's not about the clothes, Dad. It's about who he thinks we are."

Brick shifted slightly. "Sam, he was trying. Brought flowers for your mother, showed good manners. Took an interest in the house, too."

"That's one way to put it."

"He was surprised, Sam. You'd better get used to that. Your life is changing, but some people will always see you as a kid from Erietown. You're going to spend the rest of your life straddling two worlds. That's what happens when people like us go to college."

She turned to look at him. "How do you know that?"

"Coach," he said. "Coach Sam Bryant, the man you're named for. He told me when I was a senior in high school that if I went to college, I would always be a stranger in both lands."

"What a discouraging thing to say."

"Nah," Brick said. "He wanted me to go, to play basketball for—" He shook his head. "Doesn't matter. Didn't happen. Ancient history."

"I know, Dad. I know what happened. I know that you and Mom had to get married. Because of me."

"I suppose you know about Kent State, too. About my scholarship."

She lied. "Yeah. Sure."

"Sometimes I wonder what it would have been like. But I wouldn't trade you and your brother for anything. Your mother feels the same way. You need to know that."

She leaned forward to touch his arm, then decided against it. "Guess you could say I was your biggest mistake."

"No, Sam. I know my biggest mistake, and you're not it."

She held her breath and waited. They had never talked about that day. If he would just mention him, she'd tell him. Paull-two-els is a happy boy. He likes to draw butterflies. He looks just like you.

Her father was looking straight ahead, his shoulders slumped forward as he stared at something she couldn't see. The harsh light illuminated the web of grooves on his face, the white patches of hair at his temples. When did that happen? How had she never noticed?

"I'm not moving to Shaker, Dad," she finally said. "After I graduate, I'm moving home."

"Don't overreact, Sam."

"Mom's right. There are plenty of children who need me right here in Erietown."

"Your mom." He sighed. "Let's get this straight. You're not

living here. Not in this house. If you move back to Erietown, go find a nice apartment to rent. Make some new friends, too. It's time you figure out who you want to be. Away from us. It's not your job to take care of your mother, or me."

"Now you tell me." She picked up her sandals, stood, and held out her hand to help him up. He reached for the railing instead.

"Sam, that boy is not the one for you."

"You don't know that."

"You don't love him," Brick said. "If you loved that boy, you'd be defending him to me. You'd be yelling and fighting for him." He brushed off the seat of his pants. "He admires you. Probably loves you. But he's not strong enough for you. You need someone who isn't afraid of you. I'm not sure that man exists in Erietown."

"I belong here, Dad."

Brick looked up at the moon as he spoke. "It's one thing to remember your roots, Sam. Helps us keep our balance. But don't let your roots become your excuse to be stuck." He opened the door and walked inside.

Sam's legs felt leaden as she walked up the stairs to her bedroom. She changed into her nightgown and went down the hall to brush her teeth. She peeked into Reilly's room. He was a grown man, but he still slept like little Reilly. His bedding was puddled on the floor, and he lay on his back with his arms and legs spread wide, as if he were making an angel in the snow.

She didn't see the envelope on her pillow until she turned on her bedside lamp. It was thick and light blue. She ran her fingers along the typed letters: *Miss Eleanor Grace Fetters.* It was from a nursing school in Cleveland. She held the envelope under the light to read the faded postmark: *April 10, 1957.*

She flipped it over to open it, and immediately recognized her mother's handwriting: *Sam, I never even saw this letter until Grandma died. You do what you need to do, for you. I'll be fine.*

CHAPTER

62

1989

Brick knew by heart the biggest milestones of Paull's life, as reported by the *Erietown Times*.

Paull Russo attended Harbor High School, which was one point seven miles from the apartment over Sardelli's, where he was conceived. For the first three years of high school, he played forward on the Mariners basketball team. A summer growth spurt shot him up to six feet two in his senior year. Same height as his old man, same position: point guard.

Paull also played baseball, alternating between right field and shortstop and, like his father, threw "faster than a bullet out of the barrel," one sportswriter said. He did not, however, mirror his father's strength at bat. Poor coaching, Brick was sure of it. He and Paull had the same build, the same rhythm of bone to muscle. Brick knew what he was doing wrong without ever seeing him at the plate.

Paull lettered in both sports all four years, and graduated in 1983. That fall, he went off to Hiram College, about an hour south of Erietown, and majored in business administration. A private school, Brick noted with a grudging respect for Rosemary's aunt and uncle.

Four years later, Bianchi & DeLuca, the Italian accounting

firm in the harbor, announced Paull's hire as junior associate, just two weeks after he graduated from college. With a three-point-six average, Brick wanted to brag.

Brick never told Ellie any of this, because Paull did not exist. This was the deal they'd struck in the summer of 1969, in the hours after Rosemary drove off that bridge.

Brick had never thought Rosemary was capable of killing herself, and the police said it was an accident. But he'd been haunted by the look in her eyes that night, in the moment before she left. She'd looked crazed, like a trapped animal.

Did Rosemary lose control of her car, or did she drive off the bridge? He'd never know.

Brick hadn't found out about her death until the following afternoon, in the plant locker room. Gus Fazio's wife worked in the kitchen at Sardelli's and knew Rosemary well. She called Gus at work to tell him.

"Ginny's hysterical," Gus said, combing his wet hair.

What about the boy? Brick wanted to ask, his heart pounding. *Did the story say anything about her son?* He zipped up his pants and didn't bother combing his hair. He had to get out of there. He had to know. He was barely halfway to his car when he bent at the waist and vomited in the parking lot. "Roe," he said, wiping his mouth on his sleeve. "Jesus Christ."

He drove twenty miles over the speed limit to the nearest gas station to buy a copy of the paper. His hands shook as he stood by the rack of Hostess pies and Ho Hos and stared at the front-page photo of Rosemary's car dangling from the tow truck's hook, its grille skimming the water.

He threw a dollar bill at the cashier and didn't wait for change. He drove to his son's elementary school a block away and parked in the empty lot before opening the paper. He read quickly through the first part of the story. When he found it, he read the entire paragraph out loud:

Mrs. Russo was 29 years old and lived with her 2-year-old son and her aunt and uncle, Elizabeth and Daniel Martinelli. Mr. Martinelli said in a telephone interview that they were "heartbroken," and would raise the boy. "Family takes care of family," he said.

Brick pressed his forehead against the top of the steering wheel. The boy was alive. He stepped out of the car and this time made it to a rusted trash barrel before emptying what was left in his stomach.

He had to see Ellie. Sam always fetched their copy of the *Times* from the porch and set it in his recliner so he could read while Ellie made dinner. Maybe his wife didn't even know yet about Rosemary. He should be the one to tell her.

He parked on the street in front of their house to avoid looking like he expected to be invited to stay. He walked into the house through the back door. Ellie was standing at the stove, stirring something in a pot. She turned to look at him, and didn't seem at all surprised to see him. "Our paper didn't come today," she said, pointing to the rolled-up newspaper in his hands. "Sam checked."

"El, let's go to our bedroom," he said. She started shaking her head, and he held up his hand. "Not for that. We need to talk about something. Away from the kids."

When he said, "Rosemary is dead," Ellie slowly sat down on the edge of the bed.

"How?"

Brick unfurled the paper and held it up. "She drove off the Clayton Valley Bridge."

Ellie stood. "Wait for me here," she said, walking out the door. Brick could hear her talking to Sam. "Give Reilly some of the leftover stew on the stove, and let him watch TV for a while before putting him to bed. No later than eight-thirty."

Ellie returned and eased the bedroom door closed. "What do we do now?"

They talked and cried through the night. By dawn, they had reached an agreement. Paull was not Brick's son, and neither of them would ever mention him again.

"We can forget this ever happened," he said, the newspaper still lying open on the bed between them. "You always say you believe everything happens for a reason."

Ellie pointed to the photo of Rosemary with Paull in the birthday hat. "I feel sorry for that little boy," she said. "Whoever his father is, he'll never know him." She rolled up the paper and handed it to him. "Burn it."

It was necessary, Brick told himself over the years, whenever he thought about Paull. He had to walk away. He owed it to Ellie and the kids to cobble their marriage back together and get on with their lives.

Pretending didn't mean forgetting. Every time he read about Paull in the newspaper, his stomach roiled. So much guilt, so much unearned pride.

In some ways, he knew Paull better than he did the son he had raised. Reilly wanted little to do with him these days. "He's given up on me," Brick had recently told Ellie after another empty, pained exchange on the phone with Reilly, who had called to talk to his mother. Ellie had shrugged. "He took the other option," she'd said, with no malice in her voice. "He needed to find out who he is away from the shadow of you."

Brick realized he had tried too hard to mold his son into the man Brick always imagined he himself could have been. Get the sports scholarship, be the first male McGinty to go to college, be everybody's hero as a coach. Reilly wanted nothing to do with his father's worn-out dreams. He was five inches shorter than Brick, so basketball was out. He had no interest in football, and he quit baseball midseason in his junior year.

"You don't just quit a team," Brick had yelled at him the night he found out.

Reilly had reached for his jacket and refused to yell back. "Every game, I'm on the bench," he'd said calmly. "I wish you'd accept what I already know, Dad: I'm not a star athlete. I'm never going to be you." Reilly had pulled the brim of his ball cap low over his eyes. "I don't blame you for being disappointed."

Why didn't he say something to Reilly in that moment, something good about his kind and gentle son? Why did he just stand there and watch Reilly walk out the door?

Weeks later, Reilly had announced his plans at the dinner table. "I'm getting out of Erietown," he said. "Jimmy Cannon says the carpenters' union is training a new round of apprentices the same month I graduate." He turned to look at his mother, who was sitting next to him. "You always said I'm good with my hands, Mom. That I remind you of your grandpa. It's in my blood. I want to be like him."

"Sweetie," Ellie said.

Brick pushed his plate away. "The plan was for you to go to college."

"That was your plan," Reilly said, tossing his napkin onto his plate and standing up. "I'm going to be eighteen in a few months. You won't be able to tell me what to do anymore."

"Goddammit," Brick said. "Wait'll your sister hears about this."

"Sam already knows," Reilly told him.

Ellie stiffened. "What? What did she say?"

"Assistant Principal McGinty thinks my life is up to me," Reilly said. "She's glad one of us is getting out of Erietown. 'Don't be late to your own life,' she said, whatever that means."

Ellie stood up and started stacking plates.

The week after Reilly graduated from high school, he

moved to the west side of Cleveland and started his apprentice-ship with Carpenters Local 435. Reilly was married now, to a teacher, and well on his way to making good money in construction. Brick was glad for that, but he'd never felt more like a failure for his son than the first time he saw Reilly's metal lunch pail in the backseat of his truck.

Brick had read that Paull Russo got married the year after he graduated college, to a bank teller. Had a son barely a year later, and had recently been promoted at the accounting firm. Brick pictured him walking into work each day wearing a suit and tie, carrying a briefcase, and nodding at secretaries who called him "sir."

In the summers, he read that Paull played in the same softball league as Brick had, nearly twenty years ago. At Smitty Field, too. The first time Brick saw the black-and-white team photo for Sardelli's Ristorante, he knew without checking the caption which man was his son. Paull Russo, broad-shouldered and tall, stood in the back row, just like Brick always had. His hair was light, his face sunburned and freckled. He played right field, just like Brick.

Paull was not the best hitter on the team. For the rest of his life, Brick would tell himself that was why he went to Paull's game at the beginning of the second season. He knew how to help him become a power at the plate. He was doing what fathers do.

In May, Brick clipped the summer softball schedule from the back of the sports section and folded it until it fit in his wallet between the kids' high school graduation pictures. He studied the schedule to figure out the best evening to show up. He settled on game seventeen, a Tuesday evening in July when Ellie came home from work, served a quick dinner, and headed to church for her monthly Women's Guild meeting.

Just this once, he told himself as he pulled out of the driveway. It was the least he could do.

. . .

Brick sat in the bleachers behind home plate, fourth row from the bottom. He wore sunglasses and his old Mickey's ball cap, the brim pulled down. The sun had given up for the day but left the heat behind, with little breeze to move it along. Brick's shirt stuck to his sweaty back in the still air. A perfect night for softball.

Paull was the sixth batter, a spot in the lineup foreign to Brick, who'd usually batted cleanup. He leaned forward and winced both times the ump called a strike on Paull. On the third pitch, Paull popped up to short left. Brick studied his son's face after he pulled off his cap and threw it at the bench in frustration. His red hair was damp and gleaming under the lights, his freckled face screwed into a grimace.

Paull struck out the second time at bat, and popped again to short on his third try. After the game, Brick waited for people to clear out before he moved. Every inch of him ached as he slowly rose and stretched his back. He pulled off his cap and slipped his sunglasses into his breast pocket before slowly descending, never taking his eyes off Paull, who had lagged behind to gather up his stuff and shove it into his duffel. Brick walked to the edge of the backstop. He shoved his hand into his pocket and jingled his coins a few times to collect himself.

Paull shoved the folded bill of his cap into his back pocket and glanced at Brick. He grabbed the duffel and threw it over his shoulder. He took three steps, looked at Brick again, and stopped. "Can I help you, sir?"

"Nah. Just another fan," Brick said. "It's a great game. I played for a lot of years."

"It *is* a great game," Paull said, "but you'd never know it by how I'm hitting."

"Don't try to pull everything."

Paull stepped closer. "What?"

"I said, don't try to pull everything."

Paull stood in front of him and grabbed the shoulder strap of his duffel with both hands. "Is that what I'm doing?"

Brick nodded. "You're a good line-drive hitter. If you try to pull it, you'll pop up. If the pitch is outside, go with the pitch. Go to right field."

"But all my power is to left field."

"You'll get singles and doubles hitting it to right. Better than a pop-up to short, right?"

"Yeah. Right." Paull held out his hand and smiled. "Thanks," he said. "Thanks a lot. I'll try it." He tilted his head. "What is your name?"

Brick shook his hand again. "Good luck to you, kid." He pulled on his cap and walked toward the parking lot. A thin older woman in sunglasses was standing by the car parked next to Brick's. She leaned against the passenger door as Brick approached, her hands wrapped around a camera.

"A Canon AE-1," Brick said, pointing to it. "I've always wanted to get one of those."

"My husband bought it for me," she said. "He always wanted me to have the best."

He pointed at Paull, who was walking toward them. "That boy of yours is quite the athlete."

She nodded. "Just like his father."

Brick pretended to look around. "Oh, I didn't see him."

She pointed toward the ball field. "He was just here."

Brick stopped breathing as the sound of Paull's cleats grew louder against the gravel. He pulled open his car door and touched the brim of his cap. "You have a good evening." She raised her camera to her face.

As soon as Brick saw the headline at the top of the sports page, he rolled the paper and stuck it under his arm before walking to the toolshed in the backyard. He strolled past the open window and the sounds of Ellie cooking dinner and nodded to Mrs. Atkins, who waved from her yard next door with a hand cloaked in a garden glove.

He lifted the pot of geraniums and picked up the key, unlocked the shed door, and pulled it shut behind him. He reached up and tugged on the string to flick on the bare lightbulb, then locked the door before unrolling the newspaper on the top of his workbench. He smoothed the page and stared for a moment at the headline:

PAULL RUSSO'S HITTING SLUMP GONE FOR GOOD

In paragraph eight, he found it:

When asked about his new strategy at the plate, Russo wasn't giving up any secrets. "Let's just say I got some really good advice," he said. "From a real pro. I hope he sees this, so he knows I listened. I wish I could thank him in person."

Brick read the paragraph several times, rubbing his finger across Paull's name.

I wish I could thank him in person.

Brick reached behind himself for the stool and sat down. He pulled on the string and bent over the bench, his hand over his mouth as his shoulders heaved in the dark.

CHAPTER

63

1994

Sam glanced at her mother in the passenger seat. "What is it, Mom?"

Ellie turned her head away. "Nothing."

"You were staring at me. You obviously have something on your mind."

Ellie shifted to her chirpier voice. "Do you think you'll ever marry?"

"Not this again."

"I asked a simple question," Ellie said.

"What you're really asking is *why* haven't I married."

"Well," Ellie said. "Is there something you might want to tell me? Over lunch?"

"Sounds like you've already heard," Sam said, looking at her mother. "I'm not ready to talk about that yet. We're going to lunch because I thought it'd be a nice thing to do on your day off."

"Interesting," Ellie said. "Well, keep in mind, you're only thirty-seven. That's not too late these days to have children."

"I have four hundred and twenty-three children."

"You sound like Aunt Nessa."

Sam smiled. "I loved hearing about Aunt Nessa when I was

growing up. I think all those stories you told me about her helped me decide to major in education. I'll bet she would have made a wonderful principal."

"They wouldn't let her do that back then," Ellie said. "They couldn't stop you."

"Principal Samantha McGinty," Sam said, smiling, "coming to a school near you this fall."

"How Aunt Nessa would have loved that," Ellie said. "You know how proud Dad and I are of you. All that responsibility. Makes me wish all the more you had a man who loves and cherishes you. Surely there's one good man out there. They're not all like that Henry."

"He's not why I'm not married, Mom. That was a long time ago, and he wasn't right for me. It's not like I've been a nun. There are parts of being with a man I like very much."

She glanced at her mother, who simply nodded, waiting for Sam to continue. "There are too many things that can go wrong in a marriage. Most of my friends are married, and it seems a married life is never an extraordinary one."

"I never expected to have an extraordinary life," Ellie said. "I have tried to live my ordinary life in nonordinary ways. I'm fifty-six years old, and I'm working in a job I love. I know that you, Dad, and Reilly just see me as a nurse's aide, but I make a difference in people's lives."

"Of course you do, Mom."

"Here's what none of you understand. These people, my patients, they're so scared. So fragile, sometimes—even the most important men in town. Just last week I met that man who—" She shook her head.

"What man, Mom?"

"I can't, Sam," Ellie said, sitting straighter. "Patient confidentiality."

"Sometimes I wonder." Sam tightened her grip on the wheel. "You have such a full life now, but—"

"But what?"

Sam sighed. "Mom, why did you put up with it? Why didn't you leave? After she showed up at our door with that little boy."

Ellie looked down at her lap for a moment, then turned to face Sam. "We want to think there are rules in life. That as long as we follow them, everything will be all right. And then God blows up your plans. Blows them to smithereens. And you're left picking up the pieces and putting your life back together as best as you can, because it's not about you. It's about your children, and the life you've built, and not giving everyone a reason to see you as damaged goods for the rest of your life."

"I'm sorry, Mom. I shouldn't have brought it up."

"No, I'm glad you did," Ellie said. "This has been hanging over us for years." She turned to face the front and took a deep breath. "I need to say something else, Sam. It might help you, I think."

Sam looked at her. "What is it?"

"It's what I've learned about grief," Ellie said. "Not just grief after a death, but the grief you can feel after something rocks your world. Grief is that monster that bangs at your door until you let it in and sit with it for a while. When you get bored with each other, the monster leaves."

Sam relaxed her foot on the pedal, and the car started to slow. "I never thought of it that way. How long does it stay? The monster."

"That's not the question, honey. It's how long does it take you to answer the door and let it in. That's where the pain is. You have to open the door. You can always tell the people who won't. Shows up in their faces over time. The longer they wait, the longer the monster stands in their way, blocking all the good trying to find them."

"How'd you get to be so smart, Mom?"

Ellie shrugged. "I've opened my share of doors, I guess."

The back of Sam's neck started to tingle. She would never have predicted this, the mother she'd always tried to protect showing her what she had to do. Long after Rosemary Russo had banged on their front door, Sam's monster was still knocking. It was time to let it in.

CHAPTER

64

Lizzie Martinelli smoothed page seven of the *Erietown Times* on the kitchen table and stared at the two-column photo of Samantha Joy McGinty. She was dressed in a suit, smiling over the heads of a group of young children. A pretty girl, Lizzie had to admit; looked a lot like her mother, only taller. Same dark hair and pale skin, with big, almond-shaped eyes sloping ever so slightly, just like her Paull's.

HOMETOWN GIRL PROMOTED TO PRINCIPAL, FIRST WOMAN TO HOLD TOP JOB AT SCHOOL

Lizzie tapped the tip of the scissors on Sam's photo. "My Rosie was braver than you. She didn't have a father at home, didn't have much of anything. Got on that bus all by herself and moved far away to start a new life. Without your fancy degrees."

She stared a bit longer at Sam's photo and started clipping out the story. Time to tell him. Time for Principal McGinty to know, too.

Lizzie folded the clipping and carried it upstairs, hesitating in the bedroom doorway. Finally she could look at her husband's side of the bed without wishing the floor would open up and swallow her whole.

She had only recently packed up her husband's clothes, but Danny's bedside table remained untouched except for her weekly feather dusting. The leather strap of his unbuckled watch was curled in the shape of his wrist, right where he'd left it on the evening of Paullie's wedding. He was so happy that morning as he buckled on his watch and tapped his fingers on the crystal.

"In three hours, our Paullie is going to be a married man. How 'bout that, Lizzie?" He was weak and rail thin by then, but liver cancer was not going to stop Danny Martinelli from watching the only child he had raised become a married man.

A week later, Danny was gone.

Paullie had a five-year-old son now, Charlie, who was about to start kindergarten at Westwood Elementary School.

Lizzie sat on her side of the bed and pulled open the drawer of the bedside table. She lifted up the address book and pulled out the letter-size envelope tucked under it. She flipped it over: *Aunt Lizzie.*

She opened the envelope and pulled out the two photos tucked behind the letter. She studied them for a moment before picking up the phone receiver and dialing. "Charlie?" she said, forcing her voice to sound cheerful. "It's Aunt Lizzie. Has your daddy left for work yet?"

Paull Russo walked into the bar and smiled at the old man shuffling toward him. "Hi, Mr. Sardelli."

"Vinny," the man growled. "How many times I gotta tell you, call me Vinny."

Paull laughed. "Okay, okay. Vinny! It's good to see you."

Vinny pulled him into a hug. "I knew you when all you could do was eat and poop."

Paull patted Vinny's bony back with both hands and laughed again. "Thanks for *that* memory." He stepped back. "So, have you seen my aunt?"

Vinny tilted his head toward the back corner. "I can hear her." They both turned to look at Lizzie, who was half-standing out of her chair and waving her arms. "Vinny! Vinny! Jesus Christ. Get your hands off my Paullie and send him back here."

Paull waved at her as Vinny leaned in. "Just a warning. She's been here a good hour already. That's her second gin and tonic."

Paull nodded. "Thanks, Mr. Sardel—"—he held up his hands in surrender—"Vinny. Thanks for letting me know." He walked toward the back of the room. He kissed Aunt Lizzie's cheek. "To what do I owe this rare invitation for lunch on a weekday?"

She pointed to the approaching waitress. "Hi, Joanie."

"Hey, you two," the waitress said, smiling. "You know what you want?"

Paull raised his eyebrows at his aunt as he sat down. "The usual?"

"Sure."

He smiled at the waitress. "Joanie, we'll have two meatball subs, with extra sauce." He looked at his aunt's glass. "And we'll both have Diet Cokes, please."

"Got it," Joanie said. "Back in a wink."

Paull sat down, and Lizzie pulled the envelope out of her purse, setting it facedown on the table. "I have to talk to you about something."

"Is something wrong?"

"Paullie, first I just want to say that your uncle Danny and I did what we thought was best for you. At the time, I mean."

"I know that. You and Uncle Danny were wonderful to me."

She ran her hand across the envelope. "What I mean is, we

told you what we thought we were supposed to say. What your mother wanted us to say."

Paull leaned in closer. "Aunt Lizzie, what is this about?"

Lizzie slid the letter across the table. "Your mother wrote it the day she died."

The lines on his forehead deepened as he silently read:

Dear Aunt Lizzie:

I'm so sorry. As Vinny would say, I've played my last hand. I thought Brick and his wife might take Paullie and raise him so that he could know his father. I was wrong. It's Brick's fault, not hers. I met her once before, but never mind that. She was nice to Paullie when I showed up. I think she might have done it, raised him. She couldn't have any more children.

When I was pregnant you asked to adopt Paullie and raise him as your own. I was selfish. I wanted him all for myself. I'm sorry I didn't give him to you. But I'm doing it now. I'm not good for him. I know it now, and Paullie knows it, too. That's why he always runs to you.

I have $27.17 in an envelope in my drawer by the bed. I'm sorry it's not more. You were right, I overdid it when I spent all that money from Brick in the beginning. I was just excited to be able to buy things for my boy, but I got that out of my system. Brick has stopped giving me money. I was hoping to start saving some of the money he gave me for Paullie to go to college, but now Brick says Paullie isn't his. To my face, he said that. He knows Paullie is his. Even his wife could see it, I could tell.

I love you. And Uncle Danny, too. I'm so sorry. I know this will make you sad, but I don't have anything left in me, and I don't want to ruin the only good thing I ever did. Having Paullie, I mean. If he never knows me, maybe he can picture me in his mind when he gets older, and he'll like me a lot and wish I was there. Wouldn't that be nice.

Thank you for everything you did for me. Without you, I would of died in Foxglove. I would of wasted away there. I know you would say, well then Rosie just move away from Erietown and start over but I couldn't live knowing I had a son in this world who didn't even know I was his mother. I'm all played out. Please tell him I loved him so much which is why I had to leave.

Love,
Your Rosie

P.S. When Paullie grows up could you please tell him that when he was 2 his sister Sam held him in her arms + sang him to sleep? She is a nice girl. Maybe someday she'll want to know Paullie.

P.P.S. Also, please tell Paullie it was an accident.

Lizzie studied her nephew's face as his eyes darted back and forth, line by line. "I don't understand," he said, setting down the letter.

"Which part, honey?"

"Your part," he said. "Why have you never shown me this letter before now? And who is Brick? I thought my father was Anthony Russo. He died in Vietnam before I was born."

"Brick is your father," she said. "Russo was our maiden name. Your mother's and mine. Her father was my brother, as you know."

"And Anthony Russo?"

"She made him up. So many boys around here were dying in Vietnam by the time you were born."

Paull pressed his palms on the table. "Wow."

"I loved your mother like a daughter," Lizzie said. "I warned her to stay away from Brick. But she had her eyes on him from the moment she saw that picture of him in the newspaper."

"Was he famous?"

"No," Lizzie said. "But he was a big ballplayer here in Erie-town. Softball, like you."

"Do I look—"

"Just like him," she said. "It's uncanny, really, right down to your freckles and red hair."

"How did they meet?"

"Your mom tended bar here. Lived in the apartment up-stairs. The way she told it, he came in one night in a funk and she cheered him up. But she'd been waiting for him to show up for a long time."

"I'm confused."

"So was she, honey. The one guy she couldn't have was the one she wanted. He was married. Already had two kids."

He pointed to the letter. "She says here, 'Please tell Paullie it was an accident.' What did she mean by that?"

"As you know, your mother's car drove off that bridge."

"Yeah," he said, slowly. "It was raining hard, her tires slid, and she lost control of the car. It crashed through the railing."

"No, honey." She tapped the letter. "Your mother had reached her end. She wasn't thinking right. I didn't know it at the time, but she had given up. She thought she had failed you. The day she died? She had showed up at Brick McGinty's house with you in her arms."

"Because he had stopped helping her with money."

"Yes. As she says in the letter, she thought maybe Brick and his wife—Ellie's her name—would agree to raise you. But he kicked her out."

"What a prick. But what did she expect? He'd already de-nied I was his son. She says it right here."

"He knew you were his," Lizzie said. "He gave Rosie money every payday to help support you. A guy doesn't do that unless he thinks the kid is his."

"What changed?"

"Who knows? Maybe he loved your mother, but he didn't

have the guts to leave his wife. Maybe he was afraid his wife would find out."

"So, I met my father?"

"Three times. At the park by the lake, near the plant where he worked. Erietown Electric. He drove there to meet you."

"And then at their house."

Lizzie nodded.

"When was the third time?"

She pulled the photos out of the envelope. "Many years later. You were in your early twenties. Charlie had just been born." She tossed one of the two pictures onto the table. "It was after one of your games. I had my camera with me. Don't ask me to explain why, because I can't, but I held it up and took this picture while the two of you talked."

Paull picked up the photo. In it, Paull was holding the duffel strap over his shoulder with both hands, leaning in to listen to Brick. They were smiling at each other.

"I remember him. He's the guy who told me how to hit better. I thought he was just somebody's fan, a player's dad, maybe."

"Right on both counts," Lizzie said.

"Why didn't he introduce himself?"

"My question's different. Why was he at Smitty Field that day? Obviously, he wanted to see his son." She slid the other photo across the table.

Paull's eyes widened as he picked it up. "How did you get this picture?"

"I was standing by our car, waiting for you. He was parked next to us. He knew I was onto him, and he didn't seem to care. I held up the camera, and he just looked at me. Like he wanted you to have this picture of him."

Paull continued to stare at the photo. "What happened to him?"

"He's still around. The newspaper printed a list of utility

workers taking the buyout at Erietown Electric. His name was on it."

"Do you think he knew?" Paull said, holding up the photo. "Did he know my mother was going to kill herself that day? That she was going to drive over that bridge?"

Lizzie looked up at the ceiling and exhaled. "For the longest time, I wanted to believe he did. That he was just that awful. And did nothing to stop her." She looked at Paull, blinking back tears. "But if I didn't see it, living with her every day, how could he have known it? I missed the signs. I feel so bad about something I said to her, just a few days before she died."

"What was it?"

"Rosie had just put you down for the night, on her night off. She sat down next to me on the sofa and said, 'This sure isn't the life I planned when I took that bus to Erietown.'"

"What did you say?"

"I told her, 'Oh, honey, nobody gets the life they planned. We get what God plans, and we spend the rest of our lives trying not to hold it against him.'"

"Sounds pretty wise to me."

Lizzie shook her head. "No, no. If I'd been paying attention, maybe I would have heard it in her voice. The desperation. I thought she was just tired."

The waitress walked up to their table. "Here you go," she said, smiling at Paull. "Two meatball sandwiches, extra sauce."

"Thanks, Joanie." He slid the plate to the side as soon as she walked away. "Is that true, Aunt Lizzie? About me and this— this sister?"

"I know she exists. And that she has a brother. Another brother, I mean. I don't know about her singing to you, but maybe she was used to doing that because of him."

"Where is *she* now?"

Lizzie reached into the envelope. "That's why we're talking about all this today." She opened the newspaper clipping and handed it to Paull. "That's her. Samantha McGinty, the new principal of Westwood Elementary School."

He leaned back in the chair. "Charlie's school."

Lizzie pushed her plate away and waved her empty drink glass to the waitress. "Yep. When you and Megan walk your son into that school next Monday, your sister will probably be the first person to welcome you to Westwood Elementary. As I said, God's plans."

He studied Sam's face. "I know this sounds crazy, but she looks a little familiar to me."

"Yeah, well, there's a reason for that."

He looked up at his aunt. "What is it?"

"First, I need to know you're going to forgive me for all this. For not telling you everything sooner."

"This changes nothing, Aunt Lizzie. If there's one thing you've taught me, it's that resentment will eat you alive while the people who hurt you do just fine." He slid Rosemary's letter back into the envelope, and tucked in the two photos. "Now I understand why you harped on that. Because of what happened to Mom, right?"

"Yeah. Well."

He held up Sam's photo and returned it to the envelope. "Why do I know her?"

"You were eight," Lizzie said. "She was a teenager working at the old Otto's Tavern. She gave you some crayons and you drew a picture with her. She had no idea who you were."

"Butterflies," he said. "We drew butterflies."

"It was a long time ago, sweetie. Don't expect her to remember."

"Well, I was only eight years old," Paull said, tucking the envelope into his breast pocket. "And I remember."

CHAPTER

65

S am pulled off her pumps and continued to race with Lois Johnson toward the gym. "All right, Mrs. Johnson, tell me again, please, how this happened."

"As I tried to warn you, Ms. McGinty, not every family was happy about having to bring in their children's doctors' records and show them to Dr. Marino."

"We've seen an uptick in lapsed immunizations," Sam said, "particularly in the poorer neighborhoods of Erietown. You know that. Children must be up-to-date with their vaccines to attend school in Ohio. That's why I accepted Dr. Marino's extremely gracious offer to come here in person and meet with each family, regardless of income. To avoid singling out anyone."

"That's not our problem here, Ms. McGinty, and you know it."

Sam stopped to catch her breath. "What do you mean?"

Mrs. Johnson frowned. "Please don't make me say it."

"We've known each other for ten years," Sam said. "I wouldn't come to this school unless you could still be my secretary, you may remember."

"You have to admit it. You love it. Your father shows up and I tell him, 'She'll be with you in a minute.'"

Sam smiled. "I do enjoy that, probably a little too much."

"And you wanted me, at least a little, to raise the quota here."

Sam stopped in her tracks and laughed. "Because you're black? No, because I'm Lois-dependent. Nobody knows how to keep a school on track like you. And, yes, you're a wonderful role model for most of these kids here who have never talked to a black person. So, you see, we all need you." She pointed toward the gymnasium. "And now, it appears that Dr. Marino needs both of us, thanks to Jimmy McGraw's dad."

"He doesn't want a black man touching his son. That's what he said."

Sam started walking again. "Dr. Marino is half-white."

"Mmm-hmm," Mrs. Johnson said. "I'm sure that's what everyone sees when that dreamy root beer float walks into the room."

Sam stopped again. "Do you know, I've never had a root beer float that can walk?"

Mrs. Johnson smiled wryly. "Give him time. That man's got eyes for you."

"Mrs. Johnson, this is me ignoring you."

They rounded the corner and walked into mayhem. The line of parents with children stretched down the length of the hallway, their voices echoing off the walls. "Ms. McGinty," Lilah McCormick's mother yelled as she pointed up the line. "What on earth is going on up there?" Three huddled mothers turned to look at her. "You didn't say we were going to be here all day," Jeffrey Lovett's mom said as she held on to her wriggling son's collar.

Sam held out her arms and kept walking. "Folks, I'm sorry about this. We're going to get this line moving again right away. Thanks for your patience."

"Nobody asked for my patience," Jack Tyler's father yelled.

Sam smiled at him and said, "And yet here you are, Mr. Tyler, being as nice as can be."

Mrs. Johnson tsk-tsked as they walked. "People talking to you like you're their servant or something," she said. "Shameful." Sam wrapped her arm around her secretary's shoulder. "See what I mean? What would I do without you?"

Mark McGraw was standing with his son in front of Dr. Marino, seething. "As soon as my wife told me what was going on here, I had to take off work." Sam walked toward them and smiled at Jimmy, who was on the verge of tears. "Mrs. Johnson," she said, taking the child's hand, "would you please walk Jimmy down to my office and give him a Hershey's Kiss?"

His father pointed to the secretary. "Don't think I don't know what you're doing." Sam waited until Mrs. Johnson and Jimmy had left before turning toward the father. "Mr. McGraw, do you have your son's records with you?"

"He's not touching my boy."

Sam looked at Dr. Marino, who immediately returned her smile. "It appears that I'm the first African-American Italian he's met," he said.

Sam sighed. "I've got this."

Mr. McGraw pointed at Sam and Dr. Marino. "This is what happens when you hire a woman. She's never even given birth. What does she know about raising our kids? Now she's bringing in a black doctor to manhandle them."

Sam whipped around. "I will not have you talking about—"

Dr. Marino placed his hand on her arm. "You're going to need to stop talking to Principal McGinty like that," he said. The room fell silent.

Mr. McGraw glared at him. "You don't tell me anything."

"In fact, I do," Dr. Marino said. "I'm here because Principal McGinty is trying to keep your son safe from diseases that could kill him. That's how much she cares about your little boy." He turned to look at the other parents. "That's how much she cares about all of your children."

"Dr. Marino," Sam said, "you don't need to—"

"I'm a pediatrician," Dr. Marino continued. "This is what I do. We're going to go over your children's records. If we find they're missing any vaccinations, this nice nurse here"—he pointed to a white woman in a nurse's uniform standing by a table a few feet away—"is going to give your children the shots they need. That way, they can stay in school."

Mr. McGraw glared at Dr. Marino, but said nothing. "Okay," Sam said. "Let's get this line moving." The room started buzzing again.

Sam looked at Dr. Marino, her face burning. "I didn't need you to defend me, Carson."

He reached into the pocket of his white coat and pulled out a lollipop. "I know that, and so does everyone in this room," he said, handing it to her. "What I wanted *you* to know, is that you deserve to have someone stick up for you."

She looked down at the lollipop in her hand. "I prefer grape."

"As of this minute, of course you do," he said, smiling. "I'm onto you, Principal McGinty."

CHAPTER

66

Sam set the mail on the table by her front door and looked over at the blinking message light on her answering machine.

"In a minute," she said, pulling out her ponytail as she walked up the stairs. Every book for professional women said she should have short hair to be taken seriously. The ponytail was her compromise. She ran her fingers through her hair as it fell around her shoulders and she thought about her long day.

Over lunch in the cafeteria, Carson Marino had apologized for undermining her authority in front of the parents. "I was angry at that father, and showed a lapse in judgment," he said. He looked so somber and earnest that Sam couldn't help herself. She'd grabbed his hand across the tray and launched into her best Katharine Hepburn imitation. "Listen to me, mister," she'd said, her voice full of exaggerated tremor, "you're my knight in shining armor."

Sam fell back on the bed and winced at the memory of his confused face. Of course, Dr. Carson Marino never watched movies. He was too busy saving lives.

Over lunch, she'd coaxed him into talking about his family. She could tell by his quick but thorough answer that he'd had a lot of practice answering the same questions. His father was a Catholic Italian kid from Brooklyn who fell in love with a black woman from Mississippi during his residency at a public hospital in Cleveland.

"Her family had moved from the South when she was a little girl," Carson said. "She was the third nurse in her family, and third-generation Methodist. When it was clear they were in love, Mom told Dad, 'I'll give up everything but Jesus for you.'"

"Sounds like my mom," Sam said, thinking of her parents' Jack-and-Jesus wall. "She grew up Methodist, too, but became Presbyterian after she married. Still, Catholics believe in Jesus."

"Not enough, according to my maternal grandfather," he said, grinning. "Family lore has it that the first time my mom's father met my dad, he shook his hand and said, 'Hail no to your Hail Mary. In this house we praise Jesus.'"

Sam suppressed a laugh. "How did your dad's parents feel about your mother?"

"They didn't meet her until after I was born, in 1954. 'Family is family,' Grandma Anita said, and that was that. I know how to cook more Italian dishes than Mama Sardelli, because of her."

"They were brave," Sam said. "Your parents."

"My parents always joked that only an Italian boy from Bensonhurst would think it's okay to marry a black girl from Mississippi. For years, they couldn't even go visit her family. My grandparents, on both sides, were afraid they'd get killed."

"What was it like?" Sam said. "To be you. Cleveland is better than a small town, but the races still didn't mix much."

"Everybody makes assumptions about everyone else," he said. "It's just easier to figure out what people are thinking about me."

"I'm sorry about that father," she said.

He looked at his watch and stood up, stacking her tray onto

his. "Most people here aren't like him, at least not face-to-face. When they're in my examining room, or when I'm taking care of one of their children in the hospital. They get used to me."

"Still, why didn't you stay in Cleveland?" she said as they walked toward the trash bin. "Why come here, to Erietown?"

"I love my father. He's head of pediatrics. He casts quite the shadow." He emptied her tray over the bin. "Erietown needed another pediatrician, and I needed a cause, I guess."

Sam smiled at him. "Thank you for taking care of my tray."

"Thank you for letting me. I'm feeling the progress of this moment."

Sam changed into jeans and her old KSU sweatshirt and drifted back downstairs to listen to phone messages. The first one was Mandy Honkonen, 1975 senior class president of Erietown High School.

"Samantha, busy mother of six here. The reunion commit-tee is wondering if you could do those fancy class name tags again. Cahhhhl me." Sam deleted the message and picked up a pen. "Call Mandy on Walton's Mountain," she wrote on the notepad. She pressed the button for the next message.

"Sam, it's Carson Marino. Your mom tells me your Katha-rine Hepburn imitation is from *On Golden Pond*. Maybe I should start watching more movies. Any chance you might help me with that? You have my card with all my numbers. Please call me."

Sam saved the message and hit the button again.

"Sam, it's your dad."

Sam sat up straighter. Her father had never left a phone message for her.

"Give me a call when you get a chance," Brick said. "Some-thing I want to talk to you about."

The machine beeped. End of messages.

Sam picked up the receiver and dialed.

"Hee-*yell*-oh."

"Hi, Mom."

"Sam," Ellie said. "I've been meaning to call you."

"I want to talk, but first, is Dad around? He left a message for me to call him."

"Your father called?"

"Yep."

"What about?"

"I don't know, Mom. That's why I'm calling him back."

"He's not here. He's running errands."

"How was your day, Mom?"

"Crazy. Three new admissions and a patient who tried to escape, twice."

"Anything else you want to tell me?"

"Isn't that enough?"

Sam knew to wait.

"Well, a funny thing did happen on my way to the parking lot. I ran into Dr. Marino, who told me he'd just spent the day with you."

"At our school," Sam said. "Vaccinations, remember?"

"Sure," Ellie said. "What I'm trying to figure out is why you did your Katharine Hepburn imitation for him."

"Is that your real question?"

"Clever you," Ellie said. "Sylvia Manning saw me talking to Dr. Marino, and as soon as he walked away she ran up to me and said, 'I saw your daughter and him talking at a table in the cafeteria with their heads this close.'"

"She was at my school?"

"No, Sam," Ellie said. "She was referring to a lunch you apparently had with him two weeks ago in our cafeteria."

"That was a meeting," Sam said. "About vaccinations. We've had several."

"Uh-huh. Well Sylvia said you two were oblivious to everyone around you."

"Skip to the part where you told Sylvia to mind her own business."

"To be honest, Sam, I'm glad she told me. Somebody needed to tell me that my daughter was dating Carson Marino."

"We're not dating."

"I know," Ellie said. "You're meeting. Did it occur to you that by meeting about the same topic over and over again he might have an ulterior motive?"

Sam hesitated. "He's a nice man, Mom."

"Sounds like maybe you think Carson Marino is more than just nice."

For the second time in one day, Sam surprised herself. No denial, no changing the subject. "Well, Mom," she said, "what if I do?"

"I'm fifty-six years old, Sam," Ellie said. "I'll take any color of grandchild I can get."

"Mr. Russo," Sam said, bending at the waist to smile at a little boy. "And who is this?"

The child smiled, revealing a gap in his top row of teeth. "Ms. McGinty, you know me. I'm Charlie."

Sam leaned in, pointing to his mouth. "Are you sure? The Charlie I saw last week wasn't missing a tooth." The little boy giggled as his father reached down to muss his hair. "We had quite a weekend in our house. Tooth fairy came Friday night, but forgot to follow Charlie's handwritten instructions and took his tooth."

Charlie nodded. "She came back on Sunday and left it for me on my dresser. She wrote a note and said I was making her work too hard."

"Tooth fairy needs a union," Agnes Lane said. "I hope she's getting overtime."

Sam stood up and put her hand on the teacher's shoulder. "Charlie, Mr. Russo, you know Ms. Lane." Charlie waved as his father extended his hand.

"Everyone knows Ms. Lane," Mr. Russo said. "She brings Broadway to Erietown every spring. My wife and I started coming to the spring musical before Charlie was born."

Ms. Lane beamed and shook his hand. "How nice of you, Mr. Russo." She pretended to whisper over Charlie's head. "Between us grown-ups, you can call me Lane."

He laughed. "Lane. Great. You can call me Paull."

Lane looked down at Charlie and extended her hand. "And how is it that the handsomest leprechaun I've ever met has such an Italian last name?"

"We're Irish on my father's side," Paull said. "I have my mother's maiden name. It's complicated."

"Ms. McGinty," Charlie said. "All of us have the name Paull. It's my middle name. It's spelled with two els."

Sam looked at the boy's father and slowly nodded. "Paull-two-els," she said. "I knew it was you."

He nodded. "And I knew it was you."

Sam sat down behind her desk and opened her drawer. "Sit down, please," she said, pointing to two empty chairs across from her. She waited for Paull to sit before handing him the folded piece of paper.

He opened it and looked at Sam. "You knew?"

"Not exactly. Not when I was talking to you. After you'd left the restaurant and I saw your name on the drawing. The Paull-two-els."

"I remember writing this," he said, running his fingers across BUTRFLYS BY SAM AND PAULL. "Can't say my spelling is all that much better." He flipped it over and read her handwritten note out loud: *This was the second time I met Paull. 7:07 p.m., August 21, 1975, at Otto's Tavern. He was 8 years old.*

He set the paper facedown on the desk. "You were really nice to me."

"Did you know I was your sister?"

"No. My aunt Lizzie, she raised me, waited until two weeks

ago to tell me about you. She loves me more than anyone on earth, but she's as headstrong as a mule."

"I once read that a mule gets its strength and agility from a horse, but it's smart like a donkey," Sam said. "That what we think is stubbornness is really an ability to weigh the situation and avoid potential harm."

Sam could feel the heat rising up her neck. "I can't believe I just said that. I'm an idiot."

"Nervous, you mean," he said. "So am I."

She rolled back her chair and stood up. "I don't know why I'm sitting behind my desk."

"You're weighing the situation," he said, smiling. "Like a mule, smart like a donkey."

Sam walked around her desk and sat down in the chair next to him. "I don't know where to start," she said.

He pointed to the picture. "Why did you keep this?"

"Guilt, maybe," she said. "A longing, perhaps. I packed it in my train case the day before I left for college. It's always been with me."

Paull nodded slowly, saying nothing.

She started to stand up. "I don't think I can do this."

Paull grabbed the chair arms. "The last thing I want to do is make you feel uncomfortable."

She motioned for him to stay seated, and sat down. "You must hate all of us."

"No, I don't," he said. "Until a month ago, I didn't even know you existed."

"Why did your aunt tell you now?"

"She saw your picture in the paper. She knew our paths were about to cross, because of Charlie."

"Erietown is pretty small," she said. "It's amazing we never met before now."

Sam picked up the drawing and folded it. "They fixed

the railing on that bridge after she died. Did you know that?"

"It wasn't an accident. Did you know *that*?"

"No, I didn't. I mean—" She reached across the desk for a tissue and blotted her eyes. "I wondered, of course. But it was already so sad, so awful."

"She left a letter behind for my aunt," Paull said. "That's how I know she drove off that bridge on purpose. That's how I finally know, I mean. In the letter she said you rocked me in your arms and sang me to sleep."

Sam nodded. "You tried to hum along even though you didn't know the songs. Then you fell asleep."

"I met him a few years ago." He pointed to the framed picture of Brick and Ellie on Sam's desk. "Your dad." He shrugged. "My dad, too, I guess. I talked to him."

Sam shifted in her chair. "When?"

"Years ago, when I played softball for Sardelli's. He came to one of my games at Smitty Field. Gave me some good batting advice after."

"I can't believe it," she said. "I can't believe Dad would do that. How did he say it, who he was?"

"He didn't. I didn't know who he was until last month, when Aunt Lizzie showed me two pictures she took of us talking."

"There are pictures?"

He reached into the inside pocket of his blazer and pulled out the photos. "I've been carrying these around since the first day of school," he said, handing them to her. "I had to work up the nerve to talk to you."

Sam stared at the photos as she spoke. "You look like the pictures I've seen of Dad at your age, when I was little. It must have freaked him out to see you."

"He didn't say much. He just gave me some batting tips and walked away."

"Well, that's that," she said. "My father has always known you were his son. And so did Mom." She handed him the pictures. "You have a brother, too, you know."

"Reilly, right?"

Sam smiled, looking down. "Yeah. He's a great guy. He and my father don't really get along. They're just so different. He was never an athlete like my dad. Like you." She pointed to the photos in his hand. "No wonder Dad wanted to help you with your batting. He saw himself in you."

"Where did that leave you?"

She stood up and smoothed the front of her skirt. "Immune, I guess. When I was twelve, I quit worrying about what my father thought of me."

"What happened?" he said, standing up.

"You happened," she said. "I rocked you in my arms and I realized that none of us had ever been enough for Brick McGinty."

CHAPTER

68

Carson helped Sam with her coat and led her to the aisle. "Well, that was quite the romantic comedy," he said. "Makes me want to go outside and start singin' in the rain."

"Yeah, that was rough," she said, breathlessly.

"You wanted me to understand more about the Vietnam War, and *Platoon* pretty much covers it," Carson said, "although I did hear that *Hamburger Hill* is coming back to Erietown, too, in a few months. Thanks to Oliver Stone, I can now imagine why it's called that." Sam laughed, and immediately recoiled. Had anyone else ever said that to her, she would have launched into a lecture about all the boys in this town who had served in the war.

"Sam?"

She pressed her hand against her chest. "What is happening?"

"What is it?" he said, cupping her elbow. "Do you need to sit down?"

She nudged him with her elbow. "Oh, knock it off, Doc." She tipped her face and kissed him. "It's just that— Never mind." She looped her arm around his. "Let's go to the car."

She was quiet on the drive home, mulling over what she

had been trying to ignore. Carson was that *he* in her head now, that *him*. Clipping a story out of the paper because *he* would like it. Reading a parent's sweet note and thinking, *Can't wait to show* him *this.* After every shower, she'd towel herself off and think of every part of her body his fingers had touched. When did this happen?

She shivered. "Okay if I turn up the heat?"

"You don't have to ask," he said, looking at her. "You sure you're all right?"

She adjusted the heat and nodded. "Just a lot on my mind." He slowed the car and pulled to the side of the road. "What are you doing?" Sam said.

He set the gearshift in park and turned to look at her. "Sam, I'm sorry I joked about the movie. I know how you feel about the war. That was really inappropriate of me."

"Carson, no, that's not what—"

"We have relatives who served, too, you know. On my mother's side. Her second cousin lost a leg." He grimaced. "God, that sounded awful. Like I'm auditioning. Or worse, competing."

"I wasn't thinking that at all," she said. "I was thinking about how I can't stop thinking about you, and then I was thinking that's pretty scary because that's not something I've ever done. Think about a man, I mean. I'm always thinking. Mom says I think too much, but I think it's important to question things, to figure things out. To go through life just coasting? That's unthinkable." She turned to look at him. "What are you thinking?"

"I think you just used up your year's supply of every version of the word 'think.'"

She lowered her voice and spoke slowly. "If you had been any other guy I've ever known, I'd already be out of this car and walking home." She smiled at his stricken face. "But here I am." She leaned toward him. "You can breathe now."

"I wasn't holding my breath."

"Yes you were."

"I'm in training."

"Oh, really," she said. "For what?"

He touched her face. "For what I hope is coming next."

Sam turned from the stove and pointed to the fridge. "Could you get the shredded cheddar for me? There's a bag of it in the left bin."

Carson set his beer on the counter. "Yes, ma'am." He handed her the bag, and she started sprinkling the cheese into the scrambled eggs. "This skillet was my great-grandmother's," she said, stirring. "My mother gave it to me when I bought this house."

He stood behind her and wrapped his arms around her waist. "My mother's going to love you."

"Because I have Grandma Ada's cast-iron skillet?"

"No," he said. "Because you care about family, and traditions. And, yes, it doesn't hurt that you like to cook. She'll load you up with her favorite family recipes in no time."

Sam turned off the burner under the eggs and gave the skillet of home fries one last flip before turning it off, too. "You don't seem the least bit worried about what your parents will think of me, or of us," she said as she filled the plates. She handed them to him. "Not even a little anxious?"

"I'm almost forty," he said, sitting down at the table. "Do I even need to tell you how often they talk about wanting grandchildren?"

She pulled her robe tighter and followed him to the table. "Carson," she said, sitting down. "Let's not move too quickly."

"What do you mean?"

"Nothing grave," she said. "I just need a little more time to get used to all of this."

He set down his fork. "So Ms. Liberal isn't as open-minded as we thought?"

She reached for his hand. "That's not it, and you know it. I've never been in a relationship like this. I feel a little off-kilter. I can't explain it, exactly. I'm not used to caring what a man thinks of me, how he feels about me."

"But you know how I feel about you."

"That's not the part I'm getting used to, Carson," she said, pointing to her head. "Up here is what I'm adjusting to. You're on my mind all the time now."

He picked up his fork and jabbed at the eggs. "Thanks for this," he said.

"It's the cheese," she said. "Makes them creamier."

"I'm not talking about the eggs," he said. "Thanks for being honest about where we stand right now. How you're feeling."

She pushed around the potatoes, her appetite gone. "I think you're hearing something I'm not saying. I'm just asking for a little more time to get used to the idea of an *us*."

"I don't need more time," he said.

They ate in silence for a few minutes. She tapped her fork on the table. "This is old, too. My great-grandfather made it for Grandma Ada in the first year of their marriage. It was in their kitchen until they died, and then in my mother's kitchen until I graduated from college and got my first apartment."

"What's the rest of that story?"

"About the table?"

"No, Sam. About everything else."

They talked through the night, first at the table, and later in bed, naked and entwined. She told him about waiting for the deputy, alone in the house, when she was five. About Rosemary knocking at their door. How their family unraveled behind the closed door as Sam rocked Paull-two-els to sleep.

Sam studied Carson's face as she talked, searching for the slightest sign of judgment, of pity. He didn't blanch when she told him about Rosemary driving off the bridge, and when she described seeing Paull again when he was eight.

"I feel so guilty that I never tried to find him after that. We all acted like he didn't exist."

"You were barely eighteen, Sam," Carson said. "You were a kid who never got to be a kid."

"I could have helped him."

"You were still taking care of your mother, and you were about to leave for college."

"He wants to meet Reilly."

"Paull? You've talked to him?"

She nodded. "His five-year-old son is a student in my school. His name is Charlie." Her eyes welled up for the first time. "I knew who he was before he told me. Paull looks so much like my father, Carson. And get this: Dad actually went to one of Paull's games, just a few years ago."

"You're kidding."

"Showed up and helped him with his batting. He's always known Paull was his son. I'm afraid this is going to kill my brother. And my mom, oh my God, when she finds out about Charlie."

He propped up on his elbow. "Why does any of that have to happen?"

"Carson, they're family."

"They are *a* family, but they do not have to be your family. None of this is your responsibility, Sam." He sat up and faced her. "Has no one ever told you it isn't your job to take care of everybody?"

"It's not like that," she said, sitting up. "This is who I am."

"It's who you were raised to be, and if you ask me, it wasn't fair."

She was covered in goosebumps, shivering again. Carson draped the comforter over her shoulders. "What you must think of us," she said. "Of me."

He wrapped his arms around her. "What I think is that you're still trying to save your family. Maybe it's time to let them find their own way."

"Oh, man," she said, her face relaxing. "Wait'll my father meets you."

"I'm the last thing your father wants to see dating his daughter."

"It's worse than that," Sam said. "You're exactly what he expected. I hate it when he's right."

CHAPTER

69

Reilly walked through the door and Sam waved him over, watching as he weaved his way through the crowded bar with the grace of a dancer. At thirty-three, Reilly was still lean and muscular, his biceps stretching the sleeves of the faded Cleveland Indians T-shirt she'd given him a decade ago.

"Hey," she said, swinging her arms wide. "Give your sister a hug."

He set a fat paperback book on the table and lifted her up. "Look at you in your fancy suit," he said. "All dressed up and no one to boss around."

"Put me down," she said, laughing. "Buy me a beer.

"*A Bright Shining Lie?*" she said, fanning the pages of his book. "From all your notes, looks like you're enjoying it."

" 'Enjoy' is probably not the right word," he said. "All those lies about the Vietnam War; so many lives ruined."

Sam set the book down. "Clayton County was never the same. Every third house, it seemed, had a boy in Vietnam. Mom and I used to pack a dinner in the wicker picnic basket whenever another son came home. On our way to their house, Mom would warn me about how they'd changed."

"Changed how?"

Sam counted off a finger with each story. "Davey Ryan can't take loud sounds, so don't slam any doors. Elaine Dempsey keeps the blinds drawn for Bobby because he can't stand bright light. Don't ask Robbie Jackson about Clara because he called the wedding off."

"I didn't know any of that."

"You were too young. When I was at Kent State, I met a lot of students who didn't know a single person who fought in that war. First time I ever thought about what it meant to be working class."

Reilly rolled his eyes. "We never called ourselves that. Dad said we were just working, period. 'Class' was a rich people's word to make clear our ranking in the world."

A waitress came over and stood next to Reilly. "What can I get you?" she said, smiling at him.

"We'll have a couple of Dortmunders," he said, pointing to Sam. "You got it," the waitress said, still looking at Reilly, and shimmied off.

"Oh, brother," Sam said. "Do you think it would help if you told her I'm your sister, and not the competition."

"Don't start."

"Just don't tell her you're married. I can't handle another brokenhearted waitress."

Reilly snatched a menu from behind the napkin holder. "I'll let you talk to yourself while I figure out what to eat."

The waitress set down the beers and quickly took their orders. "Uh-oh, no smile this time," Sam said. "She thinks we're on a date, and we both know who she hates. Let's swap cheeseburgers."

"You're stalling," he said. "What's going on?"

"We could talk about how Mom wants to know when you're coming for a visit."

"I talk to Mom every week."

"I know, Reill, but she wants to see you. And she wants you and Dad to start talking more."

"I'm not angry at Dad," Reilly said as he unrolled his napkin. "We just don't have much in common." He smiled at her. "Until now, maybe."

Sam smiled nervously. "When you were little, I used to count all the freckles on your face. You'd lay your head on my lap, and I'd tap each freckle as I counted." Reilly pointed to the top of his forehead. "You called this one your north star." He downed the rest of his beer. "Okay, Sam. What's going on?"

She clasped her hands on the table. "What if I told you that there's another little boy who—" She cocked her head at him. "Wait a sec. You said, 'Until now.' That you and Dad had nothing in common *until now.*"

His smile was slow and wide. "Took you long enough."

"What do you mean?"

"Well, let me put it this way. Do you want to be called 'Aunt Sam' or 'Auntie Sam'?"

She squealed and leapt out of her seat. "You're having a baby," she said, pulling him out of the booth. He laughed as he hugged her. "We're having a boy, Sam. A son, can you believe it?"

"Wait'll Mom hears," she said. "And Dad."

"Right?" Reilly said. "For once, I'm the one with good news for Dad. I'm going to give him his first grandchild."

She grabbed the edge of the table. "Oh, Reilly," she said softly, sitting down.

"That's my news," he said, still beaming as he sat down. "Top that."

She thought about Paull and Charlie, and what her mother had said about the monster at the door. The ghost, Sam preferred to call it. Finally, she could see the ghost had been with her all along. The ghost was ready to leave, if only Sam would let her go.

Sam smiled at Reilly as he continued to talk. She would not do this to her brother. "Enough people have suffered," she'd tell Paull tomorrow. "Let's not hurt anyone else."

She closed her eyes and felt a rush of relief as she imagined Rosemary picking up the little red-haired boy and walking out the door.

"Sam? Sam."

Sam opened her eyes. "Reilly, I've met someone."

"Who?"

"His name is Carson," she said. "Carson Marino. And I think he might just love me."

"Holy cow," Reilly said. "How do you feel about him?"

"That's my news. I think maybe I'm going to love him right back."

CHAPTER

70

Ellie backed out of the driveway and waved at Brick, who was sitting on a porch step, sulking. He hated that she got her hair done on Saturdays now. She smiled anyway and drove off, turning right at the corner, instead of left.

What a ridiculous argument they'd had last night. He'd picked her up at the hospital because her car was in the shop. On their way to the American Legion club for supper, Brick had started lecturing her again about opening a new bar of soap before using up the old. "I'm a grown woman with a weekly paycheck. I'll buy a brand-new bar of soap for every day of the week if I want."

It was the first time in her seventeen years as a nurse's aide that she had mentioned making her own money. She could tell by the way he drove in silence that she had hurt his feelings. "Liv Ansley said that Curly Bumpus and his band are playing at the club tonight," she said. "I love that Glenn Miller music."

He shifted a bit, but said nothing.

"If they play 'In the Mood,' we could jitterbug." He gave in and smiled. "We should call Sam from the club and tell her," he said, giving in. "Just to embarrass her again."

Ellie imitated Sam's voice: " 'Dad is six feet two and you are four feet eleven. When he picks you up and swirls you, people can see all the way to the top of your pantyhose.'"

"I thought she was going to die that night," Brick said, chuckling. "The look on her face when I lifted you over my head."

Ellie squeezed his hand. "I pinched those red cheeks of hers and said, 'How do you think you came into this world?' Shut her up for the night."

"El, I shouldn't have gone on about the soap. I've got a lot on my mind, trying to decide exactly when I should take the buyout. And then what do I do?"

"I think you should do what you want to do, Brick. Retirement doesn't mean you're old. We're not even sixty yet. And last I heard, my husband intends to jitterbug with me tonight."

He pointed to her hospital smock. "You plan on dancing in that getup?"

She unhooked her seatbelt and leaned over the seat. "There's a reason I asked you to bring this," she said, propping the tote bag on her lap. She pulled out a green satin blouse, wrapped in tissue paper. "Pull the car over, honey," she said. "I need to change. You can even peek."

Still thinking about last night, Ellie pulled into the pancake house lot and thought about something Brick had said during one of last night's slow dances. "You don't need to keep working anymore, El. The kids are grown, and with the buyout and my pension, we don't need your money."

He just didn't understand her job. In Brick's world, everyone was always trying to take something away from him. Ellie got back as much as she gave to her patients. She felt necessary, and appreciated.

Ellie parked in the farthest space from the entrance and grabbed her old vinyl Women's Guild folder engraved with MRS. ELLIE MCGINTY in gold. It had been a gift from the guild membership after the church elders finally approved Ellie's resolution that women be listed in the church directory by their own names, instead of their husbands'. Sam was sixteen at the time, and gave Ellie a handmade card for "supporting the sisterhood," which was still tucked into the back flap.

Ellie had never dined alone at a restaurant, but she needed to do this away from Brick. The hostess led her to a two-top by the window and motioned for a server. "Getting a break from the family?" the waitress said, filling her water glass. "That'll add years to your life."

Ellie was not going to complain about her family to a total stranger. "I'd like the short stack," she said, looking at the menu. "And bacon. Crispy, please." The waitress scribbled, no longer smiling. "And to drink?"

Ellie sat up straighter. "I'm sorry," she said. "I *am* happy to have a little time to myself. I'm on my feet all day like you are."

The waitress lowered her pad and looked at Ellie. "It wouldn't be so bad if I didn't have to do everything once I get home. It just never ends, you know?"

"I sure do," Ellie said. "I guess that women's lib just passed us by. I'm Ellie. Ellie McGinty."

"Maggie," the woman said, shaking Ellie's hand. "Maggie McGuire. Aren't we a couple of Irish lasses?"

Ellie laughed. "I'm Irish, but McGinty is my husband's name."

"Same," Maggie said, "except in my case, Mr. McGuire is an ex-husband."

"Oh, I'm so sorry."

"Don't be. I couldn't be happier. Married twenty-five years to the slug and says he's in love with one of the cashiers at the Stop & Shop."

"Oh my God."

"I felt released. I told him he could pay me for my share of the house and I wouldn't take anything else but my clothes and my dog, Lance. He was so stunned, he gave me everything I wanted. I bought one of those little condos in Reynolds Way."

"That new development," Ellie said, "where Smitty Field used to be."

"Townhouses they call them. Shared walls, smaller yards. I never thought I'd live in a brand-new house. Everything in it is being used for the first time by me."

"Everything must be so clean."

"Spic-and-span," Maggie said. "Friendly place, too. There are a lot of girls our age who live there. Mostly divorced or widowed, but a couple have husbands. We take pottery classes together at Sullivan's Ceramics and meet once a month for book group. You get your privacy when you want it, but you never have to feel you're alone." She took Ellie's menu. "Listen to me go on. The developer says I bring in more potential buyers than that fancy marketing firm he hired."

"Lenny Kleshinski."

"That's him," Maggie said. "Nicest guy."

"A childhood friend of my daughter's. He's made quite a name for himself here in Erietown."

"Wait'll you see his brochure for Reynolds Way," Maggie said. "I'll bring you one when I come back with your food." She was gone before Ellie could tell her she needn't bother.

Ellie opened her folder and pulled a pen out of her purse. She had decided the night before to write her note like an outline.

October 28, 1994

The Duties of a Nurse Assistant on a Mental Health Unit (The Day Shift—7:00 A.M.–3:30 P.M.)

A. Admitting a Client
    1. Take patient's temperature, pulse, respiration.
    2. Fill out top part of assessment sheet.

3. Give patient an Orientation Booklet with patients' rights.
4. Orient patient to his room and the unit.
5. Give patient admission pack.
6. Check that all the patient's belongings, such as
   suitcase, purse, and all things that are not appro-
   priate on the unit, will be sent home or safely
   locked up.

Number six was harder than it sounds. It's hard for people
to part with their things, especially when they think those
things are all they have left of who they used to be.

7. If the patient is suicidal or upset, stay with him
   after admitting.

Easier said than done, because of all her other duties on the
floor. It wasn't like one of the other aides did her baths and
food trays or changed her beds when she had to spend a long
time with one patient.

B. The Duties Performed During the Day
   1. Listen to report and receive assignments for the
      day.
   2. Make sure all patients get to the solarium for
      their meals. Assist those who are unable to eat in
      the solarium.

Maggie set down a plate on the other side of the table. "So
you're a writer," she said.

"I'm just writing a letter. To my husband. Sometimes it's
easier to get him to listen if I—"

Maggie held up her hand. "You don't need to tell me." She
reached into the front pocket of her apron and pulled out a

shiny brochure for Reynolds Way. "I wrote my number on the back, in case you ever want to come visit without one of Lenny's people breathing down your neck."

Ellie opened the brochure. "It's beautiful."

"Call me ahead of time and I'll round up some of the girls for you to meet. You don't have to live in Reynolds Way to join our pottery club. And we're thinking of starting a canasta club."

Ellie smiled. "I haven't played canasta in years." She slid her finger across the picture of townhouses stacked side by side in shades of beige, cream, and soft yellow. "It looks so pretty, and calm."

"Until all us girls get together," Maggie said. "What a hoot." She tapped the brochure with her pencil. "Just take it and think about it."

Ellie got back to her note.

3. Make sure you record how every pt. ate and that their menus are completed.
4. Chart on the daily flow sheet of each patient. Also chart on the progress notes.

So much paperwork, every day.

5. Conduct an exercise class with patients every other day.
6. Act as assistant to the Recreational Therapist during groups three times daily.
7. Conduct the groups on the days the Recreational Therapist is off, on vacation, or absent.
8. Document all activities performed by patients on the activity flow sheets.
9. Conduct an Orientation Class twice a week.

Brick would only make fun of her if he knew she had to exercise with the patients. When Reilly was fourteen, he'd been so excited to use his lawn-mowing money to buy a set of barbells, the kind with interchangeable disks. Brick had laughed at him. "You want muscles?" he'd said to Reilly. "Come work at the plant for the summer."

Reilly had looked stricken, and Ellie hadn't talked to Brick for a week. "Let him make fun of me," she whispered, pressing the pen harder on the paper.

10. Talk with patients—collect information and share with the team.
11. Be able to discuss patients' progress with the doctors when necessary.

Some of the doctors sought out Ellie, instead of one of the nurses, because they knew she spent more time with patients, and they trusted her. "I heard there's something about you, Ellie," Dr. Marino recently told her, in front of all of the nurses at the front desk. "They say when you show up, patients live longer."

Ellie tapped her pencil and smiled. "Carson and Sam. Never saw that coming." There was no mistaking the happiness in her daughter. "Sam will always be a perfectionist, but there's a softening about her," she'd told Mardee. "She's wearing her hair down all the time now, even at school. It's like she's given herself permission to be more than one thing in life."

Sam had called Ellie last night to ask her to go shopping with her soon for new work clothes. "Let's face it, Mom, anyone who has a hard time with my being a woman in this job isn't going to be persuaded otherwise by those stiff old suits. I'm tired of feeling confined to a uniform."

Ellie had let that comment pass. She missed her old "urine-yellow" uniform, but most of the aides preferred the smocks and slacks they all wore now. As one of the younger aides, Tiffany Newman, put it to Ellie, "Life is a roller coaster and change is the ticket. Kahlil Gibran said that."

"Yeah, no, he didn't," Sam said over dinner that evening. "Kahlil Gibran would never have used a county fair metaphor for love. He did, however, say, 'You talk when you cease to be at peace with your thoughts.' Lay that one on Ms. Tiffany and watch what happens."

"How do you know he said that?"

"It's in *The Prophet*. Carson gave it to me."

Ellie started to pull out a pen, and Sam patted her hand. "No need to write down the title, Mom. I'll lend you my copy so you can tell me Carson's intentions."

Ellie pulled out a blank sheet of notebook paper from the back and wrote across the top, *Reasons You Should Be Happy for Sam, Period*. She'd give that one to Brick soon, too, to help him get used to the idea. The whole west end of Erietown was abuzz about Sam and Carson. It was a miracle Brick hadn't already heard.

She looked at her watch and decided to cut down the list.

12. Do not be afraid to stay with a violent patient.

Last July she'd had to stay late for a report after a patient punched her and pinned her to the floor. Brick had been sitting on the porch steps drinking a beer when she eased herself out of the car. "Ellie," he said, motioning toward her with the bottle. "It's eighty-nine degrees out here. Why are you wearing a sweater in this heat?" He stood up at the sight of the large purple bruise on her left arm.

"Where did you get that?"

"Brick, he was disoriented," she said, trying to walk past him. "That happens sometimes with patients."

Brick was livid. "Nobody should be touching you. What kind of woman wants a job like this?" She pointed to her chest. "This woman, Brick. It's my decision, and I'm staying."

Ellie folded the list into thirds and wrote on the back:

Dear Brick,

I hope this list of my nurse's aide responsibilities will help you see how hard I work, and why what I do matters.

I love you.
Ellie

She stared at her signature for a moment, and decided to add *Pint* in parentheses. She hated that nickname now, but she knew why Brick still used it sometimes. He would always miss who they used to be.

She wrote a note on her paid receipt and left it with a fifteen percent tip.

Dear Maggie,

Thank you for being so nice to me. Thanks for the brochure, too.

Ellie McGinty
555-4262

On the drive home, Ellie decided to leave the note on Brick's dashboard Sunday night, after he fell asleep in the recliner. He'd see it when he got in the car on Monday to drive to work. He was on the porch swing when she pulled into the driveway. She walked up the stairs and smiled at him. "Get much yard work done?"

"Hair looks good," he said, taking a swig of beer. "Did you know our daughter is dating a doctor?"

Ellie froze midstep. "I just heard," she said. "His name is Dr. Carson Marino."

"Italian." Brick took another swig. "Don't tell me this guy's Catholic."

"No, no," Ellie said, sitting next to him on the swing. "His mother's a Methodist."

Brick put his arm around her and started rocking the swing. "Ma was a Methodist."

She patted his leg. "She surely was."

CHAPTER

71

Brick zipped up his softball jacket and headed out to the toolshed in the backyard. It was still nippy, but the morning clouds had given way to a sunny October afternoon.

He reached for his favorite clippers and winced as he flexed the handles in his right hand. He held up his left hand, spreading his fingers wide. His swollen joints were mirror images of his mother's in her last years.

He scooped out a pile of rubber bands in the glass ashtray on his workbench and smiled at nine-year-old Sam looking up at him. Her teacher had had the bright idea of gluing kids' school pictures on the bottoms of ashtrays for Father's Day, and Sam had been so excited to give it to him. He could never bring himself to crush out a butt on his daughter's face, and he couldn't part with the ashtray even after he'd quit smoking.

He rubbed his thumb on the well of the ashtray to clear the dust from Sam's face. He tried to imagine a little brown version of Sam, with big chocolate eyes instead of blue, calling him Grandpa. This was going to take some getting used to. He blamed Motown. Maybe if he hadn't made such an issue of her music back then she wouldn't have fallen for this guy. His daughter sure could nurse a grudge.

She was smitten, of that he was certain. He could tell by her face, the way she looked happy even when they argued about politics or how he still called women "girls." *Methodist mother.* Ellie must think her husband is an idiot. The *Erietown Times* had done a front-page story on big-city doctor Carson Marino within months of his arrival. He was looking forward to Sam returning his call so that he could give her a real shock. "Bring your new boyfriend over for a cookout," he'd tell her, and then sit back and enjoy her stammering.

He reached down and grabbed the handle of the wicker flower basket he'd bought for Ellie the summer after they moved into this house. "So you can cut your own bouquets anytime you want," he told her.

She never did. "I like when you pick 'em, honey. I like looking at them and thinking, 'Brick grew these flowers, and he picked every last one of them just for me.'"

Brick walked over to the flower garden along the fence. The dahlias and goldenrod were nearly as tall as Ellie. If she were standing next to him right now, he'd joke that four feet eleven wasn't much of an accomplishment even for a flower. He still knew how to make her laugh. Ellie was at work, though, and she thought he was, too.

Their fight in the car over that goddamn soap and her job had helped him make up his mind. He would use up all his vacation days, starting today, before the buyout kicked in. He'd tell Ellie tonight, over steaks already cooking on the grill by the time she pulled into the driveway. She'd love that.

Brick had left the house at his usual time this morning and driven to the diner across town, the one where he used to take Reilly on Saturdays when Reilly was a little boy. He walked to the car planning to relax over breakfast with the latest *Sports Illustrated*—the subscription had been a Christmas gift from Reilly.

Ellie's list had changed those plans. When he saw her handwriting on the back of the folded pages of yellow legal pad, his skin crawled. This was it, he thought. Ellie wanted a divorce. The kids were grown and she had a job now. She had no reason to stay.

He was so relieved to discover a list of her job duties that he read her every word over bacon and eggs. Once again, she had misunderstood him. He hated her job. Everyone at the hospital took advantage of her.

If she wanted to take care of somebody, she could start with her husband. She was still the only person who really knew him. "You're my dream come true," she'd recently told him, for the first time in years. He'd felt forgiven. For just a moment, he'd been eighteen again, with his whole life in front of him.

"Soap," Brick grumbled as he clipped the stems of the largest mums and dropped them in the basket. That was his second surprise for Ellie. On the way home from the diner he'd stopped at the Kmart and picked up a dozen bars of her favorite soap. He'd lined them up along the edge of the bathtub stall.

He clipped six of the bright orange dahlias for Ellie, and a handful of the burgundy and dark pink for Sam, gently laying all of them in the basket. He looked at the row of helenium and remembered what Ellie had said just last night about their red-and-yellow petals. "They look like they're on fire," she'd said, pointing to them from across the yard.

He picked up the basket and walked toward the row of foxglove against the shed. They had stopped blooming weeks ago, and needed trimming. He had planted them the first spring in this house, a year and a half after it all happened. If Paull ever stood in this yard—he never would, but if he did—Brick could point to them as proof he'd never forgotten. Foxglove, he'd tell him, where she was born.

Brick grabbed a handful of stems and started cutting them

back. A spear of pain shot up his arm, and this time, bile rose in his throat. *Goddamn bursitis.* It had been acting up for almost a month now, but nothing like this. He dropped the clippers and pulled his arm across his chest. He grabbed the stems again and stumbled as he tried to catch his breath. His eyes started stinging from beads of sweat sprouting on his brow.

Maybe take a break. Maybe go sit on the porch swing.

He reaches down for the basket, but now his chest is on fire. He grabs a bundle of the dahlias from the basket and presses them with both hands against his heart.

The porch is miles away.

He counts as he walks down the driveway.

One, two, four, five

Once I caught a fish alive.

He squints at the brown dog wagging his tail.

One, two, buckle my shoe.

His right foot is so heavy. *Take off the shoe.* The thought flies away.

Harry!

His brother turns around and smiles. *My little Brickster!* He is running in the cornfield, waving for Brick to follow. *He'll never find us here, buddy.*

Little Paull has something in his hand. *That's the Johnny Lightning Chevy Camaro,* Reilly yells. *I have one just like it.*

He looks down at Sam's little hands tugging on the shirt at his waist. *Daddy, don't cry.*

Bic! Bic!

If the pitch is outside, go with the pitch.

The one-eyed dog runs up to him, yapping at his feet. Brick drops the flowers. *Patch. Here, boy.* Brick collapses backward against his car and grabs the side mirror as he slides to the ground. *This jacket is too damn small.* He tears open his shirt. Two buttons dance through the air and bloom into basketballs.

Brick! Clap, Brick! Clap, Brick! Coach grabs his shoulder

from behind. *Good game, son. Come back to the bench.* Brick runs toward the bridge. *Hit the brake. The brake!* The car soars into the sky. *Why'd you go and do that, Roe?*

She is walking toward him, her hands cupping her swollen belly.

Ellie.

Ellie smiles and holds out her hand. *Brick, look what you've done.*

His head hits the pavement.

"Ma," he whispers, his eyes wide.

CHAPTER

72

Ellie sat in her underwear on the closed toilet seat and stared at the boxes of soap lining the edge of the bathtub. An apology, Brick-style. She stood up and walked to their bedroom closet, and pulled out the one black suit she owned. She brushed the dust off the shoulders. "Hand me the lint brush," she said, reaching toward the bedside table. She sat down on the bed and started to cry.

She stood up again when she heard Sam's car door close in the driveway. She looked at her watch. A half hour before they had to leave for the funeral home. Reilly and Lisa would meet them there.

Ellie ran her fingers along the chenille bedspread and thought about her children's reaction to Brick's death. With her permission, Carson had called Sam from the ER. When she arrived, Ellie could tell she'd been crying, but Sam was who she'd always been, making it clear that she was there to help Ellie. "What do you need?" she kept asking, until Ellie finally asked Carson to take her home.

Reilly was so calm on the phone. "I'm on my way, Mom," he said, and hung up. One look at him an hour later at the hospital, and Ellie finally fell apart. Reilly held her until she was cried out, and then drove her home. She couldn't help but notice that his eyes were red, but dry. "Let's talk later," he said when he hugged her goodbye. Such an odd thing to say. Of course they would talk.

She walked over to Brick's chest of drawers. Everything was just as he had left it, including his wedding ring, which he never wore when he was working in the yard. She picked it up and slid it onto her thumb, but it was too loose. His leather wallet sat on top of the folded list of job duties she had left on his dashboard. So, he saw it, but did he read it? Maybe that explained the soap, and the thawing steaks on the counter.

The wallet had been a birthday gift from the kids more than twenty years ago. Brick had refused to part with it no matter how tattered it became. Last Christmas, Sam—and Reilly in absentia—gave him a new one. Brick held it in his hand for a moment, then set it back in the box. "I appreciate this," he said, folding the tissue over it and replacing the cover. "But I don't need it."

"Dad, it's still from us."

"But not from my children," he said, handing it to Sam. "Every time I open my wallet, I see your excited little faces on the day you gave it to me."

Ellie knew what he was thinking. Sam was eleven when they gave him the wallet. The year before everything changed.

Ellie opened the wallet and looked at the pictures. The first sleeve dated back to their wedding day: On one side, a black-and-white photo of them clowning around in a drugstore photo booth; the other side a picture of Ellie standing by Brick's truck outside their hotel. The rest of the sleeves held pictures of the kids at various ages. She pulled them out, one at a time, reading Brick's handwritten note on the back of each one.

Reilly, age 6. Lost a tooth two days before.
Sam, age 10. Hit her first home run in the backyard.

The sleeve holding the kids' high school senior portraits was chunkier. She tugged to slide them out, and the folded square of newspaper fell to the floor.

She could tell it was a team photo from softball days. "Brick," she said, smiling as she picked it up. "After all these years." She unfolded the paper and dropped the wallet.

She sat down on Brick's side of the bed and stared at the headline.

PAULL RUSSO'S HITTING SLUMP GONE FOR GOOD

She looked at the date. *July 20, 1989.*

She spotted him immediately. He was the young man in the back, tall and lean. Ellie ran her finger across the photo of his freckled face, her breathing shallow as she studied the curve of his father's chin, his narrow nose, his smile that curled a little higher on the left.

Her eyes scrolled down to the paragraph circled in pencil.

When asked about his new strategy at the plate, Russo wasn't giving up any secrets. "Let's just say I got some really good advice," he said. "From a real pro. I hope he sees this, so he knows I listened. I wish I could thank him in person."

Ellie folded the news clipping into the tiny square and wedged it back into the sleeve, between the kids' portraits. She set the wallet on the dresser.

So like Brick, to think he was the only one with a secret.

She'd never told a soul about that day. Over the years she had tamped it down until the memory surfaced only as an occasional flutter, a gnat quickly batted away.

A full year before Rosemary Russo showed up at their door, she had made sure Ellie knew about Paull-two-els.

Another hot August day, but in '68. Ellie had just pulled into the parking lot of Hills department store and was stepping out of the car when she saw him: a cherub of a baby with red hair blazing in the final glow of the setting sun. *Just like my Reilly's,* she remembered thinking as he and his mother approached. She was tall with long bleached hair, carrying him on her hip. When the woman's eyes met Ellie's, she paused for a moment, it seemed. Ellie smiled and kept walking.

A few minutes later, Ellie was riffling through the bin of discounted bras when the same woman stopped on the other side of the bin. This time she returned Ellie's smile. "I forgot about these being on sale," the woman said. Her face was flushed.

Ellie pointed to her baby. "His hair is red just like my son's. Like my husband's, too. You don't see that bright shade very often."

The woman nodded and kissed her son's forehead. "That's right, Paullie."

The skin on Ellie's arms began to tingle. Her body had been one step ahead of her, she thought later, warning her that something was wrong. She studied the boy's face and tilted her head. "Paulie? Is that a nickname for Paul?"

The woman nodded, and when she ran one of her hands through her son's hair, Ellie noticed that it was trembling. "Spelled differently, though," Rosemary said, locking her fingers together across her son's bottom. "He's Paull-two-els."

Ellie looked down at the lacy bra in her hand and felt suddenly exposed, as if she were revealing something intimate about herself. "I've only known one person who spells Paull that way," she said, dropping the bra.

The woman nodded again. "Me, too."

How long did they stand there looking at each other? Ellie could never recall. For the longest time, it seemed, her feet couldn't move. She just stared at that little boy until she couldn't take it anymore.

She looked at Rosemary. "You can't have him."

Rosemary smiled, and Ellie knew she had lost. Rosemary lifted her son to press his cheek against hers. "And you, Mrs. McGinty, couldn't have *him*."

Ellie walked away from the bin and straight to her car. On the drive home she vowed never to tell a soul that she knew. Not Brick, not Mardee, not Reverend Lubinger. If she didn't acknowledge that baby's existence, if she and Brick never talked about him, then he wasn't real.

A year later Rosemary showed up banging on their front door, and one look at Brick's face filled in the rest of the story. "Bic," the little boy called him, just as he had at Brick's game, when she had still pretended not to know.

That night, after Rosemary left and Brick left, too, she lay on top of the bedspread and never slept. By the next evening she stood at the stove heating leftovers, so exhausted that her fingers were having trouble clasping the handle of the wooden spoon, when Brick walked through the door with the newspaper rolled up in his hand.

They looked at that photo of Rosemary's mangled car, and on the spot Ellie had a plan. It was as simple and awful as that. She didn't have to tell Brick that she already knew about Rosemary, about the baby. Rosemary had written a new ending when she drove off the Clayton County Bridge.

Ellie stood up and avoided her reflection in the dresser mirror as she got dressed. She picked up the bottle of White Shoulders to spritz her wrists, and thought of the day she and Brick had buried his mother. Ellie had been so pregnant at the time, full of worries about her stricken husband and their emergency marriage. On the drive home from the cemetery,

Brick had said something she had clung to over the years. "I still don't know if I believe in God," he told her, "but if I do, Pint, it's because of you."

She unclasped her gold cross necklace and walked over to Brick's bureau. She slid his ring onto the chain and refastened it, and tucked it inside her blouse. She picked up the hand mirror on her dresser and thought about how Grandma Ada had amended the mirror's message for her pregnant grand-daughter. "It doesn't matter, Ellie, who we see in the mirror. What matters is who God sees."

Ellie stared at her reflection in the mirror. "We should have raised that boy," she said. She squeezed her eyes shut. "Please forgive Brick, and me."

She heard a tap at the door. "Mom?"

"I'll be right there, Sam," she said, setting down the mirror. She'd have to tell Sam about Carson, how wonderful he'd been with her that day. How he'd been in the ER when they brought Brick in, and raced to the patient rec room. "Ellie," he'd said, pressing his hand against her back, "come with me, please."

He was such a handsome man, so quick to smile, but in that moment he looked ancient as he stood with her in the hallway and said, "Ellie, I am so sorry to tell you this."

He walked with her to the emergency room, and led her to the corner stall. "I will wait right here for you," he said.

Ellie had slowly pulled back the curtain and closed it be-hind her. It was Carson, she learned later, who had broken protocol and tucked a sheet around Brick, instead of draping it over his body and face. Brick was wearing only one shoe. He would have hated that. She pulled off the shoe and wrapped the bottom of the sheet around Brick's feet before looking at his face. His eyes were wide open, as if he'd been surprised.

She pushed his hair off his forehead and kissed his cheek. "Sam and Reilly are on their way," she told him. A small lie. She would call them soon, but they could not see him like this. As she had done countless times before for other people's husbands, she dabbed her finger in the pot of Vaseline and sealed his eyelids shut.

Ellie stood at the dresser and patted the ring under her blouse. "Who was waiting for you, Brick?" she said. "Who did you see?"

CHAPTER

73

Sam flicked on the turn signal to turn left on Maple. "No," Ellie said. "Let's drive by the old house. It's the most direct route to Penney's."

"Mom, I can turn here and it won't add more than thirty seconds to the drive."

"I want to see the old house," Ellie said. "I haven't seen it since we moved."

Sam started to say something, and stopped. Her father had been gone for almost four months now. This was the first time Ellie had wanted to go anywhere but work or church. "I want new sheets," she'd told Sam earlier in the week. "And I want to buy some pretty towels. With flowers on them."

Sam was relieved to see her mother showing signs of life. Her father's death had left Sam feeling hollowed out and adrift for weeks, but Carson had slowly reeled her back in.

She had resisted at first; not from grief, but from fear. "It has occurred to me," she finally explained to him, "that if I love you too much, I will never recover from losing you."

"Then why love anyone?" Carson said. "Why love your parents? Why love a dog or a cat, for that matter? Your heart is too big for anything less, Sam, and you don't do anything half-way."

"But look at Mom."

"You mother won't always be this sad."

"She will always miss him," Sam said. "And so will I."

"What a lucky man," Carson said, "to be loved that much."

Sam had repeated that to herself so many times since Carson said it. *What a lucky man.* Not once had she ever heard her father describe himself that way, and her mother had deserved to hear it.

She pulled to a stop at the intersection, as Ellie had instructed. "I've avoided that house for so many years," she said. Ellie pointed at the light. "It's green."

Sam turned left and slowed down as they approached the four-story apartment building. A smattering of old people sat out on the stacked concrete porches, bundled against the cold and watching traffic. When Sam was a child, she used to love waving to the old people, making them smile. Now, they reminded her of the little figures in her childhood dollhouse, anonymous in the world.

Sam pulled to a stop in front of their old house, and they gasped in unison. A bulldozer was parked where the front porch used to be. A lighted sign on wheels blocked the driveway:

COMING SOON!
MORE PARKING FOR LOUIE'S STEAKHOUSE!

Sam glanced at the new restaurant across the street. "Wow. I knew Cecil's gas station was gone." She looked again at the house. "But I didn't know about this."

Ellie rolled down the window and faced the house. There was a gaping hole where the door used to be, offering a clear view of the fake-brick linoleum floor. "Such a long time ago," Ellie said. "I wonder if Dad knew about this."

She closed her eyes against the crisp winter breeze and the house came alive. She could see Reilly and Sam laughing as Sam pinned down his shoulders in the grass. A young beehived Ellie stood in her scuffed slippers on the porch, cupping her mouth with her hands to call the kids to dinner. *Time for my Dean Martin medley,* Brick said, patting the spot next to him on the swing. *Just for you.*

"Mom?"

Ellie opened her eyes and the porch was gone. "It wasn't all bad," she said, staring at the house. "This was our first home together. We made good memories here, too."

"Lots of them," Sam said.

"He did love me," Ellie said. "I believe that."

Sam pressed her hand on her mother's back. "Of course he did, Mom."

Sam looked down at Ellie's open purse. "What's this?" she said, pulling out the brochure.

Ellie turned and snatched it from her hand. "Since when do you rummage through my purse without permission?"

"Mom, it was sitting right there. I was just wondering what it was."

Ellie eased back in her seat. "I'm sorry. I don't mean to be short."

"But you've always been four feet eleven."

Ellie looked at her daughter and almost smiled. "Well, I see your father's jokes have certainly survived." She handed Sam the brochure. "It's for Reynolds Way, that new housing development."

"Lenny's project," Sam said, spreading it open. "Whoa, a trifold. Look at you, Lenny Kleshinski." She studied it for a moment and tilted her head at Ellie. "Are you thinking of moving already? Experts say wait six months for big decisions."

"Experts aren't living in that empty house with me," Ellie said, grabbing the brochure and folding it. "A waitress gave this to me a couple of months ago. You know how it is. You get to talking and people just tell you things. She lives there."

"When were you at a restaurant?"

"Perkins. A while ago, as I just said."

"By yourself?"

"Sam, honestly. I have done things without your father, you know."

Sam pointed to the brochure. "What did Dad think about this?"

"Dad didn't know." *He died the next day,* she didn't say. "I'll toss it out when we get to Penney's. Then you and the experts can feel better. Let's go."

Sam eased back into traffic. "Don't throw it out, Mom. Hold on to it for a while."

Ellie flipped down the visor to check her lipstick in the mirror. "It wouldn't bother you if I moved?"

"We just saw the only house that mattered to me," Sam said, gesturing over her shoulder. "Or, what's left of it, anyway. Besides, it's your life. You have a lot of years ahead of you. Who knows where you'll end up?"

Ellie looked at her. "Nobody has said that to me since I was seventeen years old."

"Said what?"

"That it's my life. The last time I heard that was when I was having lunch with Aunt Nessa at the Silver Grille in Higbee's, in downtown Cleveland. She had just handed me the application for nursing school. 'Don't be late for your own life,' she told me."

"The same thing you said to me when you and Dad dropped me off at Kent State."

"Yes, well," Ellie said, clasping her hands on her lap. "I'm not that teenager anymore. I'm going to be sixty before you know it. And a grandmother. Imagine that. I wish Dad had lived long enough to hear Reilly's news."

"So does Reilly," Sam said. "I've lost count of how many times he's said he wished he'd called Dad right after he told me."

"He wanted to tell him in person," Ellie said. "I like imagining that, Reilly and Dad standing together, talking about your father's first grandchild."

Sam pulled to a stop at the red light and looked at her mother. "Mom, you're going to be sixty anyway, so why not be the sixty-year-old woman you want to be? Who knows what's coming next? Let's go look at Reynolds Way."

Ellie studied her daughter's face for a moment. "I feel like we're talking about more than my new house," she said.

"Maybe," Sam said. "I don't know yet."

"Sure you do," Ellie said. She pointed up at the light. "It's green."

ACKNOWLEDGMENTS

This novel would never have come about without Kate Medina, my editor at Random House. Kate saw me as a novelist long before I did, and she never gave up on me—for years. There is no one like you in my life, Kate. I am so grateful.

Another person who insisted this novel must come to be is Gail Ross. Gail started out as my agent and is now the truest of friends, the kind who tells me what I need to hear. I've been told that's not always easy to do, but apparently no one informed Gail. Lucky me.

Random House publisher Gina Centrello's father worked for the railroads, which she told me on the day that she encouraged me to write about the people of our roots. It's impossible to overstate the impact of our conversation that day. Thank you, Gina.

Many readers will recognize Random House Copy Chief Benjamin Dreyer as the author of the bestselling *Dreyer's English*. I knew him long before that, as an editor, and in recent years, as a treasured friend. You bring the magic with you, dear Benjamin.

A team of other talented people with Random House helped shape this book and its future: Erica Gonzalez, Noa Shapiro, Avideh Bashirrad, Vincent La Scala, Susan M.S. Brown, Barbara Fillon, Jess Bonet, Susan Corcoran, Maria Braeckel, Karen Fink, and Allyson Pearl. Greg Mollica's cover design captured the Erietown I know, in my heart.

Other people who had a role in this endeavor: Jane Hazen sent me her wonderful books about Higbee's restaurant, the Silver Grille, which brought it to life for Ellie. Andover Public Library—in Ashtabula County, Ohio, which is surely near the mythical Erietown—allowed me to borrow, for years, several high school yearbooks from the 1950s; they were a valuable resource for names that were popular during that time in small-town Ohio. Many of my colleagues in Kent State's School of Journalism and Mass Communications have been steadfast friends and wise counselors, especially Jacqueline Marino, Candace Bowen, Darlene Contrucci, Danielle Sarver Coombs, Amy Reynolds, Kevin Dilley, Janet Leach, Michele Ewing, Gene Shelton, Thor Wasbotten, Stephanie Smith, Cheryl Lambert, Tim Roberts, Susan Zake, Stefanie Moore, Dana White, Chance York, and Jeff Fruit.

To my students at Kent State: You fill my heart. I believe in you, always.

The love of friends kept me afloat. Thrity Umrigar gave me excellent advice when I was struggling midstory: Write a thousand words a day, and your characters will find you. Long before this book was finished, Karen Sandstrom drew a now-framed portrait of me clutching it with both hands. Susan Weidenthal Saltzman designed and made a one-of-a-kind necklace for me, its single charm engraved with ERIETOWN. Jennifer DiBrienza always knows when to show up. My sister-in-law Catherine Scallen—my sistah!—has kept me focused and strong; her husband, my brother-in-law Bob Brown, is the big brother I always wanted. My many talks with Marcia

Brown, the newest writer in our family, reminds me of the mission of our work.

Some friends knew me long before Ellie and Brick McGinty came into my life. They tend to me. Jackie Cassara and Kate Matthews have helped me stay tethered to my biggest dreams through three decades of friendship. Gaylee McCracken has kept me healthy, and ever-mindful of our working-class roots. Buffy Filipell believed in me before I believed in myself. Michael Naidus was one of the first friends to read this book, and wrote such a thoughtful response that I printed it for safekeeping. For years, Sue Klein helped me brainstorm characters and the complications in their lives, without so much as a sigh of impatience. Maura Casey reminds me of who I am when I most need to hear it. Janet Newey stood in her kitchen and listened as I shared a story from Ellie's life, her eyes filling with tears as she repeatedly asked, "And then what happened?" That's when I knew.

For their many kindnesses and giant leaps of faith, I am grateful to Steve Levingston, Michael Croley, David Yontz, Peter Slevin, Dave Lucas, and Sarah Smarsh.

These women have blessed my life with their talents and their wisdom for years: Marva Register, Rosie Rosalina, and Olivia Comella Kaufman.

Three of our children—daughter Cait, son Andy, and daughter-in-law Stina—read an early draft of this novel. Their insights, gentle but unsparing, helped me cut what wasn't working and build on what was. My sister Toni also read an early draft, and kept me honest. My sister Leslie gave me a treasure trove of photographs of our childhood in Ashtabula, Ohio, which helped me infuse this story with details of working-class life in the '50s and '60s.

All of the adult children in our family—Cait and Alex, Andy and Stina, Elizabeth and Patrick, and Emily and Matt— bring so much meaning to my life, which informs my work as a writer, and as a human being. They have also given us seven grandchildren, and I am now that grandma I used to mock. I live for you, sweet children.

Anyone who has ever loved a dog knows why I'm thanking Franklin and Walter. Good boys.

Sherrod Brown is the husband I didn't dare imagine before he showed up in my life seventeen years ago. No one has believed in me more, and that has changed me. I will never forget the first time he sat across from me in our living room and started talking about Ellie and Brick as if they were real people.

I mean it every time I say this, Sherrod: You are my hero, too.

CONNIE SCHULTZ is a Pulitzer Prize–winning writer and a professional-in-residence in the journalism school at Kent State University, her alma mater. She is the author of two memoirs, *Life Happens* and *. . . And His Lovely Wife*. Schultz lives in Cleveland with her husband, Sherrod Brown, and their rescue dogs, Franklin and Walter. They have four children and seven grandchildren.